# Black Crow

# M A Cracknell

ISBN-13:978-1490327624

ISBN-10:1490327622

DEDICATION

To my inspiration – Jayne Mundy.

(What would life be like without our 5 o'clock?)

# CONTENTS

Prelude      7

Act One      11

Act Two   132

Act Three 285

Act Four   343

## PRELUDE

His morning walk had taken him out to the furthest point of the grounds, where woodlands circled the estate. Spring bulbs such as beautiful hidden Lilly of the Valleys and Snowdrops popped up their heads; however, the walker had no regard for their delicate state as he marched through and turning crushed them underfoot to get back to the main house, anxious now for his breakfast. He dabbed his sweating forehead with his white crisp cotton handkerchief.

The sun had not yet burned through the morning haze, and he knew that the Italian sun would explode and make this part of the world the most beautiful place on earth.

He had commissioned his beautiful traditional Italian landscape to be mingled with beautiful idyllic English woodland themes, and even had mock statues of imps and fairies spying out from the under growth. It was magical and he could pretend for a while that he was still at home, and that it did not hurt so much. How his heart ached for the old House and Estates, and then he smiled to himself, he certainly did not miss the English weather and the rain!

His stomach groaned and he slapped his riding crop against his thigh, impatient to get on. He had not been riding and carrying the crop was just habit. When he was hungry that was it, he had to hurry back. Hurry, hurry!

'Hello Uncle Mestor.'

'My God man, coming up behind me like that,' the porky man whirled on his heels. He was well spoken and had quite a high pitch voice. 'For God's sake!' Only then realising that the man had spoken to him in a well-spoken English accent. Then he stumbled backwards, looking directly into the man's eyes. He found his footing and started to back away. He was a fat man with height, who wobbled as he walked. He had always looked uncomfortable and was, as his inner thighs rubbed against each other and were sore. His feet were far too small for his proportions.

He could not believe who stood before him!

'What the devil are you doing here?' He felt flush and nerves set in. This could not be happening. This could not be so! Was it this? His brother's ghost? He felt short of breath. Was this the Lord's wrath hammering down now on him? The

7

similarities in his brother Troy and this man were uncanny.

'Tying up loose ends.' Came the smiled husky reply. *come*

This was Mestor Mordesan's worst nightmare came to life. He swallowed hard trying to find his voice. The man menacingly came towards him. 'Samuel, yes, Samuel, it is you? Is it, after all this time?' He pleaded as he backed away.

He was met with a punch, which collided with his double chin and he lifted off the floor and hit the ground hard. He lay on the cushioning grass and could not catch his breath. The grass was still mildly damp. His crop fell away from his grasp. With basic survival instincts kicking in, he immediately turned on his stomach to crawl away. As he scrambled to get away, he felt his nephew behind him.

There would be no reasoning.

It was redemption day.

He never thought this would happen, believing that his two nephews had died horrible deaths after being sold into slavery. He had imagined them being fondled, groomed and gang raped constantly by their peers. This had excited him no end. The image of a young boy playing with his mind at this time! God the boys had brought him a small fortune with their fair skin and blond long hair! But now the impossible was happening. He was done for! His hands were covered with grass stains and he knew his trousers would be filthy. 'Samuel, please, we can work this out? Please listen to me; I only acted on behalf of that bitch and to impress Se .....'

For his troubles, he was kicked hard in his thick stomach. Mestor screamed and pounced away with the force. His attacker kicked out again and this time, Mestor was kicked up so high, he turned and landed on his back. He curled himself up into a ball. He dared to peek over his arm and shivered at the look of hate and determination on the man's face. His nephew was the Devil himself, come to take his due. There was no escape.

The next kick winded him. The next one made him vomit and then it went hazy.

Samuel Mordesan did not flinch as he kicked and kicked his victim to a pulp. The only thing that stopped him was pure exhaustion; he stopped and nearly staggered to keep himself up right. He breathed heavily.

He was mad with rage and had waited a long time for justice. On his long trip to get there, he had considered how he would kill his Uncle when he eventually found him. He had festered his anger for far too long, and now was very glad to release it on the man who had wronged him.

He had debated how he would kill him. Be it quickly, or slowly. He had then considered torturing him for days, burning him alive or cutting his tongue out and watching him bleed to death. A thousand thoughts crossed his mind, but he knew, just pure anger would take over, as it did when from the shadows he finally caught sight of the man who had ruined his life.

Mestor waddled around, overweight, yet still wishing to dress in the latest styles, full of himself with good living and lapping up the fruits of his families' fortunes. Samuel was sick to the stomach of the flamboyant and opulent way his Uncle lived. Samuel had planned for every eventuality, however had not reckoned on the pure emotion, which swept through his whole body, when his eyes first caught sight of the over indulgent heavyset man, heading towards him. Nothing could stop that blackness which came over him. His rage was intensified to a point where all time stood still. He was calculating and had no remorse. The man had wronged him and now he would die for everything that had befallen him and his family since that dreadful day all those years ago. He had been denied a father, denied a home, and denied his name.

Slowly he lowered himself and removed his dagger from the back of his belt. He leant down and pulled Mestor's head towards him, gripping tightly into his hair. Mestor was semi conscious and Samuel cursed as Mestor pissed himself in fright. He swept a blade across Mestor's neck, mocking him. He casually sat on top of him.

Mestor was far too weak to move. He tried to flap his arms, but Samuel just laughed as he slapped his arms away.

Samuel then lent across him and held his left arm down, and with his right hand swept the blade across his wrist. Blood gushed out like a fountain and squirted across and over the two men. Mestor screamed. Samuel then went to the other arm and casually did the same.

Mestor screamed and screamed. He screamed for mercy and the blood they shared, but Samuel was past caring. His eyes were black slits and his face set to such harshness.

9

Mestor's focus slowly started to haze from the man, who he remembered thinking was a wonderful and beautiful as a child, and now so brilliantly forged by God, his thoughts drifted, and he laughed at the irony of it all, that a devil disguised as an angel had came to avenge all his wrongs.

Samuel retreated and leant against a nearby tree and watched as Mestor's life ebbed away. Mestor was desperately trying to keep his eyes open and say something, but there was too much blood and gore everywhere and frankly, Samuel did not give a damn for what this man wanted to say. He retrieved his dagger, and winking at the dying man, he proceeded to wipe both his bloodied hands and dagger across the dying man's frock coat to clean them, and then replaced his dagger in his back belt. He noted that the material of Mestor's coat was of pure royal blue silk, trimmed with lush pink velvet. It was now covered in grass, mud, blood, and gore whilst his black silk pants were covered in the same, as well as his waste.

Death was never attractive!

'You bastard,' Mestor mouthed with tears in his eyes.

'Tell me something I don't know.' Samuel knew Mestor's death would be soon now. He kept eye contact and whispered. 'In the words of a great man I repeat, - you Mestor, are a fat pompous poof, who I despise and mark my words, this is not the end;' Mestor remembered the words spoken to him many, many years back. His mind's eye took him to that day and it was as clear as if it were yesterday. 'And in my words, this is NOW the end.' Samuel choked through gritted teeth. 'God, I'm going to love remembering this. You pissing and shitting yourself and at deaths door, and me the Lord of all I see.' Samuel spread out his arms and found himself whirling around in triumph again and again. Slowly he stopped and tutted at himself for twirling around like a child. He grunted in displeasure, but then laughed at the obscurity of it all, he needed to get home.

He spared a thought for the dying man and whispered over his shoulder as he made to leave; 'Bye, bye.'

## Act One

## Chapter One - 2 years previously

He head butted the man out of the way and lowering his body, run at the next man who charged ahead with bat in hand, to bring down on his back.

Shem's whole weight thundered through his shoulder and knocked the second man flat. As the man went down Shem was already drawing back his leg to hammer home a stiff kick to the first assailant. He then whirled round and literally jumped onto the other man, he then positioned himself over the man and angled his dagger across his neck grabbing him by the hair and drawing blood.

'Who sent ya?' He hissed in the man's face. You could see his breath, as the temperature continued to get colder. The man had closed his eyes, rigid with fright knowing his life was held in the balance, he had been at death's door many a times, and this time, he really would not mind if this was it. The man shook in both fright and cold. Shem felt the man physically give in.

'That was so fucking pathetic, if I'm going to be killed, I want the honour of a professional, not fucking arse holes. Jesus!' Shem roared, 'I'm that fucking embarrassed for ya.' He was disgusted. 'Paully!' He called and from the shadows, a taller man than Shem swaggered forward. He smiled as he approached one of Shem's attackers, who lay virtually unconscious, he kicked him in the head for good measure and walked towards his boss nodding his head in appreciation of the beating he had just witnessed the two men get.

Shem could not believe that the two men had been that naive to walk into one of his local haunts that were known by anyone who cared to do a bit of digging, and expect to do him over and walk away. On further scrutiny, it was apparent that they were low life amateurs from London, down on their luck. They had obviously been spun a yarn and in their need for the money had gone in haste to do a job that they were ill prepared to succeed in. The person who had hired them surely knew this and they were just bait, a distraction, and testing the waters.

In any event, they looked haggard and tired, full of too much drink and desperately trying to forget the wars they had fought and the rejection received when they returned home. Shem shook his head in disappointment at their plight. It was not

11

the best night to be out and making mischief.

Before the attack, Paully had left the alehouse, on the pretence of wishing to have an early night, which had raised cheers from the parties within, knowing that Valentina's paradise waited next door. Shem, who was assuming a position of worse for wear, shortly followed him.

As he hit the cold night air, he had second thoughts and wanted to turn back and forget all about the men. The night air caught his breath and his whole body went quite stiff.

The cold had been creeping in all day and had wrapped its arms around the village. The temperature was plummeting.

Pockets of frost were taking hold and turning the dark into a powdery white. He smelt the fires from inside the homes and again thought of the warmth of the Inn and how quickly he would get this over with, so he could get back into the warmth. 'Need some company love?' Shem had stopped in his tracks and assessed the situation, not expecting his little plan to meet a distraction quite so quickly. He looked at the little strumpet who had fire in her eyes and smiled to himself that she reminded him of someone, but this was not the best of times to reminisce.

'Good evening.' He offered still walking away from the Inn. He was a man whose identity was a mystery. At this time, he used his normal low husky laboured well-spoken voice. He spoke well when needed to, or adapted to the environment when required and more than often could be heard speaking in a local accent or a common French dialect.

'Well ain't you posh? Me thinking you was a right geezer!' She smirked. She smooched up to him and rested her laced gloved hands on his chest, seeing that his frock overcoat was indeed of a fine cloth. 'Are you of a mind to visit the Mint House?' She referred to the local Whore House in the village.

He lifted her hands from him and slightly pushed her away. She was obviously new to Valentina's establishment.

'Very nice to meet you, however I have business to attend to,' with that, he went to turn away, not looking directly at her but assessing the situation, and stealing a look at the Alehouse door.

'You look down your snotty nose at me, ya fucking prick.' She found herself blurting out offensively.

Shem sighed and slowly turned back to face her, this was not the time for this. She caught the darkness in his eyes, and knew that she had overstepped the mark. She stepped back. He leant forward. Her whole body froze and he witnessed the freeze. He pretended to lurch forward, as she skipped back, like lighting he gripped her by the throat and pulled her forward. He felt her whole body become rigid and set. He smelt the staleness of her and gave her the most evil smile she had ever witnessed in her life. Fear set in. She thought he was going to kill her and she felt faint. His one hand held a firm grip on her throat and she could feel him apply pressure while with his other hand, he stroked her cheek. He let her go as quickly as he had grabbed her, and without saying another word, dropped her from his hold and casually walked away, as if she was nothing. She crumbled to the floor, having no strength left.

She felt gentle arms behind her, helping to hoist her back to her feet.

'You're a lucky bitch,' Paully moved round and whispered in her ear. She watched her target go on, and in a shaky voice, shrugging her shoulders she tried to get some bravado back.

'Well you win some, you lose some.' Her cheeks were crimson with embarrassment.

'Best you keep well away, I've seen him slit a girl's throat for less; you caught him on a good day. Now piss off and tell next door to keep the coast clear, we got some business here.'

Paully quickly escorted the girl back to The Whore house front door, noting to himself that she was quite fetching really. She was a warm colour with light brown frizzy afro hair and deep-set brown eyes. She had an oval face and many dark cute freckles over the bridge of her nose. However, her best asset was, well, he left that hanging and smiled as he focused on the job in hand.

He then skirted back across the yard to the hedgerow, where both he and Shem could watch and see when the Inn door would creak open.

It had not been too hard to pretend to be legless, and Shem had taken the time waiting for the men's exit from the establishment, to find a nice place just in front of Paully, who was hiding behind the other side of the hedge. Shem decided that now was as good a time as any to relieve himself. He started to chuckle to himself and deliberately started to aim at Paully, knowing he would hardly penetrate the hedge and get through it. He slightly turned his head and from the corner of his eye saw, the two men leave the Alehouse; he smiled in pure pleasure and joy at what he was going to do to those two lairy bastards. The two suspect characters sneaked out and started to look for Shem.

Who did they think they were attempting to attack him? The bear cheek of it all! Shem had calculated exactly what would happen and what he would do. He was in his element and these amateurs would pay.

With both men barely conscious, the other members of Shem and Paully's gang had came out and took the men away for further questioning! They would not be seen again! Paully rubbing his hands together in utter delight.

'He's getting abit fresh, ain't he? He is an idiot, the dosey bastard.' Claude observed as much later they had returned to the warmth inside the Alehouse. He carefully removed his doublet and folded it nicely over his chair. The Castle was a small Alehouse cradled in the small village of Pevensey. This was the main thorough fare for trade from the main fishing port of Hastings through to Eastbourne and Brighton.

Claude Bohun was a French migrant who had come across, as did many of his family, when the Huguenots had been persecuted back home. His family had originally settled on the outskirts of Canterbury, and his family trade of carpentry had taken him along the coast for work and building boats to Hastings. It was there that he had met up with the Hawkins Brothers, which eventually led to Shem. No one would have known he was French if he did not say and no one held it against him, as many had other matters on their minds rather than wars being fought.

Claude was one of Shem's main men. He was a wiry man, tall and skinny with short sandy blond hair and lovely blue eyes that were always smiling. He was firm and logically minded, he observed quietly and was thoughtful and acted like a true gentleman.

Paully Fiennes Lennard was a local man from Herstmonceux, and was the bastard son to Thomas Lennard, the Earl of Sussex and was Shem's enforcer. He got rid of any problems and made them go away. It was a job and he did it well. He was a giant of a man, heavy set and he too kept his dark hair cropped. He looked like a lovable rogue, but that was his exterior. His father had declared he did not have a heart and lacked emotion, but he was the one who looked after his father and his crumbling estates. Paully and Claude were the best of friends.

Shem, Paully, and Claude were part of a smuggling gang that run out of the south coast. Many lived in terror of them and certainly, the local Customs officers were so frightened that they hardly dared to perform their duties if they knew they were in the area, and the magistrates themselves were equally frightened to convict smugglers, as most were in their pockets anyway. The only one who ever stood up to them was George English, a local Riding officer and Paully and Claude constantly mugged him off. Yet George had the admiration of many, including another member of the gang, Jason aka Jesus Jordan, which was a rarity of ever there was one. Jesus was a man who hated everything and everyone, and believed that everyone was a sinner and should repent. It was rather out of character that Jesus genuinely liked George and vice versa, although, they had known each other all their lives.

Shem had built up a web of spies and informants on his payroll; and Claude controlled the network, and the feeding of rumours to scare people into deluding, hoodwinking, and at times submission.

Paully was in such high spirits after Shem had allowed him to clear up his mess that he thought that he would reacquaint himself with the lovely mulatto lass he met earlier that evening.

Shem returned to the Alehouse, which he had previously seized on an opportunity in investing in, with the current owner, Gideon Moseley. Gideon had fallen into a slow decline after marrying his beautiful bride and lost himself in drink and was bitter against the world and everyone in it. He did not much care for people and enjoyed to hear about others hardships. He had thought that he had captured a true gem in his second wife Valentina. He was over the moon when she consented to be his wife and had ignored the concerns of his friends that he did not know what he was getting himself into. Time had shown the truth of the matter. He was a man in his forties looking like a man twice that age with the bitterness of life edged onto every wrinkle on his face. However, he was an expert brewer and with some persuasion from Shem, he had picked himself up a little and together they had re-established the adjoining out buildings into a brewery, which had not been used for years. Gideon having been previously depressed had resorted to buying his ale in many years ago.

With Bob Hawkins, a founding older member of the gang, and Claude's logistic skills, the newly revived Ale had proven to be very popular in the area; they had regularly orders for shipments to be made across the South Coast. throughout

So overall, the move to the South Coast for Shem had proven to be a sound investment and the only one who moaned at him was Valentina. She had wanted Shem to rid her of her bad penny, Mr. Gideon Moseley, and Shem had never encouraged the conversation or indulged her in any of his business. He had never given her cause to suggest that he was capable of such things!

Valentina had resigned herself to sulk.

Shem nodded his head at Claude, confirming he agreed with his earlier observation. A man in his position was always a target and Shem was glad to have such a good band of men around him to protect him, but this time their new little annoying Captain of the Riding Officers had overstepped his mark. He had hired men from out of town to do his dirty work.

Shem was absolutely offended by being attacked by such useless amateurs that his ego had taken such a massive dent! This needed to be sorted.

'He is short of a dozen ain't he?' Claude left the question hanging in the air. 'The man's as thick as shit, God, is he all there? That attempt was feeble; you would think he would have a bit more savvy and suss your strengths out a little bit better! He has no idea, which is good in one regard but so naive in another. Does he think, if gets rid of you, that the business folds?' It was unlike Claude to ever talk for much, but when Shem got him on tactics and motives, he relished in it.

'Obviously he does.' He then raised his eyebrows at Claude, who very quickly followed through with - 'You know we would be lost without you.'

'You arse licker.' Shem grinned at his friend. 'But rest assured, Bob will jump back in the saddle should I suddenly decide that I am bored with you all!' He pointed to a small man who appeared to be asleep, his chair slightly away from the table, legs outstretched and crossed. His arms too were crossed against his chest holding his coat together to keep him warm. His head was tipped forward on his head covered by a large black fur hat. He hardly looked like a man who could carry anyone, let alone the authority of a successful smuggling gang!

Bob Hawkins was slightly chubby and looked like everyone's lively old granddad. He had a baldhead with just small patches of grizzly hair around his ears yet a full beard. His skin was dark leather brown where years of being exposed to the sun had darkened it. He did not have eyes, just black slits. He carried a clay pipe in his pocket and no one could remember him actually smoking it, only rather chewing at it.

'We can't just assume it is him.' They returned to the conversation in hand and Claude added. 'I'll get Larry's crew to do some digging.' He could not believe how stupid Hartright could be.

'It was him, he is a prick, and do not assume he is playing us, or this is a deception. He is a coward because he can't face me himself; he's always been under handed and look at him over the last few years.' He checked himself and stopped. More slowly he continued. 'However in the meantime, let's pull Rafe to us, I can't afford for him to go off and get himself beat up again, or God forbid even killed, silly bastard.' He sighed at the image, which came to life in his mind of Hartright. It had plagued him for so long, and his bigger picture to make that man pay, was wearing on him. His patience had been tested just recently, and he had to rein himself in and tell himself to wait just a little longer.

'Who killed, am I needed again?' Paully joined them and with Shem's permission sat down.

'Now pup, calm down, you will be sick from all this excitement.' The sleeping man retorted. They all laughed at that, even the offended.

'No, you can go and get Rafe.' Shem told Paully. He sat back smugly and waited.

'Oh, why me?' He cried like a spoilt child. No one bothered to answer and just looked at him. 'You know he'll just run rings round me and talk and talk and I'll have to chin him one.'

'He is not that annoying.' Shem found himself automatically trying to defend his younger brother and regretting saying it before it came out.

'Oh you would say that.'

'Now, now girls.' Bob giggled still not having moved from his comfortable position.

'It will be good for you, go get him, have a drink together, have a laugh, you may bond.' Claude tried to make it sound better for his friend.

'Only if you come too.' Paully pleaded with his best friend. Claude just shook his head.

Claude was the one who was the middle man when it came to Rafe and Paully's relationship. Rafe constantly wound up the huge giant and Paully could never quite get one back on him, and it was only a matter of minutes before Paully would have  to result to violence. (resolt

'What are we twelve?'

'I'm warning you Paully, I don't want to see or hear of any fighting otherwise you will have to pay.' Shem warned still laughing.

'Oh, for God's sake, man.' He looked at Shem with an appalled expression.

'I mean it.'

'What, what will I have to pay? This is worse than going to Church!'

'Well as that doesn't work anymore, we will have to restrict the level of violence you dish out every month.'

'What like, only two slaps, one kicking and only a stabbing every 3 months. God a man could just go crazy with that level of limitations.' He got up in mock anger, flinging his hands in the air, and staring at all of them and pointing his finger at each and every one of them in turn, and he told them, 'I am seriously thinking of taking up another career if these are the rules under this management.'

 'What like - Sheep shagging?'

'Bird watcher?'

'Hangman?'

'No, goat herder?'

'Milk man?'

Came the chorus back of laughed suggested alternative employment. He watched his friends spill out all these jobs while patting each other's back as if to say, that was a good one.

With hand on his heart, Paully looked so hurt and sorry for himself; he actually started to pretend he had tears in his eyes. They had missed Theatre player out completely. He bowed his head acting and keeping in character. They gave him their attention.

'You have no respect for my feelings.' And with that, they all laughed raucously whilst proceeding to throw all manner of objects at him from all directions.


Rafe had the cheek of the devil in him. Wherever he went, there was sure to be mischief. He could wind anyone up, get into a fight at a flick of a coin, and charm the pants of any one. He had two passions in life. One was women and the other was horses. Since an early age, he had been naturally attached to horses and many a time, he could be found in the family stables asleep in the hay with his favourite things in the whole world. It had been laughed at amongst the servants that the young master was an unpaid hand. However, that life had been snatched away from them, at a young age and Rafe and Shem found themselves deposited into the care of their trusted butler Gunthorpe's gypsy family who had been travelling around Europe. Rafe had taken up his training with Marcel Vargas, who was the leader and main breeder and dealer, for the Romany gypsies. His specialty being in breeding the fine Gypsy Bohemian Horses and being a main trader along the South Coast of England and Europe.

Now Rafe and Marcel were responsible for purchasing different types of horses and ponies for their different functions to suit the need of the south coast smuggling gangs and their operations.

It was also a good ploy, as a decoy, for Rafe to herd loads of horses around their favourite cargo trails. The militia had taken the bait and could be seen scouting Rafe and his party, and too often had been giving misleading information that Rafe was carrying a cargo, for this to be determined that it was a ruse. However, they had not let him off and Shem thought that had been rather clever. At times had actually used Rafe to move only small things, when the militia were fed information which they clearly were not going to act on, thinking that Rafe was just that a decoy. It was a chicken and egg situation and one that Rafe relished, and one that Shem panicked to himself about for Rafe's safety.

Rafe was enjoying the company at The Woolpack Inn at Burwash and drinking heavily with one Theo Hawkins, who was one of Bob Hawkins's nephews and Idris Speck who was one of Shem's Captains. Theo was a tall man who looked powerful and stern. Being tall was not a family trait, so there was always alot of speculation around who his father was, much to his annoyance. Theo was a man who did not like to be made to look a fool. He had thick dark hair, which he grew long with a matching dark beard. Idris was smaller and had a balding head with light stringy pieces of hair. His eyes were everywhere and he looked creepy and on edge all the time. He was one of those men who always thought he was funny. No one whoever met him trusted him. The Woolpack offered exceptional stable facilities and Rafe had needed all the space he could muster, having bought quite a few ponies and horses from his cousins at Horsendon Horse fair.

He especially liked this part of the world as Theo had a daughter called Amelia. She was small with jet-black afro hair that spiralled out of control. She was a very dark brown and had beautiful dark black eyes. She was so out of bounds. Her mother was called Sade and was from the Kingdom of Dahomey, and how she ended up in Burwash was another story. Rafe kept a good distance away from Sade for good reasons, but he could not keep his distance from Amelia. He was so in love, that Paully said it was absolutely embarrassing to watch, and he felt physically sick just listening to Rafe gushing over her when his other fancy piece, Daisy was not next door who had bore him a daughter. borne

Paully was not one for his sensitive side.

Theo's father Harry Hawkins and Idris Speck were the main men of the area, both reporting to Bob Hawkins, who was trying to convince everyone that he was semi retired and that Shem was the main man. Harry, like his brother, was of old sailing stock and controlled the galley traffic of export and importing contraband, Idris was the inland man and he took over as soon as the contraband hit dry land.

Rafe could never quite get over how Bob and Shem could control all of these separate gangs. They organised business from France to the South Coast and had a regular army of between twenty to thirty armed men available each time a shipment was due back. It was like clockwork, their gangs knew when to load and get the

* import and export of contraband

20

cargo ready for departure and at what time to rendezvous for the return shipment. The gang controlled and worked the whole South Coast, and what held it all together were the family connections. Everyone was related in some shape. (way?)

As Rafe had been warned off his beloved Amelia, Rafe had taken to the lovely Daisy and his eyes kept following her as she worked. She was a sweet girl and besotted with Rafe. She was very pale, with long thin white blond hair, big blue eyes, big bosoms, and a big plump bum. She was not the prettiest girl you would ever meet or the brightest, but she had such a lovely nature that you just could not help but love her.

Although she was working that day in the pub, at every opportunity she would wave, grin, or just lust after Rafe who she had had a crush on since her eyes had first witnessed the joy of him. He would look up from the table knowing her eyes were on him, he would curl is long hair behind his ear and beam at her every time and her heart would melt and she would sigh in delight. She and Rafe had an understanding and had done for a few years but she would die if he did not make a good woman of her soon and had paid no heed to the gossip about how he lusted after Amelia also.

Theo would look at Rafe in disbelief and shake his head. Rafe would have the biggest grin on his cheeky face and though they wanted to hate him for his luck with the ladies, all they could do was laugh at him and the things he got away with. He put it down to his fantastic personality; however one or two had said that he was well endowed which helped. Rafe could not possibly comment on that, because that would be vein! Vane

Whereas Shem was, either up or really down and broody, Rafe was light and bouncy. Many wondered how two brothers could be like chalk and cheese. Shem was determined, calculating, and cold, whereas Rafe was more laid back, happy go lucky and went with the flow. He was spontaneous and on more than one occasion, Shem would have to bail him out of one of his adventures.

Shem was a foot above most men's average height, lean, dark, with green eyes, and blond wavy long hair, which hung to just above his shoulders. He tried to grow a beard, and just ended up with stubble. Shem was not handsome; however, he had an attractiveness that made women look twice and men envious of him. He had a menacing and ruthless air about him.

Rafe was shorter, lean, and tanned. His eyes were hazel and his hair the same colour as his brothers however, his hair bounced around his head in natural curls, and hung well past his shoulders. He tended to pull it back into a ponytail. Women melted in his presence and men wondered if he was indeed a man. He had a magical charm.

The brothers had similar mannerisms, a certain way they walked, which was filled with confidence, and both shared a smile that charmed and had a bond that was undeniable. They were brothers that loved each other a great deal, would do anything for each other, and were the best of friends.

Rafe was lead by Shem, and would do anything asked of him he would not ask questions, he knew his brother had a game plan and he would be looked after. Rafe had no great ambitions himself, just to be happy, be comfortable and have a good time. Rafe just knew that Shem loved what he did and he did it well. He was respected; he looked after people and had a good reputation. However, Rafe tried not to reflect too much on the darker side of the business and the things he had witnessed his brother do and had done, nor what they both knew needed to be done. Nor did he waste time on regrets, as to what had been and how Shem had brought them where they were today.

He chuckled remembering a few weeks prior when he and Shem were both on the move, Shem was off on one of his jollies, and Rafe was going to Mayfield for the Horse fair.

'While I am away, please try and be good. Because, I don't want to have to send Paully after you.' Shem had said to Rafe. He was just finishing washing and getting dressed and Rafe was still half asleep in his bed. Shem turned to see if Rafe had heard him, leant over, and whacked him on the leg.

'Oi, bully!' Rafe had cried.

'Well, did you hear what I said?'

'I am a grown man you know, and can look after myself. And I don't need that silly wanker hanging around or being sent for.'

'You two had another row?'

'No, we had a fight and I won.'

'You still dreaming, dick head.'

Rafe began to laugh, no matter how much he would love to smack Paully one, he knew it just was not going to happen!

Rafe knew how much Shem thought he could look after himself, which Shem would never allow him to be exposed. The last time he had received a right beating. They had not taken too seriously the introduction of the New Riding Officer a while back, and certainly, Shem had been finding his feet establishing his authority over the gang and the area. The boys other personal business would have to wait.

It had not taken the New Riding Officer in charge long to make a name for himself, had immediately started to put his weight about, and even had arrested some of Shem's crew for lesser charges. However, it all became evident that Shem and company had bribed the local magistrate to get their men off and actually planted men and contraband that they wanted to be found. The men, who volunteered to be captured, were looking to be transported to the new world and grasp the excellent opportunity. It was apparent that Rafe was also a plant, and many a time he had been followed on a wild goose chase.

The brothers laughed at this however, they did not know whether to laugh or cry when Bob Hawkins's had told them the new man's name. It was Captain Hartright Mordesan. He was a Mordesan from Cornwall.

It was only natural thereafter that Shem put a spy on him constantly and his gang had started to work on him. And be it that Hartright was adamant that he personally would ride the whole of the South Coast of the smuggling vermin and restore order; it had not taken long for him to be in the gang's pocket.

However, when Hartright had set about Rafe, the die had been caste for the next chapter and Shem had to be constantly restrained by Bob.

It was bitter sweet, having waited for so long, to put things in motion and avenge the wrongs committed against him and his brother. They had needed to gain strength, to prepare and then have destiny meddle and make them step back and rethink matters. Plan, plan, and then plan again Bob would repeat and whatever you do, remember to keep emotions intact. They would be allowed to come later.

'How long will you be?' Rafe remembered asking his brother.

'As long as it takes!' Shem was not committed to a time scale. He yanked his last boot on and stood up to thump it into place.

'Hoodwinking Hartright then?' Shem looked across at his brother and grinned. 'Well don't leave home for too long, I will miss you and get lonely. I may even get married while you are away and then what will you do?'

Again, Shem said nothing, not letting on until later that he had just come from meeting Hartright who had had the cheek to threaten him!

'I can't be left alone for too long, you know, I just can't be trusted to look after myself.' He remembered his brother shaking his head listening to the same old lines.

Shem grabbed his long coat, which was lined with fur. He threw it on and headed for the door and turning to his brother just murmured. 'Grow up, ya prat!'

'Nice, yeah nice, love you too,' Rafe had shouted as the door shut behind his brother. 'If that was humour, not really getting better, maybe wanna work on it?' Rafe heard his brother chuckle as he made his way down the narrow stairs; Rafe went to one of the only glass windows in the whole inn and watched out for his brother who was making his way to the stables. Shem masked his expression. He knew exactly what his brother was thinking as he checked himself, now being outside and on show. Shem did not need to get himself a reputation for smiling now could he?

The spring day was still chilled, and Shem started to do his buttons up and wrapped his collar close to his chin.

Bob was in the stables preparing for the day's trip. He turned as he heard Shem approach and with hands outstretched remarked;

'What time do you call this?' He put his hands on his hips, mocking the young man. Shem just breezed past, heading to the stables.

'Do you wanna die?' Was all he said.

Rafe had watched as the stable lad decided this was a good time to move to the back of the pens while the two men bantered.

It was just dawn and the sky had that pinkish air about it; the ground was crisp with moisture. Shem could be seen stamping his feet against the cold and Bob laughed at him.

Bob Hawkins was semi retired and had handed the reins over to Shem. Bob had taken the young man under his wings and brought him up through the ranks. He was Shem's teacher, mentor, his protector, friend and more like an Uncle.

Bob was not a tall man, but was solid. He could put you down with one and you did not mess with him again. People tried to take liberties due to his height, but initially he let it go and only really got back at people if someone really got on his nerves. He could be a nasty bastard, and you did not mess with him even if he did look happy go lucky.

He led the horses out from the stables and mounted his horse with ease for a man of his ageing years. Shem took the reins offered and walked the horse to the edge of the stables where some of his men were waiting instructions. He looked once back up at the room he shared with his brother then mounted and was off.

Shem had sowed the seeds for Hartright Mordesan to be off on a wild goose chase and he was preparing for the biggest haul he had ever organised.


Now back in the present, Rafe's attention was drawn to the lovely Daisy and he was just about to make his move when the pig loud figure of Paully and his crew entered the tavern.

'Did ya miss me?'

Rafe lowered his hands in his head, sighing and nearly cried.

'Go away and leave me alone.'

'No!' Paully said too chirpily. 'Orders, my love.' Daisy smooched over and poured him some ale. He shook hands with both Idris and Theo and then did not take his eyes off the lovely wench. He smiled wildly at her, at which point Rafe kneed him under the table.

'Babysitting?'

'Yes, and before you start,' he looked at him viciously for kneeing him. 'I did promise not to cause any trouble and behave like a saint!'

Both Theo and Idris nearly choked. He looked at both of them and winked.

He then took a serious stance and leant forward as did the others on the table.

'Shem sent word, Idris, for you to return with us and to ensure the crew take extra precautions here, ya not going to believe this but Hartright has gone and got himself a set of balls. He must have been hit over the head or had an epiphany, as Shem said.'

'That's a big word for you Paully.'

'I'm impressed that I remembered how to say it to be honest Idris.'

'So what's it mean?' They all looked to Rafe, as he had been educated.

'Rafe?'

'You dick head,' Rafe found himself laughing at his friend who volunteered to be the idiot. Then Paully held up his hand indicating for Rafe not to speak.

'It means, a moment, a realisation, all of the sudden it all makes sense sort of thing.' Paully finished seeing his comrades' nod in appreciation. Paully may play the idiot but Rafe knew that Paully's father had insisted that his illegitimate children were educated. He just was too lazy to think half the time. 'Well anyway, Hartright only went and bought some low life to try and off Shem at The Castle. Can you believe it?'

'He did what?' Rafe stood up in shock.

Paully sipped his drink while they all took in the implications.

'Is he for real?'

'Got too big for his boots'

'He must be getting pressure from on high.'

'Or impressing a woman!'

'I hear his sisters fit.'

'She's a bitch.' Rafe offered and then curbed his tongue.

'Know her do ya?' Theo nudged him suggestively.

'Oh, ya know...' Rafe tried to steer away from the conversation, he most certainly did know her, and still it left a bitter taste in his mouth.

'She blew you out!' Theo concluded at which Rafe shrugged his shoulders and pretended embarrassment.

'Well, I never!'

'Anyway.' Paully said over the top of them. 'So, home we go to see what happens next.'

'It was definitely Hartright's men?' Rafe asked and Paully nodded. 'You sort 'em out then?'

'No, Shem had that pleasure, he was that pissed off that the twat had sent amateurs. I just sat down and had a rest.'

'But why?' Rafe questioned Hartright's motives.

'That's what we need to determine.' Idris offered as he then got up and affectionately smacked Paully on the back.

Hartright Mordesan had been especially commissioned to head up the Land guard and with the government backing was now in charge of a troupe of 50 riding officers. Previously the coast was just overseen by a handful of men, and this clearly was ineffective.

In addition to the extra riding officers, the government had sponsored over 20 new naval ships to target the sea smuggling aspect and Hartright in line with the Navy and Water Guard were to work hand in hand.

Hartright soon discovered that his riding officers were country people, and not very partial towards the officers of the Customs or the Naval sections, so between the two grades many smuggling bands were allowed to carry on their work almost unmolested.

He had looked to employ someone with the experience to whip his men into shape and he had enlisted the talents of Joshua Clay. He was a man in his early forties with a strong military background, having just returned from the Netherlands and was more than able. He was committed and a diligent officer. He was a long man with a drawn gaunt expression. He wore his hair short and his side burns were black and tightly curled. He always looked ill, sweaty, and unwashed. He was a vicious, ill-tempered angry man.

Hartright felt that his presence was enough to frighten people, and he found that he could not bear to look at the man, and more than once felt himself ready to gag. Hartright hated dirt and always tried to turn out looking immaculate.

Traditionally, the riding officers were paid a pittance and tended to turn a blind eye in return for payment of a small fee and Hartright could see this as being irresistible. He had wanted to set a standard and not have anyone on the take, and wanted to weed out all the original riding officers, but this had proven harder than he thought, and really, he had to rely on the experience of Clay to keep his men in order.

Hartright prided himself on his appearance and took ages over his toilet. He was of medium height with silver blond hair that was very fine. He had sharp features and a very sharp noise. He wore his hair long and pulled back into a ponytail. He could not abide wigs and had so far stayed away from that particular fashion. He had a good complexion and very rosy cheeks.

Hartright was a man on a mission; it was his duty to try to make some sort of name for himself. He did not wish to just inherit from his uncle and have it all laid out for him. He wanted to make his family proud of his achievements, and have his sister Constance swell with pride.

He was under the impression that he could win the war with the smugglers, and had no idea that these men, if you can call , scum of the earth, men, could give him lessons in how to be successful, how to manoeuvre, how to manipulate situations and work as a unit for everyone's benefit. For him, smuggling was a selfish trade, motivated by greed. He did not see the other aspects of what it gave the community, the camaraderie, the need to survive. As far as he was concerned everyone involved were low life vermin, he was a noble man through and through, and that was the only criteria he needed to succeed.

He would not admit that he was jealous of the success of the smuggler leaders. Jealous at the way they had successfully organised themselves. The vast amounts of money they earned. He thought if he became just as devious and deceptive, to show the locals he meant business, they would fear him more than the smugglers. He had not bargained on the fact that even the magistrates and Lords of the areas all had a hand in the deceit. That everyone's lives touched smuggling in some shape or form, and then to learn that people had volunteered to plead guilty for crimes that they did not commit, knowing full well that the magistrate had been bribed to send them to the Carolinas, where they were held in servitude for as little as two years and then were free. They knew that their families would follow, all had been protected, and they had jobs waiting for them. He did not understand their mentality.

Slowly it had dawned on him that he was losing and what could he do, to reclaim some sort of face? Everyone earned from this smuggling while he chased fairies. He was not wholly stupid and grasped that Rafe Smith, Shem's younger brother was a decoy. So why could he not earn in turn?

It had started subtly at first without him even realising that he was on the payroll.

He would wake up and find a nice deposit of rum by his bed. His men would receive special favours from the ladies; to this, he was never grateful and found he would take his frustrations out on the whores.

He and his men could also expect a hot free meal here and there. Then when he was in certain Inns he would be approached and given back his purse, which unbeknown to him; he had apparently dropped on the floor. Then he would receive little messages from passersby who he never knew, and was never likely to see again. They would approach him at the market, or in a crowded place and say that he had a gift waiting at a certain place.

He could not believe that he was given to turn a blind eye and over time he knew his men had became complacent, the drive had been lost, yet Hartright's pride still pricked him. He still tried to gather intelligence and still made arrests, although irregular. Clay was good at getting little snippets of information, but even he had became accustomed to the good life and could be found in the local whore house. His reputation for being nasty had been watered down and the Madams had warned him to behave. Whenever he now visited these places, he soon found that local Hench men would suddenly appear and watch blatantly his every move. At this time, he was naive to that fact that there was a permanent spy reporting on his every move.

Hartright had grown more and more bitter at being made to look like a fool rather than a hero. He had even started to exaggerate his successes to his family. He was living a lie and now in his anger at getting a result, he had thought that attacking the main men would send a ripple through the gangs. However so far this had not been overly successful which added to his frustration.

He did not know which way to turn. He had to show them that he should look like he was attempting to bring in some smugglers and get a decent conviction every so often.

He was becoming rash and this lead to mistakes, coming away from the game plan and becoming unpredictable. He had tried to ruffle a few feathers of the key players in the smuggling community, but they had been feeble attempts and had just resulted in Shem tightening his security even further.

If Shem had his way, he would have knifed Hartright the first time he had set eyes on him. However, he had learnt patience. He gathered his evidence and worked his plans behind the scenes. He would have his day. He would ensure that Rafe was safe. He had waited so long now and the fire had smouldered for too long, it needed to be put out!

As they made their way into the Castle Inn, they felt all eyes on them. They peaked their tricornes and woolly caps in greeting and then moved nearer to the warmth of the hearth.

The Castle Inn crowd whispered amongst themselves at the identity of the newcomers and then after speculation and confirmation, they all resumed their previous conversations although there was still a tension in the air.

Ned and Ray Cavendish, with some of their crew from Alfriston, felt like they had walked into the Lion's Den and Ray knew that lesser men would have succumbed to the level of scrutiny that they were the victims of. The hairs on the back of their necks stood to attention and Ned thought he would die of fear. Ray just scowled angrily, as was the norm.

Shem had requested that they meet at The Castle, which was nestled on the High Street in Pevensey. That evening the place was packed to the rafters with all those of a less savoury kind that made up Shem's many different crews. There were his bodyguards, his sailors, his local cargo carriers, the locals mingling and loads of loads of lose women of the night. They worked the local Ale and Inn houses and reported to their madam who run the local whorehouse, which was called the Mint House, which was across the road. The atmosphere usually was vibrant and loud with laughter. Slowly this took hold again.

Ray and Ned Cavendish broke away from their own men who had started to mingle and found themselves being welcomed by Claude, who nodded in greeting and then directed them towards his guvnor's table.

Without a word, Shem's company left and Shem remained with the ever-watchful Bob in the corner. Whilst he motioned for the brothers to sit down, the Landlord's wife Valentina served drinks. She liked to keep an eye on her working girls.

Ray could not believe how beautiful she still was. He remembered seeing her years ago. The famous whore of Sussex! She was tall and slim with long black silk hair that was loosely plaited. She was of Spanish Ottoman descent and she moved like a dancer, very gracefully, slow and purposed.

Ned felt that although everyone had eased back into their drinks and conversation had resumed, that eyes still were peering across, curious to see what was happening. Ray could not keep his eyes off the whore.

The Cavendish brother's and their gang landed contraband along the South Coast, mainly at Cuckmere Valley and surrounding area, with Alfriston Village being their main base. The gangs earned a good steady living and they liked to think that they had a good working relationship with Bob and now Shem. There was enough meat on the bone and if everyone agreed their turf then no one lost out.

Shem had earned a reputation for being unyielding. Ned felt out of his league sitting opposite the younger man who was determined, ruthless, and full of energy. He was a great technician and was unsurpassed in organisation. He believed in delegating and was greatly rewarded with loyalty from his men, clients and the general public. But Ned knew about the dangerous menacing side and Ned was weary.

He looked about again taking in his surroundings and was anxious being in such wanted company. He thought if the local militia were about, they would have a field day. Then he breathed more easily, having seen the amount of security outside.

Yet he did like Shem. Whether Ray did was another matter. He looked across at his brother and he could see that he was calculating how to get out of there in one piece.

Ray was a fighter, if in doubt; he just lashed out and thought about what he had done after. They both sipped their drinks and Ray found himself getting quite apprehensive.

He had hated the way that Shem had ordered William Devereux (their business partner and friend) and Ned to report to him, and hated the way that Shem had still not remarked on William not being there and he in his place. Nevertheless, Shem already knew what the score was.

He felt intimidated and, due to that fact, considered how he could do Shem if it all went pear shaped. Ray had matched up many times with Paully in the bear knuckle tournaments and even though Paully had the slight upper hand now, he had heard that Shem was just as good. But if he could beat Paully, he could do Shem.

Ray had not listened to the conversation thus far and caught the back end of Ned's report. He was advising Shem about Hartright's activities in their area. There was nothing of great importance to convey, other than he had been staying at the Devereuz House over in Lewes, where he had an open invitation to stay for a few weeks.

Ray and Ned had been told the bare bones of a job that was coming up and told what was expected of them, what the terms were and had not been given an opportunity to decline the favour. Unlike some of the gangs, they were further down the food chain and did not get involved in more of the hard-core activities. Their function was mainly transporting the goods and using their good contacts.

Ned was rather pleased that he shared the table with Shem, as usually it would be Claude giving those orders, and he became quite comfortable and they started to discuss other aspects of the business which Ned found as an opportunity to put forward some ideas. This may lead into him asking if they could expand, but timing was everything so he held back for now. Whether Shem had a further motive did not cross his mind.

All the while Ray just sat ideally thinking of ways that he could take Shem down. His crew was far smaller and by doing that, he would get everyone killed. It was just the idea of having one up on this lairy bastard that was helping to increase his confidence.

He could do Shem; he was puny compared to him. Ray was a big man, who was robust but still he knew Shem would do him, and then would kill him. Then he imagined Shem would have a field day and walk all over his men, his farm, his tavern, and his Grandfather, Shaun Cavendish. The operation would be absorbed into his and this was all for wishful thinking. Ray hated it when he confused pride and his ego. Why was he thinking in such a way anyway? He hated to admit that he was slightly scared and out of his league.

Shem's crew run the whole show on the south coast and therefore they answered to him. The gangs were run like a military organisation and once in, it was very hard to get out. If you grassed you were dead, if you thought you would be protected and in hiding then your nearest and dearest were next in line. Therefore, no one snitched. Why would they? They had work; they had money and so far a good prosperous living.

Shem's reputation was growing far beyond the boundaries of the South Coast. He posed a mystery and as such, gossip and stories emerged.

Ray found it hard to look at this man and the man Shem had become. He remembered the first time he had met him, that seemed like a lifetime ago and he certainly remembered his sister had been taken by him too!

Ray decided to appear focused and just concentrate. To be alert as Shem was lethal but as the conversation had flowed between Ned and Shem, Ray had begun to get impatient and without realising, it had blurted out what they had wanted as part of the deal that Ned had just laid on the table.

Ned immediately looked at him with such loathing that Ray was tempted to look away. He knew it had been inappropriate and his timing could have been better. However, he had asked anyway, he knew his nerves had got the better of him. Their Gang was longing to expand, seeing an opportunity and he had just asked for permission to do a job and go across one of Shem's other Captain's territory to transport some goods.

Shem respected anyone who wished to get on and he would do business with most, subject to gain and respect. Shem tapped his fingers on the table and smiled at Ray who he genuinely liked. He knew Ned was more diplomatic and would have asked when the time was right.

Claude sat forward, his whole body language alert and ready to bounce on Ray for being so out of order. Shem smiled and held his hand forward and stopped Claude from physically whacking Ray for his disobedience.

'Tell me why you are asking and not that cocksure wanker who plays at being your Leader?' Ray was delighted that Shem had not told him right away to get stuffed and that Claude had not managed to get across to him. Then he felt the presence of Paully behind him.

'He couldn't make it.'

'Take this seriously then does he?'

'Look Shem, we came so while we're here, I'm asking? So no more fucking about, what will it cost us?'

Shem leant back on his chair and swung back on two legs. He drunk from his tankard and looked at Ray intently, whilst still smiling. Claude and Paully knew Shem was playing with him and were waiting for Shem to put Ray in his place.

Shem knew that Ray loved the chase and that he was a little too impulsive. He then looked at Ned. Ned was the thinker, the one who reined him in, the pragmatic one. Ned was laid back and moved with an ease that many thought boarded on laziness, but to Shem it was the sign of a man who just knew what he was doing. He would get there when he was ready.

He needed to keep these two in line, but on his side. As to the other one, William, well he was another story. Shem certainly was not a charity; but he did like the Cavendish brothers. He smiled to himself, and reminded himself not to mix business with pleasure. Paully clocked the change of smile and the sparkle in Shem's eyes and knew it was coming.

Shem observed the way that Ray did not beat about the bush, was not going to grovel, and was rather brash in his request. He liked the way that Ned did not butt in and let Ray take over and sent a small smile to Ned while Ray was not looking. Ned immediately let out a breath he had been holding and started to relax back in his chair, taking it all in his stride. Shem noticed at that point that all the Cavendish's, Ned, Ray and their sister Rosie, all had the same hazel coloured eyes.

'Idris will handle from Burwash.' Shem watched Ray's conflicting emotions, - disappointment, not too surprised, yet ready to do battle.

'So that's a no?' Ray had the right hump now, and again felt like smacking Shem one. This wasn't going so well and he hated to lose. Why was he here anyway, he was rubbish at this sort of thing, Ned was better? He looked at his brother for support, but Ned with effort, waved his hand as if dismissing him. Well he had decided the quick abrupt no nonsense approach worked well for Ray. In fact, he couldn't remember the last time he did not get his own way. Well he never did with his wife. Shem was a hard taskmaster and he could easily take it all away, he had the muscle, the power, and the connections. Ray had to tread very carefully indeed. If only he had just kept his mouth shut.

'Did I say that?' He goaded Ray and again looked at Ned with a twinkle in his eye. Shem banged his chair down. Ray sat back. *Hello, what was happening here then?* Shem held out his hand for Ray to shake. Ray firmly took Shem's hand and they shook, but as Ray went to release his hand, Shem brought his other hand round and smashed Ray's arm down on the table. This brought Ray's whole body forward. Then as quick as a flash he felt Shem's power and his hands went to his head and smashed his head on to the table. Tankards of Ale jumped up and everyone in the tavern knew that something was going on, but pretended not to look. Shem held Ray's face firm against the table and then for good measure smashed Ray's head down again. He leant over him and whispered in his ear. 'I do like you Ray.'

Then as quick as a flash he released him, stood up, and brushed himself down. He really did want to make more of a show of the man for his disrespect but knew it would get back to Rosie, their sister, and he really could not handle the grief she would give him when they ran into each other again. He smiled at that, he missed her; she was one of the only people who spoke to him without any inhibitions.

'Ned come and see me soon.' He then casually walked away, his men following him all but Bob remained. Bob calmly sipped his ale and nodded intently.

'He likes ya boys, don't mess it up.' Bob raised his drink to Ned in a salute. 'Well done lad.' He winked at Ray who was still aghast at what had happened.

'You call that liking?' Bob held up a hand to silence Ray who was still bright red with embarrassment.

'I'll be coming back with ya to talk with Shaun, and boys, remember.................' They waited. 'Forgotten what I was going to say. What was it?'

'Need a top up Bob?' Ray was beginning to get a little too sarcastic, trying to divert the attention from his comeuppance from Shem.

'I ain't that drunk to know when you are taking the piss Ray and I can still knock you for six you saucy pup, or better still get Shem back hey? Oh, lost me thread, that's it, now be extra careful with that dick head, whashesname? We need to talk

35

about this relationship that your young Lord and Hartright have. Remember the bit you deliberately left out of your report! Word of warning, cos we like ya, do this right! No hanky panky.'

Ned left out a long breath and tried to apologise to Bob who held his hand up and dismissed it. Ned knew that they already were aware of everything about the friendship that had developed between their friend and business partner William Devereux, and it was wise in future to never underestimate the power of Shem. They had just scratched the big league and Ned was unsure how long they could swim and whether he really wanted to get in this deep.

Ned also recognised that Shem had deplored divide and conquer tactics and the Cavendish boys had been given the go ahead for a new run, however their current absent Leader – William Devereux had been left out in the cold!

**Chapter Two**

'That Hot head of a brother of yours…' Hartright left hanging in the air. Shem had decided to give the new Captain of the Riding officers an audience finally.

Hartright had only been in the area a few months and was determined to make his mark. It was their first meeting.

The gangs had all been watching to see what would happen as a consequence of the government commissioning a few more riding officers to patrol the South Coast.

Shem had asked Bob to gather as much information as possible on Hartright. He already hated him, but when he found out his name, he could have spat kittens. He had been tempted to just get his dagger out and stab the man to death right there and then. But fate had dealt him a hand and he would milk it.

Shem slowly turned round to face the officer from his stance observing the buzz on Hastings harbour. They had met in one of the local hilltops, away from preying eyes, where they could talk.

He had taken a few trusted men to this first rendezvous and they made a picket line for security. Hartright had also brought his trusted Clay, his right hand man along with and a handful of men, and both gangs eyed each other suspiciously.

Shem glared at Hartright waiting for the next line. Hartright knew he was playing with fire; and his confidence had begun to increase with every new dare and he found the opportunities of a riding officer most rewarding when one mixed with the right gentlemen. Yes the pay was bad, but the opportunities out weight that. He tried to read the man before him, but was hindered to fully look at his face by the way he wore his tricorne His hat was a deep green and pipe lined with black velvet and deliberately lowered to shadow his face. He wore a scarf around his neck, which reached to his lower lip.

His hair was long and plaited thinly at the sides and constantly whipped against his face as the wind took up.

'He will get caught.' Hartright smirked milking the moment. Shem chose to ignore the man and not belittle himself with the challenge. Therefore, Hartright still liked to play games and play people off on each other. They both knew that they were on tender hooks and Shem found his mind wondering on how he would kill the man. He rather liked the idea of a long, slow death for the man, which incorporated being stretched, quartered, sliced and then perhaps some nails being ripped out! He could see the man calling for his Mummy, and he grinned to himself. He had certainly seen that before.

If only Hartright knew who he really was! He knew that Hartright considered him a jumped up lairy bastard, with limited intelligence, who just happened to be in the right place at the right time.

Shem looked at Hartright with contempt. Hartright was vein and smug and this was evident in the way he wore his uniform and conducted himself. Shem saw a man who liked everything to be just so and his shirt was clean and crisp, his shoe buckles and buttons sparkled and his tricorne was of the best quality. His hand kept a tight grip on his sabre and he looked like a man who knew how to use it. He also wore a pistol across his chest and looked every part a professional soldier.

Shem had been both looking forward to meeting Hartright and dreading the encounter. Every fibre of his being screamed out to kill the bastard right now for previous wrongs, but Shem knew this was the greatest test of all. How he could look this man in the eye, keep calm, and calculate how he would manoeuvre the situation to his advantage and ultimately the long thought out plan?

He could not believe that history was repeating itself and Hartright had the cheek to threaten his brother Rafe. That Hartright had the nerve to say that Rafe would be caught, he said. Caught for what exactly? The only thing Rafe would be caught for would be with his trousers down and in the wrong bed! He was desperate to get it off with the beautiful Amelia, the local forge masters daughter in Burwash. Rafe had the luck of the devil and always had good old Daisy the Burwash Bar maid, to fall back on. God knew who else he visited at the Mint House, which they appeared to be using more and more as a home base!

Hartright had no inkling of the scale of the South Coast operation and was led to believe that Shem run this small little outfit, and was like himself, a Lieutenant in an organised field. He took orders from above.

Hartright always fancied that he would someday meet the main man, and be seen as the Hero of the Day, by arresting this exclusive man who run the whole South

Coast Smuggling ring. He visualised how Her Majesty, would reward him handsomely, he would be glorified and made an Earl for his troubles, rather than having to wait for his uncle to pop off.

He did not feel he was doing anything wrong by dipping his toe into the water. He could twist to his advantage and kill anyone who got in his way. He had the power and the confidence to be immortal, and no scum was going to get in his way. In his ignorance, he believed he was invincible.

Shem turned back to the sea and shrugged his shoulders; Hartright thought that as an admission of defeat but to Shem it was, let this be over soon so that I can just kill the bastard!

'Rafe is his own man, and has business ventures all over the county, all above board with papers.' Was all Shem said and left that hanging in the air!

Bob bit back a grin. They could not believe that Hartright had so under-estimated them, so they let him continue to believe how they were just small fish in a very, very big pond.

During the meeting, Hartright formed the impression that Rafe, the spoilt little prat had been sent packing, so his persistence to Shem had hit home, and he felt he had scored a point. He believed to himself that his actions had caused Shem to act and for Shem to appreciate there was only so much covering up that he could do to stop Rafe being put up for the gallows. He did like to acquire a horse or two that had not been up for sale at the local fairs, which had not gone unnoticed!

Hartright felt himself swell with pride and that now he felt that Shem was in his debt, that he owed him something, because he had listened to him about his brother's behaviour and the attention it was bringing and he had acted.

What had really happened was that Shem had used his annoying brother as a decoy to persistently get on Hartright's' nerves and harass him and pull him all over the place. Rafe would brag that he was purchasing this type of horse for this type of work. That lead people to talk that the gangs were perhaps looking to use this or that point for their next drop, or use so and so's farm to hide things. Rafe would tell everyone, who would listen, his business. In fact, he had been given permission to just make stuff up as he went along. Moreover, Hartright had fallen for it, unaware there was no way that Shem would ever put his brother in a situation that they could not get out of. Rafe would probably do that himself! He had the charm of the devil.

Shem was starting to feel that he was losing control of himself at the meeting and his patience; he could feel his hate for the man intensify as they stood there. He kept having flash backs and found himself squeezing his hands tight.

He concentrated so badly, on not killing him. The emotions drained him thoroughly. He caught Bob's eyes and both agreed without saying a word that this was getting tedious, and could they just kill him now? Paully would be pleased!

'We will be in the Marsh Lands between Wednesday and Thursday.' Shem left hanging in the air and started to walk away to where the horses were tied. Bob stepped nearer to Hartright and whispered. 'You are a bit clumsy ain't ya? Look you've dropped something on the floor!'

Their meeting was over. Hartright watched as the party rode away, smacked his crop to his thigh, and grinned. What a good days work! He was being given another gift and that would do nicely. Very nicely, indeed! He was not a greedy man, just a man that wanted it all.

'At least we know where the shit head is.' Paully remarked having knocked at Shem's private rooms above the main bar in The Castle. The Inn was a few hundred yards down from Pevensey Castle and Paully could see the great entrance through the small glass window. 'He's playing cricket.'

The gang were cramped into Shem and Rafe's small room discussing the latest crisis that had befallen them because of Hartright and his men's meddling. Bob's two nephews had managed to escape by the skin of their teeth after an attack on their prized boat, The Three Brothers.

Bob did not care one fig for the contraband and was heartbroken about his poor boat and both his nephews, thought it was abit rich that he hadn't asked them once if they were all fine and dandy!

They were one of many gangs that were wholly sponsored by Bob and Shem, and sailed back and forth to Guernsey. They purchased goods that were to be smuggled back, such as brandy, tea, and rum.

Unfortunately, the crew had been spotted and after hours of being chased and fired on, the cutter had heaved too.

Customs held a deputation to seize prohibited goods, and had been watching for an opportunity to cease one of Bob's known runs. After a tip off, they laid in wait with Hartright's men giving support on land.

Bob could have easily dismissed the contraband, as for everyone he lost; they were better being beached and moved on to more than cover the costs lost. Nevertheless, it was his beloved boat, his ole girl, and he had loved and nurtured for many a good year.

His nephews had trailed the cargo, which had been taken into Rottingdean, a small village off the larger town of Brighton and along the coast from the Alfriston Gangs area. There was tons of tea, casks of brandy and rum, together with a small bag of coffee. They just could not let it go and watched as it was conveyed ashore and locked up safely in the Rottingdean Custom House.

Bob had ensured the contraband was watched night and day and after a few days, he had made his way to The Castle to discuss the next plan of action with Shem.

'You're joking?' Bob sighed. 'Ain't the fucking nobility got anything better to do?'

'Well suits us.' Claude analysed.

'Do you wanna know the scores?' Paully asked innocently.

'What?'

'Well, who's winning? Is there a stake? Who do we want to win? My Dad's team or the Magistrates Team?'

'Are you for fucking real?' Shem gazed at Paully as if he had two heads. Shem had started to wash himself and poured his warm water from the jug to the vase bowl.

'Well, could be an earner.' Paully shrugged his shoulders, instead of taking a seat went straight to the made bed, and threw himself across it.

Valentina had followed him up and proceeded to put some hot tea onto the table. Paully raised himself on his elbows and winked at her. Bob went across and slapped his legs; Paully looked at him aghast and mouthed, - 'What?'

'Shut the fuck up you prat.' Shem warned shaking his head and turned back to finish washing his torso. Valentina left silently, aware that she held a trusted position being able to come and go as she pleased and all knowing that she would never dream of saying a word to anyone on what she overheard.

'That's nice, motivational, inspiring.' Paully stopped thinking he was beginning to sound like Rafe.

'He ain't had enough tea yet.' Bob started to laugh; it was far too early for all of them.

'Will you lot just fuck off! God almighty, it is like working with a bunch of kids?'

'You love it.' Paully moaned as he closed his eyes to have a doze.

'Fuck off.' He heard Shem again moan and then next minute he cried out in pain as the whole lot of them bundled onto him on the bed.

It was late in the night.

Paully, Claude and their men were sent ahead to picket. Meanwhile Shem and Bob waited in the freezing rain and dead of night for news. Shem found his mind wandering from the task, and as always since his last encounter with a certain young woman, he found his mind's eye resting on her and how she was and a warm fuzzy feeling would come all over him.

Her memory was like a breath of fresh air and always had him laughing. She made him act young and carefree. She was a cocky one, and wore her heart on her sleeve. She had been so glad to see him, asked him how he faired and was genuine. He laughed remembering their very first encounter when she had been anything but lady like! She enjoyed to talk and sometimes even laughed at herself when she got carried away with the conversation. She was all his, his little pixie.

He was perched down in the middle of an ancient wood, the rain falling on his head, he was soaked through and just waiting until they received word that all was clear. It was pitch black; the stars sparkled in delight and the only noise was the soft wind singing through the trees and the horses shifting their weight.

He pictured her at the Fair, a smile on her face, as she wondered around exploring all the fun of the fair. Watching, observing wondrous things and making him participate in all sorts. He remembered she was especially good at the bow and arrow and had beaten him fairly when they had a wager. She bragged that she had always been better than her brothers had.

She took nothing for granted and marvelled at all the beautiful trades and workmanship that was brought to the fair and was in awe at the wonderful horses and ponies on display.

He remembered her darting around from place to place, with her hair all over the place. It had a mind of its own and, no matter how tight it was plaited and pinned up, it was forever falling out of place. He remembered looking deep into her eyes, her hazel eyes.

'Why you smiling like the cat got the cream for?' Bob mused as he elbowed him. Shem elbowed him playfully back and shook his head, coming back to reality.

'Shut up and mind ya own.' Shem spoke casually being lazy with his speech.

'It's a woman.' He whispered to no one in particular.

Shem raised his eyes in protest and Bob nodded into the night, again at no one.

'Knew it! Can't keep nothing from me.'

'Will you shut up, or I will cut ya tongue out?'

'It is that lass, that lovely little thing, at the fair isn't it pup? Said it, didn't I? Whashername? Caught by thunder! When's the wedding?'

Shem turned on the balls of his feet and as quick as a flash grabbed Bob by the neck and mouthed to him playfully while grinning wildly.

'Just shut up or I will.....' He pretended to squeeze the old bloke's throat, and Bob fell back onto his bottom, onto the wet grass. He picked himself up and wiped his backside leant then leant over to him and cheekily whispered.

'All talk, you love me, and you won't kill me.'

Shem chuckled at Bob, who playfully punched him in the arm. 'That hurt.' He mouthed pretending to be mortified.

'SSSSHH,' come from up the ways, at which both men's immediate stance changed to alert and all business.

A whistle floated through the air and Shem signalled to Bob who returned the call. Slowly from the night, Claude made his way forward.

'There's a sloop-of-war lay opposite to the quay,' he reported and explained that her guns could be pointed against the doors of the Custom House. Shem looked to Bob who conveyed the news along the line. They nodded to each other and slowly the party made his way to the Custom House.

'I said whatdoyou call it? You know? Didn't I?' Bob started.

'No I have no idea.'

'The thing.' Shem just looked at Bob with a blank expression.

'Don't get annoyed.' Bob moaned seeing Shem getting impatient again with him for not being able to get his words out.

'Well for fucks sake please.' He indicated holding his hands out to show Bob they were in the thick of it, it was pitch black and spitting with rain, they were waiting to do a job, and Bob couldn't get his words out.

'The sea, water, ......thing.'

'Oh my word!'

'The tide, tide, tide!'

'Thank fuck.' Shem knew what he was going to say.

'The tide, its low, low ebb.'

'You know its fucking torture working with you.'

'I can say the same.'

'What, I get on your nerves?' Shem questioned playfully.

'No, I get on my own nerves; you don't have to live with me!' He then pointed out to sea impatiently. 'It's an ebb tide tonight, look, we're in business.' Bob grinned.

Shem was still trying to suppress a laugh and shook his head, Bob patted him on the back and winked at which Shem mused. 'You ain't coming on any more jobs, I'm putting you out to pasture.'

Through local intelligence, the gang had been advised of what times the tides were and had ascertained what time would be a good to get their goods back. The gang proceeded in picket fashion towards the customs house.

All the men were alert for any sign of danger, and confident from their scouting that there were no parties protecting the valuables, only a man of war out at sea, who could not have a good and clear shot at them with a low tide, which was against them.

The Custom services were so confident that no one would bother to attempt to come and steal back the goods. Hartright had immediately been authorised to oversee the investigation of the crime and capture of all known ringleaders. To date, all he had managed to arrest were petty thieves who had been given across as bait, having been thrown out of the gangs. As the Customs officers thought that the House was well protected from the sea, no guards had been posted. Claude immediately went to the locked front door and with hatchet in hand, proceeded to attack and get the door open.

'Can you make any more fucking noise?' Paully jeered. The door collapsed with an almightily thump and Claude laughed in triumph.

'Fermer, le cochon anglais !' He responded.

'Give it a rest girls.' Bob tried to tell the children off.

Claude waited for Paully to join him at the door and then mocking his friend he bowed down, made a big flourish, and motioned for him to go first.

'Not so brave now are ya?' Paully whispered.

'Oh if that's the case, you idiot, I'll go first.' He went to move his friend out of the way. But Paully stood his ground and gave Claude a dirty look at which he backed off.

The giant of a man poked his head through the doorway and in a woman's voice called; - 'Hello, any one home, is there any one 'ere?' He cheekily looked back at his friends and poked his tongue out at Claude, who gave him the two fingers; he then turned back and marched into the lion's den. 'I've just popped round to get me stuff...' They heard him joking in the blackness of the house, Claude followed, and they heard him call back.

'Clear'

Shem and Bob just looked at each other as if to say, do you believe these two?

As quickly as they had come, they had rescued the cargo, and an organised file of men headed back up the road to the waiting horses.

The band was divided into separate sections, with the intention that all went their separate ways to off load the merchandise in the usual way.

'I don't much care for coffee... .' Paully observed to no one in particular, watching as the men slowly disappeared into the night.

'I don't care that you do not care, will you just get a fucking move on.' Bob groaned through the night. He could hear them all start to move off. Bob just wanted to get away as quickly as possible and think about how he could ever replace his precious boat the Three Brothers.

'There's no need to take that tone with me.' Paully sulked like a child looking back over his horse at his partner in crime. Claude was sure he would have stuck his tongue out playfully again if he hadn't warned him off.

'If you don't move your fucking arse, there will be no fucking tea, shit, or sugar.

45

Now move it you plep.' Shem hissed and at that, they all moved forward in complete silence, as they had approached conscious that they had sufficient scouts along the way and that the man at war was none the wiser.

'For fucks sake George, you scared me shitless.'

'Sorry Paully, been hiding out here for ages and anxious to get it over with and all that.' Paully could not believe that George, single handily would be able to even consider arresting even one of them. In fact, how was it that he was here? He was far off his normal patrol area. They had been making their way back up the valley to meet the coast road.

George was wet, frozen, and shuffling from one foot to the other. Yet his stupidity still astounded Paully.

'You can see I'm in a hurry and need to get away. Don't fuck it up mate!' Paully tried to reason being discovered by George English, the local Custom man. George's hair was plastered to his head and al his clothes appeared to be soaked through. He was a tall thin man with a pleasant face. Everyone always commented on how well mannered he was. He talked to everyone in the same manner and was always respectful. No one had ever heard him curse in his life. He slowly walked towards Paully with his musket held firm, all the while looking out for the others who he knew were in the shadows. George, unlike many of the existing riding officers was not ostracised by his community because he was genuinely liked.

George was predictable, amicable and gullible, and many believed that he deliberately spent many hours away from home, as a ploy, not to show he was willing to catch the smugglers, but purely because he was scared of his wife, Bella. She was a force of nature and no one messed with her.

'Well I'm sorry, but you know...' George found himself saying. 'I am awfully sorry and all that, however duty does call Paully, I have to show ....'

'You are taking the piss?' Paully shook his head and watched as George hesitantly stopped before him and started to shift from one foot to the other again, all the while, trying to keep the pistol on Paully, and with his other hand hid inside his coat  to keep warm. His eyes shifted all about, trying to catch shadows. Paully lowered his head shaking it all the while and placed his hands on his hips, sighing. He needed to sort this whole mess out! He then went for something in his pocket, at which George immediately drew back in fright.

'Have some of this to warm you up.' Paully handed him his brandy flask. George backed up and held his pistol out firmly. Then, seeing it was indeed a drink, he relaxed, just a little, and took the drink with appreciation. He put the flask to his mouth and with his teeth, undone the flask and took a generous swig.

'God, I needed that.'

'Well I'm freezing me bollocks off here too, I am wet through, and I want to get back to the Inn. You should get home yourself. You know its Prudence shift tonight and God in heaven; you could just die in her tits.' Paully was grinning from ear to ear with the memory.

'Now is that any way to talk?' Paully could see that George was trying to be serious, and a hint of a grin was evident, so he failed to see it coming.

Claude had been creeping forward from the shadows and landed a thud with the back of his pistol to George's head. He went down like a sack of potatoes.

'You didn't kill him?' Paully looked appalled and his eyes nearly popped out of his head. He leant over George all the while thinking that Bella would kill him. Claude also bent down to feel his pulse. He grinned back up at Paully who exclaimed. 'Thank fuck!' He heard the others making their way towards them as quietly as the night and only the rustle of their clothes and horses snorts giving them away, they all appeared to have witnessed what had happened and had huge grins on their faces.

'George is a diamond bloke and God, could you imagine our Bella if I had accidently done him in. No, I just can't bear to think of it?' Paully shuddered to himself whilst Claude looked at his mate in disbelieve and wonder, all the while shaking his head. The rest of the gang went by snickering and making jokes at Paully's expense. Claude retrieved George's weapon and placed it his trouser buckle, whilst Paully hands on hips, started to re assess the situation.

'What shall we do with him?' He called to Claude, who was already moving away. He was worried now.

'The idiot dosey bastard's your brother in law!' Claude flung over his shoulder.

Paully couldn't believe that Claude had just left him to sort it out. So he grabbed his blankets from the back of his horse and flung them over the unconscious George. He then decided to leave some rum and some tea for good measure with him and hoped to God that he didn't catch his death of cold!

Overall, the raid had been a complete success, it was now the next stage which always gave Shem the greatest satisfaction, seeing all the contraband slowly drift away, mingle into society and weave its magic and bring them all a tidy penny. Wherever the contraband went, it was invisible to the locals, who all shied away from looking in that general direction.

Shem knew that after the discovery of the empty Custom House, that the likelihood of the Custom men making a fuss wasn't realistic and knew it would be a long time in coming should the Queen proclaim there was any reward for the apprehension of the men concerned in the deed. He knew that by nature, Hartright, always on the make, would like the sound of the reward and put it about secretly that his door was open to any one anonymously to give information. Likewise, the general public knew it was not in their best interest to get involved.

He had other matters to attend to before he could celebrate. He had received the confirmation that Hartright was looking to take a young man called Chater into custody for questioning. He needed to get to him first.

Paully was a man who loved his Ale and appreciated the skill, love, and attention it took to make a good one. He wanted to work with Gideon on producing some alternatives recipes for beer, but never found the time. Claude would drink anything and just loved the sensation of letting go. However, when it was time to call it a night, they both hated that it had to end.

Both men were hanging onto each other. Claude the scholar of the two was explaining to Rafe the aftermath of a good night's session. The only time Claude ever really had a conversation was when he was drunk and tonight had been no exception.

'The effects may include dizziness, nausea, vomiting, incarceration, erotic lustfulness, eemmm, loss of body control, loss of clothing, loss of money, loss of virginity, although that's only on your part, as I don't believe you have scored. I personally think you're gay, but Paully reassures me that......'

'Fuck you, you half talk bollocks when ya pissed.' Rafe announced.

'Well I disagree,' Claude tried to sound intelligent, ' however to get back to the point in hand, delusions of grandeur, which I have in abundance, table dancing, I am soooo good at that, headache, dehydration, dry mouth, and a desire to sing at the top of your voice. Although again, I do not and have never done this, however......'

'For fucks sake man, shut up.' Paully cried.

'Just because you know that I was making an observation and you general need to be heard, and we have all agreed that you may think you have a good voice.....'

'I'm not listening any more, go on, fuck off.' Paully removed himself from his friend, trying to cover his ears with his hands. However deciding that was not a good idea, held out his arms, and found Claude coming to his aid. They then proceeded to hold each other up and attempt to walk along the lane in a straight line. Their lodgings could be found in the Priory House, which was a stone throw away from The Castle.

'Play all-night rounds of Strip Poker, Truth, or Dare, which alternately end up with him losing everything, cos he loves to show off his tackle.'

'Jealous!' Paully declared.

'Is he still talking?' Rafe laughed.

Both men had been attempting to hold the conversation in whispers, however as they had progressed back to the lodgings, it had grown in volume.

'Ah shut up.'

'I know you love me.' Paully declared.

'I know, you know, I love you.'

'He's my mate.' Paully turned to Rafe who was walking slowly behind them keeping watch shaking his head in wonder. 'I do love you.' He whispered to Claude and thumped him in the chest.

'Well there really is no need for violence, you dosey sod, and stop spitting in my face. You're an idiot.' Claude wiped away the spit and rubbed his hand across his friend's clothes.

49

'Ya know I hope George is alright.' At which they both burst into uncontrollable fits of laughter with Claude re-enacting hitting George over the head. Paully took to the part and pretended the hit had made him whirl around, around and around again and finished by falling on the floor playing dead.

Rafe nearly pissed himself laughing at the two clowns. Try as he might, with Claude's help, they just could not get Paully back up on his feet, and all three kept looking at each other and just roaring again.

'Will you lot kerb it?' They heard from Valentina's whorehouse. They all stopped laughing after being told off, however could not suppress their giggles. They looked up at the old Mint house, which stood on the High Street, to see if they could see who it was who was mouthing off at them, but then gave up as none could clearly see a thing in their condition. They were having such a great time.

Rafe sighed with relief when they finally got back to their digs and once he had helped them into their room, the pair just collapsed on to their beds fully clothed. If only he had been at the Woolpack in Burwash, he could have slipped away to see his beloved Amelia. Oh well, he could always go across the road to the Mint House.

He chuckled to himself as he made his way from the room, and shook his head at himself for closing the door very quietly behind him. As he turned into the small passage, he fumbled loudly down the small wooded staircase and nearly crashed through the door. Why he thought he had been in any fit position to take them home was news to him! As he hit the air again, he started to giggle to himself. He headed back the way he had came and then having felt he was no longer alone, turned round with a grin on his face, to find the next second, that it all went black.

He slowly came too and discovered he was tied to a chair and his whole body was stiff with the upright position. He could not move and groaned as the throb in his head absorbed his every pore. He could not bring himself to open his eyes, his whole head was ringing, and he just did not wish to move anything.

'Now, now master Rafe. What have we here?' Hartright groaned. 'Out and about without any great protection, what has the world come to? Truly, I am surprised that your brother let you off the lead. He did say that he was going to take much better care of you from now on and here you are enjoying my hospitality.' Hartright drawled in amusement. 'Rest assured, we do have a warrant for your arrest, which is for your involvement in the Rottingdean raid. However, as a reasonable man of standing, we could come to some arrangement? Are you game?'

Rafe could not comprehend what Hartright hoped to achieve by this move? Hartright had played a major card by kidnapping him. He had taken Rafe to an old shepherds hut towards the small village of Eastbourne, heading towards Jevington. It was a perfect spot to see for miles in all directions. The hut just had the one room with a large fire and kettle. They had no wish to bring attention to themselves and had not lit the fire, yet the candles they lit, flickered and gave their location away.

'Oh Harry, you don't know the trouble you've got yourself in now.'

Hartright double checked himself at Rafe's over familiarity with his name and found he was put out. No one other than his immediate family called him Harry.

Rafe could not believe that Hartright could think that he knew anything about the business. Surely, he had determined after all this time that Rafe was just a ruse! Surely, he knew that Rafe wasn't a player? If it was now a personal vendetta against Shem, then Hartright had most certainly achieved that. Shem would not rest until Rafe had been found. If Hartright laid one finger on him, Shem would kill him. He knew that his brother was looking for any excuse to put his plans in action, and be it that Bob constantly reined him in and reminded him of the bigger picture.

Rafe had begged Shem to get more involved in the business and running the livestock was great but he never really knew anything about the jobs. He was just told, get this and that, and tell so and so this. It was all word of mouth and never anything specific.

He knew Shem was protecting him and what he did was to keep him out of mischief and any real danger. It was Rafe who caused the most amount of danger to himself by acting out and pushing it always. Rafe was a horse expert, his skills were used to buy and sell the horses, as well as maintain the stock they had at Pevensey and cultivate a separate business enterprise. Admittedly, he was a decoy at times, but not always. He would steal a few horses here and there, and then replace them with poor substitutes; he would run amuck and with his cheek get away with it. But his last little game had seem to get him into abit more trouble than he had bargained. He knew he would probably get a beating from Hartright and his men and that would hurt like hell, he just wished his brother would find out he was missing, sooner rather than later.

'I have it on strict authority that you personally gave Benny Chater some tea that was from the haul at Rottingdean. You gave it in additional payment for some leatherwork he had done. He was so impressed by the gift that he let far too many people know.' Hartright declared. 'Now with some persuasion Mr. Chater has agreed to testify to that fact.'

'Has he now?'

'He is under our protection, and if he should go missing and be found floating with the fishes then we will know what has happened, won't we?'

'You're using the poor soul as bait? And you're the one who will get him killed!'

'Now, now, Master Rafe, as if?'

'Benny Chater is a simpleton and will do anything for a kind word. What have you promised him?'

'You are not in a position to ask me questions now are you?'

'You have played the wrong hand here Harry.' Rafe could not believe that Hartright would be that thick. The raid had only just taken place and Rafe had not seen Chater for weeks.

'My name to you is The Honourable Mr. Mordesan and you seem to forget that I am the law and can do whatever I like. Isn't that so Mr. Clay?'

Mr. Clay came forward with a delightful smirk on his face and with that swiped his bat across Rafe's knees. Rafe screamed in pain and Hartright laughed nervously at that.

'Maybe not quite so hard next time Clay, we have all night.' Clay smiled venomously back at his boss.

'I can't tell you what I don't know.' Rafe spoke through gripped teeth. His heart was beating wildly.

'Now, now Rafey, this isn't how one plays the game. You give me what I want and I give you what you want.' Hartright almost sung the words. He felt so confident of success.

'And what if I have nothing to give?'

'That's not going to happen is it?' Hartright had bided his time and knew he'd get them eventually and if it were through the weak brother. Then so be it.

However, far be it that Shem would ever be complacent; he had already received word that one of the leather workers from the area had been arrested on suspicion of handling stolen goods. Ned Cavendish's gang were keeping an eye on the proceedings and sending reports via Claude.

All over Cuckmere Valley, there was gossip that Chater had been heard to remark that he had seen the smugglers on the night that the contraband was rescued, and that one of the smugglers had given him an extra lot of coffee. This was as he had done such a good job on the new leather saddles that he had commissioned to make.

Everyone knew that Chater wasn't the full ticket and that no one had clapped eyes on anyone on that night, at that particular time. It was not uncommon for people to boast, but Chater had got himself in deep and seem to embellish his story every time it was heard.

Chater had been delighted to be singled out, but had bragged in the wrong company. Chater's story had made its way to Hartright via his sister's maid, Maisy Howlett when they were visiting the Devereux's. She had waffled on and on and Constance had ordered her to obtain a batch of the lovely tea and coffee to take back home.

Constance had mentioned it to Hartright and that's when Chater just fell into his lap. The poor man did not know whether he was coming or going and soon found, himself escorted from his home and business in the middle of the night. Word immediately had to Ned, who in turn sent word to Claude.

They had no idea that it would lead to Rafe being picked up and to say that Hartright was delighted at the outcome, was an understatement.

Hartright had immediately sent a word to the Justice of the Peace for Sussex who was based in Lewes to give the authority to serve papers. Hartright intentions were to acquire as much information on the smuggling gangs as possible from Rafe. He did not care that he had put two and two together and come up with six! Hartright wanted to use this time to get a better picture of how the organisation was run, who were their suppliers in France, who were their contacts here? Who were the nobility involved? What Bankers did they use? The questions kept coming thick and fast and Rafe's mind whirled with confusion. His whole body screamed as a further punch, kick, smack connected. Hartright promised he would not charge him, if he gave him the information he needed, even though he had evidence and a signed statement from Chater that he had given him illegal goods. He also suggested that he had a signed statement from a publican over East Grinstead way, which alleged that Rafe had stolen his horses. In addition, as Hartright pointed out, that was a hanging offence and he would let him go, if he gave Hartright what he wanted. He wanted everything in order to crush the ring and the nobility who were involved and ultimately to make a name for himself. He wanted power, but he also wanted reassurances that the information Rafe would give would be genuine, and so he made his threats. He said that he would rape and kill Rafe's little plaything, his favourite little whore at Burwash, Daisy, and if that wasn't enough, he'd fling in the delightful Amelia too.

Shem lay naked with his hair lose and everywhere. Cuddled up against him, lay Valentina. Her left dark leg covered his and her jet-black shiny hair made a blanket across him. He had been dozing when he heard the creak on the stair and men whispering. This was then followed by paws patting on the landing and he could then hear the dog scratching and groaning to gain entrance. He smacked the woman across her backside and she groaned as she moved off from him. Slowly he got up to find his pants. There was a soft knock on the door. The dog had become more excitable now, knowing that entry was to hand.

'Shem, its Claude, you awake?'

'Well I fucking am now!'

Valentina had slid off the bed. She found her beautiful silk robe and flung it on. She had flicked back her hair and looked at him for some sort of smile or comfort before she left, but he totally ignored her. She rushed past Claude and Paully as Earl, the dog, bolted through and immediately flung himself at his master and was welcomed by a fuss. Claude and Paully rather sheepishly entered both having shared a thought and little look at the woman descend the stairs.

The dog was proceeding to circle Shem's legs as he whirled round looking for his pants. He stopped, and putting his hands on his hips, smiled at his friends in defeat.

Both looked away and then down at their feet. Shem was immediately alerted, they did not usually get embarrassed at seeing each other naked, so there was something else. Both had looked back at him and the tiredness in their eyes was evident, he knew something was up. He hunted further for his trousers and proceeded to pull them on.

'Well?'

'You're not going to like it.' Paully started.

Shem closed his eyes waiting.

'Do you want to get dressed and then we'll talk down stairs, have some breakfast and that?'

'Why you being a prat?'

Claude took a step forward.

'Rafe's gone.' Shem crossed his arms and waited.

'And!'

'It would appear that he has been taken.' He uncrossed his arms and at this point noticed the dog also stood waiting.

'I'm assuming he ain't got lucky?' Claude shook his head at that and Shem nodded his head at Claude to continue.

'We found some of the guards tied up. Rafe's bed has not been slept in. None of his horses are gone, he ain't at Valentina's, and me and Paully were the last to see him.'

'Best find him them, ain't ya?'

'Larry and the boys have already ridden out. I've sent Little Paully to Idris.'

'That comforts me already.' Shem sarcastically replied and turned his back on them to hunt for his shirt. The two knew they were being dismissed.

As Paully and Claude descended the stairs Paully whispered;-

'Went well,'

'You think?' Claude stopped. 'I seriously think that if we had stayed another moment, he would have beaten seven shades of shit out of us.'

'I love it when you speak slang, sounds so funny you being French.'

'Oh for fuck sake, we have a crisis going on and you talk gay.' Claude infact had no hint of an accent. 'You're an idiot.'

In fact, Shem had stopped what he was doing and was staring into space. He could not comprehend what they had just told him. He could not believe that under their noses, Rafe had just disappeared. Where was he? He found he could not breathe, and sat down at the end of the bed and tried to calm himself.

Slowly he felt the warmth engulf him.

He knew it was Hartright. He obviously had his warrant already and Shem was mad with himself for under estimating him. Still, the man had made a stupid move. Did he really think he could get away with this? What did he think would happen now?

Shem had been told to tread carefully, all good things came to those who waited, and Hartright had given him an excellent opportunity to wipe the floor with him. The fires were smouldering. His breathing was now under control. Slowly he begun to smile, he was under no illusion that Rafe would be found, and that extra wood could be flung at the fire.

It hadn't helped that everyone had been so drunk to see what was happening under their noses, and if he was being honest to himself, Shem felt he was also to blame for Rafe's kidnap and assault. Shem silently had concerns that Hartright had a mole in his camp. He hoped that wasn't the case. But someone had to have let them know where and when they would be about and when was a good time to snatch Rafe.

It wasn't long before they had discovered where Rafe was being held, and why and who had given the information to the authorities for them to pick Rafe up for questioning.

The man was hired as a go between to tell Hartright and his men where to locate the main bulk of the gang and what likely security they had in place.

'He said it would not be wise to disappoint him. I'm new to these parts, I need to earn a living, and I've got children, a sick wife.' The captured man moaned.

'I am not interested in you. Just answer my question.' Shem was getting impatient; he slapped the man around the head.

'Why should I trust you any more than him?' The man looked long and hard at Shem and knew it had been the wrong thing to say. He had heard of Shem, but thought it was all talk. 'Please, he said he would kill my children.' The man bent in submission, begging for some compassion.

'Do you wanna die? Do you want me to set Paully on you?'

'Please Mister.' Shem sighed and Paully came forward and as Claude let him go, he punched the man around the ear. He lost his sense of balance, which Paully had intended, and as he tried to correct himself, Paully head butted him.

As the man leaned over, Paully followed through with a left hook, into the man's stomach. The man lifted and then crashed to the floor. He stood over him like a big black cloud, the man unable to move with the shock of it all. Paully lowered his foot onto the man's neck.

'Waiting!'

'Yes, he paid me to give the information to Hartright.' Paully leaned down and picked the man up as if he was of little weight and then grabbed both his arms and bent them to the back of him.

'Now tell us what we want to know.'

It hadn't taken long for them to find out everything they needed to know. They found out about where Rafe was, whether Hartright had the warrant and where Chater, the young man who had been pulled in to make a statement about Shem and his gang, was being held. Shem and Paully had a little fun along the way and beat the grass just enough for him to understand he was indeed lucky. Shem then ordered one of his men to take him out of the village and dump him. He did not want him dead and ordered his man Jesus to put a man on his tail and see where the trail lead them.

Shem rode out after also giving orders for Claude to attend to other business and report back, whilst Paully went to gather back up. Shem was slightly concerned at the name given by the hired hand. It did not fit and he knew that someone else other than Hartright was playing with him. Hartright was clearly not intelligent enough, so Shem had a new foe to contend with. Why was life always so complicated?

'Fuck me he's here. ' Clay nearly pissed his pants and was clearly forgetting himself.
'Who?' Hartright asked.
'Shem!'
'Ridiculous.' Hartright was not convinced.
'He is coming down the valley as we speak, we'd best.....'
'We can take him.' Hartright announced with all the confidence in the world, standing tall.
'Sir, with all due respect, the man is coming with his Hench man and we don't know how many others he has. Our men are not equipped to deal with this sort of attack. Look our men are already running scared.'
'They will not run.' Hartright said abit too quickly, watching with his own eyes, as his troupe were mounting their horses in panic and looking over their shoulder to see where he was, and to be assured that they could leave.
'I think you will find they are.' Clay was disgusted but he was also ready to bolt and thankful when Hartright motioned for them to go.
'What are you waiting for, get the bloody horses.' He screamed like a girl.

'Tossers.' Shem was disgusted. They pulled back their mounts and watched as Hartright and his Riding officers left the scene sharpish!
'Look at them run.' Paully spat. They could not believe how cowardly they were.
'I'll get Rafe.' Shem started forward again. 'You lot watch that pair of prats.'
'They can't have a brain amongst them.' Paully mused shaking his head in disgust.
Shem anxiously made his way to the hut pondering on what made Hartright make that move to kidnap Rafe. What was his motivation? He had always thought that Hartright was a mug. A stupid man who had been given every privilege that money could buy. He had the arrogance of a gentleman and no common sense at all. Strategic had never been a strong point and all Hartright wanted was glory and to be the centre of attention. If he did not get that, he tended to have a temper tantrum and through his toys to the floor. Then he would just act out. There was

no rhyme or reason and no thought to the consequences.

To that end, he was dangerous. He mixed business with personal pride. That would be his downfall, not working matters through. A slapped wrist would wind him up and he'd go hell for leather. It was a vicious circle and one that Hartright would never admit that he was the maker of. He would always say he was innocent. It wasn't him. It was always someone else's doing. He could never admit defeat or that he was vulnerable or ever at fault.

Shem smashed through the door and found his brother hunched over and tied to a chair. He had not allowed himself to believe that he would be seriously hurt. What would Hartright have expected in retaliation?

Rafe painfully lifted his throbbing head and tried to focus on the huge figure in the doorway. His thoughts were everywhere and he had lost track of time, however he slowly recognised his brother's form.

'You took you're time?' He joked croakingly.

'Can't leave you alone for five minutes, plep.' Shem came forward and fell to his knees in front of his brother. Rafe was hurt and he was mad, mad, as hell, but Rafe needed him more than his anger at that moment.

He cut him free, loosened the bonds gently, and watched as Rafe flinched and shifted into a better position. Rafe sighed at the release and groaned with all the pain. Shem remained on his knees and he placed his hands around Rafe's face. He loved his brother so much and look what that man had done?

The brothers looked at each other and Rafe tried to grin but he was too hard. Shem smiled and kissed his brother on the forehead. Then they leant against each other, head to head.

'I'm so glad you got here.' Rafe whispered. Shem could have cried for him at that moment and promised that this time he would have vengeance.

'I know I'll get you out of here and sorted.' Shem replied full of emotion; he started to lift himself up.

'No it's....'

'Don't worry Rafe, I know.....' Shem knew his brother was frightened at what had happened and as to what would happen next.

'No, it's not that.' Shem looked back down at his brother. They spoke in their normal voices.

'What, what then?' He tried to encourage his brother who he could see was slightly reluctant. Rafe tried to smile through his pain.

'Well I'm dying for another piss and I can't wet myself again, quick help me up.' Shem laughed at that. Trust Rafe to make everything into a joke!

'Ehhh, you dirty bastard. Couldn't you hold it? Ehh I can smell it now!' Shem flung himself away from Rafe looking at him in disgust now really sniffing the air and played along whole-heartedly to steer away from what had really happened.

'Shut up you Nancy. I have been tied up.' Rafe was trying not to laugh at his brother's reaction, he was in pain, but Shem's face was cracking him up.

'Ehh, you weak feeble girl.'

'Stop it, help me up, come on.' Rafe tried to grab hold of Shem's arm.

'No, get yourself up you pissy fart. Ehh. Nasty.' Shem had backed away pretending to be mortified. 'I am not touching you again.' He was covering his nose.

'Oh shut the fuck up. Stop laughing at me. I have been brutally beaten. I may never walk again.' Rafe rose himself to his feet and felt a little faint when putting all his weight down.

'You seem to be doing all right. Stop walking towards me, you filthy bastard.' Shem held his arms in front of him.

'I swear, if I catch you I will do you. Look, I am struggling here, I am in shock, I am hurt all over, and you are fretting over abit of piss. I've got broken kneecaps. Get some laurels man.'

'Oh that's rich, that's fucking priceless, I've rescued you.'

'You ain't yet! God look I am hurt, if you haven't forgotten.' Rafe was losing his temper now and feeling faint with all the effort.

'Just get the bishop out here, sort yourself, then let's get you home, and then if you are really lucky, I'll have Valentina sent over the new girl.' Shem was enjoying his brother's discomfort now but it was a disguise for how he really felt. Regardless of what anyone said he had to do, he would kill Hartright and if that meant all the Queens men hunted him, then let them try.

'Is she as pretty as Daisy?'

'Got bigger tits.' Shem gestured, play acting just for his brother's sake.

'Well if that's the case, fuck off, and give me abit of privacy. Turn away'

'Thank fuck you don't need my help to find it.'

'I never needed your help in that department, thank you; I think you will find, I'm the looker in this family.'

'Not today you ain't.'

'Did I say I love you?' Rafe was near exhaustion now.

'Oh come on, let's go.' At which point Shem went forward to help his brother.

## Chapter Three

Shem knew he would have to act quickly and he had to play this one gently, be it that he had sent his wildest men to apprehend Chater! He found it was all too easy now to lose his temper and fight to contain himself. He was mad as hell.

Paully, Claude and Jesus Jordan were ordered that on no account were they allowed to kill Chater. Shem advised that this was a test as all three had no souls and were condemned to spend infinity in hell if by accident Chater were to die. They were renowned for not giving a flying fig and showing no passion.

Once Chater had been found, Shem's men sent word to Ned Cavendish that they were in the area and to ensure there was assistance should any be needed.

'Can't we just kill him?' Paully was bored and just wanted to get it over with. Claude raised his eyes to the sky.

They had been playing with Chater, visiting at various times where he was locked up and taunting him. He had been locked up in one of the cellars in one of the local pubs in East Dean, just along from Ned and Ray in Alfriston. The landlady there was ever so accommodating in all aspects of their business and Paully had been especially keen to meet back up with the landlady's daughter. She had always been nice, well-endowed lass who was in mourning; having just been told her husband had passed away having gone to the Netherlands to fight in the war.

Jesus pulled the simpleton Chater up by the scruff of the neck from the damp and rank floor. They had apprehended Chater easily along with his escorts and all the boy kept doing was crying, which irritated both of them no end.

Paully had previously kicked him severely and he had curled up in a ball. His head and hair were covered in his own blood.

Jesus was waving around a large knife and uttering an oath exclaiming: 'Get down on your knees and start-praying mate, because you see this, I am gonna butcher you with it. I'm gonna rip it into ya belly and cut through ya ribs and yank everything out and burn the shit. Forgive me my Lord.' Terrified at the menace, and expecting shortly to die, Chater knelt down on his knees and began to say the Lord's Prayer between gulps of sick, blood, and fear. Paully immediately pushed Jesus out of the way giving him a filthy look, while Jesus just laughed menacingly at his own antics still waving the large knife around like a plaything.

'Oh behave.' Paully was appalled at the spineless idiot who cried on the floor. 'You surely do not believe in that old fucking nonsense. There is no God. For Christ sake?' He looked across at Jesus to make his point. 'You should be in fear of me, I'm the fucker who has ya life in me hands!' Jesus still looked at him disapprovingly, as far as he was concerned Paully was going to hell no matter what he did. There was a God and he had better start watching over his shoulder. Paully pulled Chater up from his knees. 'If you tell us everything we will let you go, you fucking moron.'

'You'll kill me anyway.' Chater sobbed.

'Oh for God's sake, give me a bloody bible and I swear on it that I won't.' He looked at Jesus who was appalled at him again for mocking the Lord. He remembered Jesus had not been so religious or pretentious in their youth and in choosing this line of work, he was hardly going to make it to heaven!

'You said earlier that you would kill me.' Chater pleaded.

'That's cos I knew you'd piss ya pants. You ever heard of anyone having a laugh?'

'I did not mean to get anyone in trouble.' Chater moaned swaying on his knees.

'We know that.'

'Hartright said he'd rape my sister and slit my mum's throat. He wrote loads of things down and I gave it my mark. He has versed me into what to say.' He blabbered.

Jesus shook his head and put his hands on his hips, the man was a blabbering coward, and he hadn't promised Shem that he would not kill him. His full name was Jason Jeremiah Jordan and both Paully and Claude nicknamed him Jesus. He was of medium height and had long black shiny hair that he wore in a long ponytail. He had a small goats beard and was very dark from exposure to the sun. He had a taunt face and sharp features. His clear blue eyes had that delirious madness about them and both Paully and Claude agreed that if he had got the calling he would have been a formidable Vicar and scared everyone shitless into attending his Sunday service, because if you did not attend, he would have stalked and killed you! They were surprised his brother, Jonah Joel Jordan, across at Alfriston had not asked him to perform such a duty and get more souls to seek salvation.

'Look I swear we are not going to kill ya.' Paully wanted to give him a little comfort also.

'You promise?' Chater pleaded. Chater was a young man, too inexperienced who relied on the good will of others and his mother to tell him what was best for him.

'Look. Claude will arrange to go and get ya mum and sister.'

'No, you'll kill them.' He was adamant that that was what they were going to do.

'No, no listen, we only wanted to scare you.' Paully wanted to laugh at that, any more beating and the boy would surely die.

'Please don't kill me Paully; I won't say nothing to no one.' He begged and cried.

'Its abit late for that you silly sod.' Jesus yelled.

'Listen stop crying, Chater, stop crying, once we get the evidence we will send you away.'

'You're gonna kill me Paully.'

'No, we just said we were not.'

'You're gonna kill me,'

'Oh for fucks sake, let me kill him, he's getting on my fucking nerves. I can't stand it.' Paully looked back at Jesus for the nod.

'No I'll do it. Forgive me lord for my weakness.' Jesus again tried to get in between Paully and Chater and Paully turned on him.

'Children please.' Claude declared from the back thinking the whole thing was turning into a farce.

'Well I'm bored.' Paully announced. Jesus backed away still shaking his head and started muttering to himself. Paully decided to try again.

'Listen Chater.' Paully started calmly to explain to him, as if he were a child. 'Shem has given specific orders that you are not to be killed. He gave orders for you to be sent to our man out in France to start a new life. We were going to set you up and obviously, we will get your mum and sister. I promise Hartright will not touch your sister. Shem will cut his dick off first.'

'I know you are gonna kill me.' At last, Paully lost his patience and jumped forward to grab him. Claude then shoved him aside and with a look warned him off. He then turned on Chater and punched him so hard that he fell unconscious. Claude slapped his hands together in satisfaction. Jesus fell about laughing.

'Why is it that some men just whine and whine? It's just so undignified, what an idiot!' Claude spat disgusted with his charge. Paully could not believe what Claude had done.

'Is the fucker dead?' Paully kicked Chater in the side, he groaned. Paully then turned on Claude. 'I'm the one who hits and kills; you're the one who prances about on bloody look out.' He shouted at his friend who merely just looked at him and shrugged his shoulders in his casual manner. 'You are one selfish bastard.'

'What, I can't have fun too?'

'No.'

'Spoil sport.'

'French dick head.'

'English arse hole.'

'No, please don't cos when you say it, it's just silly.' Paully waved Claude away and was laughing at him now.

'Stop laughing.' Claude tried to suppress a grin. 'We have a job to do.' He needed to regain an element of seriousness to the proceedings.

'English arse hole.' Paully repeated mimicking a French accent of which Claude did not have. Paully in his deluded world, always imagined him speaking with a French twang. At this point Claude jumped into a sparring position, inviting Paully to play box.

'Oh just stop it, I'll piss me self!' He turned back to their charge and kicking Chater again cried.

'Wakey, wakey!'

'Should have let me kill him!' Came from behind, and they heard Jesus continue to mutter in pray, whilst suppressing a cheeky grin.

'Jesus, just shut it.' They both roared in unison.


'So what did the boys say?'

'Had them wrapped round my little finger.' William referred to seeing his friends back in Alfriston. He wanted to sound confident and hoped it worked and fooled

Hartright. William Devereux had not helped matters and tensions had been mounting somewhat over recent months when he had not taken himself to Pevensey when summoned. He had left that to Ned and Ray Cavendish to attend and still they had not forgiven him. They resented him for his newfound developing relationship with Constance Mordesan, Hartright's sister. They also appeared to blame him for their sister leaving home. For many years, he had been playing around with her and all knew it was a doomed relationship from the start and would fizzle out eventually. However, they were even more miffed, when they had come home from a job one day to discover that their sister had decided to go away for a time and stay with a relative of Shaun Cavendish's wife. They all missed her terribly, but life moved on. William hoped she would be happy. She had always been so much fun and still he found himself thinking what she would think of this and that. He knew she would hate Constance Mordesan, not because she would be jealous. Oh no! He just knew she wasn't someone she would like and he chose not to reflect too much on that. In fact, she would not have liked Hartright either. He found himself more and more in turmoil about where his life was now heading and found that the grass wasn't always necessarily greener on the other side.

'I'll bet.' Hartright drawled.

'No, really.' Williams' eyes twinkled. He wanted Hartright to believe he was in charge.

'William, if you believe they believe you, then you are a fool.'

'They cannot resist the Devereux charm and my contacts?' William exiled with confidence and authority. He was a handsome man with cold blue eyes and was average height with blond hair that was turning brown, as he got older. Even if his relationship were currently strained with his boyhood friends, they would all make up in the end.

'Yes, your contacts.' Hartright burred. 'Well, the fruits of our partnership have been and are still slowly making their way across the channel, and I am not disappointed with the results. Rather feel this venture is going to be most profitable.'

'If Shem doesn't get wind, or hasn't already and is awaiting his moment.'

'Yes, a minor detail.' Hartright tried to sound dismissive.

'Minor. Hardly. The man is becoming a legend!'

Hartright really did not need to know how popular that Shem had become since he hoodwinked him at Alfriston. He listened to William prattle on about how everyone was talking about Shem's exploits and how such and such of the high society had bought this much brandy, this much tea. The gossip was endless.

'Well if I had my way he'd be rotting in a jail in London, but seems he has disappeared of the face of the earth. For all we know he could be dead and his band of merry men haven't exactly been paying much attention to me in any event. He seems to disappear very often.' He mused. 'I couldn't get any head way with the band and everything I try to do, I get nowhere.' Hartright sulked. He at least would have thought there would have been retaliation for his attack on Rafe. But as yet, nothing had happened. This did not bode well for him, but then on the other hand, maybe it had scared Shem off. Maybe he wasn't such the big man after all. He wrestled still, whether that had been a desperate move on his part. He constantly doubted himself and found that William was tedious and although he initially had liked him and thought he and his sister were well matched, the jealousy had started to creep in.

'So you will quit?'

'Yes of course, as soon as I can, can't flog a dead horse. Anyway, Shem has not been apprehended yet and will probably kill me so I have to keep on my toes and lively. Once we have made more capital, we can look into some proper investments.' He padded his pocket indicating the wad of cash that he and William had made. 'But it would be delightful to leave on a high. I have something up my sleeve!' William did not want to know and doubted if Hartright would tell him anyway.

'Well, say the word. We have our man in London for the investments?' William dismissed his last remark and went back to talking about the money.

'Yes, young Saltdean. God that man is like Midas.' Hartright recalled the young man. 'So with that in mind, my next venture is to carry myself off to the Carolina's, buy some land and by then, hopefully the old fart, would have died of too much excess and I'll have a title, an estate and would have established myself with property in the America's. And you my loyal partner, will be looking out for all our money over there while I come back and sell it all.' Hartright looked hard at the man who had won his sister's heart. He could not believe that William was milking every word. He would use him and dump him in a heartbeat.

'You'd sell the Mordesan estates?'

'Without a shadow of doubt. - Holds nothing for me. Even kill off me old Granny to close that chapter on that one.' William laughed at that, but strangely, he had the feeling this venture was not going to end well. None of this was, so why did he just not back away? Shem was more than likely playing them and William was deluding himself. He found that Hartright wasn't really such a good friend and how had he got in so far? He was in too deep and everyone was warning him to get out while he could.

'Ah Mordesan, good of you to come. Good of you to come.' The Earl ushered the man into his study.

Hartright did not like anyone calling him just Mordesan.

'Take a seat, sit down my boy. Naomi, will you bring some tea and cakes my love, that's it, make yourself comfortable. Wanted to talk to you about your progress in these parts.' He flapped his tails and too took a seat, while his granddaughter, who also stepped in as housemaid, skipped off to do her grandfathers bidding. Hartright watched her go and pursed his lips in delight. She was a fetching little thing.

He then turned his attention back to Lord Lennard who wore a wonderful banyan, which was of natural linen and embroidered with purple and navy flowers. The man was living in the lap of luxury. This was evident as every room he had past had a full-lit fire with spare logs to the side and waiting. Everything was clean and tidy and spoke of money. The house was immaculate and the estates well, just beautiful. Hartright wasn't aware of the family connection between Lord and servant, and did not like the familiarity the Lord gave the servant. 'Hard, I should imagine hey. Hard?' The Earl spoke in a short snappy way, which Hartright found very off putting. His mind had turned from how he treated his staff to actually concentrating on the lovely looking Naomi. He licked his lips again.

'I'm finding my feet and as you are aware have been managing to secure some convictions.'

'Yes Magistrate over at Cuckfield Manor tells me so. Very keen to make a name.'
The Earl nodded to him enthusiastically. The Earl was much respected throughout
the whole neighbourhood and Hartright had been warned to keep him on side. He
had rarely ever met the Earl and had expected long before now to be invited for tea
rather than summoned to his very lovely country estate in Herstmonceux.

The estate went way back and the opulence as he rode in was evident everywhere.
The driveway leading to the main house was of small shingle and the house itself
was nestled and surrounded by wondrous woodland that was magnificent. The red
brick house, was surrounded by a moat, and had a delightful European style
courtyard in the middle. The lawns were immaculate and all the grounds men and
staff appeared chirpy. How they could be that happy was beyond Hartright and no
one ever had a bad word about the Earl. He provided many local people with
regular work and he looked after people. He had a huge estate but hadn't a clue as
to how to manage, never had, never would. The big secret was that Paully, his
bastard son, paid for everything and Bella his daughter, run everything. Their father
was a lazy man and unknown to most lived far beyond his means and was getting
into deeper debt by providing huge allowances for both his legitimate daughters,
until Paully had stepped in. Lennard had no real head for business, so was not
surprised when his second wife decided to return to her family estates in
Hertfordshire, and still required to be kept.

As Paully was not the legitimate heir, the Earl had been persuaded that the best
course of action was to take his son's money and in return split the estate up. He
had his relative in London, Saltdean draw up the papers. The estate had been
divided to leave the family title to his eldest daughter who was his heir, and the
house and the garden and woodland it stood in. The surrounding woodland,
grazing, and farmlands had all been sold off to Paully.

Hartright had proceeded by foot over the small moat bridge and a small door
opened inward from the main gate. He had bent down and found himself in the
gate room and was then hastily manoeuvred up the flagstone staircase surrounded
by oak casing into the magnificent hall where the Lord sat by the huge fire. He
mused over the fine furniture, his memory had drifted back to his own old
ancestral home, and how it had always been full of light and laughter before

everyone died and or made to move on.

'Yes, I want to be more successful.' Hartright mused. He would say whatever the Earl wanted to hear. The Earl did not like the fact that Hartright would not hold eye contact.

'Good, good, good, stands you in good stead for the market hey? Talking of which, I hear tell young Constance is a fine one. Been out of the country for a time after her husband's death?'

'Yes, she recently came back from Italy.'

'Italy? Remember it well, lovely, divine.'

'My Uncle is settled there.'

'Thought Mordesan's were Cornish stock, boy?'

'They were. Uncle has relocated; the Italian air suits him better.'

'What about the lands, title? I heard was a great place.'

'Yes certainly, well, as you know, I am the oldest male, and will inherit should Uncle not have any issue.'

'Really thought that title was held by the Dowager?' He raised his eyebrows and before Hartright could continue he added, 'Throws you a bone then does he?' Hartright was becoming uncomfortable.

'Well, I could not possibly live on this salary alone.'

'No, no quite.'

'Lord Lennard, you called me here for a reason?' Hartright was keen to get to the point. He circled his cup with his forefinger.

'God yes, yes I did.'

The Earl drank his tea while Hartright waited. The Earl thought it was rather ironic that they drunk Hyson Tea which Shem and Paully had smuggled and smiled to himself! 'My people have been doing a bit of digging.'

'Ooh yes Sir.' Hartright tried not to show how alert he had became.

'I understand that you've come into some property in London.' The Earl looked straight at him and clasped his hands between his legs.

'And what business is that of yours?' Hartright was immediately on the defensive.

'Well, I need to know where the money came from. You just said the salary was poor and as an officer of my guard and I am wholly responsible. You must understand?' He looked straight into his eyes and Hartright looked away feeling very uncomfortable.

'Well, Uncle remortgaged Mordesan Hall.' Hartright found himself playing with the edge of the Earl's desk. He felt he should not have blurted that out quite so quickly.

'Be it that your Grandmother still has an interest? How so?' Hartright pursed his lips and looked at the old man with loathing. He hated the fact that the Lord was playing him. The Earl had all the information he wanted. He watched as the older man held his hands up in the air and lost patience. 'You are a fool Sir. You hide your money until it can be attached to an episode, so as not to bring attention to yourself. You don't flaunt it. So what have we here? Lies and deceit, and you, an officer for her Highness?'

'Lord Lennard with due respect, I don't know what your agenda is here but I do not like its tone.' Hartright stood up, ready to leave.

'My agenda is to try and have some order here, but Sir, I have been lead to believe that you have been quite happy to accept back hander's from some of the South Coast Gangs along with many of your men. Remortgage, what nonsense! Are you denying it?'

'That is a lie.'

'Oh Sir, behave you have been caught out and I have sworn testimony and eyewitness accounts that you have been taking bribes.' Hartright nearly choked. How could that be so?

'I am being framed?'

'No, Sir you are being blackmailed.'

'What do you mean?'

'I have been put into a difficult position myself.' The Earl played his hand. He wanted to calm the situation before it got too out of hand. As it was, he was a hypocrite himself.

'And what is that?' Hartright decided to sit back down. 'Are you too being blackmailed or indeed taking bribes?' Lennard chose to ignore the accusation.

'This is not about me, I asked you hear to try and protect you.' Hartright did not believe that for a moment. 'Sir, you would be wise to reign back your enthusiasm somewhat on the local merchants shall we say. They are concerned that your eye has not been turned very well lately, and that you have been over zealous in your handling of fellow merchants and taken quite a high hand to them . It is not liked.' He let the message sink in. 'If you do not play cricket my boy, they will bowl you out.'

'Are you mad?' Hartright could not believe what he had heard and from a peer of the realm. He could not contain himself.

'No quite serious, I have been informed to advise you that you will be given information on what you can and can't confiscate and you will do it without any fuss. You are lucky he let you live this long.'

Hartright stopped in his tracks and stared at The Earl in disbelief. He knew exactly of who the Earl referred. So, The Earl was Shem's man. How could that possibly have happened? What did Shem have on the Earl?

'I could have them all rounded up and hung tomorrow.'

'How so, Sir?'

'How so, I too have witnesses, I could make them all provide me with evidence.'

'Again, how so, Sir, you seem to forget one major obstacle. To the people you are the enemy.'

'I am the law!' Hartright was astounded at the Earl.

'Don't make yourself look stupid. Who's the one here with the Earldom?' Lennard spat. He had decided he really did not like this young man.

'I came here to do a job and I will do it well.' Hartright had worked himself into a frenzy believing in his own lies to himself.

'Well, now is the time to leave, because you are bringing unwanted attention to yourself, and you have let your ego get the better of you?'

'I will crush this gang and by God, bring you to account also.' Hartright was screaming at him and wholly offended at the cheek of the man.

'No, Sir, you will not, you have been warned. You over stretched yourself when you beat up Rafe Smith, you could have served your time, had a few nice convictions under your belt and got out with dignity. Now you have taken it too far, and so are to be reined in. How dare you suggest that you could bring me down, that you could begin to bring down the organisation and the livelihood of the local people for your vanity?'

'You think that I am going to let a low life scum of the earth get the better of me, and tell me what to do? No one gives me orders, I am Hartright Mordesan.'

'Am I supposed to be impressed? You forget your father was the third son on the pecking order boy! No, you are a fool, who has gotten in too deep and has not the brains to get out while you can.'

'So Shem has you in his pocket. Perhaps I had best have a word with Lord Justice in Lewes in London and Lord Monmouth in Wadhurst and have you removed from honorary post, a charge of lack of confidence in your ability to serve justice, in these parts.'

'Oh man, shut up. Just shut up.'

'Hit a nerve there have I? Well I do not quit and run away with my tail between my legs. I came to do a job and I will have Shem Smith and his gang hanging from the Gallows, mark my words.'

'Sir, you have neither the intelligence nor the man power to take on such a foe as that. You would have been better just minding your own. Cut your losses and go, because believe me when I say, you have no idea who you are dealing with.'

'This conversation is over, I wish you good day.'

'Harry. Be forewarned, be careful. He has been humouring you. You have tested this man's patience; do not push it anymore.' Hartright stopped at the door and turned back. Who was this man to call him by his first name and be so informal to him? Who was he to rein him in?

'Sir, I think we have nothing more to say to each other.' Hartright tried to remain calm. He made his bow and the Earl sat down and heard the door crash shut. He scratched his head then removed his powered long wig and flung it to the table. He had not expected that to go well, and wished that Bella had been there. She would have given that young man what for. He laughed at that and this made him feel better. It would be even better if he went to see her and the children. Yes, that's what he would do. He needed to smile and delight in his families company. He dare not think what Paully would have done if he had been there to see the way the upstart had spoken to him. Paully would have leaped across the table and ripped the man's throat out, and that would not do. His boy's vicious nature was a constant surprise to him, and the way his Bella scared grown men was a great shock. He often thought how a man like him could have produced such children when his other children through his legitimate marriage were so sweet and humble, like him! He just wanted the good things in life and did not want too much trouble at his door. He enjoyed his title and the power that brought, he knew how, and when to use it. However, all he really wanted now was a peaceful life. He would speak to Paully and Shem later.

'You spoil me so.'

'You deserve it.' He pulled back her curled blond ringlet hair and laid a gentle kiss on her neck. She sighed in pleasure and leant up against him. They parted as they heard the door to the parlour open and Constance Mordesan's young maid, Maisy proceeded to bring in some tea and cakes.

'Will that be all Ma'am?' The young girl asked keeping her eyes down and not looking at either of them. The maid was burning with embarrassment, knowing what the young couple had been about, and did not see it as fitting. She also knew that if she tripped up in any way, that Constance would have no hesitation in physically reprimanding her.

'That will be all. Thank you.'

The girl almost run out of the room and William Devereux watched as Constance played hostess, pouring the tea for the both. She then sat back and sipped her tea seductively.

William looked at a woman who was vein, beautiful, rich, and popular. She loved to take risks and was adventurous. However, she had a spiteful streak that William chose to ignore. She made up excuses not to mix with his associates, and endured meeting his very good friends at their Alfriston Estate, Shaun and his wife Nana Cavendish, but was all too eager to meet with his family at the Devereux manor house in Lewes. She would change the subject if he were to mention the names of his other associates, as they were to base born for her liking and made it more than clear, she did not favour the association.

Constance was a snob and did not like to meet and talk with people who were beneath her social standing. She could be heard to announce, 'Really to be expected to acquaint myself with such vulgar dirty people!' She would cry out. 'Well I can hardly breathe in their presence. How you ever can even begin to converse with them is beyond my understanding. One assumes you make all the necessary precautions and cover your face with a handkerchief just in case the wretches have diseases?'

She chuckled to herself at her observations. Oh, she thought she was ever so clever and everyone else seemed too as well, joining her to laugh the matter off. Her friends were all very obliging and she loved them all dearly, because they loved her dearly. She mused over her tea and wallowed in her lovers looks. Although his attire was not of the latest bright fashions, all rather drape, and dull, she still felt her cheeks go red with desire. Oh, he could stoke her fires at any time, and she found herself having to force her gaze away in case she just snatched him up and out into the garden for some more fun. She turned away with the memory and physically had to calm herself down. Her brother Hartright would be so jealous, but it was so good to have such a fine catch. If only she could get to the bottom of William's inheritance and allowances, she would be even more than happy.

Oh, she knew when her Uncle died, that she and Hartright would be so well off, and knew that it wasn't as far off as she originally thought. She had visited her Uncle in Italy and was satisfied that with his life style, if he did not have a heart attack with all his activities, he would soon die of over indulgence. The man was a glutton and pig. He continuously pink and puffy. He looked like he would explode out of his skin.

He drunk like a fish and his nose was turning to purple where his nerve ends were busting. She had purred in delight at the thought that it would not be long, and remembered with delight the gaiety of his life, the wonderful parties, and the ever so lovely men.

William was torn between his loyalty for his position in the smuggling world, and his new friends. He found he was on tender hooks, because Hartright could crush all his dreams if he let his secret out. William had rather hoped that the romantic side of being a smuggler overshadowed the criminal aspect of the smuggling trade. If he were caught, he rather hoped that the authorities would see it as a passing fancy, child's play, - because now he was courting, a lady and he had responsibilities and a name of his own to make. It was all getting a little too hot.

'Tut, tut Master William, I have to tell you off for your lovely gift of tea. My Brother is trying to up hold the law in your area and purge the earth of the reckless smugglers, and we lap it up.'

'If it were not for the reckless smugglers, as you say, I doubt you too have that silk on your back either.' Being with her made him forget for a moment all his worries.

'Would you prefer I discard it.' She played with her dress and flirted shamelessly. He grinned at her knowingly.

'Maybe again later.' He smirked and she laughed softly. At that point, there was a small knock on the door. Constance was not happy and assumed it would be Maisy again, but a footman appeared holding a message for William.

He opened and scanned his missive and sighed in agitation.

'What's wrong my dear?'

'My father insists that I return immediately to the house.' His brows had creased and he looked perplexed.

'Whatever for?'

'It would appear that we have been broken into.' His father would not let this go.

'And how does this concern you?' He looked at her discreditably, how could she be so dismissive of this?

'They have trashed all the winery.'

'Whatever do you mean?'

'The ruffians have got into my father's wine cellars and smashed every bottle. Every barrel left to drip open, and what else have they done? Which is unbelievable? They have taken back all the brandy.' She could see that he was becoming annoyed with her and she did not wish to displease him.

'I can't believe that they got in without being caught. Where were the servants, the dogs? Does Hartright know, maybe he can apprehend.' She tried now to sound genuinely concerned.

'You do not understand Constance?' William was beside himself and was working himself up into a state. He could not believe her naivety with the situation.

'Then tell me.'

'It's a slight at me.'

'What?'

'They have taken back all the contraband that I have had a handle in obtaining.' He confessed.

'Then get it back!' She shrugged and sipped her tea.

He looked at her as if she was mad. She really did not get it and he was concerned that she had not even asked how everyone faired!

'My love, it is not quite that cut and dry.' He had to escape before he erupted and so he tried to remain calm.

'William, dear boy, if it's yours and it has been taken, then you get it back. Is that not what those dirty smugglers did to Hartright? I'm sure if low life like that can organise robbing your family, it should be quite simple for you to outwit them.'

'My love, with all due respect, this isn't the work of some low life scum.'

'Oh William. Behave, Hartright says.....'

'Constance, please!' She did not like his tone and this new manner of his was not what she expected. She did not comprehend fully what he was saying. Shem had sent a message that he knew about his extra work dealings and William knew this would not be the end of it. Why had he gone down that route? Why had he wished to impress his new friend? Why had he not been happy with what he had got? He was a man who could walk away from it all at any time, whereas his friends could not. But what he had done had put them all in it now. He knew this was the work of Shem. Shem was sending a message. Now he would have to deal with his family, his friends, and especially Shaun Cavendish. What did he really think was going to happen? He had been taken up by the buzz of it all and hadn't been rational and methodical. He was a fool! 'If you do not mind, I will take my leave of you.'

'You are returning to the Coast.'

'Immediately, before my father has a heart attack and disowns me completely.'

'Surely it cannot be as bad as that. How could he blame you? Surely, Hartright can be of assistance. Ask him to help.'

'Constance, my love, I know you mean well and are wonderful. However, you really do not understand all what is happening here and to be honest as much as I do not wish to go, I must. I will explain later. Say you forgive me.' Why did he feel he needed to butter her up when she had really annoyed him? He was angry now and just needed to go.

'I have a mind to follow you back down.'

'I have a mind that you will stay put and I will return shortly.'

He could not believe his luck when he had met her. It was as if a light had come down and struck him, and all he had known before, was nothing in comparison to this woman she was everything a woman should be. She was sophisticated, mature, experienced, rich, and very, very attractive.

At first, he found he could not get enough of her. Her face, her smile, her voice, her smell. He had been besotted. Again, he had deluded himself. He had chosen to ignore how he had started to become irritated by her on occasion and now he found at the first excuse, he wanted to run from her presence.

William and Hartright had initially met when William's father had thought it only right to invite the new Commander of the Riding Officers to dinner when Hartright had first been introduced into the area. They had formed an acquaintance and then when William's younger sister Daphne had almost had a fit when she understood her old friend Constance was Hartright's sister, they had immediately corresponded and the next thing William knew was that the lovely Constance Mordesan had graced their home. The ladies had been acquainted through family relatives since they were teenagers and Lady Mordesan had recently returned from abroad, having spent time away with her uncle after the death of her husband. He was very interested and the Lady Mordesan was a real beauty. This woman had captivated him. Now the lustre was wearing thin. Everything seemed to be crushing in on him. Shem had him!

Constance on the other hand had been immediately drawn to William; he excited her and was full of surprises and a man that she thought she could so easily manipulate to her will. He had been easy pickings, she needed a good family name to marry into, and he seemed to fit the bill perfectly. He was handsome and his family was all of good fine stock and had taken to her. William had shown another side to himself with his little outburst and Constance swayed in satisfaction, he had shown how assertive and commanding he could be and she found she rather liked that!

William Devereux and Hartright Mordesan had formed quite a friendship. They made a good pair. One, an established gentlemen and the other the younger son of the Earl of Lewes, Mortimer Devereux, and his mischievous wife the Lovely Lady Victoria Eugenie. Rumour had it that she had been very lose with her favours and no one could quite deny that William Devereux did strike a stark resemblance to the right honourable Shaun Cavendish of Alfriston – Charlton House. Both had blond hair and blue eyes. Whereas Williams siblings were all dark, taking after their mother who was of Spanish and French heritage. Everyone forget that Shaun Cavendish and Lady Victoria's mothers were first cousins and that Victoria was therefore his second cousin and so shared similar genes, be it too pale by comparison.

William and Shaun's household were near to each other, so it was no wonder that William had struck up a relationship with Shaun Cavendish and his family. However, this was not encouraged by the rest of his immediate family.

William's father had not felt the need to send any of his younger children away to school, and lavished the money on educating his two eldest sons. So he very much left their schooling to his wife. She was constantly at her wits end, and nine out of ten times, allowed them to finish their studies early, so William immediately went looking for adventure and found it with his two friends, Ned and Ray Cavendish.

William had always been adventurous and having met the boys, thereafter whenever he could he would be off to the Cavendish homestead for some good old fashion fun. It hadn't taken him long to be accepted into the fold and was seen as an accomplished asset in many of their outdoor extra curriculum activities. They had all been inseparable and it was only now after all this time that the cracks were starting to show.

William now had a new friend who he wanted to impress, who had a good-looking sister, who happened to be an acquaintance of his sister Daphne's. His attention therefore had been more focused on his socialising to his mother's great joy. He was now returning to the fold and was trying out to be quite popular amongst the opposite sex.

There was never a quiet moment for Shem, and with running a successful business that had arms in both legal and illegal activities, dealing with every day issues, and now having Hartright physically assault his brother, he was just about holding on mentally.

He dreamed of what he would do to Hartright. What torture he could inflict, how he would make him pay. How he would scream for his mother and Shem even visualised her being beaten senseless. He hated everyone at that moment and needed to vent his anger. He had waited too long for pay back, but that was a great weapon in its self. Bob had taught him to pull your enemies into a false sense of security and then chip away, slowly, slowly until there is nothing left.

Shem felt like his whole life was a whirlwind and to keep the balance he let his mind wonder to his pixie, and then he dismissed her as his attention centred on his men.

'Oh God, don't tell me, he just had to kill something?' Shem asked as Claude and Paully returned to The Castle Inn after being across country to visit their neighbours in Lewes. They looked so pleased with themselves that Shem was expecting them to report that their plans had gone up in smoke and blood lust had been allowed to reign.

Shem had sent them across to Alfriston and Lewes on the quiet, to gather intelligence about what William and the Cavendish's were really playing at. He had given his men a free hand to have a little fun and keep everyone on their toes and looking over their shoulders and hopefully away from his other objectives and plans afoot.

He hoped their scheming would make an example of William Devereux, as he would not let it go, no matter what Shaun Cavendish said on the matter.

Bob had been sent to France, and Jesus was sent to find Chater's statement and to investigate the state of play in East Grinstead.

'NOOOO.' Claude answered outraged that Shem could suggest that they had killed someone off the cuff. Shem chuckled. 'We acted with great restraint and you would have been proud of the way we conducted ourselves.'

'My arse!' Shem retorted. 'Soooo?' He mimicked his friend.

'We did as requested and uncorked every last barrel.'

'Did you nick any?'

'For fucks sake, truly,' Paully came to his own defence. 'I am here, why does everyone always assume I will have to kill something. It's not an addiction. I don't have too? I can go without killing. In fact, when did I last kill anyone? See I can't recall. It's a blur. Really, anyone, can anyone tell me? Cos you can't, you just can't. So nah.'

Both Shem and Claude looked at Paully with blank expressions; they then looked at each other and continued with their conversation.

'We did not take any, although I have to say, if I had been a gentleman, I would be so upset. I would cry at the loss. But there, it's gone, I don't give a shit. It's all vinegar.'

'And you're French!'

'A mere peasant, I am scum, a rat from the gutter, the son of a carpenter. What would I know?'

'Does anyone ever listen to me?' Paully was asking.

'No.' Shem answered flatly.

'So, what next?' Claude asked trying to divert the subject.

'I don't believe you didn't nick something!' Shem sat back and sighed. He looked long and hard at his friends and noticed their unwillingness to look at him. He knew they would crack.

'Only what was owed!' Claude could not contain himself. Shem knew them too well.

'I knew it.' He shook his head in disappointment at them still with a grin.

'Alright, for God's sake, we stole back some of the Brandy.' Paully said dismissively waving his hand to indicate that it was of no significance. The thought that it could be traced was not even considered.

'You fucking pleps.'

'We got some for you.'

'Oh that makes it all better then?' Shem retorted sarcastically.

Claude proceeded to swipe at Paully, who chuckled at his attempt whilst ducking out of the way.

'Do you forget what we do for a living?' Paully tried to sound also sarcastic.

'Can we get back to business now?' Shem ordered, however still laughing.

'Can't we just get drunk?' Paully knew it was the wrong thing to say before it left his mouth. Shem choose again to ignore him and started to smile as he looked at Claude. They all new another plan was in hand.

'Fire!' Shem suggested with light in his eyes. They all looked at each other liking the idea and all licking their lips in joy. 'I do love a good fire.' Shem mocked in his impressive quipped accent. 'Right – o, in next few days, let's torch the Barn.' Shem was grinning wildly in glee, enjoying the play-acting.

'God, Mortimer will have another pissy fit.' Paully observed. Lord Devereux was William's father and a good friend to Paully's father, Lord Lennard. Shem certainly wanted to rock the boat with William.

'Horses out first?' Claude stated and Shem nodded.

'Yes, otherwise Rafe will have a pissy fit as well.' They all smiled at that.

'Can we nick 'em?' Paully was already adding up the potential profit from selling off the Manor's horse stock. He loved that Shem was in fine form.

'Noooo.'

'Silly question for me to ask, really?' Paully sulked. If there had been any good stock, they would have taken them and replaced them with an inferior breed long before, but obviously there had been little gain to do and plus they were not out and out criminals! However for the line of business that they were in, usually if there was a local job, it was only to be expected that sometimes Lord Devereux's good working horses would go missing for a few days and be returned as good as new after the job was completed.

'Yes, it was.' Shem agreed with his friend.

'Don't make me feel any more foolish.' Paully remarked feeling slightly sorry for himself.

'I don't have to, you do that all yourself.'

'I sometimes get the expression that I am just here for your entertainment.'

'Well, it would be pretty dull wouldn't it, just listening to all this moaning, the shit and the bragging, but with you we get that extra richness to the proceedings.' Shem held out his arms in wonder to put his point across 'Such a sense of the world, the culture, and diversity you experience on a day to day basis.'

'Again, you are taking the piss?'

'Well you just open yourself up for it, time and time again, and I just have to bite.'

'Ladies!'

Both the men looked across at Claude who was playing referee instead of the usual Bob. Shem slapped Paully in the stomach and Paully responded while chuckling, in grabbing Shem round the head and manoeuvred him into one of his headlocks. There was no way anyone could get out of it, but both knew that Shem knew his weakness and Paully was leaning forward trying to keep his stomach away from Shem who even then had him. He had managed to swing his body round somehow and was attacking him with tickles, he couldn't stop giggling like a girl and Shem was trying not to chuckle, they both lost their footing and begun play wrestling on the floor.

Bob walked in at that moment, to witness the men playing boys games. He spread out his hands in amazement and glared at Claude, as if to say, in my absence I rely on you to keep order, but Claude just sat back and laughed at their antics.

'I just can't leave you lot, alone for one minute.' Then at Shem, he barked. 'My God! How are your men going to have any respect if you persist in playing with them? You know what I mean? Do you want to hear me report or what?'

Both Shem and Paully were lying on their backs in the middle of the room panting for breath.

'Bob, nice to see ya, we missed ya, how ya been?' Paully asked.

'Stop taking the piss and come up here and sit down.' Bob couldn't look at them. Sometimes their play-acting just worked him up no end and when he was grumpy, they knew better.

It was time for business and they all immediately jumped to attention whilst still digging at each other as they made their way back to the table. Bob needed to report to Shem privately about his trip to France and what he had discovered after speaking with his contacts. They also needed to get up to speed on Shaun Cavendish's position now he was back and how that would affect the area, what the Cavendish's would do They also needed to talk about what they were going to do with Chater. He noticed that Jesus wasn't around.

Bob and Shaun sat in the comfort of Shaun's warm parlour. He had stacked more fire in the grate and the room was comfortably warm, and smelled of pine nuts. The fire was the only light in the room.

They both held a glass of brandy and sipped occasionally, each lost in their own thoughts. Bob chewed on his pipe. Throughout the years, the two had found themselves settled in this room for a night of drinking and remembering times gone by.

They were old friends who could tell a tale or two. They had sailed the Caribbean's looking for their fortune and come back rich men with pardons. They were both growing tired and weary but still could not give it up. Bob knew he was on borrowed time, but the sense of fun, intrigue, deception and madness was just too much. He still had so much to give and knew Shem still needed him.

Shaun had expected a visit from his old friend and before long they knew their topic would turn to William and his almost desertion of the gang. Shaun loved William with a passion, but it was becoming evident to him that all the time and attention that they had given him had been lost. William's visits were fleeting; almost as if it were a burden. He had hurt those who cared dearly for him and turned his back on them for the sake of a better class of people, it would seem.

With the backing of Shem, Ned was now the main man in Cuckmere, be it reluctantly. Ned was lucky that he had grown up with the majority of their gang, they all looked out for each other as a big family, it was natural for him to take over, and so the problem of William was left to him.

'If you and Ned do not sort, then we will step in.' Bob left hanging in the air. The implication very clear. Shaun could not agree to those terms.

'I think you have already been having a little fun if I am not mistaken.' Shaun referred to the attacks on the Lewes Estates and the taking of all of the houses various alcoholic beverages. It was not a conversation that both ever wanted or needed to have and both were equally awkward but Shaun followed through with a youthful grin at the antics.

Shaun had to concede that he had tried his best, that William had just wiped his hands of their protection, and so he was on his own now. Shaun sighed thinking he was getting too old for this.

He had already been summoned across to Grays Mill in Lewes, to see Mortimer Devereux, William's father for some answers on the attack on his house and the destruction of his cellar. Of which, Shaun obviously had no answers to give, so instead he chose to send across to Mortimer some brandy as a peace offering. He wasn't surprised to hear that Mortimer had called across for the Magistrate at Hooe and Lord Lennard of Essex to bully them into doing something about the awful foul fellows who had dared to trespass his property, tie up his servants, and steal his fine wines and brandy! He had made his thoughts clear on the current Riding Officer and that in his wisdom he had no control and that Mortimer was going to have him dismissed. He had had enough! He was most put out that Shaun had not dared to come and see him after he had summoned him. This did not sit well, and Shaun really did not care either way. Mortimer had always looked down at him and Shaun did not bow to men who did not deserve his respect. Mortimer was a hypocrite. How could he tell him to look closer to home for answers? William had made his bed and would suffer the consequences once Shem got bored of stringing the man along.

So Shaun would not be concerned then, that at Mortimer's home of Grays Mill, it had been targeted again and they were all tackling a small fire which had started at the back of the stables. It wasn't a big fire and would soon be under control but it would appear that some of the horses had gone missing and could not be found! But Bob knew!

## Chapter Four

'Daisy's pregnant.' Rafe said out of the blue. They had watched the sun settle and had sat in the inner bailey, which was curtained by a roman wall. The wall was a layer of defence for the people who had originally lived inside Pevensey castle walls. Over the years, those who had settled there had added additional defences. Some bright sparks had also tried to destroy the castle, but time and neglect had found its footing and the main inhabitants were the pigeons nesting in the crumbling walls along with the cows and sheep. The grass was covered with cowpats and sheep and rabbit droppings.

Shem and Rafe had brought some bread, cheese and Ale, which Pissy Chrissy, the old village drunk had put together for them. Gideon, the Inn Landlord, had started to find little jobs for his friend to do and slowly over time, she had become the boys' helper. She cooked, cleaned, and did their laundry. Nothing was too much trouble and she just wanted to be busy. More and more she helped in the Castle Inn and Gideon was glad that after so many years of her wallowing in self-pity, she had a purpose. He was not naive to think she could have bad days and fall back on her woes, but at least she had something.

Shem and Rafe cherished the moments they had on their own and smiled to themselves lost in thought, soaking up the last of the sun as it decided to head for bed. Rafe thought of Daisy and his little girl Phoebe. Since Rafe had been attacked, he had been pampered silly, Daisy had immediately decided to move to Pevensey, and nothing was going to stop her fussing. She had also bought over Rafe's daughter who was now coming up for two. Phoebe had a wonderful nature about her. She smiled and laughed at everything and waffled on and on without making any sense at all. She had been a delight and Rafe had started to feel guilty about how he had hardly seen her when now he could not imagine life without her. He was glad he had them close to hand and wanted so much to protect the women in his life, but he still would not acknowledge that Daisy was his woman. As far as he was concerned, he was free. Now Daisy had told him she was expecting again.

On hearing the news, Shem had merely turned to his brother and shook his head. It was a standing joke how many children Rafe could possibly have. 'I like her, marry her.' He ordered in his normal voice.

'Don't be daft, she's common.'

'What did you say, you fucking snob!'

'Can you really imagine Gunthorpe opening the door and seeing Daisy standing there? He'd slam the door in her face and just berate me for the rest of my life.' He referred to a man from their previous life. Shem shifted his position to look at his brother incredulously. He gave him such a filthy look. Rafe looked away in embarrassment.

'I was hoping a good kick in would knock some sense into you!'

'That's lovely, that's just great.'

'Well, you haven't exactly been forth coming about what happened.'

'I did say. What are you trying to say? You think I talked. You think I let something slip.' Shem waved his hand in dismissal, he hated arguing with Rafe. Rafe always took exception and would never let it go with him. He'd play on how hurt Shem had made him feel. Why had Shem opened that door? 'Do you really need to ask?'

'Well?'

'You're becoming paranoid and I don't much like your tone to me. I am a wanted man I will have you know. He has an arrest warrant for me. He has Chater over at Alfriston ready to testify. And really, I'm the innocent one, I got a kicking for you, and what do I get. I get accused of being soft.'

'Oh shut up plep.' Shem dismissed his brother's rant as mockery. He looked hard out to the horizon. 'You really think, I think you said anything. You know I'd kill you.' He produced the smallest of grins. 'You're not that weak, that you'd bubble. You think I'd let anything else happen to you? I'm fucking mad as hell that I allowed this to happen. It won't happen again. He'll be dead before long if I get my way.' Rafe felt satisfied that Shem was backing him. He settled back against the grass. 'Anyway, I've got Chater and Jesus is fetching both your statements. But I still need to get to the source of this shit over that way.' He nodded towards the southeast.

'You got Chater? You bloody kept that quiet.' Shem never ceased to amaze his brother.

'I'm telling you now.' Rafe could not believe him.

'I'm not going to came running and tell you everything, that would definitely then get you killed you prat.' They both were a little peeved at each other at that point.

'What are you talking about, the other stuff?'

'The gentlemen who grassed on you was not a spy for Hartright. So we have another bloody problem to solve, as well as this shit from over that way!'

'As well as sorting out Chater?'

'Oh Chater's a piece of piss.' Shem was dismissive of him as a real threat.

'Don't kill him Shem. He's alright really?' Shem raised his eyebrows at Rafe for defending the man.

'Are you for real he could have had you killed?'

'He did not mean it.' Rafe offered but he could see his brother's mind working overtime again. He was deep in thought.

'Who did he really talk to, and why is Gunthorpe's name being kicked around? They won't play me for long.' Shem pondered and Rafe knew he referred to the grass that had been sent to Hartright. One thing he knew, Shem would find out.

'You haven't told me what Bob said about France.' Shem sighed at that. Rafe smiled seeing his brother's discomfort.

'I have been ordered that on no account am I to kill Hartright for what he did to you. Infact, I have been told I will never get the go on that.' Shem was disgusted that the main man in France, who had rescued them and made Shem into the man he now was, but who still held the strings. It was only a matter of time before Shem cut the ties to France.

'But soon, we won't need them to say either way, will we?' Shem smiled at his brother's insight. He had tried not to get Rafe too involved in the business, but respected his brother enough to give him snippets of information on their finances and Rafe was not that naive that he could add up that that meant also what their strengths and future plans would be.

'No, and that's what scares them. I am too big for my boots and they know I do not need them anymore. You watch me play with the little poof; they can't do anything to stop me. You watch me make a success of the Pevensey job and see their faces.' Shem's face snarled as the image of Hartright entered his thoughts.

'You show off!' Rafe tried to lighten the atmosphere.

'I'm the one with the muscle now and Mr. H knows that.'

'You think he sent the grass!' Rafe asked.

'I know he did.' Shem did not know why he believed it to be him. Nevertheless, his gut told him so.

'He wouldn't try and wipe you out?' Rafe laughed at the absurdity of the accusation.

'It's a family trait.' Shem smiled sarcastically.

'He would not do that to us?'

'Don't count your chickens, or in your case your daughters.'

'I've only got one.' Rafe laughed.

'That you know of.'

'There isn't anymore.' Rafe tried to sound sure. 'Well maybe there are two...'

'Three, four....'


Shem threw the man's ear to the ground and heard a rustle as the rats ventured to investigate. The man was howling in pain and Shem paid no heed, he was enjoying himself. The man was now tied to a chair in the centre of the room, his once coiffure look, now in complete disarray. His silvery blond hair caked in blood and his scalp covered in bruises. His whole body ached from the beating he had got.

All Shem could think about was an eye for an eye. Retribution.

Hartright did not know how long he had been there, the air was foul, he had to soil his own clothes, as he was tied and had no mobility. Rats and other life form seem to have taken up residence.

Hartright had never experienced true fear before, but know he had. He could be locked in here forever and no one would ever know. It was ironic how the tables had been turned and he had been the instigator of a similar act on Rafe. So this was the reprisal. He felt no remorse for others, for how he had put others in this situation, especially Rafe Smith; he just wanted to get out of this. This was becoming out of hand. He had been warned.

The one consolation was that if they had wanted to kill him, they would have by now. These sorts of men did not mess about, so to that conclusion he knew he was either being held for ransom, which was hardly likely with his family's futures, or they were teaching him a lesson after Rafe. Perhaps he should have listened to the Earl. He reasoned with himself that he had a value and be it, it seemed insufficient now, he was needed, so he had advantage.

Shem was the only real one capable of ordering this and if that was so, he knew that he could outwit the man. Shem thought he was clever, but he did not know him. Hartright was a gentleman and Shem was scum. Shem was a bully, playing at being a hard man and Hartright would have him!

Shem had been lucky with the Rottingdean job, and Hartright had been pissed that Shem had had the cheek to go and retrieve back what he had so painstakingly planned to confiscate. Admittedly, he had had a back hander to avert his eyes from the whole convey of galleys going backwards and forward from France, so it had been agreed that he could at least claim a little of the cargo. So a little give and take. What was the harm? It wasn't as if no one did not know what was going on.

By God, Shem had regular shipments coming across from France every few days. The Cavendish's had cargos being dropped off as and when at Cuckmere and Shem's inland gangs run by Harry and Idris's were overseeing the runs off Fairlight and Lydd. The whole area of East Sussex now reported to Shem. The traffic was unbelievable and Hartright's' resources had been stretched. He needed to catch them with a big run and then had been handed information on a plate. He thought he had Rafe by the balls, but the pup had given nothing of importance away. Rafe was just a soldier in the gang, nothing more, he had no authority and just happened to be the leader's brother. He had not thought it all through and realised that the information given by Chater did not directly link in with Rottingdean, but previous shipments. Therefore, he could not connect the two events. Then to top it all, he had run like a frightened rabbit being chased by a fox when he had seen Shem come to rescue his brother. He had humiliated himself. He would have to win some pride back.

He remembered throughout Rafe's capture that he had kept singing a pathetic childhood lullaby that reminded him of his own youth and even now, he could not get it out of his mind.

'Hush-a-by baby

On the tree top,

When the wind blows

The cradle will rock.'

Shem had proven to be quite a planner and Hartrtight was beginning to appreciate he had under estimated his foe. He had stolen back the Rottingdean confiscated goods, whilst Hartright had been chasing around trying to get his witness to make a statement in front of the Magistrate, and now Hartright knew that they were all in league together and no matter how hard he tried, nothing would ever become of this commission. He had to take whatever he could, and then get as far away as possible. He had become complacent thinking that Shem perhaps was avoiding him, seeing how he had the power to kidnap his own brother from beneath his feet, but all the time Shem had been waiting and playing him.

He had been livid to have been summoned to the Earl's House for a telling off and that had got him a little annoyed and started to think that maybe he should get some payback. Then to add insult to injury, this all powerful Shem had then sent house breakers to his new home in London and had cleared the house of every piece of furniture, cutlery, bed linen, his clothes, his wines; the wood for his fire.! Soon after, he discovered his horses had been stolen from the local stables where he paid for them to be kept whilst in London.

Then to add insult to injury, he had seen Rafe ride one of his horses. The man had blatantly produced a certificate of sale; the legal's were stamped and signed by Magistrate Pelham, of Cuckfield Manor, as confirmation of a sale between the South Coast gypsies and him. Hartright had wanted to strike him down with his crop there and then, but now Rafe rode with a party of others. He was now better protected.

What could he do? He would have that flash bastard Shem. Innocent, his arse, the man was mocking him!

They had also started to attack his new business partner William and it had not stopped there. He had been sent on another fool's errand, missing a certain arrest by an hour, only to discover that he had been hoodwinked, by all accounts, he had missed apprehending all the men of the local parish's for participation in one of the bigger hauls that landed every now and again. Apparently, as that idiot George English had advised, there had been over 300 horses alone ferrying the cargo at Cuckmere sands. Shem was rubbing his face in it.

Then he had been summoned to London to make his report. He could not let that lie. They had played him well and waited a few months so that his confidence was restored and that hopefully he would have deluded himself that Shem thought of him as a great threat after all, and by attacking Rafe he had made a point. He had also been brave and told the Earl to stay out of his business. He had seen this as winning a small battle and was confident with the way that events were running, he would win the war. However, he had let his guard down and easily succumbed to an ambush. He was locked up in a disused Fishermans wrath on the beaches near Eastbourne. He knew he needed to barter for his life. But what could he do, when he was tied and beaten up?

'If you let me go.' He spat through bloodied teeth, 'I will release Chater. I will destroy his evidence.' He wanted to weep in agony at it all. He was disgusted with his own weakness and shook his head in pity at himself.

Shem was contemplating taking off one of the man's little fingers, or pulling out a tooth when Hartright had made the proposal? Shem choked on his laughter.

'I'll do anything just let me go.'

'How do we know you will not run to Lennard or one of the other Magistrates?' It was the first time Hartright had heard his attacker and did not know it was indeed Shem. Shem had deliberately disguised himself and his voice to sound so large and more common.

'You have my word.'

'That means nothing.'

'I have information.'

'I am listening.'

'You let me go, I release Chater, and I swear I will give you a name.'

'I'll tell you what. I'll just kill you, cos I don't give a fuck.'

'No. No. No. Please!' Shem stopped; he did not intend to kill him just yet.

'I'll give you Chater.'

'Harry, don't be so naive. We have Chater already.' Hartright looked dumbfounded.

'Chater is under our protection now.' Shem wanted the point to hit home.

'No, he is safe. I have him secure.'

'No, you went back to Lewes, after you fled when you saw the gang coming for Rafe Smith, you fled and failed to check your insurance, and left him with your hired help.'

'No, you could not have!' Hartright tried to convince himself it could not be possible. He had been too complacent.

'Yes, we could have!' Shem was enjoying this. 'Chater, his mother, and sister are all under Shem's protection now.'

'I don't believe you.'

'I really don't care. So you have nothing to barter with.'

'I do. I do.'

'No, you really don't.' Shem decided the cut off his finger.

'Tell Shem. I want to speak to Shem!' Hartright tried to lean further back in the seat as his abuser moved towards him. 'I have information.'

'Listening.'

'It's William!'

'Old news.'

'No you can't know. He is in league with me!' Shem could not believe how low Hartright would go to save himself.

'Old news, you ship from Bologne to Newhaven via Old man Samson, Shaun Cavendish's old contact and the transport is overseen by Jacobs's gang. They in turn sell on to Idris' man at Hooe and make a profit from the Newly Lads in Morden!'

'How can you know this?'

'They are all Shem's men.' Shem said.

'But you can't know that.' Hartright cried in disbelieve.

'No, what we want from you is the name of the man who told you when to get Rafe?'

'I don't know what you mean.'

'You do not have the intelligence to stalk him yourself, you were spoon feed when to kidnap and attack him. Who sent you the man?'

'It was one of my Uncle's friends.' Hartright knew he had been too quick to give the information, but he wanted to go. He could not stomach anymore. He would die.

'And who is he?'

'You don't know him. None of you will.' He hesitated to say any more. He wrestled with himself, just to tell them. Maybe they would then let him go! He hurt all over.

'Who is he?' The torturer kept shouting.

*Just tell him; just tell him'*, Hartright's mind called out. *'I want to go home.'*

'Tell me who it is!' The torturer roared again.

'He is Gunthorpe!' He blurted out. Shem's jaw dropped. This could not be so. Impossible! Yet, it could be true!

Jesus was still gathering intelligence and Shem had been taught to expect the unexpected. But to suggest it was Gunthorpe, could it be him? What was the motive? He analysed the information. Who would gain from this and who knew Gunthorpe enough to use him so? There were still more questions than answers. Nevertheless, his gut gave him the answers. He then heard a whistle from outside. He tutted at the inconvenience and before he went outside, he kicked Hartright in the shin. How he hated him!

The wind was up and it was drizzling. The cool air hit him and he hunched his shoulders. He pulled down his scarf, which previously had been hiding his face.

'What?' He moaned as he walked out onto the shingle beach to be greeted by Paully. They walked a distance away so their voices would not be heard or carried and took shelter between the fishing boats.

'Look at ya, enjoying yourself silly, ain't ya?' Paully laughed and punched his friend in the arm. 'Please let me take over?'

'Again, what?' Shem crossed his arms and looked impatiently at his friend, not in any mood for any tomfoolery. Paully pulled himself together and became serious although Shem noticed he was in some discomfort and kept rubbing his privates.

'Bob's back from France, he's with Rafe. He said he had disturbing news.' He advised. Shem nodded and turning back put his scarf back on and re entered the building, indicating to Paully to stay outside. He was not the only one with news!

Shem was disappointed that he had to go, yet a part of him had been thankful, because he knew that he would have eventually lost it and killed Hartright. He was battling daily with the need to make this man's life a living hell, and to torture him at every angle. Death would be too quick. It would bring Shem peace and closure but he knew it would not be enough. Hartright could not be allowed to get away with the crimes he had committed.

The fire was not quite ready yet to flicker.

Hartright looked up with pleading in his eyes, tears streamed down his face. Shem was disgusted at the weakness of the man who in real life was a spiteful bastard. He was a cowardly grass who would do anything and had time and time again to save himself. He had no shame!

Shem casually walked towards him and ungraciously pulled his privates out and proceeded to urinate all over the man. Paully watched from the doorway and grinned at his Boss in satisfaction. Hartright burnt with humiliation. Even in his weakened state, he was thinking of vengeance. Trying to convince himself that he was a brave man and he would have his day.

They knew what he had done and they were showing him who ruled. Taunting him. He could suffer more or he could just run away and leave now, and at least he would have his life. But running wasn't something he was used to doing. Oh, so he led himself to believe. But his mind whirled and he swore they would pay, he would have all of them hanged, no tortured first, like they had done to him. Tortured for an eternity, then hung, and quartered, yes that's what he would organise. He would have each and every one of them. They had no idea who they were dealing with and what he was capable of doing! He had no idea his thoughts mirrored those of his torturers.

He had been warned to get out of the fire and paid no heed. He would never admit that this had been his fault, that his greed had caused this. He was arrogant. He had seen an opportunity and gone for it. He never looked at the damage he left behind, he just went for it. Now, now they would pay. If they thought that scaring and deforming him was going to make him run, they had another thing coming. He would kill them all and their families as well. He had the power of the law behind him; he had his name and his title. He knew influential people. He was Hartright Mordesan, no less. Son to the deceased Hector Mordesan, brother to the current - Lord of the Mordesan House, Mestor Mordesan. He would not run now.

The bigger man came back and unceremoniously he kicked Hartright from the chair. He sprawled across the floor. Hartright nearly died when the man pulled a dagger from the back of his trouser belt. His previous thoughts vanished in a flash and pure fear set in. He could see the man was grinning through his disguise. In one quick movement, the man had him face down and in the next second, his wrists were set free. He could not move. He heard the man walk away, calling to the other man, and laughing. He heard them mount their horses and heard others join the group and as he held his breath, he heard them all ride away, yet he dare not move from the floor. He was free. They had set him free.

'You alright mate?' Rafe had been watching Paully all evening and there was definitely something amiss.
'No.' Paully answered sullenly. He had been drinking all night to ease his pain.
'What?'
'I got a bit of an itch.' He whispered into his drink.
'Itch, you don't say? You ain't left it alone all day.' Rafe tried to make light of the delicate subject.
'I am in pain.' Paully moaned. He leaned back against his chair and stretched. Not wishing to look at Rafe.
'Pain, what do you mean?' Rafe knew exactly what sort of pain he was in.
'Well the other night.' Paully started going all quiet with his voice and looking to see if anyone else was in earshot. This was indeed awkward!
'Oh No, no, no, no.' Rafe sat back and started to tut and lapping up the moment.
'You don't know what I was going to say.' Paully leant forward.
'Too much information. You been well and truly done up. You want to go and see Hattie in the woods for potion to clear that. By God, Err you've put me off my dinner. I told you before if you want any tips all you had to do was ask.'
'It's not that, Nancy.' Paully growled through gritted teeth
'This jealousy you have to me is so unfounded. Infact I am offended. I offer my

hand in friendship and you mock me.' Rafe knew that if Paully had not been in pain, he would have thumped him one.

'Stop giving it large and fucking listen.'

Rafe suppressed a grin and cocked his head forward, loving every minute of Paully's discomfort.

'I know the difference between that and this.'

'You've lost me. Are you saying you been caught out before. You dirty bastard.'

'Oh someone give me strength.' Paully declared.

'What's going on? Why are you not fighting yet?' Claude came and sat down.

Paully raised his eyes to the ceiling.

'Tell him!'

'Tell him, I don't want the world to know me business.'

'Tell me what?'

'You're supposed to be best friends.'

Claude looked from one to the other and became conscious he was not going to get anywhere. 'Fuck this for game of soldiers.' He immediately got up and went back across the bar.

'Rafe, seriously it is killing me, will you have a look?'

Rafe leant back against his seat and tutted again. 'You are gay! You just want me to see your tackle.'

'Oh for the love of Mary. Please God let me kill him.' Paully went to get up and Rafe could see he was flush with embarrassment.

'Alright, alright, come on.'

Claude watched the pair go into the back room privy and curiosity got the better of him and as he went to bang on the door of the back room to gain entrance, he heard Rafe yell.

'You moron!' Claude barged through the first door and stopped before he had an opportunity to get through the next door, as he heard Rafe crying with laughter.

'What, what?' Paully was pleading and then through the door he heard Rafe shriek.

'There bloody teeth marks, someone's tried to bit your knob off!'

'Who?'

'What do you mean who? I don't know who you were with.'

'Nor do I, it's all a blur.' This got Rafe off more and he was laughing so much, he could not breathe.

'You're joking?'

At this point, Paully had done his trousers up, shoved through Rafe, and opened the door to find Claude standing there with his arms folded not believing the conversation he was over hearing. He stepped back and Claude watched as the very red Paully went a further shade of red and then purple with rage.

'I'll torch the bitch and everyone in that house! He charged through his friend and headed out towards the front of the Inn.

'This should be fun!' Rafe darted after him and Claude sighed knowing he would be the one to sort the stupid pair out.

'Mr. St Clement, how wonderful to see you, how are you.' Both men bowed in unison and then Shem flicked his coat tails back and sunk into the beautiful carved chair with ease. 'Mr. Saltdean, thank you, I am in high spirits it is an honour to see you Sir.' Shem spoke in his gentlemen voice in fluent French and felt comfortable and at ease with his disguise. He was in London as St Clement to discuss his business ventures and receive his reports and later he had other more unsavoury business to attend to. He watched as Mr. Saltdean sat down at his desk and from his drawer pulled out a file. He opened the file and found his papers as he had expected at the top. He smiled up at Shem and handed him a paper.

'Your annual statement, however I do have some disturbing news about one of your investments which I only received word on yesterday.'

'If you refer to the Warehouse at Dieppe, I already know.' Saltdean was taken aback, and noted how calm and collected the gentleman's body language was with this news. He impressed him.

'My man confirms that everything was burnt to a crisp. I await the inventory books on that property and its stock, and then I can make adjustments to the ledger which was prepared and finalised for last week ending.'

'Just deduct the property value; it held no stock at that time, thankfully.' Shem smiled at him.

'Hah, understood. Shall I order tea?" Shem smiled back in acceptance and spent the next few hours going through all of his papers and figures.

Bob had confirmed that their main warehouse had deliberately been torched; and Shem had sent Jesus out to France with Bob on his last trip, securing the Chater family in their new home with protection and at the same time, keeping an eye out. Many a time through the trip Jesus had wanted to push the ever-grateful Chater over board as all he kept saying to anyone who would listen was. 'I really thought they were going to kill me. They assured me they were not, but I did not believe them. I should have had more faith!' Jesus knew he had passed a divine test when he had left the simpleton, his mother, and sister to their new life.

Jesus had reported back to Bob on what the underground rumours had been and Bob had decided to get shot of all the stocks from the port as quickly as possible, hence the extra new runs and agreements with the Cavendish's and Jesus had also set up a new route with his contacts further along the coast line to Poole. They had deliberately kept a run of wagons off loading to the French warehouse, and only Bob and Jesus had known that it was all empty.

Shem knew full well who was behind the attack, but Bob was not being convinced at this stage, so Shem had made further investigations.

Shem was more than happy with the arrangement with Mr. Saltdean, and found that doing business with him was reaping its rewards and he had diversified his portfolio.

Mr. Saltdean was Lord Lennard nephew from one of his younger sisters and had taken the decision early in life that to get anywhere he best get sponsored by his Uncle or rather Paully and placed in a position that he could develop. It hadn't taken Lord Lennard long to see how clever his nephew was and before long, the young man had a good reputation. He was a great networker and he had wisely worked with the East India Company and bought shares in the company-shipping yard where they build their own ships for purpose. This had turned into a sound investment and in addition, he and Shem found themselves investing in commodities from India and Asia.

Both men realised if Lord Lennard had not had influence with the Company that neither of them would be sitting where they were today. However, both also knew that this would not have been possible either without the small capital injection from their other associate, Meir the Jew.

Mr. Saltdean had established that the young French man had no qualms about where he invested and paid no heed to political sensitive's and just agreed to invest in whatever Mr. Saltdean deemed fit for purpose. Shem had plans and he wanted his dreams to be fulfilled sooner rather than later.

The next few weeks were going to be particularly trying as Shem and his men had put together a plan to off load a massive amount of the stored contraband and even more in one great run. It was planned to land at Pevensey Bay and the operation would include every able bodied in the whole area and the collaboration of all their families and some. In conjunction, there would still be the normal every day runs which would continue and the plan to hoodwink the riding officers whilst all this went on.

Shem's mind was constantly working overtime and he just wished he had more time to take a step back. He needed to see a certain someone and he found his heart aching for that mischievous smile. He remembered as he had walked to the office that he had looked up to the sky, knowing there were no stars, just smog covering everything and making him feel sick. At least for a second he could pretend, that he was anywhere other than in London. God, he hated it so and all the memories it conjured up for him. Mr. Saltdean's offices were placed in Billingsgate, which offered also the ungodly aroma of both fresh and rank fish, being that the fish market was just to hand.

The whole place made him want to bring up his insides and he constantly had to divert his path from dead animals and drunken people littering his path. He always felt as if the whole world was caving in on him as he made his way through the various small streets, which were like a labyrinth. Every street and alley held a secret and the blackness did nothing to help.

As hard as he might, he could not win the battle and his mind's eye kept returning to the familiar scenes of a dock and the blackness that brought. It had been dusty and stifling hot on the docks on the Congo. It had been years ago, he remembered the sweat pouring from him, the smells, the sights and sounds, the loneliness and despair of it all.

He had been no more than a boy and remembered he had to be constantly alert, always holding his brother's hand, giving him reassuring cuddles and hugs, and watching as each and every day Rafe drew into himself. Rafe started not to speak, he was petrified at any movement, any sound and of anyone speaking to them. He would curl up and looked to Shem for protection. It had been horrific and he was more shocked at himself for finding he had been shaking all over and had to lean against a wall for support. He had tried to control his breathing and wiped the sweat from his brow. He was exhausted and had stayed against the wall until he composed himself.

Then he sat as a gentleman going over his holdings and stocks in Mr. Saltdean's offices as if nothing of consequence had happened. His attack had scared him but he had no time to dwell on it. How far they had come now with all his preparations and how far would he have to go?

'I take it that you will keep me informed of this issue with the loan at Mordesan Manor?'

'I have already scheduled a meeting for Friday to discuss with the Bank Manager.'

'Excellent.'

Later in the day, Shem strolled arm in arm with Lady Barbara Skelton, while her husband Charles Skelton, Esq., Lieutenant-General in the English service, walked beside them. They made a striking group. Charles was very dark and was a man always on alert and currently fighting in the War of Succession with Marlborough. He had a condescending manner about him and he wore a smirk on his face that he put down to the sun and sky being too bright for his eyes! He was conceited and full of himself.

His proud wife was of similar height and wore herself regally. She was the eldest daughter to Thomas Lennard, Earl of Sussex, and looked very much like him and shared many of his mannerism, which was also that of her half brother Paully. She had a delightful air about her, however as Shem had quickly observed, she was vein and if she caught her reflection, would give herself a small reassuring smile.

Both Lady Barbara and Charles had formed an easy friendship with Mr. Samuel St Clement aka Shem Smith, having accepted that he was a distant relative of Lord Lennard's from Britanny. He was very good company and never overstayed his welcome. Charles had heard of his family name and no suspicious was ever directed at him.

The couple had been informed that Mr. St Clement would be staying for a few days and both relished the opportunity to re affirm their recent friendship. Lady Barbara had no idea that Mr. St Clement was the infamous Shem, her brothers Boss and friend.

Lady Barbara rather missed living in England and wanted nothing more than to return home to Herstmonceux, and Charles, whose family was originally from up north, was of the same opinion.

Shem looked very dashing in his highly fashionable justaucorps knee length coat, which was of rich blue and mixed black velvet. His waistcoat was black and had been embroidered in silver metal thread with small petals and leaves. His breeches were matching and his whole appearance screamed of money, power, and nobility.

His shirt was white and crisp and he had a black solitaire tied around his neck. His leather shoes were fastened with solid silver buckles, and he wore white silk stockings. He wore his swordstick concealed beneath his coat and for good measure, his trusted dagger was held fast to his side. His hair was greased back tightly and knotted at the nape of his head with a black ribbon and he was clean-shaven.

His tricorne was of a similar colour to his coat and was trimmed in silver. He looked magnificent and Claude remarked he should watch out for the ladies! This had made Shem grin even more and he thought today he would really play up and was rewarded with very warm and welcoming smiles.

'Well, well what have we here?' Shem remarked as they strolled towards an oncoming young couple Shem looked back to see that Claude had been driving discreetly behind as they had walked and nodded to Shem that he had seen the people ahead.

'Oh look who it is, Lady Barbara, Lady Barbara dear.' They heard a young woman call from the other party.

'Oh Charles, can you believe it, its Constance!' Lady Barbara screamed in glee and with no further ado, both ladies run to each other, kissed, and cuddled. Both Shem and Charles shared a look.

The two ladies gossiped, giggled, and admired each other's attire before they remembered themselves and the introductions begun. Lady Barbara introduced Mr. St Clement to Constance Mordesan and Master William Devereux.

'Pleasure Sir.' William had a firm handshake and Shem was happy that he hardly looked at him, his eyes clearly on Constance all the while. She seemed to scan his face and smiled sweetly and he sighed with relief. They had rarely met before and Shem was thankful.

Claude by this time had covered his lower face with his scarf, hoping that William did not recognise either of them; otherwise, a hasty exit would be called upon.

Shem kept himself conversing with Charles as they proceeded with their walk and outwardly could be seen at ease, however inwardly he was on high alert with Constance never far from his thoughts and view.

She had always been very pretty, but now she radiated a vibrant passion and beauty, that obviously had caught William, hook line and sinker. He could not keep his eyes of her.

She was a few years older than the party and had been married and widowed. She did not seem deterred by being a widow and seemed to lap up all the attention. William was obviously smitten and at her disposal. Shem felt sick.

Her hair was curled tightly in the latest fashion and she looked elegant all in a pale pink. She carried herself in that sophisticated manner and played at being in love. She was attentive and socially engaging, however all too often he caught her smooth down her dress, play, reset her hair, and raise her head in defiance. Herself arrogance shining through.

He remembered her devilish laugh, that seductive all consuming deep laugh, he never forgot, she was poison.

He turned his attention away from the blackness and found in his mind, his little pixie and he pictured her all dressed up and looking elegant. He laughed to himself, she would act the part, be in her element while all the time, he would see in her eyes that she was not taking it seriously. He knew, as soon as she was out of sight of any of them, she would kick off the silly shoes, as she would call them, she would let her hair down and rip the finery away and be comfortable and free. He missed her so much. It was time he found the time to see her. She had better not gone and got herself married.

'Jesus that was close.' Claude observed later when they had found themselves in one of the better Alehouses in the middle of the most notorious Red Light district in Covent Garden, which was run and owned by Shem's very good friend Luca Bravio. Shem had excused himself from the Skelton's and would return later. He and Rafe knew Luca from their previous lives and they had complete loyalty to each other.

Luca Bravio owned and run all the criminal activities in Covent Garden. He was a ruthless leader with a network of informants over the city and beyond. He was a barrel of a man with a shiny baldhead. He had numerous businesses such as, Alehouses, coffee shops and whorehouses and all had a reputation of being extremely clean. He hated dirt and untidiness and it was no surprise that he also owned Laundry Houses. He could control many things but not the stench, the outside brought and this he hated.

Luca's main Alehouse was situated off the main square, which held a daily small open-air fruit and vegetable market. The aftermath of the market was still evident when Shem and Claude had made their way across the square to Luca's, treading through the waste and rats looking for scraps. The place was rank and smelt disgusting. Shem smiled at the rats and thought of Hartright.

Taverns, theatres, coffeehouses, and brothels surrounded the square. The various establishments and prostitutes milled around the square, and the whores stood in groups being both crude and cocky. Shem found himself fighting to get beyond the ladies, who like the square had seen better days. The evening was drawing in and a small mist had begun to descend. Shem had shivered in anticipation.

Shem had changed back into his old attire to see his friend and to all and sundry he was now Shem Smith from the south coast and not St Clement.

'I wanted to wring her bloody neck.' Shem whispered into his drink. The Alehouse was packed to the rafters with very unsavoury characters and all keeping an eye out on everyone and everything that walked through the doors.

'What, I thought you wanted to wring his neck.' Claude observed thinking he had just mispronounced. 'But God, what a woman!' Claude closed his eyes and visualised the beautiful Constance in his arms, not taking Shem up any further on his previous comment. 'God, I bet she keeps our young Mr. Devereuz sweet.' Claude laughed at that, thinking she could keep him busy anytime. He eyed a lovely creature across the way and indicated for her to come across.

The woman melted into his lap and he smiled warmly at her. She was long, thin, and as white as plaster with crinkled ginger hair. She was no beauty and not in any league near the intoxicating Constance but she certainly made a change from the dark women he tended to favour. His thoughts touched on Paully, and he laughed to himself. Paully had been ordered on no account to go near Valentina's establishment or threaten to set fire to it or anyone in the house. Paully had eventually found out who had bitten him and his rage could hardly be contained.

Claude liked that this woman of the night on his lap, did not have that sadness in her eyes that many of the London girls acquired after a time on the game. It was a quiet forlorn look, which would lead them to the blue ruin and a quick death.

Shem sipped his ale, eyeing everyone who came into the pub and looking for one man in particular. 'As long as he stays busy and stays here for the next few days.'

'Luca will sort it, either way.' Claude sat with one eye wooing the woman, and the other watching as his Boss left him to it, having just been nodded at by Luca from the bar. He turned back just the once and nodded at Claude who understood. He was not to breathe a word of this meeting to anyone outside of this room.

Claude watched as Shem made his way towards the bar to a handful of men who greeted him. He watched him embrace heartily a very handsome dark man with jet-black hair and a moustache and beard. He was immaculately dressed and his company suggested a more Spanish influence. They were obviously very close and known to each other and he witnessed Luca also greet him like an old family friend, by roughly embracing him. All three men proceeded to greet and speak in French then disappear through the back with some others. Claude knew better than to ask, but what caught his eye were Luca's younger brother Jo Bravio and another familiar face to him, Mr. Benedict Brown, who was a notorious pirate, watching the party also intently. His gut told him to be weary and with that in mind, he averted his concentration back to them rather than the lass on his lap. The next few days were going to be very busy as Shem' s master plan was nearly upon them and there would be very little time for fun and games thereafter.

The day had arrived. It was dawn and a crisp morning with clear views all the way to the horizon; the sky was that wonderful white merging into a blue haze. The sea was calm, just shifting ever so slowly in rhythm and the tide was out and low. Pockets of Sea gulls rested and floated atop the sea whilst Terns wobbled along the beach.

Shem stood on the top of the shingled beach looking out across the immense bay and keeping a sharp eye on the three large cutters anchored. He could not have asked for better weather, and knew that no one could see the inner turmoil he went through watching the proceedings. He rubbed the hairs on the back of his neck and wiped the sweat off his brow.

He looked like every other man on the beach, ready for work, with hair plaited, and loosely tied back and an unshaven look with dirty working clothes on, which had seen better days.

He watched intently as the cutters were being unloaded, and the goods ferried to shore. Each gang unloaded the cargo at great speed, protected by a half circle of the gang armed with muskets, who would then defend the rear of the column of tub carriers and pack horses when the cargo left the beach and headed for the marsh roads. Shem was thankful that the usual boggy marsh was dry and so cargo could easily be carried across and avoid any hold ups. Shem stood in awe looking to his left along the whole stretch of beach, watching as his men manoeuvred. He still could not believe that he had done this and knew that his father would have been so proud.

He followed the trail and his eyes took in the wonder and excitement of various arrays of activities. The helpers along the beach, reminded him of hectic ants in haste as they loaded the cargo onto the back of the horses, men and wagons. The shore was lined with over 700 men who all looked to Shem and his gang for their orders. He made fists in anxiety.

They said that this was the biggest operation of its kind ever mounted and no one had witnessed the like before. Shem had worked his magic and pulled in all his gangs and connections from the flat beaches at Romney Marsh in Kent, to the white chalk face clefts around Beachy Head to Cuckmere, along the South Coast. Even in every village and hamlet, the locals played their part in the operation by ignoring and just carrying on with their everyday lives and paying no heed to the scores and scores of horses, wagons and men, plus all the noise and attention they brought with them.

Shem was in no doubt that, anything would go wrong. He had assessed every aspect; risk assessed everything and had contingency plans at the ready. It had taken so long to plan. It was a military style operation, and everything had been thought of right down to if any injuries occurred. Shem had Doctors on the pay roll in each region that could be called upon at any time. All the gang members knew that for their loyalty an allowance was paid to the man's family should an accident occur and he was unable to work or indeed if for some unexpected reason, the Revenue forces ever captured them.

He and his gang had planned it that the riding officers were off on a fool's errand across to Romney and had ensured that there was enough rumour and supposed action to warrant an investigation.

Shem had arranged to have spare wagons, horses, men, and doctors, to hand and was in awe at the efficiency, which the gangs worked. It was all quite unbelievable.

The younger men were handling the horses, under the watchful eye of Marcel and Rafe. The strongest men of the gangs had then been tasked to unload the cargo and this was under Claude's remit. While under Larry, Bob's brother, the older men were there to keep security tight and formidable. There were batman on the beach, up on the ridge and as many men guarding the roads through the villages as there were loading on the beach. There was a network of men in the surrounding area and every avenue had been covered.

Determining the safest time to run goods, when the riding officers were not in the neighbourhood, required a system for gathering and conveying intelligence, and all together Shem and his gang had spent hours assessing the information to ensure the run went as smoothly as possible. No stone had been left unturned. The last piece of the puzzle required an organized network for the distribution of contraband goods. Over the years, Bob had established a good network for the disposal of goods, as well as shares in the transport for the goods, distribution, horse stock, and local pawnbrokers to buy and sell off the smuggled goods. Slowly these contacts had started to trust more and more in Shem and everything seemed to be heading in the right direction.

With assistance and help over the years, the French contacts had also been developed and with hindsight, Shem had encouraged his Boss, Mr. H, and Bob, to invest and buy into French Warehouses to store their wares. There was a thriving community of ex pats in the French ports, especially good shipbuilders, who had seen a market and were making a killing from supplying galleys to men such as Shem. Everyone profited from this arrangement, which included the ship builders having a regular demand for galleys. Bob and Shem had invested wisely in as many galleys as they could afford, and found it fascinating at the high speed crossings the sailors made of the Channel, especially at night, taking five hours if the tide was favourable. A galley could lose a pursuing cutter by turning into the eye of the wind and taking a course that it was impossible for the cutter to follow. Bob only wished his beloved Three Brothers had outwitted the cutter and the contraband had not been seized.

None of this would have been possible without the co-operation and influence of those in high places which included Lord Lennard, Paully's father. Shem laughed nervously at the cheek of it all. Scores and scores of men had made their way to Pevensey under the noses of the authorities. They had pitched up camps, taken all the rooms available in the local Inns, and made it impossible for anyone of the local stagecoach travellers to acquire a room whether they were high or lowborn. And all this done within a stone's throw of the law!

It was all so ordered, so beautiful and uniformed. Shem had every reason to swell with pride, but still his body was alert. Paully patted Shem on the back and he too took in the whole scene.

From behind, Shem heard the crunch of shingle as a party of men had dismounted their horses and stepped onto the beach to observe and look across at the magnificence of the venture. Bob was among them and could be seen to be pointing out different things and Shem watched them all follow Bob's direction. The party acknowledged Shem and Paully and soon after with a salute they turned to fetch their horses from the edge of the beach where the moss weaved into grass and then rode away.

Shem let out a breath. He had contained himself well and not let rip at them. It wasn't the time or place to start making accusations and start trouble with his so-called Bosses.

Claude had been coming up the beach and in his haste had decided to head straight for them, rather than walk up the pebble beach at an angle. Consequently, as quickly as he was making head way, the pebbles drew him back a fraction. Paully folded his arms and sighed at his friend.

'And I supposed to be the dim one.'

Claude was breathless by the time he reached them and bent over to catch his breath. He pointed towards the leaving party.

"Oh oui.' Paully answered for both of them, 'Had a great chat, Bob and his highness, nice bloke,' Paully tried to look important and tried to rock back and forth on the pebbles, only to slightly lose the rhythm. Claude just gave him a dirty look, as if to say you are so full of it, and then smiled at Shem.

'Tout court facilement'

'Aucuns problèmes à tous ? '

'Non.'

'Excellent.' Shem looked over his shoulder again and said not another word about the visitors, however intrigued to see that along with Mr. H, the party included the trusted Gunthorpe and the ever elusive Kebo and Pasha. No one would have known who they were, as their faces were covered, but Shem would be able to tell them anywhere. To anyone who asked they were brothers, be it that Kebo was a very tall fine dark skinned man with heavyset intelligent eyes. His hair was very short and he was heading towards his forties. Pasha was slightly shorter and a few years older. He was a dark olive brown with black hair that he kept to his shoulders. He had a well-kept moustache and beard, which was cut into a point. Both were lethal swordsman, and were perceived as loyal, trustworthy, and good to have on ones side. However, looks were deceiving and they had a reputation of being horrible nasty bastards.

Shem knew that somewhere amongst that pack of men was the answer to who it was playing him and he swore he would have whoever it was!

'Told ya.' Paully added at which point Shem shoved him playfully remembering Paully also could speak French when he had a mind. His father had tried his hardest to educate all his illegitimate children; however, Paully had a habit of getting bored easily. Paully recovered his footing, looked across at his friends, grinned, and humbly stated. 'Ya made us proud today Shem.' Shem looked long and hard at his friend and a small grin began to surface. He nodded in appreciation and let out a huge sigh. He had done it, they all had done it, and Mr. H and his party were witness to the waking of a new dawn, where Shem showed how powerful he and his gang had become!

Felicity Mundy looked with loathing a Paully Lennard and convinced herself that this man did not scare her so, yet when he made towards her, she gathered up her skirts, her bag with papers, pencils, and charcoal and run as if he devil himself was after her. She had planned to spend her time off from work drawing again around the village, but she thought she'd best run for cover abit further afield. She had pushed it with him and had a habit of causing trouble wherever she went. She had certainly made an impression on his guvnor and now she had upset one of the main man's Hench men. The stories were rife about Paully's exploits and Felicity found that she should consider getting out of this neck of the woods, as soon as he had enough money. She had pushed it too far and he was livid with her and would not let it rest.

She had tried to keep out of his way and when Claude had approached her to find out exactly what had happened she hoped that he could persuade his friend that she had not meant to be quite so aggressive. He had offended her badly and she had retaliated, but agreed she had taken it too far. Claude had said the best course of action was for her to apologise, even though she said she would not, that Paully owed her an apology. Claude had explained, if she did not wish to die a horrible death she would do as she was told. After the success of their latest venture, Shem and his gang had become legends to the local people and in that alot more dangerous. The celebrations were still in full swing and she started to learn more about the men and appreciated Paully did not mind being the fool with those he loved and trusted but when it was an outsider that was not allowed to happen.

They had almost collided outside the Mint House and she had just been about to leave, and was looking back laughing and joking with one of his men. As soon as she had registered who it was, she panicked, then thought better and a defiant streak of fire run through her, which Paully saw and quite liked, but still she needed to put back in her place. He reminded himself that he was absolutely beside himself and then he went for her. However, she was too quick, and darted off. He sighed, did not have the energy after all to chase, and was glad of it really, so he returned to the Castle Inn across the ways sulking.

'How's ya willy?' Bob grinned calling to catch up with him. Paully could not believe that his friends had told Bob.

'Don't laugh at me Bob.' He called over his shoulder seeing his old friend make towards the Castle Inn also.

'Hattie soothe it for ya did she?' Bob was lapping up the moment with glee.

Paully turned and pointed his finger in temper at Bob and was too frustrated to say anything and in a fluster he found himself lost for words. Bob entered the Inn laughing with Paully in tow.

Rafe had been in the Castle Inn already and seeing his friends and the expression on Paully's face, he made a beeline for Paully.

'She said I was an animal.' Paully further sulked remembering every word that Claude had related back.

'That's nice.'

'That's nice; did you hear what I said?'

'Course, course, keep ya hair on.'

'Am I an animal?' Rafe looked at Paully who had a sad expression on his face and knew that he only just had into the Castle Inn, so he wasn't drunk yet.

'Well on occasion....' Rafe started but Paully wasn't listening.

'She really has hurt my feelings, I thought I was thoughtful, attentive and well you know...' Indicating to his lower regions.

'Well-endowed?' Rafe finished for him.

'Yes. God it's so nice to be able to talk to someone so easily about these sort of things, you get it.' Paully opened up and Rafe could see the tension lift from him. Paully was rarely serious and Rafe was waiting for the catch. Paully just could not be this affected by the whole thing.

'Well my friend, if you've got it, you've got it.' He thought this would cheer him up. 'Well obviously not. The bitch fucking bit me!' It obviously did not work. They sat down.

'You really need to get over it.'

'Get over it? Do you know how traumatic that whole experience was?'

'You are joking?' Rafe could not contain himself any more, he laughed.

'Joking? Rafe I had a near death experience. I could have been dickless.'

'Never bothered you before.'

'Oh you are gonna get it,' he turned on his stool and pointed in warning at Rafe. 'Go on run, have a head start cos when I get up and catch ya, believe me I will do ya silly.' Rafe hadn't even attempted to move.

'Paully, how many times, I am not that way inclined.' He knew then he had pushed it too far but he just could not stop giggling.

'Oh that's it, that is it.' Rafe wasn't silly and was gone in a flash, Paully had knocked tables, and chairs flying as he tried to get up. His bulk was far too big to be as quick as lightening. The drinks toppled over and in the end, Paully just threw tables out of the way.

Rafe skirted out of the Castle Inn bending over giggling and cheerfully waved at Shem who was walking towards there. Shem stopped in his tracks as Paully thundered through the doorway screaming after his brother. He watched as Rafe kept running and looking back trying to control his laughter, and raised his eye brows when Paully stopped to catch his breath and then started again.

'Anything I should be worried about?' He entered the Castle Inn and stopped in his tracks at the destruction caused. He kicked a chair out of his way and sat down with Bob indicating over his shoulder.

'Oh the lovers had another tiff.' Bob was dismissive and continued to sip his drink. 'Let's be thankful for the quiet.'

Everyone knew that William was on borrowed time, and although Shem had made no further moves against him, William did not help himself and found himself getting a little peeved at being given orders from Shem. He wanted to feel important and not have to bow down and appear quite so low on the food chain, and felt a little rebellious, so had acted like a spoilt child, which Ned and Ray were not impressed with. He had made himself and everyone around him paranoid. He really had started to miss Ned and Ray and was becoming more and more disillusioned. He was jealous of his friends' success without him and that they had been offered a golden opportunity and if they served Shem and his gang well, then they could get more off the back. Did William not want more success and better runs? Isn't that they had all wanted to originally ask for? Ned and Ray had even helped out further by providing additional decoys for the main run across at Pevensey Bay and William had not played a hand in any of it and kept well out of being told about any of it. Bob had not given them specifics about the Pevensey Bay job; as they did not need to know as the rumours beforehand had fuelled everyone's imagination. The Cavendish's were instructed to keep Hartright and the Riding Officers busy across this way on empty runs and after had been awarded with a good regular run with Idris Spike.

'Where's he's highness then?' Ned and Ray along with their men had nearly finished loading and were making ready to leave, Idris had checked their calculation of the goods, and neither Ned nor Ray were happy when he had asked them the dreaded question. Both gangs now met up regularly with Idris and the brothers grateful for any new business and chance to earn, but not once had William made an appearance.

'We done?' Ray answered totally ignoring the question. Bob's nephews, Theo and Kish Hawkins attended and smiled at Ray. Ray had a cocky swagger, known for being a lairy bloke, but everyone liked him. He held court, could drink you silly and generally wanted to have a good time. He was straight talking, glided over troubles, and tried to leave the worrying to Ned. So it was only natural that he wanted to get back home to their pub, The George Tavern.

'Can't imagine its easy?' Idris was determined to wind Ray up and again watched as Ray tried not to say anything. 'He still shagging your sister?' At which Ray stepped forward to Idris. Ned then stepped in between the pair.

'I don't care who you think you are, you've overstepped the mark!' Ned looked down at both men, being over six foot tall. He was also lean and strong. He had an air of dignity around him and an arrogant face that said, do not mess, but everyone knew of the two, he was the peacemaker. He had mousy brown hair that was wavy and long to his shoulders, he had the family trait of a huge mole, which rested, on the side of his face. Ray was shorter, stockier, and cockier and hair was shaved and slightly darker. Ray had a mole on his neck and well only, a few knew where their sister Rosie's was.

'Just abit of friendly banter.' Idris winked at Ned who chose to ignore him. They all just wanted to get out of there. 'A word before you go, though boys.' Idris went towards his horse and his voice was less cocky. 'Shem thinks it's time to wind William in, wants to see him at the Castle. So tell him to get his arse across.'

'What!' Both boys said in unison.

'You heard!'

'We got all this to sort out, and you want us to get word to him, wherever the fuck he is!'

'And I am supposed to care?' He grinned at the boys, who both individually found that they really did not like him after all.

'Well, William may not make it.'

'Well we won't hold our breath but I am sure he does, when he's sucking Hartright off.' His gang laughed and mounted their horses. Idris could not resist a further dig. 'I think you will find that they're all at Lady Barbara's little do. In Herstmonceux. You should know better and keep ya ear to the ground.' Idris spat in their direction and Ned held out his arm again to warn Ray back. 'She'll be fully returning home soon, with a shit head of a husband, by all accounts, who we all need to watch as well as your fuck up. War hero he is, looking for a new job. I thought you were told to get rid of William? What no bottle?'

Ray went to grab Idris's horse's reins, but Ned literally pushed him away and glared at him to defy him. 'Are you finished, because we have?' Ned was getting more than annoyed; he did not need to listen to Idris prattle on. Ned's gang headed for their own horses and knew this could not go on. Idris may be a main player and way up there but he could push it too far. Ned needed to sort and soon otherwise, he would lose face with his men and he would never allow that to happen. He would have Idris.

'Go on, on ya way and dickheads.' Idris called and was going for the ultimate move. Ray rolled his eyes in dread. They turned back in their saddles and Idris pulled his horse alongside them, and held fast on to the reigns of Ned's horse. 'If you wanna play with the big boys you have to learn to take it mate.'

'Take it from you?' Ned replied quietly.

'You know I thought you may be of sterner stuff, but ya Dad pissing off as he did, left you a little light on the man front.' He never saw it coming and Ray watched his brother land a punch on Idris, which threw him back. His men immediately came forward and everyone was on tender hocks waiting for Idris to react. Idris pulled himself forward and stroked his hurt chin. He grinned at Ned. 'Finally some balls. I like it pup.' Ned did not relax. 'I'll give you that one boy; you are so fucking lucky I like ya.' Ned found he did not care whether Idris liked him or not. He was a bully and a thug. Ned and his men just sat there watching as Idris' gang slowly moved away and out of sight, only then did they allow themselves to breathe easy and after Ned's men started to giggle nervously at what he had done. He was still shaking looking over his shoulder all the way home, thinking that he could quite easily have got everyone killed by playing the hard man. He wasn't sure this was really, what he wanted.

They tore into The George tavern, which stood along the High Street of Alfriston. Shem had positioned his men outside and around so that no one could escape unless he allowed it.

He was angry and in no mood to be messed with. The gang stood in the centre of the Tavern and looked about menacingly. The threat of violence, a heartbeat away. Ned and Ray's men had cocked their weapons and held concealed beneath the tables. They were scared and out of their league. After the incident with Idris both Ned and Ray were on tender hooks.

Shem stood and surveyed the Tavern, looking at each and everyone with such menace. He oozed power and no one wanted to breathe. There was total silence waiting for the man to make his next move. He had heard about Ned and Idris little tete a tete and thought good for Ned, but that did not sway the fact that they still had not produced William. He marched towards Ned and Ray who slowly rose to their feet.

Silence loomed and Shem slowly bent down and rested his hands on the edge of their table. Both Ned and Ray obeyed the command when Shem flicked his hand for them to sit back down. Both could feel the sweat tickle on their necks.

'William missed his appointment?' He whispered not once looking at them. The only movement was from Meriska, their dog. She came towards Shem without a care in the world. Shem watched her approach.

'He ain't 'ere Shem...' Ray offered and was immediately stopped by Ned. Shem straightened up.

'I ain't blind Ray and certainly not stupid.' He shook his head in shame at them. The tension intensified in the Tavern, every one waiting for his next move. Meriska sniffed him and then rubbed up against him in comfort.

'At this very moment, the shit head, has his dick inside her Ladyship, the right Honourable, butter wouldn't melt in her mouth, fucking whore Miss Constance Mordesan.' He let his voice be heard by the whole room intentionally.

A nervous laugh went around the room; he found himself crouching down and stroking the dog. He smiled seeing the guns under the table, cocked and aimed at him. Meriska licked him all over the face and he cooed at the dog holding her face and rubbing her long shaggy ears. Still not looking once at the boys, he again resumed a quieter voice but still with enough tone to carry and said. 'Now, the shit head has played his last hand. I am not happy.'

The implication set in around the room and the men begun to murmur among themselves. Shem had given William every opportunity to make amends and Shem knew these men relied on each and every cargo for his livelihood, and knew that William's indifference could affect them all.

William had not concealed his plans and everyone knew he was in league with Hartright and that they had been undercutting some of the regular gangs business. A few of his supplier's had started to come to Shem in protest and explain how they had been threatened and wanted him to sort it out. He was more than happy to oblige.

They knew that Shem did not need to come, he could have sent Claude or Paully, but by being there, the message was clear. If they were to be taken seriously, then they had better start acting seriously. He wasn't carrying anyone and had more than enough men to move into the area for the work.

Everyone's eye seemed to stare at Ned for answers; he looked to Shem for moral support. Shem was sighing inwardly. He raised himself and still stroking the dog murmured in boredom.

'I ain't got time for this shit. We need to get going. So sort it Ned and report back to Bob.' He bent back down to stroke the dog. He lent back across the table and smiled as he saw Ray flinch. He whispered to both brothers ever so quietly. 'Less of the guns next time, I could think I am not welcome!' And with that he left, the dog trotted off behind him.

The door was left a jar and the cold wind blew in and made every man shudder. Ned found himself shivering whilst everyone still looked at the door in fright. He tried to compose himself and thought, what would he have done if he were in Shem's shoes?

God he would be livid that William would have the front, but Shem would not let that lie and should he warn William of the consequences, William was no fool. Why was Shem being nice to him and Ray? He looked at Ray who looked back at him and both sighed in relief. Shem had made it clear that he was mad, but he had not been as harsh as he could have. He had been known to walk into a pub full of a rival's men and batter their leader for lesser offences. It was just as well the Pevensey Job had been such a success, which must account for Shem's current mood being not so harsh. Ned knew that Shaun had Bob's ear and had spoken up for William, but everyone had limits.

Ned got to his feet sighing with relief that his men were now returning to their ale and chatting amongst themselves. He went to the door to close the visit away, however instead found himself outside for a few moments. He watched Shem's party start to ride away. There seemed to be loads of them and obviously were carrying cargo, as they seemed to have loads of extra horses. So Shem had decided to make a stop off in transit.

Ned noticed that Meriska was hanging around Shem's horses feet while Shem conversed with Bob and then he watched as Bob moved off towards Shaun's large house just off to the right. He whistled for the dog to come back but the dog paid no heed, it wasn't like Meriska to wander off with strangers.

'Here girl, come on girl.'

Shem checked who had called then reverted his eyes back to Bob as he entered Shaun's house and then his eyes scanned the whole house as if he were searching for something, he come to his senses and then become aware again of the dog. Shem acknowledged that the dog wanted to be made a fuss of, but he had no time and motioned to the dog to return, but Meriska just appeared to look back and then back at Shem.

Shem shifted his position in the saddle and looked back at Ned standing waiting for the dog.

He shrugged his shoulders at Ned then commanded Meriska by name to return to the Tavern in a very demanding manner. Meriska trotted back but kept looking back in earnest at Shem, who in turn grinned back and then waved goodbye, following his party who had headed towards the Newhaven coast road and not homeward. Ned found himself returning the gesture feeling foolish as he did it. He wasn't friends with the man!

He returned to the warmth of inside and was so conscious that his men may still be worried for all their future, as was he. They had sent word across to William again as soon as Idris had left them on the previous evening, but he had failed to show up again. Ned had requested that his messenger keep an eye out for him and hoped that William was already on his way to meet up with Shem being across that way apparently. Regardless that Shem was heading towards Newhaven; if he ordered you to him, you would go and wait. Ned did not know what William was playing at? Surely, he did not think that by having Hartright as a friend that would give him weight? Hartright was on borrowed time as it was. He further mused at what Shem's game was? He had to make an example of him and Ned knew this would not end well.

'He is mugging us off.' Ray was already in extreme panic mode.

'I can't think straight when you are like this. Just shut up and let me think. I just don't know what people want me to do?' Ned placed his elbows on the table and rubbed his head.

'We need to talk to William. He will listen to you.' Ray urged.

'So what do I say? Look mate, know you found a new bird and all that but can you came back and play.'

'I don't think you appreciate the ramifications of what is happening here. Shem is playing us; he has already attacked William's home and God knows what else he has done on the side. Apparently he disappeared again a few weeks back and rumour has it he is seeing his accountant in London. Getting ready to sail away when it all goes tits up! He can squeeze us out anytime. We will be ruined if he doesn't crush us first. Look at how he mugged Hartright off before.'

'So we get squeezed out, we've earned ain't we? Look we have this place.'

'For fucks sake, you gone soft on me?' Ray asked.

'No give over, it's just....' Ned tried to reason.

'What, I don't understand?'

'It's not the same without William.' Ray was sure that Ned would have shed a tear if they had been girls.

'Look, he's made his bed, really, we knew he'd fuck off at some stage, he's been playing at being one of us, but he ain't, you know it Ned.' For a long while, Ned digested the information.

'Not like you to be so insightful Ray?' Ned laughed. Ray smiled at that and allowed the tension to disappear and be replaced with a cooler head.

'Yeah, well I did fall over the other week moving the barrels and knocked me self silly.' Ray offered smiling. 'Didn't see you run to my aid, you fucking pissed yaself. I could have died.'

'Not with all that weight, cushioning the blow.' Ned laughed nodding in gratitude that Ray had changed the tone.

'Fuck off.' Ray laughed with his brother. He grabbed his expanding belly and squeezing it said 'Good living mate!'

They both knew that they may be earning well at that the moment, and at the throw of a die, Shem could pull the rug from under them. The situation with William needed to come to a head and Shem expected them to sort it out. William had let everyone down and it was not to be tolerated. Shem had given them orders that needed to be obeyed and life was going to get hellish.

Rafe had been dying to get to the bottom of who had caused Paully so much grief. He had been constantly busy with Daisy and running errands back and forth up to Burwash recently. He grinned at himself, as that held another allure that made his heart sing. The lovely Amelia was oh so beautiful, he was in love, she loved him, and they would live happily ever after. He sighed in pleasure at life in general.

He entered the whorehouse and Valentina winked at him as he made his way into the back room thankful that Paully had seen reason and not torched the Mint House after all.

Someone handed him a drink and he grinned in appreciation and started to mingle amongst the lovely ladies who attended. They all were half-undressed and the aroma of the room was pleasant with fragrance, not too over powering. The Mint House had been decorated to a high standard. It was not gaudy as many whorehouses tended to be. Valentina wanted it to be classic and stylish and with a homely feel. Valentina indicated to a young lady who was leaning against the stair well, just outside the room to entertain Rafe. Rafe had seen her on many occasions and knew that he would eventually get to her.

'Hello darling.' He purred and Felicity eyed Rafe all the way up and all the way down. He winked at her cheek and said, 'I hear you are quite a wild cat.' He put down his drink and moved towards the doorway. He spread both his arms out to hold onto the door skirting.

'Oh I can be whatever you want me to be lover.' She was a cocky one.

'Oh you saucy mare, I am intrigued.' She was a pretty little thing with frizzy hair and freckles and she obviously loved to flirt as much as he did. This was going to be fun.

'Well be intrigued this way.' She gestured for him to come closer. He swaggered towards her and as he come very, very close he whispered in her ear.

'I don't do rough, so keep your biting soft. I like to take my time and girl, after tonight you will be begging and paying me to return.' His arrogance and confidence oozed from every pore and he had that cheeky expression on his face. He was gorgeous and Felicity knew she wanted to die in his arms, but dare not let on.

'You are so full of yaself.' She hoarsely whispered, feeling a wonderful glow all over her body. He was beautiful, smelt fresh, clean, and lovely. He shrugged his shoulders at her remark and ever so gently, she felt his hot breath on her throat, his breath teased her and filled her with desire. He had not even touched her and yet she felt her whole body arching forward for his touch. What was he doing to her? His long hair tickled her neck and her senses were on fire, she closed her eyes in lust. He had her then. He blew on her neck and she swayed. They both then looked into each other's eyes for an eternity. Both their worlds seem to merge into one, it was smouldering with tension. He licked his lips and she groaned. She grabbed his arm fiercely and without another word, she pulled him towards the stairs and Rafe laughed in anticipation thinking, - *Caught ya*! Neither was seen again until late the next day.

## Chapter Five

She flew through the undergrowth with all the speed she could muster, having had to run for her life on many occasions with her brothers, when they had been hunting or poaching on Devereux land. She had not expected to hear the thunder of hooves behind her giving chase. She still run and tried to look over her shoulder to see her foe, but every nerve in her body warned and told her to keep going, flee! She needed to divert them from Hattie and try to get word back at the village and hopefully alert everyone to protect themselves. Birds escaped the trees as she made her way through the greenery.

She tried to out manoeuvre the horse, which she knew, had great speed and stamina, it was a question of time before she would be overhauled. She had hoped that the thickest of the woods would slow them down.

She needed to change direction, disappear in the dense undergrowth. The trees were thick with foliage, and she hoped that she could be lost to sight. Her breathing was heavy, laboured and she was so scared.

She could hear the horse, or now horses; they had now begun to trot through the undergrowth. She could hear the riders' sabres thrashing the undergrowth. She could hear the thunder of her heart. There were no other sounds.

'Here pretty, pretty.' She heard the taunt. She moved off again, caught her face in the thick bushes, and wiped away the blood from the small scratches. Her hair had become lose and caught in the branches.

She knew the secret was to remain cool. Even though she was trembling uncontrollably. Ned, her brother had taught her to stay focused, stay alert, he always said that you must believe you will escape, you must escape, there is no alternative if you are being chased. He would say remember to breathe, count your breath's evenly. They will not catch you. There is only escape. If they catch you, you are dead.

What was she doing?

If she and Hattie had just kept still would they have noticed them? She needed to escape to get back to Seb.

She could not find a hiding place.

She run on and on, dodging bushes, jumping logs, her breathing deafening. The thunder in her heart ready to explode, she looked from right to left and did not see the horse, which smacked into her from the side. A foot ramped into her chest. Her body flew through the air, while the wind was whacked out of her. She landed heavily on her back. She turned to get up and pushed on all fours. A foot pounded into her back. She smashed flat against the ground hitting her face. She heard the thud of the man dismounting. She could not breathe.

'What have we here then?' She felt the speaker press harder into her back with his foot. She tried to resist and turned to look at the man. 'Well Hello?' He grinned and at the same time brought his crop down to swipe across her face.

The force of the blow flung her down. She felt the sting of her left cheek, and slowly felt the warm blood from the opening creep down her face. Her whole body started to shake and then the nightmare begun!


'For fucks sake, what's happened here?'

'Look at it. Fucking animals who've been here!' All around was chaos. The cottage was well ablaze by the time they had reached the scene. Everything had been ruined. The livestock slaughtered, the garden and vegetable patches up rooted, there were no flowers, herbs, trees, or crops left untouched. The stable had been pulled down, and ditches had been dug looking for hidden contraband.

'Was there anything left here?' The Guvnor enquired to his men, looking at the once lovely cottage, which was smouldering and spitting in rage. One of his men approached him and shook his head.

There had been no attempt to try and put the fire out, a portion of his men, had just set up a circle around the building to monitor the wind position and smoulder where they could, but still it was far too hot to control, and so it had just collapsed into itself.

'No, Larry had got it out ages ago.' They referred to the contraband from the Pevensey run. Both men continued to look into the fire when they heard a call from behind. Shem had just about to ask if the owner of the property was unharmed.

The gang had been making there way back to Pevensey after their visit up the coast to Newhaven, taking in the Cavendish camp over in Cuckmere Valley. But they had seen the burning buildings towards the small Hamlet of Hankham and rushed over to investigate, not believing that there was a fire burning not far from their own home.

'They're looking for the girl.' One of his men said as he approached them.

'What girl?'

'Larry's little lady lived here, with her niece and kid. Hattie got to Larry with the kid but the girl was going to get help and alert Gideon. She never got there!' He pointed back towards the small woodland.

Paully had previously arrived and sent some men through the woodland surrounding the small dwelling, which headed back towards the coast and the villages, to see if they could locate the girl.

'Oh fuck, fuck, fuck,' murmured one of Paully's men, he then begun to panic and screamed. 'Paully, Paully, she's here, I have her here.' The men started through the woods towards the scream of anguish.

'For fuck's sake, someone cut her down!' Everyone heard Paully roar as he run towards her.

It was barbaric, horrific. None of them could ever say they were angels and had seen and done many bad things, but this, this was horrid. This was sickening. They all seemed to stop as one, and stare in utter shock, no one could move forward. Some of Paully's men turned away in disgust. Paully hesitated.

The girl had been found. She was hanging by her wrists from a rope, which had been thrown, over a branch of a tree. There was an eerie silence around her. She was covered from head to foot in blood. The floor beneath her was saturated with it. The air reeked of it. She was still.

As Shem and Bob approached the whole form of Paully impaired their vision, each of them stepped to either side of him.

'Oh Jesus, love her. Get her down.' Bob roared. The small man leapt forward and checked her neck for a pulse. He thought he was going to be sick.

'Is she dead?' Bob shook his head at Shem's question.

The whole woods seem to be still.

'Still breathing, just?' Bob was shocked to discover just a hint of life. Bob found himself shaking his head in disbelief. He had been cradling her head and stroking her head. He felt her move, when Shem came towards them.

'Then best to put her outta of her fucking misery.' He whispered into his ear, and he turned to go.

'We can save her, I'm cutting her down.' Bob called after him. They had all seen horrific things, but not like this. This was sick.

'We ain't got time for this.' Shem warned, just then stopping as he thought he heard the girl groan. Shem half turned round and took a step back ward. He looked at Bob to confirm he had heard right. He walked around so he stood facing her. He looked again at Bob and waived his hand to dismiss him. Bob could not look back. He carefully wiped his eyes, not caring who witnessed his tears.

Shem slowly looked down at the pitiful girl and knew he had her life in his hand. The gang are waiting for his judgement. Slowly he withdrew his dagger from the belt at the back of his trousers. He needed to be away to finish his work. He really did not need this. He grabbed hold of her blood soaked hair and yanked her head up. This was the best way for the poor thing.

He felt her coming round.

Slowly she became more aware, although it was hazy and she felt like each breath was her last and that God was being merciless with her and torturing her so. She knew she was due to go to Hell. Who were these people now? She felt a presence over her. Someone stood right in front of her. She could feel the power that oozed from him. She shook with anticipation; he was going to finish her. Kill her. Put her out of her misery. Every fibre of her body was alive, screaming to burn. She wasn't going to have it. No way. He would not determine her fate. She would not be defeated, she would live and she would make them all pay for this. Her whole body ached and she could so easily just let the sleep take over and lose herself in that wonderful contentment and forget everything else. However, that defiant streak would not let go. Life burnt through her, fired her will. They were all bastards.

She had Sebastian and by God, almighty no other woman was ever going to raise him other than her. She would piss all over them.

From somewhere deep, deep inside, she strained with all her power, all her will, and slowly she moved her held head and focused her eyes to the force before her.

With every movement, her body screamed in sheer terror pain and fire of resistance. Her neck muscles intensified with the strain, salvia run down and mingled with the blood congealed on her chin.

Her breathing was arduous, every breath sheer agony, but she was determined and she slowly met the man's gaze. His green eyes tore into her and she shivered with the evil she saw there. She had thought that no one on this earth could ever be as worse as her attackers, in particular that one man with the sarcastic laugh. Oh, he had enjoyed himself. 'There, there my beauty.' He had mocked. But this man looking down at her had her fate in his hands. Life or death! Black like the pits of hell and damnation. But those eyes! They were green.

That green!

His stare tore into her soul, willing her to drop her eyes, so that he could see her weakness. She swallowed and pure will power made her glare back at him. She would not let go. She snarled at him. It took the last strength of her character to hold on, she gritted her teeth, and this could not be the end. She felt the blade come towards her face, he grabbed a handful of her hair and yanked her head back again and put the knife to the side of her neck, ready to swipe and end it all. He felt her tense.

It came to her in a flash, the last few hours all hit her in one great wave. She remembered that all throughout her ordeal, time seem to stand still. The pain was unbearable, she remembered then they had gone and the stillness of the coming night crept into her and slowly the cold took hold. Her whole body had cried out. She could not call out and was too weak to even spit the blood from her throat. She opened her mouth slightly and let the blood trickle to the floor.

She was hanging by her hands. Her whole body suspended with her toes just touching the ground. They had flung a rope over a tree branch and left her hanging. Her wrists were cut through with the weight of her on them. This blood had run down her forearms. Her toes were wet with blood that had oozed into the ground. Her face was a fire of pain, being split open and slowly turning black and blue. Her dress lay ripped around her body, and everywhere on her body showed the signs of a severe assault. Her breathing was harsh and every breath caught her, as some of her ribs had been broken. Her back was a mass of scars from the crop. Blood had long since stopped and crusted itself. Blood handprints were all over her lower body and she still bled between her legs. She was lost, it was hopeless, and she could easily just slip away. She let herself drift away.

She remembered time seemed to stand still, she could hear nothing but numbness. She had tried to focus her hearing, but there was nothing, just a blank. No birds, no wind dancing through the trees, and letting the leaves whisper in delight. It was cold, black, and silent. Her whole body ached with such an intensity she knew at any point she would vomit again and again. But there was nothing left inside to give. She tried to black out the flashing memories and focus on the sounds she should be hearing. But that voice, that man, everything just kept coming back again, and then coming back time and time again, like in a reoccurring circle. She was in so much pain; her mind whirled with the sound of her attacker's crop, his cackle, and that sarcastic laugh! Her mind repeated a man softly saying as he had thrashed himself into her. 'There there my beauty.' He had yanked back her head by pulling hard on her hair. She could feel the grunt, and had no more tears to shed; her body was lifeless, broken. But her mind's eye heard that cackle; it kept coming back, again and again. He had laughed all the while.

Her head was painfully yanked back and a blade pricked her neck. She was now fully aware that the nightmare wasn't over. This was now and reality. She was no animal to be put out of its misery. A single tear slowly made its way across her face, down her chin, yet she held his gaze. Her eyes started to focus and her power, seemed to get stronger and stronger as the stare progressed. Then it came back to her! It could not be. Her mind was playing tricks.

Was he holding a blade to her throat?

Was it him?

It was him.

'Shem!' Her voice croaked. Her world went black.

He let go and stepped back. He looked to his hands covered in her blood. His arms fell to his side. He let the blade fall. He looked for Bob and stood back in disbelieve. *No. No it could never be. No. Don't say it could be?*

Bob rushed forward and came to stand next to the younger man, who was struggling to keep it together. He nearly collapsed, but checked himself.

Slowly he moved back to face the woman, he crouched down and so gently he pushed her curtain of hair aside and cupped her chin. Time seem to stand still.

His breath held tight.

He needed to really look at her.

Slowly he raised her head slightly. She had blacked out and had now no fight left at all.

Was she dead?

He felt the panic rise in him. *Oh by all the Gods, it's her!*

Then the world came crashing down.

He let out his breath and with venom and the devil exploding inside, let loose on everything that was alive.

He roared like a wounded animal.

Everyone stopped and looked in utter shock at Shem.

His whole stance was black with doom and no one ever messed with him when Satan took hold. No one had ever heard him roar with just abandonment and raw emotion not even when Rafe had been badly hurt.

They all twitched in anticipation and awkwardness, not knowing quite how to respond. So when in doubt they just looked at each other to see what would happen next. Then they looked to Bob.

Shem was shaking from head to foot with such anger and rage, they all thought that any moment, he would turn red and Lucifer would be reborn. But to everyone's amazement, they watched him crouch down to the floor.

His strength seemed to fail him.

Bob stood beside him and placed his hand on his friends shoulder for comfort.

'For fuck's sake, get her down.' He pleaded with Bob as he rested on his heels and put his head in his hands shaking all the time.

Bob hurried forward and a few of the men came to assist. 'Get the cart, I need to get her to the Inn, get the Doctor there now.' He looked back at Shem in wonder.

Who was this girl? One minute he was about to slit her throat and end it all for her, and the next he was roaring like a wounded animal.

With all the care in the world Bob cuddled her to him as her bonds were cut free, her body fell limply to him and Shem heard him coo to her. 'It's alright now my love, Bob has ya, it's alright now.'

He watched as the older man cradled her and tried to cover her body with the ripped remains of her dress. Her blood covered his whole front.

Not many things in this world ever effected Bob, he rarely showed his hand, and he felt overawed with emotion at what he had just witnessed, he failed to hold back tears for the girl and kept looking at Shem anxiously.

Shem just stood there as if transfixed, his eyes glazed over and his expression lost to the world, he then lowered his head to his chest.

At that point, Claude come into view having sent there men out to gather what information they could.

Bob jerked his hand to keep him at bay.

They looked across at Bob in confusion and seeing their Boss with his head on his chest and eyes shut, they rethought their approach.

Shem fought to control his composure. He raised himself up, sighed, and shook his head. He removed his long fur lined leather coat and stepped forward. With as much gentleness that he could muster, he wrapped the small woman up in it. Bob looked to him for answers.

Shem took her from Bob and effortlessly held her to him, cuddling her as if she was the most treasured possession. He motioned for Bob to get into the cart. When Bob was positioned, he handed her back to Bob, who softly cradled her in his arms. 'She will not die.' He whispered to Bob. Was it a threat or hope? Shem then knocked on the side of the cart and without any further words; it rolled off, taking her away.

Shem's eyes never left the cart as it slowly ebbed away, after a time, he motioned for his friends to speak, his composure returned.

'It was Hartright's men, looks like he's feeling us out?' Paully confirmed. 'Old man Elijah down the road watched them retreat after they had their little fun.' He seemed to want to say more however, Shem flinched at that remark and thought it best to shut up. Claude shook his head at him. 'Asked after the boy?'

Shem turned his whole attention to Paully in question.

'Apparently Hattie's niece came to stay and had the baby a while back.' At that moment, one of the men come running towards them.

'We found the old women and boy, there all at Larry's.' The man leant over to catch his breath, 'Larry thinks the shock of everything is too much for her, he fears the worse. It's bad.'

'I am surprised she ain't dead already.' Paully remarked for all of them. Shem outwardly appeared more focused now.

'Get Larry some help for her, bring the boy to the Inn. Chrissy and Daisy will look after him.' Larry would have enough to deal with and was too old and frail as it was. Shem gave his orders and he turned to see if he could still glimpse the cart, but all he could see was a dancing pixie whose hair whirled and whirled and whose laugh had filled him with so much joy.

He could not believe she had been a stone throw away all this time and there he was thinking she would be at Ned and Ray's and when he had looked up at her window last night hoping to catch a glimpse. He had felt a little disappointed when he had gone there and he thought, she must have known he was there and she had made an effort to come and say hello, but at least the dog had remembered him and greeted him. It seemed little comfort now.

He could not believe that his path would cross again with her under these circumstances, but concerning Hartright Mordesan, the die had been cast many years ago between them. Revenge was always a calculated business, but now it had moved up a stage. He felt faint again with the sheer intensity of his emotions.

The cart had disappeared but still Shem stood there. Did Hartright know about her, how could he? It was just a chance encounter, a desperate man lashing out at being made to look a fool. He had always been a bully, and now he could add rapist, along with all the other things!

Further fuel had been thrown onto the fire and now that smouldering was just set to flame. Mr. H may have stopped him before, but no more.

'I will kill him, mark my fucking words,' he said through gritted teeth. His hands were fisted and his stance menacing and his face full of black evil. 'I will kill him slowly, painfully and I will enjoy every fucking moment of it. I will kill his mother, his sister, his Dad if I have to. I'll burn everything of theirs. He won't have his fat protector to watch over his little puny arse for long. I'll have his head on a stick and a shaft up his arse. I will have him for this.

**Act Two**

**Chapter Six**

'How much did you bung him?' Shem asked as Jesus had returned from seeing his brother the Vicar at Hailsham, who held the parish of Hankham.

'Don't be so bloody harsh, it was a contribution to the church.' Bob barked from the corner before Jesus could reply. Tensions were high and Shem was growling at everyone in bitterness. He was hurting and everyone was on tender hooks.

'Religion, in all its glory!' Shem remarked dryly.

'Regardless, you will still be called upon to repent all your sins, as will we all. Forgive him my lord.' Jesus offered at which Shem snarled at his cheek. As if he would! God had played no hand in helping him in his life no matter how much he had prayed!

Shem had decided that no one, but his immediate circle, needed to know that Rosie Cavendish was still alive and under his protection. He had felt there was no need to alert Ned and Ray Cavendish's as to the full extent of what had really happened and so let it be believed that she along with Hattie were dead. They apparently did not know about the boy! His gut told him it was the wrong hand to play but the Cavendish's had enough on their plate without fretting over their sister and possible revenge antics. So if she allegedly died by accident due to a fire, that would suffice for now. His main aim was to keep her secret and safe. He was not naive to believe that at some stage, someone would let something slip about her and then Ned and Ray would get wind and Shem did not need any further aggravation.

Rosie was a witness and victim to one of her majesty's officers overstepping the mark. If Shem had not known her as he did, he would have no hesitation in using her as bait. Now she had moved from bait to his scorecard against Hartright. He could not stand the fact that this man had touched her, it sickened him to the core, and he would pay dearly for that! How many more things was the man going to be allowed to get away with it before his vengeance could satisfy his blood lust? Shem fought with his own demons; he had to work with time and patience.

Rosie needed to be protected from the man, who had left her for dead. Why was she in Hankham? Why did no one know who she really was? She needed to explain herself, which in the circumstances, with a child in tow was not hard to put two and two together, but until she was ready, he would protect her secret and so would everyone else. Why had he not heard a whisper about her not being with the Cavendish's? He sat trying to analysis, and pondered all these questions, but they kept churning and churning in his mind. Why had she not reached out to him when she was in trouble? Did he mean nothing to her? Did this mean what he thought it meant about the boy? He stopped and his mind tracked back but kept coming back to rest again on Hartright. He had brutally raped Rosie and knew without a shadow of a doubt that if the boy had been there, he would be dead along with the poor Hattie.

Hartright was already a thorn in his side, and had been swanking around lording it up trying to be liked in the area. He wanted to make a name for himself and within that, try to sway the tide of loyalty away from the smugglers and even now had the cheek to start to imply that the smugglers had killed the women because they believed that they had given the authorities information on where contraband was being stored.

Obviously, everyone knew that was a lie, but it still lead to some of the locals becoming more paranoid about looking after themselves and their families. Hattie was a local woman and had been respected and liked. Her loss was greatly felt. She had been found with the boy at Larry's but had succumbed to a collapse at hearing what had happened to Rosie and subsequently never recovered consciousness. As far as the gossip went, Hartright had brutally killed her along with the girl. He was not a threat, just a nonsense who would get his come-uppance. However, no word was ever to be said about what really happened, it was a tragedy in any event, and the gang let it be known that what had occurred was an accidental, dreadful fire.

The whole episode also showed how desperate Hartright had become. He was a liability and why had the authorities not already replaced him, as was rumoured to be about to happen? Shem knew he had to build the locals confidence back up and had ordered that everyone became more cautious, to take extra care. Too, lay low for a time, and revert to contingency plans. If anyone needed extra help or reassurance, they were only to say. He knew he needed to keep the people on his side. He had made it clear that Hartright was his, and that he would make him pay.

He had let it be known that he was going to play with the man and make him suffer, and no one was to interfere and try and get to Hartright before him. Hartright belonged to Shem and he wanted to further humiliate, crush, and destroy him, even more than he had before when he had toyed with him over Rafe's abduction.

He could not believe that Hartright would make such a move after Shem had attacked him and warned him off. Why did his spies not see this coming? He wanted answers but knew that at the end of the day, he was responsible. He alone had failed to protect those nearest to him.

However, what did he do about the boy? The locals knew the girl had a son, so Shem had made up a story that the boy would be returning to far off relatives. But as yet, he had not made that move and the boy was at a loss to what had happened. He also thought that Rosie and the boy were still too near to their old home for comfort and to get away with it. There would be gossip. As soon as Rosie was better, she would be moved for her own safety. He was not quite convincing himself that if he allowed her to stay, it would play havoc with him. He needed to focus on the job to hand and not let emotion get the better of him. He could not endure the torment and explore what Hartright had subjected her to. He would see to it that she got better.

He knew too that he would have a summons from Lennard and there would be further questions raised which he had avoided answering to Lennard so far about the dealings with the stolen horses, which was a hanging offence, the stolen brandy, a small fire and the talk about this big job. As well as the issue with Chater! It was just as well Lennard would only want answers to this incident, to get his peers of his back.

'Jesus, Mary, and Joseph. A fucking shiver went through me then!' Ray made the oath and Ned glared not too kindly at his brother's remark at the dinner table. They were having dinner and all the family were to hand.

The children around the table giggled behind their hands and Ray's wife, Sharon come forward with a large wooden spoon in hand to whack him across the shoulder. He ducked at the right time and laughed at her attempt, but then become serious again too quickly, which was out of his nature.

'Just when I think I have pulled you from the gutter, you bring it back home.' Shaun, the head of the house tried to make a joke and deflect away from Ray and his unease. Ray looked to him apologetically and shrugged his shoulders. Shaun Cavendish tutted at him and wagged his finger at him. This made the children laugh even more as he was told off.

Sharon managed to get in another whack and looked back to her stepfather for reassurance that the smack had been hard enough, as Ray bent over and tried to massage his back. He looked at his wife in mock horror and then slowly smiled at her, but she could still see the unease there. Her stepfather, Shaun tried to suppress a grin.

'Seriously, I gone all cold.' It was hard for anyone to take Ray seriously.

'Here we go, doom and gloom again. What is this time?' Ray's brother Ned grinned.

'Ned!' Shaun warned. Trying to steer away from one of Ray's prophecies, as much as they joked about things, Ray was known to be able to sense certain things and many a time, his feelings had proved to hold true. They certainly did not want any more doom, gloom, as the house had been on tender hooks since Shem, and Bob had visited them.

After the meal, Ray had retreated outside to take in the evening air, still feeling apprehensive. It was still warm mid way into the night and the sun was still trying to hold court but slowly losing. He sat on the old crumpling wall by the side of the old Manor House and took in the beautiful view across the field towards the valley and sea. Ray looked across at the sheep and cows grazing in the fields and he watched as a couple of swans glided onto the far off sea, which melted, into the river which zig- zagged through the valley. It was a wonderful sight!

Ned sat next to him and patted his leg. Ned very rarely witnessed his brother have anything to deep on his mind and was a wonder when he did. However, Ned knew when Ray was like this, it was best to give him the lead and eventually the words would tumble out and Ned would put the pieces together.

'Rosie just keeps coming into my head; I know she is in trouble? It's not like before, when I felt relieved and happy for her. Something has happened.'

'You can't be sure.'

'Well I'd rather be certain.' Both looked at each other sharing without saying that a visit was long overdue and the guilt had set in about how they had neglected her. They both sighed in pain.

'I know.'

They did not attempt to justify their actions this time; by saying, they had been too busy with work, their families, or anything else. When their sister had not been there when they had returned from one of their adventures, they assumed she would be back soon. They had received messages through Hattie that that was the case, and also telling of how Rosie had been a great help to her, that she has settled in and she did not know what she would do without her. It seemed that their sister had made a new friend in a new community and was finding herself.

The brothers' had lead to believe that Rosie's trip had been a short visit to Nana's older sister, who had lost her husband years before and would benefit from the company. It would be good for both of them. But the months had rolled on, she hadn't returned, they had got caught up in the business and before they knew it, time had flown by. It wasn't as if she was that far away!

They had not bothered to write and she had stopped sending messages, although they still got tip bits from Nana. Rosie had not been a great writer and all the letters were in Hattie's hand.

'I think we should go across.' Ray said and Ned agreed by nodding.

They had arranged to go across a few days later and were going across to the main house to say their goodbyes and just as they stepped foot through the back door to remove their dirty boots they heard the wailing of Nana. Both Ned and Ray's wives barged through on hearing her mother in such grief. Nana was at the kitchen table bawling and Shaun was at the kitchen fire just staring into space. The dog, Meriska was whimpering.

'Mum, mum?' Sharon cried and immediately noticed the crumbled letter in her hands. On the kitchen table sat the envelope addressed to the Kin of Hattie Charles.

Ray peeled the letter from his step Grandmother and unwrapped it. The feeling of doom washed through him. His mind screamed in anxiety, he could not read it, his vision had became blurred, Ned took it from him.

*To the Kin of Mrs. Hattie Charles*

*It is with great regret that I have to inform you of the most tragic of occurrences in our most humble parish.*

*I regret to advise that your beloved sister, Mrs. Hattie Charles did leave this mortal world for a better place. Even now, she is at the side of our most humble Lord who wraps her in His most warm arms and comforts her for being taken away from those she loved, but who, He has proclaimed will be forever, a light shining in the sky.*

*Mrs. Charles was taken to kneel at His holiness's feet, dying of a broken heart, when hearing of her niece's tragic departure.*

*Her niece, the respectful Mrs. Rosie Smith was overcome with smoke and taken away to our Lord when their home caught fire.*

*I understand that this was a tragic accident and we having investigated the said cause, and have concluded that it was a simple house fire sparked no less by dying embers in the cottages hearth in the middle of the night. No other reasonable explanation can be determined other than a cruel twist of fate at the hands of that most dark of men, who shall not be named.*

*The local Magistrate, the Earl of Essex has verified the above.*

*I have had the pleasure of the acquaintance of our beloved sister Rosie at church and found her to be best of women, being in the company of such a rare gem as our beloved Mrs. Charles.*

*Both will be sorely missed from our small community and I am happy to confirm that they were both well supported at the ceremony held in their honour today when we sent them on their path to our Almighty.*

*Further words cannot express the loss I feel and I wish that I had written to you under better circumstances than these.*

*Yours faithfully*
*Mr. J J Jordan*

None of them had heard anything about any fire across at Hankham and were in total shock at the depressing news. Nana wanted to ride across at once, see for herself, her beloved sister's home, and pray over her grave. As for Rosie, they could not believe that she was gone. She had been so vibrant in life and only now when she was really truly gone did they realise how desperately they had missed the little minx who had been called Rosie Smith in the letter!

Why had she been called Rosie Smith? What had happened? Why had no one in the gang been in contact? They needed answers and Ned and Shaun agreed to send a message across to have a word with Shaun's old friend Bob Hawkins but he arrived shortly after.

It was all too much. Their world seemed to shatter and squeeze them hard. Both Ned and Ray thought that the guilt they felt would surely kill them and they would follow her and Bobby, their younger brother, into the afterlife.


Shem heard the church bells toll six times and thought of the poor woman who had been laid to rest. Larry Hawkins had been devastated by the death of Hattie and had immediately set about burying her in style. He knew the funeral would have to be rushed but still for those who were able to attend, he wanted the best send off.

Shem's emotions were at a high. One moment he was lost in guilt, then all consuming hate. His mind worked overtime on what he should have done what he would do. His mind kept circling back to Rosie and her smiling face. He had to get her better. She was his responsibility and he could never have that on his conscious too that he had caused the death of his pixie.

Chrissy, Daisy and even Valentina with other women of the village were helping and caring for her and surprised by Shem's attendance to the poor young woman.

Valentina at first, had wrongly tried to make him leave, saying it was women's work, but he had merely snarled at her to back off. She had backed down and watched as he had taken over, she knew without him saying that the girl was known to him, and slowly it dawned on her, his heart was with this woman, and that he really did not care for her at all.

Valentina had always held Shem in high regard. He was the Boss and she his occasional lover. She was at his beck and call and would do anything for him. She had learnt to keep her mouth shut a long time ago about the comings and goings of the village. She had an entirely different relationship with his brother Rafe. She adored him and they flirted outrageously with each other and had such fun. He made her feel young again, whereas her husband Gideon was a walking corpse, a man who drunk constantly, who was unhappy and bitter and took it out on others.

Her husband, Gideon's was a man lost, his eyes drooped in boredom, and he wore a permanent frown. He hated everything and everyone and the less time he spent with Valentina suited him best. The only passion he had in his life had been brewing Ale, but he had let that go by the by and the only person he loved was his sister. Valentina had watched as Shem had tried to coax Gideon out of his moods and after a while seemed to have succeeded, and she found she resented Shem's attention to her husband instead of her.

She watched as Shem touched the young girl with all the care in the world. It was as though she was the most delicate flower and any wrong move would break the petals from the bud and all would be lost. She watched his emotions, the hurt, the sadness, the tenderness, and love and it stung her so deeply.

This tenderness was a side she had never witnessed before from him. She had seen him be playful and full of fun with his friends, but he always held back with her. She wished with all her heart that he would just give her something. She felt she could suffocate with the pain of it all. If she had known what this woman to him was, she would not be standing there now. How could she tolerate it so? She believed that he was hers! She wiped her nose with the back of her hand and scolded herself for being quite so selfish and unladylike in her gesture.

Bob's younger cousin, Doctor Simeon Fox, had come and taken over and all of them watched with baited breath as he had examined the patient and at one point, Valentina thought, Shem would have throttled him, with the way he just pulled her about. She knew he had never really been hers, he had just used her, and she had allowed her hopes and dreams to get the better of her. She had lost herself in them and did not know who this man was anymore. She was trying so hard not to be bitter that her hopes and wishes had blown away in the wind.

Shem held back the bile in his throat, as he had carefully washed Rosie's whole body clean and then he had watched over her when Doctor Simeon Fox had started to examine her and advise how to treat each wound she had been inflicted with. Doctor Fox's assessment had not been great, and if she pulled through the next few days, he said it would be a miracle, but Shem knew better. He had seen that look of determination on her face and then the recognition of him. He knew that alone would be enough for her to rally all her strength and will power.

There was no getting away from the fact that the poor girl would be scared for life. She had a scar running from her left ear lobe and curled round her face to her chin. She had been repeatedly whipped, all over the back of her body and legs and she had lost a hell of alot of blood. She had been cut with a sharp blade repeatedly all up her arms, however Doctor Fox felt these would heal and have no scars in time, if she survived.

She had a few broken ribs, and her whole body was a mass of bruises. Shem was sickened, by the imprints and bruises, which were clearly of hands and fingers. Where someone had held her so tightly and inflicting so much pain. The Doctor had stitched her up as best he could, and had known with Shem over his shoulder, watching his every move, that the job had best be good. He had filled the girl with Laudanum and taking Shem aside, and said she probably would never have children ever again!

How could any woman survive such an ordeal as this? This had been savage, cruel, and brutal. Not just a rape but a torture, a ritual of satanic hard hate, and what struck him most was the fact that he knew Hartright had enjoyed every vile moment of it.

Shem had always intended to kill Hartright regardless of orders and he had wanted that pleasure to last until he had his ultimate revenge. Now he had hurt the one woman he had truly ever really felt anything near love for. What was love? If this was it, then it was pain and suffering, again and again and it hurt every part of his body. How could he be expected to let this lie? There was too much at stake. He knew the madness would engulf and overwhelm him. He needed to keep calm. He had to achieve certain goals before he could kill the vile worm. All in good time, he kept repeating to himself. If only he could manage to control the smouldering, it was going to be so hard. What was he going to tell her? Tell his men? What did he tell Rafe?

He was torn. It was not an experience that he was used to. One moment making plans for Rosie's future, the next arguing that why should he? He felt responsible, but then should he be? She was not his. Why was he protecting her so? What was he going to do about her? What time could he give? Why did he feel so bloody guilty? Why did his already big burden have to carry now an extra load? Why did he not just return her to her brothers to sort out? Why had he not looked yet at the boy? Why was he lying to himself? Rosie had meant everything to him and not a day went by that he did not think of her and then scald himself for being soft. She was his to protect. He should have protected her better. He had failed again to protect those he loved.

His blood boiled with such intensity that he felt at times he could explode with all hate he carried. He constantly battled with his temper and found that all reason and sense of justice seemed to be ebbing away, he felt continuously lost in this blackness, this all consuming fire, he would make them all pay.

When Rosie screamed, he comforted her. When she moaned in agony, he gave her Laudanum. When she cried for Ned, he lied and said he was on his way. When she cried for him, he choked up. He watched her night after night, after night. They kept her calm with Doctor Fox's medicines. Shem was worn, torn and in a spiteful and fretful temper. However, slowly she was getting better. He took reports from his men and let Bob take on the main duties whilst he watched over her. He had sent Rafe and his man, Little Paully to meet Rosamund and knew any day she would arrive. She would take over as she usually did and sort everything out and put him straight. She was their surrogate mother.

In the meantime, Chrissy had again proven to be a Godsend. Rather guiltily, he hadn't taken much notice of her before; but over the last few months she had became part of his and his brother's life. A motherly figure in the background. When they first met her she was a shadow of her former self, thin and gaunt, however she had started to fill out and had rosy cheeks and curly brown hair that was tinged with a hint of ginger at the ends. Chrissy had settled in nicely and did not judge, speak much, or hover when not needed. She even managed to look after the dogs, which all seemed to come to her without any fuss, knowing that she would spoil them rotten and give them all so much love.

Many years ago, her husband Arthur Gray, had been one of Bob's main men had been a right one by all accounts and after he had drowned on one of the runs, Chrissy's had fallen to pieces.

She was known as Pissy Chrissy, as she was always out of her brain drowning her sorrows in Ale and Gin. She just could not cope. Gideon had always had a soft spot for her, having known her all his live and he looked after her. He gave her a home and asked nothing of her. He gave her work and over time, he had started to give her more to do, but he could not control her demons. She would drink herself silly and could be found lying on top of her dead husband, Arthur's grave, which lay beside all of her dead children. She had no one else in the world. She had craved for death, but had always been too weak and as she said, too fat to walk all the way to Beachy Head and fling herself over the edge of the cliffs and end it all!

Just recently, her mind had started to clear and she found herself being called on to help more with the mysterious Smith brothers. She liked both of them, as they never judged her. They were so polite and over time, as her confidence built, she started to look forward to seeing them and having a sense of purpose. She could not believe that she was needed. Every now and again she would find herself with a bottle of blue ruin, and go to have a sip then put it aside. She felt better about herself and finding a new strength for it. Her drinking had become all consuming and a habit that she could well do without now.

She had been like a shadow in the background when both Gideon and now Shem had brought her back into the light through purpose. Shem needed all the help he could get and she had not even had to think twice about offering. She had shared the load, and tried to make him look after himself and giving him food and hot drinks, she had made him go out and get fresh air. Her presence was a comfort.

She fussed over Rosie, who was making slow progress and she had the patience of a saint when it came to the boy. Through Rosie's suffering, she had found further purpose and direction.

It was late and Chrissy was tired and on edge. Try as she did, the poor boy who had been placed in her charge, would not settle even though he had been with the other children in the village and had taken to Phoebe, Rafe and Daisy's little girl.

'Poor lamb.' She kept fretting. He was beside himself and just wanted to see his mother. She had tried repeatedly to explain that his mother was very ill and needed rest, but he was relentless and kept going on and on. It had reached that point where she was losing patience and both were becoming more and more agitated with each other, but she was too good natured to give in. He did not know a soul, only Larry and he was too full of own grief, and kept hiding his face and crying.

'I want my mum.'

'I told ya, Mummies not well at the moment and you'll be able to see her in the morning when she is feeling just abit better.' She could not recall how many times she had said the same thing over and over again.

'I want my mum.'

'Seb, I did say....'

'I want my mum.' His voice started to whine.

'Now come here and sit down, look I have some lovely warm milk for ya.' She tried to keep her voice calm and low-pitched.

'I want my mum.'

'Please darling, I am trying my best here and you're not helping.' She wiped her brow feeling a little too pressured. Her hair was all lose and needed re plaiting. She felt worn out and old.

'I want my mum.' He said again and this time stopped in his tracks.

'Oi. What's all this racket?' Both Seb and Chrissy jumped out of their skin as the door was flung open and a huge figure emerged in the kitchen door way. Earl rose to his feet in greeting, wagging his tail at his master. Sebastian seemed to shake and stand to attention and ever so slightly move back, then stopped as he felt the heat of the kitchen fire on his back.

Shem strolled into the room and Chrissy got up to let him sit down on the chair by the fire. She handed him the warm milk and he sat and slouched tiredly back. He looked so worn; the day had seemed to drag on forever. The dog moved nearer the boy.

'Do you want something to eat Shem?' She asked. He shook his head.

'Will you go up to keep an eye?' She nodded needing no excuse for a few moments free of the boy. Shem sat back and closed his eyes, however kept them open enough to watch the boy.

He could not see any of Rosie in him. He was a young toddler, who was just leaving his puppy fat behind. He had the look of a child who was contented, however not so this evening. He had dimples in his cheeks, with wavy dark blond hair that curled just above his shoulders. This reminded him of Rafe's hair as a child and how their cousin had sat for hours practising plaiting his hair and putting it up in pony tails all over his head. Rafe had loved the attention.

His eyes were true Cavendish, that soft hazel colour. He obviously was a little stubborn and spoilt. He smiled to himself and was a little put out that Earl had rather taken to him. However, that was to be expected! Shem sipped the milk and got a reaction from Seb as he flinched as if to say, that is mine. 'Why are you being a plep?' Shem checked himself remembering that he was talking to a young child. Seb became alert at his words and looked at him as if he were mad. Shem leant forward in the chair and rested his arms on his legs. He wiped his forehead and Seb could see how tired he was. Somehow, he knew this man was not going to mess about with him. At this point, Earl moved forward and was rewarded with a warm welcome and a rubbing all over. The dog cooed in delight. 'Your mum's not very well, and if you keep on making a fuss you will wake her up.' Seb watched as Shem looked into the fire. He did not like the way this man spoke to him. 'As soon as your mum's better, the sooner you can see her.' Shem was struggling on how to speak to him. He knew he should have made more of an effort with him but he was just so tired and sometimes being direct with children worked best.

'I want my mum.' Seb whispered feeling a little frightened of the man. The child was out of his depth in a strange place, and struggling not to cry in front of him. Shem's heart went out to him and he so wanted to comfort him, but he should not make assumptions that the boy was his! But every fibre in his being told him that it was so.

'If I let you see her, will you be good?' He asked the boy and as a peace offering in a much softer tone, he held out the rest of the milk, trying to avoid Earl's large nose from sniffing over the edge. Shem was proud of him for keeping it together. Seb nodded and took the milk and watched Shem over the rim of the cup. The boy swallowed back tears. 'Finish your milk and then promise me you will go to bed straight after you see your Mum.' He knew he was taking a chance with the boy, he laughed to himself, remembering his father and similar words. 'She be better in morning?' The boy stated as he handed Shem back the empty cup and watched him wipe his lips with the back of his shirt. The boy slightly edged towards him.

'I'm sure, if she knows you have been good.' Shem knew that was a lie.

'Can I see her now?' Seb went towards the back kitchen door, knowing this lead to the stairs and waited.

'Seb, you haven't promised me you will be good and go to bed after.'

'Is she asleep, I be quiet?' Shem nodded watching and waiting for the boy to promise. He could not believe the young pup thought he could negotiate with him! 'I go bed and look after her.' So that was that. Seb had made up his mind and completely ignored everything that Shem had just said.

'Seb, your mum needs rest.'

'I want my mum.' Shem then had mixed emotions, he wanted to laugh and cry and at the same time and could have killed the young upstart, but he resisted the temptation and sighing, got up, went, and stood by the boy. He held out his hand and Seb slipped his into his. His hand was so small, warm, and gentle. Shem had the desire to swoop him up and cuddle him. He was his boy, he was sure and if he could, he would not let anything hurt him. They looked into each other's eyes and Shem felt warmth run all through him. The boy gave him a smile that was like angels and Shem checked himself, it was like looking at Rafe. He motioned for the dog to remain.

Shem had the impression that he had lost the battle with this cheeky little one and his heart swelled.


They quietly crept up the stairs and slowly Shem opened the door to the bedroom. He leant back down to Seb and whispered, 'Remember your mum is very ill, she is asleep, and we do not want to wake her. You will be brave?' Seb nodded and at the same time whispered ever so loudly.

'I promise I be good.' Shem liked him more and more. He was trying to be brave but did not understand what was really going on. He tousled his hair. Chrissy watched them creep in and softly and silently, she moved away from the bed and left them on their own. Seb tiptoed to the side of the bed; he could not clearly see his mother and tried to get on the bed. He felt Shem lift him gently on to the bed, a little way from his mum. He was so soft and light.

'Be careful Seb.'

Seb sat and looked at his mother. He did not flinch at her bruises or the bandages and slowly moved his little hand forward and rested it over her shoulder. He slowly stroked her and ever so slowly lent forward. He curled himself up by her side and then softly he put his arm across her to protect her. He turned his head to look at Shem, who had resumed his place in the chair by the bed.

'She will get better Seb.' He assured the boy and watched as he cuddled back up to his mum, trying to move softly and so as not to disturb her. Shem thought it best to let him fall asleep and remove him from her side later. He lent forward and placed a warm blanket over the boy who had closed his eyes.

'Night, night.' Seb sung.

'Goodnight Seb.' Shem whispered back.

'Don't let the bed bugs bite.' He heard him whisper and he chuckled at Seb's cheeky grin. He leant forward and shuffled the boy's hair again.

Rosie was a strong girl and if anyone could make it, she could. She was getting stronger and stronger and she needed to pull through, for him and Seb both.

Her eyes lids were so heavy. Every part of her body ached so. Both her cheek and back constantly throbbed and she woke with her hand between her legs protecting herself and in a mad way holding everything in place. She knew she was cocooned and protected but she still felt scared and frightened. She felt weak and paranoid all at the same time; she could not sleep and panicked if her son was out of her sight for too long. After the attack, she did not want to open her eyes and come back, she wanted to die, but then she knew she could not because of Seb. Slowly she came round. She hardly talked, everything was a haze. They tried to talk to her in general, and she just answered wherever possible with a yes or a no. Everything was such a trial. They had asked no questions about her attack and welfare, and in return asked for nothing.

She would wake and find Seb curled up by her and Earl the dog at the foot of the bed. Earl would creep up to her, kiss her with his nose, and offer comfort. She would reach out, stroke him, and softly speak to him. However, there was one presence she felt without ever having to open her eyes. She remembered she had woken once and knew he was not there. She had hit beneath the sheets and tried to keep her eyes open, waiting for his return.

As she woke now, she was wrapped in his arms. Her head was resting on his chest and she felt her whole body move in time with the rhythm of his heart. Just like it used to be and how it had been since he started to nurse her better. She wriggled her nose, smelling his sweat, and then she scolded herself. She was hardly in a position to moan, she had been constantly sweating, and her hair felt damp and hard. Her skin was so very pale and clammy.

She so wanted a bath. She seemed to be able to focus better and things were clearer now and so were all her emotions. She relied less and less on the laudanum, it helped her sleep and her nightmares were fewer. She would give anything to just stay wrapped in his arms and not endure the pain of what was to come. He had said he would never let her go. She would always be in his heart.

But hadn't he put a knife to her neck?

What manner of man had he become?

The boy she had fallen for all those years ago seemed a world away. Had their love really survived over all this time? She wasn't a fool to what he was and who he had become. She knew his ambitions, who he run with, what he felt. Nevertheless, seeing him as a potential lethal killer, with such evil in the depths of his eyes was not someone she wanted to see again. She felt the dog at her feet and watched as Earl poked his head from beneath the sheets and look up at her still sleepy and slightly upset that he had woke up sensing she too was awake. He padded up the bed in between both their legs. Shem grunted in his sleep and then tutted as the dog rested his whole body between their legs and his paws and head were laid firmly on Rosie's chest.

Earl then started to lick her, seeing and sensing she was in better spirits, but she was denying how weak she really was. 'No, stop it, stop it!' She moaned grinning trying to push him off and having no luck. 'You're licking my booby.'

'That's my job!' Shem muttered and she felt herself blush and watched as Earl turned his attentions to his Lord and Master. Shem manoeuvred the dog away from her and then kissed and stroked the dog in greeting. He then rather reluctantly got out of the warm bed, she watched his naked form stretch and let the dog out, while at the same time scratching himself and calling down the stairs to Chrissy to let the dog out. She looked across to see Seb fast asleep in his cot, and noted he had not made a move when Shem had called down the stairs. She noticed how dark Shem's skin had become where exposed to the sun and how lean he was. His hair was a mess and all fluffy with sleep. He crouched before the smouldering fire and carefully placed a few more logs on the fire. Whilst he waited to see if they caught, she watched as he checked on Seb. Satisfied on both counts he turned back to bed. They caught each other's eyes, he smiled warmly at her, and she lifted the sheets for his return. He quickly got back in and they cuddled up to each other as they had during her recovery. Both had been anxious, on tender hooks, and steered clear of certain subjects. Shem knew when she was ready she would confide but until that time, everything centred on her and getting her out of bed.

'I'm not hurting you am I?' He was so gentle.

'You nearly did.' She whispered curled up in his chest. He sighed heavily and she wished she could take it all back. She had needed him and he had been there. He had constantly held her hand stroked her forehead and just kept touching and she was grateful. It was only his touch she could bear, as he would never ever hurt her intentionally.

'I can hear you are on the mend!' He jested with her.

'You wait until I am fully recovered, then you'll get it.'

'Emmmm.' His interpretation was obvious.

'Oh behave.' She felt him stroke the side of her back.

'Shut up and go back to sleep. It's too early. You need to get better.'

'I am better.'

'And getting on my nerves, already.' He groaned.

She thumped him. 'Look just let me have another half an hour. Just half an hour, then I'll be as right as rain. We'll get up and have breakfast.'

'I am hungry.' She said. He had closed his eyes and murmured. 'In a minute.'

'Can't I have something now?' She pestered.

'Rosie, please.'

'Can't you hear my stomach?'

'I can hear your gob!'

'I am the patient.'

'You're a pain up the arse.'

'You are supposed to look after me.'

'You'll wake the boy.'

She thumped him again at which he gently grabbed her hands.

'Don't do that again.' He laughed not angry at all with her.

'Or what?' She raised her eye brows mocking him.

'For the love of God! Why me?'

'Waiting.' She used one of his phrases, and he laughed at that.

'It may have missed your notice, but I am the Guvnor round here.' He loved it when they played, and this time it was working to avoid the real issues!

'You ain't mine and I'll get it myself.' She whipped the sheets away and all too quickly tried to get up forgetting herself.

She felt her back rip and she lost her breath and felt every part of her body scream and cease up. She collapsed back down on her knees and still fighting for breath caught his hand in panic and tears streamed down her face as the pain hit home.

'You stupid, stupid cow.' He caressed her face and she leant back into him.

'It's not going to go away that easy is it?' She cried into his chest. He held her so securely and gently, and felt her heart wrench in pain. 'I can't pick up the pieces and pretend it didn't happen.' She clenched her teeth in pain.

'SSSHHHH.' He gently rocked her back and forth and let her cry and cry into his chest to smothered the sounds, so as not to wake Seb, and then she tried to punch her head knowing all the thoughts were jumping around and running riot. She looked down at her arms, where the wounds had started to fade and then touched her face. He held her hands down and she tried to fight him off. He firmly held on and would not let her go. He felt her give in and succumb. She cuddled deep into him and let him soothe her. He rocked and rocked her until she fell back to sleep exhausted with it all. It was just as well that Doctor Fox would be here soon. He needed to get her to see sense and not fight too hard to get better too quick. She had all the time she needed. He needed her to get better. His heart was torn and all he could then think of was how he would make all his enemies pay.

He felt like he was floating on water, floating through a world that was so far away. It was bliss. He sighed in pleasure, Rosie was by his side and he could feel the water lap around him and he could stay suspended in this heaven forever, he was not going to open his eyes to that soft golden glow that was just peaking through. This was his Eden. His eyes would burn if he opened them. Burn and cause so much pain. So why bother?

Ever since he was a boy, he had been able to close his eyes and picture himself in that wonderful place where there was always someone there to hold your hand. He remembered it had originally been his father's warmth that had comforted him. He would lay for hours and hours stirring and fidgeting until he felt his father's presence. His father would come and curl up with him and his brother and then sleep would come.

In his dream, he was cuddled up with Rosie by the side of a stream. They were cocooned in the roots of a great tree and the leaves sheltered them from the wonderful sunshine. He could hear all the excitement from the fair across the way. She was warm, so soft, and cosy. Her need of him had got him through the darkness and the whirling oblivion of torment that was brought in the real world. She would get better and they would be happy.

'Oh it's so touching, seeing you here watching over her!' Shem jumped out of his dream and tried not to wobble as he focused on Valentina as she sailed into the room carrying his supper. He came to his senses, grabbed the food from her, and looked away as he placed it on the side table. She wore her favourite day dress, which was a deep crimson. An underlay of beautiful Spanish Lace had been stitched into the bosom and the overall effect was beautiful. She wore her hair lightly tied back and even if she was not welcome, she still was good on the eye. Whilst Shem's back was turned, she took the opportunity to walk to the other side of the bed. She looked over the sleeping patient and smiled wickedly at Shem. 'I've missed you.'

'Get out.' He snarled checking to see that Rosie had not been disturbed. That would be hard; the Doctor had given her more Laudanum to ease her pain. He had been with her for ages and she seemed to have slept all day and night with Shem never far from her side.

She was taken aback by his harshness, but thought she would try again. He did look so tired. She had decided she wanted him and he needed to be comforted. She had waited and bided her time.

'Why so touchy?' She made towards him seductively swinging her hips. 'I seem to recall you liked our reunions so very much.' His whole body tensed and warned her to halt. That was not going to happen. She needed to do this and before she had come, swallowed at least three glasses of brandy for courage. She had tried to ask who this woman was, but not everyone who may have known was certainly saying anything to her. Valentina had been there for Shem, helping him initially, then when the creature had been brought to them and she had wanted to show him how she could always be there. Shem only had eyes for this woman it would seem now. It could not be so, that the little trollop held him in the palm of her hand.

Everyone was tripping over themselves to ensure that Shem had everything he needed, and that the whore's son was catered for. She was the only one who felt she had been left behind. Her husband Gideon did not even pass the time of day with her now and his disgust at her was far too evident. She was made to feel awkward now if she dare entre the Inn to help her husband, and only once did he actually speak to her and say that her assistance was no longer required. She had only offered to help Chrissy with the invalid so that everyone could see she could help as and when required that she wanted to help the community and not be wholly shun for what she was. Nevertheless, when she started to comprehend how much this creature meant to Shem her jealousy got the better of her. She realised all too late that she had played this all wrong. She felt very stupid at that moment. She sucked in her cheeks and as always, when she was trapped she went on the attack. 'Who is whore to you anyway? Is the boy your bastard? What's the secret? Who are you trying to protect?'

He took a step forward and she stepped back seeing the menace. Why did this man make her act in this way? She slowly stepped back towards the door; his eyes fixed on her every move. She felt for the door handle behind her. Ever so slowly, she opened the door knowing at any moment he would pounce on her. She was choking with grief for herself and the situation. Never before had she felt so vulnerable and small. 'Why can you not see how much I love you and you hurt me so. Do I really mean that little to you?' And without another word, she fled.

She stopped at the top of the stairs panting in fear, annoyance, anger, and frustrations. He had made her feel so worthless. All she had wanted was to comfort him and he had been so cruel. Her cheeks were burning with humiliation. She tried to calm herself down and as she checked herself, however Chrissy was at the foot of the steps holding back the dog from running up the stairs to his master. Chrissy smiled weakly at her, as Chrissy would believe it in comfort; whereas Valentina recognised it as a knowing, spiteful rebuff and felt her cheeks go even redder!

Shem slowly allowed himself to calm down and looked across at Rosie, who was still fast asleep. He sat down and rested his head in his hands. Valentina had been a great help initially but now he did not want her in there and why had Chrissy allowed her to bring the food up? No doubt, Valentina had forced Chrissy into it. He could not blame Chrissy, she tried very hard to please, and the more he thought about it, the more he recognised he had really put on her with the boy, the caring of Rosie, him and overseeing the Coach House where they had all had moved into. He was mad at himself for missing all the signs with Valentina. She had been a passing fancy, someone he could take comfort from and discard without a thought. She was deluding herself if she ever thought there was going to be anything to get out of this. Did she not realise that? By God, she was a whore and it was not as if he had said or promised her anything. He always thought he had made his position clear. He needed to set Valentina straight. He sighed and placed his head against the back of the chair. Why was everything so complicated? He was worn and tired through it all, he just needed to get Rosie over this set back and then once he knew she was well, he could make decisions about their future.

He had no idea that Rosie had awoken and had heard every word and found that she was green with envy. This Valentina was incredibly beautiful and oozed such sensuality that she became overcome with envy. Rosie thought she could not compare, she had nothing to offer, no looks, any pride, or dignity. She had been raped and the man she loved had been prepared to put her out of her misery before he realized it was her and then subsequently had rescued her and cared for her. He had been there constantly, each and every hour that she was ill. But none of that counted for much when she lay feeling so dirty, so vile and that everyone would look at her and say she deserved what she got. Now the truth of the matter hit her. Shem had a life, which included other women too, and whereas he had never openly confided in his jealousy about the way she lived her life previously, she could not abide the fact that he was too familiar with the beautiful woman. She could never compete with her. Rosie had felt that she would never be able to feel anything again after her ordeal, but slowly Shem had shown her the way. Was it all for nothing? He just felt sorry for her and as soon as she was better, he would send her packing for the love of that woman. It was too much to bear. She never wanted to open her eyes again.

Shem leant against the kitchen door drinking his tea; Chrissy came up behind him and stroked his back in affection. They all lived now in the Coach House.

The Coach Inn was shaped in a big square, just off from the main thoroughfare. It was a double fronted massive house with a coach tunnel to the right. Both sides of the house had been over time extended to form a huge square enclosure and embrace the stables and courtyard in the centre of the premises. The house was made of the traditional flint stone, which was familiar in the area and mainly grey in colour, with the black glistening of the flint. From one of the side wings, Shem had extended the house for the private quarters after he had bought into the business. Old Man Mole was believed to be at least seventy and could still run with the best of them. However when his wife had recently died he knew that he needed more help. His own relations had long since moved away and his main family were the people who remained and had worked a hell of long time with him. He had good people working for him and Shem had not wished to upset that and so the business and the living quarters for Shem and Mole's respected families had been divided up.

Chrissy, without having to be asked, moved in as Shem's housekeeper and told Gideon she was only a stone throw away if he needed her help at the Castle Inn. Gideon was sad to see Chrissy go, as she was one of his only true friends. As she had got better in herself, this had transferred to the Castle Inn and she had created a homely feel about her, which made the atmosphere in the Alehouse more than comfortable and that would be missed.

Paully had also managed to swing it and had got placements for his sisters two eldest.

Rafe and Daisy seemed to have settled in nicely and got into a routine and although he had not offered marriage, Daisy felt secure with a home and it had been a Godsend. She loved Rafe with all her heart and was not naive to the fact that he loved her in his own way, however not the depths she to him. Daisy just loved being with these people. She had a home, was wanted, and had especially everyone mucking in to care for Phoebe. It also helped that she had hit it off with Chrissy. She felt as if she belonged and she seemed to be accepted by Shem who made her welcome and she knew he would always look after her. She was pretty much in awe of him

'You alright pet?' Her eyes followed his and landed on Rosie.

Rosie sat in the sun watching as Rafe played with Phoebe, Seb and the dogs. Daisy sat beside her shifting her position at regular intervals, not once moaning, which was not in her nature, about her condition, just waiting patiently for the day and the baby to come out. The baby was well overdue and what with Rosie still recovering and a baby on the way, everyone was on tender hooks.

Why did he feel this way? Feel like he was always doing something wrong? Shem tried to act all hard and tough to show her who was in control when all he wanted to do was wring her bloody neck and tell her to snap out of it. Then he could kill himself for thinking like that and remember what she had been through and then he would physically have to sympathize and that made him feel silly and weak. Previously they had been getting into a routine and the trust had been there. Everything had been so natural, they spoke without having to say anything, and then it had all came crushing back down after she had recovered from the set back.

Rosie smiled weakly at the children's antics and he watched as the breeze took whispers of her hair and fanned it away. Her thick hair was plaited and fell down her back. It was so thick and looked so much better now, all clean, and soft and he could just imagine, that it smelt of lavender. She was dressed warmly and colour was back in her cheeks. He hated that they were so close in body but so far apart mentally. One minute he wanted to love her and the next kill her! Laugh, he wanted to scream, she was driving him mad, and if something did not happen soon to solve this problem, he would explode!

He promised himself that he would make her life hell; he would not talk to her unless he had to, and he wanted her where he could see her but wanted no friendship, no mock pretence. But she was ill and she needed him. She needed to be surrounded by people who cared and loved her. But he needed answers, not just about the attack and confirmation on who it was, he wanted answer about Seb.

His son, the son he had been denied. He hadn't seen him being born, seeing his eyes open for the first time, see him sit up on his own, see him hold his own cup, and try to feed himself. Start to play and interact with children his own age. He hadn't seen him hold hands with one of the older children trying desperately to catch up with the others. What had his first reaction to the sea been? Did he like bread, did he like apples? Was his favourite drink milk, like his? Did he prefer to sleep in a cold bed that hadn't been warmed up? Did he bite his lip when he was anxious about something? Did he hate being all alone? Did he thrive on company and want to be one of the lads? Wanted to be loved?

He knew when he first laid eyes on him that he was his. It all made sense now, how he had not seen her over the last few years. Rosie had known Rosamund, his gypsy adopted mother and she had mentioned knowingly over the last few years when Rosie would be visiting, but each time he hadn't managed to make it, being pulled from one place to the next, and then he looked back with regret that so much time had elapsed

Rosie knew he was there and watched him from the corner of her eye. This was the man who had had her life in his hands and who casually was going to cut her throat open and leave her hanging at Hattie's for dead. His whore had paraded herself in front of her. She felt humiliated still. A shudder went through her and at that same time, it was as if he had felt it. He had been watching her and their eyes connected. Her body let her down and she flushed all over, she tried desperately to divert her eyes but his stare tore into her, it was menacing, it ate into her, challenged her. Then it was black and empty, - gone. He looked away and she felt discarded. Both pretended that they did not care but both longed for the same thing.

How could she go on? She was in turmoil. The energy that oozed from him was magnetic. She could feel the pull. Feel the butterflies and her whole being turn to jelly when he was around. Then she had to remember she hated him and be deliberately spiteful, however it was wearing at her. She couldn't eat, she found that the nightmares slowly crept back and to make matters worse, she had started to call out for him to rescue her! Of course, he would be there and she hated him even more for that. He would creep into the bed when she was fast asleep and he would be gone by the time she woke. She could feel his presence and they would cuddle up to each other as if nothing in the world mattered.

She felt like she was drowning, being cocooned in a world where everyone cared but were smothering her to make everything look roses. Painting a lovely picture not to expose her to what was really going on. She was having a breakdown, which wasn't any wonder after all she had been through and any moment now, she would just lose it. But she could not let go. Sebastian needed her. He looked at her with such love, need, and at the end of each day carried his stories to her with such enthusiasm and growing love for this new family.

She could hardly run away again and get away with it a second time. *Make the best of what you have;* she kept trying to tell herself. Like hell could she! The sun shone and she tried to feel at ease, but her mind kept wondering and then she found herself smiling to herself as she recalled a time a few years back.

The air was fresh, the rains having come and cleared all the humidity away. Everywhere was lush and green and everywhere that Rosie went, white butterflies could be seen hovering around. The lavender bushes were abundant and blooming, and fierce with bees. Starlings circled the sky above and made wonderful waves and patterns. It was breathtaking to watch.

She loved that time of year and could think of no better time than sitting up on the beach with the sun on her face, watching the surf and the men hunting for worms. The occasion galley would beach and off load its cargo; she witnessed the odd Custom man come down to investigate, whilst having a laugh, joke, and then walk away being a few coins better off. Life moved on and it settled her to just witness the everyday coming and goings.

Then she remembered those glorious days when the August fair was upon them. She looked forward to this every year. Oh, it was wonderful. She had a full day to herself and could do as she pleased. She remembered one year when all the family had come except William, who had to return to Grays Mill in Lewes for some family member's birthday celebrations! Well whatever. She had already spent some time with Rosamund, and given her yet another handkerchief, which she had painstakingly embroidered. Rosamund had held out a full minute before she nearly bowled over laughing so much.

Rosamund had eyes that were like black slits and she wore a multi coloured shawl across her head and shoulders. Her hair was plaited to her thighs and was still strong and full. Her features were hawk like and you could just look at her and know from that stare, she did not take any prisoners. Her brown face was well leather beaten, and the grooves in her face told a tale or two. However every now and again you'd see a sneaky little twinkle of the cheeky young girl she once was. She was a proud woman and loved to brag she had no grey hairs! She loved the young feisty little madam and could not stop chuckling at her cheek. Rosie was useless at embroidery, but she promised Nana and her sister in laws that she would practice and get better. However, try as she might, her embroidery was always a laughing matter and looked as if it had been a child's first attempt.

'Really my sweet, the torture must be too much for you to endure. I think its best you try something else. A little less fancy perhaps.' Rosamund had tried to sound not so sarcastic.

'You are very ungrateful!'

'Each year you give me a handkerchief and its getting boring. What I am saying is next year, give me something else.'

'You may be dead next year and then you'll be sorry and miss my surprise.' At which she got a smack around the head.

'I told you before, I'm not going anywhere.'

'No, the devil never takes he's own.' And with that, she skirted off. Rosamund pointed after her in mock aggravation. She waved back at her and followed through with blowing a kiss from her hand. Rosamund sarcastically pretended to catch and pressed it to her heart.

She turned around and just like the first time they ever met, collided into him again. She never thought that she would ever see him again. And here he was! They had just somehow come to be in the right place at the right time. She remembered feeling her insides somersault a million times over. He was grinning at her like the cat that had the cream. She looked up into those green eyes and just found herself melting. Time had been good to him; he was no longer that tall lanky blond hair boy. He cocked his head to one side and winked at her. She had bounced off him and his strong arms had caught her. The touch had been like a spark through her whole body, like lighting, all-powerful, magnificent, and scary.

To him the touch had sent tingles all up his arm. It was like thousands of butterflies, landing, and then fluttering off, all at different times. His whole body rejoiced at seeing her and this was genuinely seen in his eyes. But she also noticed he looked tired. His hair had been pulled back and put into a bun at the top of his head. It made him look severe and he was unshaved. He had an air of confidence, a knowing that was not there before. He was a man who looked as if he lived on the road, tanned and ever ready, and there was something else to him that had not been there before. An edge. She could not quite place her finger on it. He wore warm practical clothes of good cloth and he rested his hand on his sabre.

She melted at his gaze and felt her knees wobble. She shook her head in wonder and laughed at the silliness of it all.

Her man Shem was standing in front of her after all this time! The one man who she spoke to in her head, her friend, her companion and her soul mate, who she never thought to see again. In a few quick seconds, he had become the centre of her universe and no one else mattered at all.

He gave her the most precious of smiles and heard his deep voice make his excuses to his friends, she never focused on them at all.

When Shem remembered that incident he could see Rosie swaying in front of him, and he rocked back on his heels. She was his little pixie, all rosy and so cute. Her hair was long and plaited down way past her back, as always it was untidy and spilling out everywhere. She had far too much hair! He remembered running his fingers through it and it being so thick, but so soft and as he recalled it always smelt of lavender.

She had grown fuller, and he could feel that he liked it and groaned. She looked good and even though her clothes were old and frayed, she held herself up with dignity and pride. She was becoming a woman. He thought he had died and gone to heaven. His heart was pounding so, and he just could not explain the feeling that run from his head to his toes. A tingling sensation, he had flatters in his stomach, he felt warm and that he had come home. How could he ever let his mate go again? He had opened his arms and she had melted into him and cuddled into him. She was so small. His hug felt so good. He kissed the top of her head.

He knew he would always love her and he would try to see her as much as he could. The Fair would be a regular feature, but no way was that ever going to be enough!

Her mind came back to the present. She missed him. She would try harder and make amends.

His mind came back to the present and at that moment standing in the kitchen, he decided he hated her, although his heart ached and his head throbbed. He would keep well away from her, but he knew that was not likely to happen any time soon.

'You can't go killing everyone who has pissed you off Shem.' Bob warned.

'Says who?'

'I say.'

'That means jack shit to me.'

'You will hang.' Bob wanted Shem to slow down and see the wood from the trees.

'Like fuck I will. They tried and look what just happened; my very good friend Lucifer keeps protecting me.'

'Please, think on, you have Rosie, Sebastian. A good future and your men love you. You know what I mean? Don't throw it all away.' Bob knew that Shem was not even listening now. His words of warning were wearing thin and Shem just did not want anyone to interfere with his plans. He tapped his fingers on his desk and looked hard out of the window.

'They are the reasons why I have to finish what was started.' He looked back at

Bob sternly, his expression also saying, you should know better than anyone. 'If not, people will think I am getting soft.'

'No one will ever think that of you boy.' Bob laughed. Shem sat down and closed his eyes, placing his face in his hands for a second and then sighing. 'I need for my woman's eyes to be free of that constant fear. To have a home and a life. For me, to have some remembrance of normality. I need to protect her, as I should have done ages ago. I will not have any other fucker, pissing on my shoes and telling me it's raining.'

'When will it stop? I am frightened for you.' Shem sent Bob a small smile of thanks and then winked.

'You should be frightened for all the other fuckers!' They had come full circle and Bob just felt that Shem had given him lip service. He knew that Shem was now the main man in charge and all his schooling had paid off, but this man's revenge, his lust for it, was all engulfing, and a topic that Bob could not even contemplate ever understanding.

Shem knew he was worried for him, he wanted to see justice done, and Bob knew that Hartright had a price on his head and Shem would see him dead.

Bob sat back and thought what he would have done if he were in Shem's shoes. Probably killed alot more people in his prime if that had happened to him. Shem needed to show that Hattie's death had not been in vain. People were beginning to see the pay back and he was on the warpath. He had a plan and was acting it out. Bob had given him clear orders from on high that Hartright was not to be killed, but how far could a man be expected to suffer without retribution? Shem was just holding it together. He needed Rosie to confirm it was Hartright, although he knew. Now the body count had started. Would he be able to contain himself and hold off on Hartright regardless of Mr. H and what he wanted?

There were rules in business and Bob knew Shem as a man who could carry such tragedy and lock it away and bring it out to use as fuel when needed. Shem was remarkable that way and a better leader than he ever was. He had resources that he could pull on, that Bob never had. Bob knew he was getting old, he had started to worry, and fret like an old woman. He laughed at himself, is that what he had become, a sentimental fool? Better a drunken fool, he left Shem pondering in his study and headed along the passage to the kitchen and a comforting word from Chrissy who he noticed had just acknowledged Rafe as he entered the back room.

'Cup of tea and a hug when ya ready, girl.'

'Oh Rafe!'

'Oh you love it, get ya arse over here for a big squeeze.'

'What are you like?'

'Stop pretending to be shy, woman.'

'Ssshhh.'

'When you gonna make my mate Bob happy?' He dived straight in.

'Whatever do you mean?' Her mouth was wide in mock shock.

'Don't give it all sweet and innocent.'

'I don't know what you mean.'

'You know exactly what I mean.' Rafe winked at her and laughed 'Just get in there girl.'

'That's abit inappropriate Rafe and I will not discuss it any further.'

'Oh look, she's gone all red.' He teased, and then sung. *Chrissy's in love with Bobby.*

'Why do you have to do that all the time?' They both heard from behind. They both turned to see Bob in the doorway

'Oh hello Bob.' Rafe said innocently.

'Hold on to the tea then Chrissy, I think ya man wants ya.' Rafe winked at her and run through the kitchen to the back stairs and up to the rooms, he shared with Daisy.

'I, what?' Bob stood flabbergasted.

'Oh behave Bob; just get in there my son.' They heard him call out.

'I'll fucking swing for him, I swear I'll fucking hurt him.'

'Well, Bob that's not nice, here have his tea, sit down and take the load off.' She managed to get him to sit but he kept looking over his shoulder thinking that at any minute that little pup would come back down to wind him up again. 'It's going to be a hectic week with Rosamund due, Shem and the boys off on business and what with Daisy's baby about to drop. You want some bread and honey?' He smiled at that. She had a way of making him feel at ease whereas that little upstart! She was more doing it for herself than him. Her face was indeed crimson, that Rafe was such a so and so!

He sat back and relaxed watching her fret over him and knew he liked it, he liked her, but by God, wasn't he abit too old for all that hanky panky?

'You took ya time.' Shem remarked as Rosamund's cart pulled up by the coach House. Half a dozen men on horses to protect and escort her to Shem's, along with Jesus and Little Paully surrounded him.

'Nice to see ya, Nan.' She retorted sarcastically back at him. Her son, Marcel was already at her side helping her down; he winked at Shem and handled the special cargo with care. Marcel and Ziggi were the eldest boys of Rosamund. She had four sons and three daughters. Her husband Martinez had died rather suddenly of a cold not two years before and was sorely missed by all. Marcel, her eldest had become the leader and was a natural, however many would have said that his mother pulled the apron strings. If she barked, then her boys came running.

'Well come on, where you been?' Shem persisted standing folding his hands and questioning her.

'My bloody whereabouts is of no concern to you young man and ya be right to get of ya high horse and welcome me accordingly. Ya ain't that mighty that I won't smack ya one for ya insolence.' Her Romani accent was thick and clipped. He came towards her, burst into a huge smile, cuddled her up to him, lifted her off her feet, and whirled her round. He planted a kiss on her lips and whispered. 'You old cow!' She pinched him, slapped him, and then to finish, kicked him in the shin, for his previous rudeness. She made him yelp in pain and her sons just let them get on with the banter. Their welcomes would follow.

'Where's me baby?' She cut straight to the chase.

'Oh I knew it, haven't got time for me have ya, I'm the one who needs you and the first thing you say is where's my baby, where's my Sunshine?' He mocked. Rosamund had looked over his shoulder and was looking around for Rafe. She shoved him out of the way and he tutted at her. She was so short compared to him, but whatever she said or did, he would obey. Marcel just laughed at Shem and their play-acting, but all could see the relief Shem felt at her being there.

'He is with his ray of sunshine.' Shem pointed out.

'That man does not love anyone like he loves me, who is the bitch?' Rosamund barked.

Everyone was laughing at her retort, except Jesus, who shook his head and prayed to God for her forgiveness. Rosamund was never conventional and Shem was finding it hard to speak.

'If you must know, he is with Daisy.'

'That's alright then. Daisy is such a sweet and lovely angel. Does that mean she's here with the littleun?'

'Oh my God. Marcel did I hear right?' They could not believe that she would succumb to actually declaring she liked any of their women.

'Stop ya stupid nonsense and fetch me boy now.' Shem tutted again and she went for him and he quickly backed off just as Chrissy brought forward some refreshments. 'And who are you?' Chrissy nearly jumped out of her skin at the woman abruptness; however, she smiled nervously and looked to Shem for help.

'You be nice to her.' He warned to Rosamund and she could see from his look that he held this woman in high regard. 'Chrissy, this is my Nana Rosamund and don't be getting the wrong impression on the woman, she is evil.' The two women smiled at each other and then Chrissy was introduced and everyone else greeted each other.

Chrissy noticed that all the gypsies were so tall, lean, and dark. They were olive skin coloured with eyes that were bright and sparkly. They all had black shiny air, some left it lose while the younger ones, favoured pony tails. All had beards; however, Chrissy noticed that none of them had bushy beards, just fuzzy stubble. They all wore gold in their ears and wore bright coloured neckerchiefs.

All of the men were clearly related and of various ages, only one appeared slightly lighter, and a mere baby in comparison to the others, later she would find out this was Marcel's youngest son Rye.

The leader, Marcel had a quiet air about him that was quite appealing. He seemed to just move his hands and his party seemed to know what was expected. Although Chrissy did learn later that they did talk in sign language, which was very useful she imagined in various adventures that they would find themselves in.

'You still here?' Rosamund said impatiently to Shem. Chrissy laughed aloud and then looked away embarrassed and covered her mouth. 'Go and get my boy and his family and then after you will get my pixie hellcat and the cub for me.'

Chrissy was overawed by the love that Shem had for her and the way that Marcel hovered over her to ensure she was well looked after. This woman was respected and she could see she meant the world to her family. She had never seen Shem jump so quickly.

Rosamund had arrived!

**Chapter Seven**

Hartright had decided to escape to London knowing that everyone and their mother were suspicious of him. He had thought he had covered his tracks, but there were still rumours and accusations. He had enjoyed the taunt, the chase of his last mission, be it unsuccessful in getting an arrest of one of the gang members, he had got a greater prize and then shared after! He felt empowered and grinned at the memory. He had to admit that he would not have gone so far if he had not been so frustrated and been lead up the garden path again! He had received reliable information, that the smugglers were collecting in and around Hankham through to Hailsham's way and no reason to disbelieve the intelligence. He had an understanding with some of the hierarchy of the local gangs that he had to get some results.

He had been made to look a fool, they had the whole area covered, and nothing had happened. He had been frustrated and he had let his men ransack the old woman Hattie's cottage in Hankham. They had license to destroy and took full advantage of that.

After the event and the subsequent aftermath, he decided a change in scenery was the best remedy for the way he was feeling. He would review his options for the future. He had a mind to request a deployment, even though he was on his last legs, and was aware that would jeopardise his business venture with William. He needed to keep that income revenue just a little longer, then plan for the future, as well as keep his sister happy.

He had been enjoying himself immensely in Covent Garden in the heart of London and found that contrary to what some were saying, he found the area not so squalid and that the Landlord of the establishments he found himself in, was a complete gentlemen! There wasn't many people called Luca and the name rang a bell with him from his ancient history, but he chose to ignore it and found that the Landlord Luca made him very welcome. He had drunk himself silly trying to forget everything and was in no condition to see himself home and had started to talk to himself and giggle as he made his way, when from behind he found himself manhandled and pushed into the back of a carriage. As soon as he raised his head, finding himself on all four's at the bottom of the carriage, a fist had bounded down and knocked him senseless.

He woke slowly, finding himself in his own front room, comfortably laid out on his new sofa. His head mildly ached and his month was dry, however he was comforted that he was home. He thanked god, having for a moment thought he had been kidnapped again.

The fire was roaring, and there was just one candle lit. He felt his cheek throb with the pain of the punch he had received. He quickly opened his eyes in fright and could not believe the bear face cheek of the man who sat before him.

He sat with his legs flung over the chair, drinking his brandy as if he owned all he surveyed. He looked every bit the gentleman. He was dressed immaculately and the height of fashion. Hartright felt inferior at that moment, being worse for wear with all his clothes ruffled and creased. Shem gave him a grin but there was no feeling there. Hartright went to get up, but Shem was quicker and before he could even straighten his legs, Shem was over him. Hartright leant back as far as he could in the chair. Shem smelt fresh, with a subtle cedar fragrance. He hadn't seen him this close before, a sense of familiarity crept in, and he felt a shiver go up his back. Shem immediately backed off and without warning; he backhanded him across the face. Hartright's head smacked back.

'Did you enjoy yourself?' Shem mocked and then checked himself; he had used his natural voice and reminded himself to be careful. Tonight be it that he looked every inch a gentleman, he could not betray his identity and use his given voice. He moulded back into Shem.

'What are you talking about man?' Hartright automatically responded then spat the blood from his mouth.

'Your little adventure, down the coast?' Hartright hesitated and then found he could not breathe with fear.

'What are you...?'

'Killing and raping under her majesty's banner? A new low for you.'

'I don't know what you are talking about.'

'I warned you.' The devil was back.

'I don't have to justify myself.....' Being scared and backed into a corner made him attack.

'No, I think you do when you kill good people. Fun was it? A lovely old lady and a young girl with a babe? Not the first time you've bullied people is it, you cowardly bastard. My God, mind ya don't piss ya self again!' Shem was back.

'No I haven't.' Hartright roared but still looking down to make sure, he hadn't anyway! 'Get out of my house.' He screamed going quite crimson in defiance. Why had he reacted to the taunt? He was on his feet now.

'Or what?'

'Or what, I'll have you, oh yes, mark my words, I will have you gibbeted and hanging from Pevensey Castle.' Hartright was recovering his composure.

'Oh don't Harry, you'll get me started with the giggles, and I just won't be able to stop.' Shem mocked him in his own voice.

Hartright tried to step forward and ended up walking into a stomach punch.

'You will leave now!' Hartright choked, bent over his stomach. Both knew his bravado was a sham. Shem laughed at him.

'Harry, you're trying to grow some balls at long last? But come on, we know you really prefer young boys, don't ya?' Hartright looked straight into his eyes knowing there was something he could not put his finger on. 'Do I know you?' He pleaded, it seemed such a silly question, but then he felt himself losing his breath and crying in pain as Shem grabbed his privates and started to squeeze.

'Like that don't ya, abit of rough? You dirty bastard!' As quick as a flash he drew his blade and let Hartright go. Hartright started to wriggle and bring his hands up to fend the man off. He fell back into his chair. Shem placed the cold steel against his cheek and using his weight, he pressed his leg across him. He then grabbed him by his hair yanked his head back. Hartright could not defend himself. He was frozen with fright.

Shem was completely lost now, just seeing the vision of a laughing pixie. The red mist whirled and he sliced lightly at Hartright's left cheek. Hartright screamed like a girl. Then Shem pulled the blade free and with a lighter swifter movement scared the man all the way through his cheek to his jaw.

'I've had ya ear, and pricked ya pale corpse face, next time I'll slice ya dick off.............cos there will be a next time, oh I'm not gonna kill ya, not just yet, it's gonna be slow. I know you will fuck up again, and I'll be waiting, you fucking poof.' He grabbed Hartright by the hair and threw him across the floor. He followed him and kicked him in the side. He then casually went back to finish his drink. He slowly looked down at Hartright withering on the carpet in all his blood, and watched him cry like a baby. He was slightly satisfied seeing that Hartright had wet himself after all.

God! How he hated him. He wanted so much to kill him there and then. The seeds had been planted. The rest of his plans were now in motion. It was time. He calmed the blackness and then he flung his empty glass into the fire in temper. The smash made Hartright jump. He turned to see Shem open the door and welcomed the arrival of a large bald man who was grinning from ear to ear. He recognised him from earlier. The Landlord!

'You know my friend Luca, don't ya? He took a shine to you.' And with that, Shem left.


'Here he comes,' Claude whispered.

'I can't see him. '

'You going blind?'

'There is fog and mist.' Paully tried to defend himself.

'Where?'

'Look there.' At which Paully just pointed in the wrong direction completely.

'That's over the Downs and twenty miles away, you idiot. You need to get some spectacles.' Claude moaned.

'And look like a freak?'

'Least you'd see.'

'Oh shut up.' They both lurched forward and within seconds had caught their prey unaware. Paully jumped and grabbed Clay by the lapels while Claude grabbed the horse to stop him from bolting in shock.

'Hello Clay, how are ya?' Paully pulled him down and held him fast as he thumped onto the ground. Paully proceeded to lean down and put all his weight across the man. 'Up for a little fun are ya? Now, what are we going to do to you?' He mocked. Clay tried to fight free and was constantly beaten back down. Claude came from behind and swiftly knocked the man out by whacking him across the head with his baton.

Clay woke to find it dark. Even after his eyes adjusted, it was still dark. He found himself tied up with his arms outstretched and tied to iron hoops embedded deep into a stonewall. He felt sick with dread. His whole body was numb, his mind churning over all the horrible things he had done in his life. He whimpered and started to mumble in panic.

The air was foul and damp. He tried to calm down and take stock of his surroundings. He made out the walls, and could just make out that they were green and black with water stains and moss. A small glimmer of light and hope came from the entrance, which was above the exposed stone stairs. It was cold and Clay started to shiver. He tried to concentrate on how everything he had been done had been for his country. He had followed orders, he was obedient and trust worthy. He could be relied upon. He was a soldier through and through.

'Oh Hello.' Came a voice from above. Clay looked up and could just make out Paully leaning down the stone stairs carrying a torch. He proceeded to place the torch in a sconce hoop on the other wall. They were in the depths of Pevensey Castle and the dungeons that would appear to have been long since forgotten. Paully turned back to face him and with a lovely grin said. 'You have been no real trouble at all, have you? Bless you.' Paully looked up hearing footsteps from above and smiled as Claude approached him. 'Oh look, here's Claude. I hope you don't mind? I am going to see if I can crack your leg in half with one swift swipe of the hammer. Oh don't wriggle, no, don't do that. Don't be silly. Bless him. Thank you Claude.' He took the sledgehammer from his friend. 'That's my boy.' Paully slowly approached Clay with as much theatre and dramatics as he could muster. He then swung with his entire might, and both he and Claude winched as they heard the crack of bone. Clay screamed as if the whole world had fallen upon him. 'Perhaps a little more pressure on the other side? Shall I try again?' Paully taunted. He thought he heard Clay say something. He pretended to lean forward.

'No, sorry Mummy not's coming today, she was shagged by the night watchman and loved it so much she left ya scrawny little arse to go back for more.' Claude looked away and grinned. 'Oh bless, look he is sweating buckets. You can scream more for your Mummy if you want, we won't hold it against you.'

His arms against the wall were just holding up Clay. He was groaning in agony. 'I should stick the other end of this up your arse after what you did to that poor lass. The one you raped and left for dead.' Paully's tone had changed. Clay was frantic now. 'Shall we turn him round Claude and stuff this up his arse? Or I know one better, get a burning poker and stick that right up and see how far it goes?' And with that, Paully made the decision just to swing the sledgehammer at the target. This was just pure pleasure for Paully, as Shem did not need any information from Clay whatsoever.

Claude backed away as Paully took another swing. He slowly made his way up stairs to return to the Castle Inn and leave Paully to it and all he heard has he left was swing after swing, thud after thud, then squirt after squirt.

Shem had planned his attack on Hartright to coincide with simultaneous attacks on all of his men. Those who had been riding with Hartright on that dreaded night had been cornered and captured without mercy shown. Lord Lennard nearly had a heart attack as reports come in from several villages of discovering of the dead corpses of Hartright's troop. The villagers had been awoken in the dead of night as dogs had barked at the goings on outside. But none had dare to venture out and look and only in the early hours did they discover the dead officers hanging in gibbets, from either the local court house or local public house. The children had screamed in horror initially, then later before the corpse were pulled down, could be seen throwing rocks and sticks at the bodies, which in turn had made the Black Crows fly off having been feasting.

Lord Lennard thought that Shem had gone too far dishing out his form of justice and needed to be reined in. He immediately sent word for Shem to visit him and felt quite perplexed at the whole thing.

He had to deal with the Hartright situation also and that in itself was a challenge with the Mordesan family still having some family ties at parliament and him receiving word from the powers that be, that they did not wish to see Hartright decommissioned and so no final decision on the young man's future had been made yet! The Earl knew he had to work smartly and by God, he would remove the man from his region and get him deployed to the Highlands if he had too. He was a menace who had inflamed the whole area and to top it all, had manipulated his son into such drastic actions of revenge.

Paully had always been wayward as a boy and God knows he had tried to steer him in the right direction but to no avail. Paully had a vicious and sick nature and Shem had seemed to contain it and see to it that Paully was controlled in using it. Underneath, the Earl mused, Paully was quite a good-humoured fellow, and he did love him so. Look at what he had done for him! God they all had faults and Lennard had to keep reminding himself what his bastard children had given him, whereas his two other children had done nothing but take.

He was at a loss, he had wanted Lady Barbara, his daughter, to come home, feeling guilty that he did prefer his eldest children and had rather hoped he could give his son in law, Charles Skelton, Hartright's post, as a kind of carrot. That was the plan and by God, he would do his upmost to succeed. He wanted Barbara home and near, desperately ignoring the fact that trouble was afoot once she found out that she really had no real inheritance at all and could not even entertain what her reaction would be when she found out after her father's death, that Paully would cease her allowance altogether.


Hartright could not move. His life was in turmoil. He had never felt so much pain. So much humiliation. He had woke after his ordeal and found the house completely empty. He thought he was going to die and like a mad man had managed to alert his neighbours to his attack. They had been mortified and he had told them he had been attacked this time, after being recently burgled. They had wanted to call for the local magistrates however, he had assured them that the culprits were long since gone and not to worry. Obviously, he had not disclosed the full horror of his attack and in no time at all his sister had arrived and promptly removed him to her own home. He had also decided to write to his mother and ask her to come to him in his hour of need. He doubted she would.

He could not look at Constance in the eye. He refused to get up. He wanted to remain in the room forever. Constance tried every tactic to make him feel better, to try to rebuild his confidence. She worked on his arrogance. How anyone could dare attack her brother. How dare they beat him up? Who were they to attack him in his house? They had scarred him for life. She would send a message to her Uncle Secomb; he could always be relied on.

Constance was in turmoil and Hartright could not have had a better sister. She was his rock, his best friend, his love. He would never tell her the full extent of what had happened to him. He would never tell anyone. It was too much to bear and did not give a thought to those who had suffered the same fate, - at his hands!

'Just kill the cunt.' Shem said as he put his head in his hands and shook his head in denial.

'Now do you mean, kill the cunt, or kill the cunt?' Paully asked with hands outstretched. Claude was looking at him shaking his head as if to say, shut up now, what you doing, you are digging a hole....? 'Well I mean, what do you mean?' Paully asked his boss again. He had just been trying to give his latest report and Shem had jumped straight in losing patience and just kept saying that he wanted everyone dead.

'I don't believe this.' Shem said to himself, he remained with head in hand; eyes closed hoping it would all just go away. This was turning into a comedy. Rather that, than the reality of what his plans entailed. He sat back in his chair and looked to the ceiling; he was so tired having just got back from London.

'Well you say kill the cunt all the time, and if this keeps on, everyone will be dead, because you don't like anyone. So what I'm saying is, can we have a code to what you really mean,' he smiled and finished with, 'is that too much to ask?'

'So have you killed him or not?'

'Who we talking about now?' Paully asked still with hands in the air, he looked to Claude for help, and Claude covered his mouth with his hand. 'Because when I came in you were talking about what's he's face, and then we went to Chater.'

'Do you wanna die?' Paully looked away and shrugged at that and then Shem continued. 'You plep, you know I mean Clay.'

'Yes, of course Clay, daahhh.' Claude was sure that Paully when he leant forward was going to stick his tongue out. 'Where do ya think we've been for the last couple of hours? On our jollies, but I'm telling ya, ain't going back there. I refuse to work under such conditions ever again, they say there's ghosts there, well I tell ya, got a chill right through me I did, and to think, next you're insist we go back to that other bloody shit hole London with ya!'

Shem leant forward and Claude was sure that he was going to get up and smack Paully one so he added, 'Jesus has just left to take the cargo to London.' Shem smiled wickedly at that and nodded his head in satisfaction. He then returned his gaze to Paully. He closed his eyes and mockingly tapped his fingers together as if in real thought. He then put both his hands together in prayer. Jesus would not like that.

'Why me God? Why me? - Is it me?' He looked across at Claude with a glint in his eyes, who shrugged his shoulders defeated in everything; they both teasingly looked at Paully, who with hands on hips looked from one to the other. Shem needed to let go and relax a little and enjoy these moments with his friends as his other plans were set in motion. He started to chuckle at the whole situation. Claude smiled wildly and said to his friend Paully, 'you are an idiot.'

'What? What?' Paully grinned. They all just looked at each other and fell about laughing. 'Don't laugh at me, I'll get stroppy and have to do ya.'


It was early, before the house would normally stir. The servants had just started to totter about and make the house ready. The Doctor had visited Hartright and had not been made aware of the full horror of his attack. Hartright could not endure the humiliation of it all. He had stitched his face up as best he could, but said there would be a scar and was prescribed to have total bed rest. Constance could not have been any better and was at her brother's beck and call all day and all night. When she had left, his side he had lay hidden beneath his sheets and listened for footsteps as Constance and her staff made their way around the house. It was so quiet. He was frightened. Slowly he took in sounds from outside but nothing soothed his conscience. He was lost in turmoil and shook in fright when he heard Constance have another go at her little maid. She would not give the girl any quarter and after each outburst, he heard Constance slap her. He flinched.

Feeling extremely sorry for himself he had confided only to Constance that someone had got to all his staff, as one by one, over the previous weeks, and that they had disappeared and left him. He had assured his staff that he was going to pay them however, the ungrateful low life had decided to take payment in the form of his goods, and so had stolen from him. He had hardly anything left after he had been previously burgled in any event. It was all too much and then to be attacked in his own home. He would never admit that he was a bad manager when it came to his finances in any event and just about everything else he put his hand too if the truth be known. He was in denial.

One of the young maids had just walked out from the back kitchens to the hall to start lighting the fires when her scream penetrated the whole house. She had fallen to her knees and as she tried to scramble away from the mess left in the middle of the hall, she had vomited everywhere and all over herself.

From the top of the stairs Constance rushed out and stopped dead in her tracks as she saw what looked like the remains of a dead body laid out in her hall way. The body lay like a cross with arms outstretched with only a Riding Officers issue sword next to it. The body lay on a blanket that was once blue, but now red.

No face could be made out on the corpse, and the body was all lumpy and bumpy and just caked in dried blood. The smell had engulfed the whole area and Constance too made to vomit. The maid continued to hysterically scream and scream.

Hartright had pulled himself out of bed and he too now just stood frozen in sheer shock, panic, and overwhelming fear. It dawned on him, who it was at the foot of the stairs!

How had the body got there? Who was doing this? Hartright was petrified, he needed to escape and get away as soon as possible. His whole body shook in panic. It was obvious who had done this. He was telling him he knew where he was. He was mocking him. He could not cope. He felt the bile rise to his throat then it all went black!

'Who we waiting for again?' Rafe was so tired.

'Are you having a laugh?' Shem could not believe his brother sometimes.

'My arse is killing me on all these stones.'

'I know someone else whose arse will be killing them.' At that they both laughed.

It was late in the night and the moon was high so the view was clear and crisp. Shem scanned the darkening horizon. He sat with his knees up and his elbows resting against them. Rafe set next to his brother and had kept having to jump back out of sleep. They were on decoy duty. There were temporary Riding Officers deployed and George had been told to tell them there was an expected run due at Pevensey Bay. Shem thought it was still important for him to do his part every now and again and spending time with Rafe, because soon he would have to leave for a while if his plans went as expected.

Rafe had sensed that his brother was more on edge lately and thought this time together would help him relax. It had seemed like ages since they had just sat quietly looking out to space. Rafe loved being up at the beach on silent nights like these. When the air was just starting too moist and without having to be told, you spoke in whispers against the shadows. The bay was still and every so often Rafe could the sight of the white surf against the curve of the bay, as the water hit. The air was warm. It was a lovely night.

'You didn't stay long in London.' When they were alone, they spoke in their normal voices.

'I did what I had to do.' Shem answered flatly.

'You should have just killed him, finished it all.' Shem just tutted at Rafe who did not want to annoy him. It was the last thing he wanted to do. 'We could have been sitting here free of this shit. And Rosie free of ever seeing that prick again?' Shem turned to face him and shook his head.

'You really want me to sit here and justify our motives on this?'

'Well, you know.'

'No I don't. I'm doing what needs to be done. End of.'

'You can be a right prick sometimes.'

'Seems to run in the family.'

'Oh you're so funny.'

'You started it.'

'I said you were acting like a prick, and you certainly aren't acting your age.' Shem looked at him waiting for what was coming next. He waved his hand to encourage his brother, knowing his ways, far too well.

175

'Well you been acting like a right prat around Rosie.'

'You talk shit.' Shem was immediately on the defensive. He had Bob in his ear and now Rafe!

'Shit, I don't think so, you seen yourself around her. Every time I looked at you, you were looking at her, like some love struck fool.'

'Bollocks!'

'Bollocks! You are so protective over her. I feel like being sick. And if anyone else goes near her, you almost have a fit. I'm sure if any one laid a finger on her you'd have it off.'

'Well there is no chance of that, you seen her if she is touched. God she goes mental!' Shem knew he was exaggerating.

'Can't say I noticed?' Rafe was smiling; he had managed to wind Shem up and knew it was a lie. Shem slept with her every night.

'Shut up plep. She isn't my woman.' Shem said in his own warped defence.

'Now you're having a laugh! It's great you are looking out for her but honestly you need to stop pussy footing around her, that approach really isn't helping.'

'I am protecting her!'

'She needs to be weaned off the drugs and given things to do. Give her more responsibility around the place.'

'Hark at you, old wise one. Seeing you this mature is terrifying.'

'Seriously we need a plan of action.' Rafe was taking charge and Shem grinned at him in gratitude. They both fell into silence. Rafe was just airing what constantly went round and round in Shem's head.

'Don't you think I want to get her better,' Shem whispered into the night. 'God, to see her as she was! I'll do anything to have her just speak to me, to look at me without that sadness. God, I was on top of him slicing his face and I wanted to put all my weight behind it and slice through his whole fucking head!' He spat and then physically calmed himself. 'You should know better than anyone how hard it is.' He spoke more softly now.

Rafe lowered his gaze. Rafe could not ever remember a time when Shem did not have a plan of action up his sleeve. Everything else was planned to the last T, but not with Rosie. It was an open book. Rafe thought he would mellow the atmosphere.

'Tell me about Rosie.'

Shem looked at his brother in wonder. Rafe wasn't one to listen usually. He was so wrapped up in his own selfish ways, and latest exploits.

Rafe watched his brother look out to sea. It was so bright, so empty of everything. The surf glowed as the stars shone down. They were so clear, glistening and seemed to sing to him. It was one of those nights when all heaven shone in all its glory and made life feel and look wonderful. The stillness was bliss.

Shem sighed. He flung a stone and watched as it silently rippled over and over across the water.

'Years ago.' He started quietly. 'I think I was seventeen or eighteen, just shortly after our return from Europe, we had been to Lewes, for something, I think new straps at the leather merchants. Anyway, it was market day,' Rafe smiled encouragement. 'I remember it was mad, you know, everyone buzzing around, too many faces, too much going on, people having fun, all in a rush, that's when I met her.' He looked at his brother, shrugged his shoulders, and started looking amongst the pebbles for his next missile.

Rafe watched as his brother went into himself and started to smile at his own memories. Shem very rarely opened up his heart and Rafe felt honoured that his brother was letting him in just a little bit. 'Well?' Shem was examining a flint stone and turning it around in his hand. He snapped out of it.

'I thought, I'd probably never see her again, but I did, we run in to each other again and again at the August fair and other places. It seemed fate had a hand.' He laughed to himself remembering her uncontrollable hair and that look of excitement and mischief at the same time. The way his heart had literally somersaulted at seeing her and the funny feeling that had engulfed him and made every part of his body on edge with anticipation. Rafe smiled, loving to see his brother so natural. 'It's fate. It's those moments people talk about and you know you have met a soul mate. No matter where, when, what, you know that person is your friend for life.' Shem said. 'Her eyes were always so full of life.' Rafe let him look to his memories for a time.

'She'll get better, and you and her will make a go of it.' Rafe thought that fate could be so cruel. What if Shem did not really want her now? She was damaged. A wreck to her formal self. Did he want and have the time for this? He certainly had time for revenge. He could not let Hattie's death go unpunished and it had started. It was becoming too dark. Over the years, he had watched his brother turn into a silent calculating black hearted man. Only amongst those, he really trusted could he be himself and those moments could be filled with fun and mischief.

'You do love her Shem?' He asked the awkward question.

'I'm hardly in a position to have a life and all that am I?' He did not want to mention what Doctor Fox had said.

'Speak for yourself; my Amelia knows I'll always come back to her.' Rafe tried to lighten the load.

'Amelia? After you've shagged everything that breathes? Does she know about Phoebe and that Daisy is pregnant again?'

'I can't help this pull I have on women. Daisy should be honoured. But hey ho, I can't help it if they find me irresistible, you should try it sometime, put yourself about abit.' Shem threw a stone at him.

'Behave.' He warned and shifted his position. 'Rosie is too much of a distraction having her so close. I have to put her away from me for her to get better. And for my sanity, so I can focus on the job.' He sighed. 'What am I saying? She is always on my mind. One minute I want her with me, the next I don't. God help me!' Shem laughed for arguing with himself.

'Focus on the job? Shem, all you ever do is work, work, and work. You need to stop and take a breath. You have been running around like some demented lunatic. Plotting, avenging, torturing, and gathering intelligence, you need a break. You need this woman!' Shem eyed him and shook his head knowing that Rafe was trying to make light out of the situation.

'Yes you are right, I do need a break from it all,' Rafe grinned at that silent confirmation that he made sense, but then Shem changed his tune and snarled in sarcasm, knowing the truth of the matter and that it hit a nerve. He would have to leave soon. 'I'll just get me stuff together and go on one of those grand tours. Take in Paris, Milan, maybe go across to Athens, you'll be alright for a while on your own, yes? Good. Excellent.' He snarled at Rafe and then with a huff, he lost himself in thought and played with the stones, shifting them between his fingers and only after a fashion said. 'You're right. I do need her.' He sighed. 'She is never far from my thoughts.' He took a handful of stones and let them fall between his fingers. 'Sometimes I did not see her for an age but I was always thinking, what will she be doing, what would she think of this? And if I went with others I felt slightly guilty and always compared them.' He held up his hands in the shape of a pair of breasts. Rafe laughed as he got the picture and Shem joined him. He looked out to the sea. 'Can I really have her with me and still have this sort of life? Will she have the patience still? What do I have to do? What plans do I make?'

His world was full of darkness, death, and destruction, he fed off others weakness, and if truth were known, he did enjoy it. He knew he was brutal, but he knew he too was good at his job. Rosie had been like a ray of sunshine, a pleasure that had been given to lose himself in. She asked nothing of him, and that's the way he liked it. However, too many times, while he had been away, she crept into his thoughts more and more. On cold rainy nights when boredom from waiting on a job had set in, she had crossed his thoughts. He had slowly learnt to indulge for a few seconds then get back to business in hand. He had to be alert, on top form. He could not afford to be absent minded on his part, for a few warm thoughts and memories.

'Plans can go wrong, why can't we do and have both now? The revenge and love? And home? I miss home sometimes; it was wonderful there, wasn't it?' Rafe lost himself in his memories. 'When can I go back? I promise I will grow up if you say I can go home. I have plans.' Rafe rushed his words and still managed to make everything sound like a joke.

'Yes and we all know it's just too bloody escape.' Rafe grinned acknowledging that Shem saw right through him. 'For the life of me, I really don't know how you get away with it.' Rafe had certainly made his bed along the south coast. He was doing rather well for himself and his reputation. 'But seriously, it may be wise to put you at arm's length from any further trouble.' Shem was weary. 'So I may send you away from all this for a time.' Rafe smiled wildly and slapped his brother in play and thanks, but then he shook his head and sighed seemingly to wash away the child play.

'As much as I would love to run away, really I am not going anywhere.' Rafe declared in a serious voice. 'Together until the end, that's me and you brother.' Shem smiled in appreciation. 'If there is more shit to come, I will be there for you.' Rafe could be sincere on occasions and this was one of them moments. They looked long and hard at each other and both were touched by the brotherly love they shared. 'We have faced all manner of shit, we have had shit on shit and then more shit. Shit soup.' They laughed at that together. 'However, seriously though Samuel. Can you really ensure that we will be able to cope with anything else?' Shem was not going to let Rafe return the mood back to doom and gloom.

'Oh I will be ready, but you'll be still in the shitter with your trousers down your legs shouting, Samuel, Samuel, wait for me, I ain't finished. You got anything to wipe my arse with.' He ended by sounding like a streaking old hag. At which Rafe lunged at him, and both brothers found themselves wrestling on the beach. Rafe managed to land on top pretending to batter his older brother while Shem was killing himself laughing at Rafe's poor attempts.

'You can be such a wanker at times.' Rafe chuckled.

'SSSHHH.' Shem spat and then jumped up and started to look out to sea. 'Oh my God, look its Oliver's frigette, he can't be back this quick? ' Shem pointed out to sea, Rafe immediately got up.

Rafe was still looking out thinking they had better not have missed anything. No ship was expected! Why could he not see anything on such a clear night? Bob would go mad at the amount of noise they had just made!

'Sucker!' Was all he heard and shock his head in disappointment at himself for being lead down that road again. Why would he think that their cousins ships would be anywhere in these waters when he was doing business for them in the Indian Ocean? Shem darted off down the beach, tried to contain himself, and did his usual shake of his head to rid himself of the giggles.

Rafe put his hands on his hips and sulked watching his brother laugh at him and wishing that just once God would favour him and make Shem trip and fall over and hurt his pride. No. As if that would ever happen. Now it would to him. Why was life so unfair?

'I can't believe you would allow him to get away with that.'

'Constance please'

'You can't just run away.'

'Constance I.......'

'No, you can't let that low life make a fool of you. My God, he is intimidating you. My God all these accusations, your attack, this killing, My God. The audacity of the man to blame you for something his gang obviously did. He has cut you to pieces.' She turned to face him. 'Does he think you are capable of such wretched behaviour?'

'Constance, you forget who you are talking to and what we have done previously.'

'My God, you'd drag that up. We did nothing.' She spat at him adamantly. Striking her arm away in defiance. She refused to even consider bringing up the past.

'No?' he smirked at that. If she wanted to forget something, she most certainly did!

'No and you'd best put that out of your mind and focus on the task to hand. You best wake up and retaliate against this man before he gets you fired or killed.'

'What are you saying?'

'You know damn well. You have every right to look out for yourself and my God, you certainly would be a hero if you got rid of that scum. He is a low life dirty smuggler. A criminal! You have already helped put a case together to have him hung. What more do they need? You could say it was in self-defence. He attacked you again and you had no choice.'

'You forget my star witness had disappeared. He's killed Clay and God knows who else from my troop!'

'But you have something to get him with? You have a written statement?'

'Did have.' That too, appeared to have gone missing.

'You surely have contacts that can help with that legally?'

'You forget most of them are in league with the smugglers, my love.' They both pondered for a while lost in their own thoughts. What he had done originally did not seem so sweet now!

'Perhaps Grandmother will know of someone reliable?' Constance suggested.

'Grandmother?' He looked at her in shock. 'The woman hates us.'

'Don't be so absurd.'

'You may recall that Dear Uncle Mestor  threw her out of her own home and left

181

our dear mother in charge and made us promise never to allow her to set foot into the Hall again. We only now are not there because it is so far gone. We can hardly go grovelling to her for help, this time; she'd more than likely let Gunthorpe wholly lose and you have heard the stories, he would pay no heed to hiring men to knock the pair of us off, given half a chance!'

'Oh you make Grandmother appear so odious.'

'Have you ever visited her at Croxley Manor?'

'I've been far too busy. Remember I married that dreadful man and well, time seems to slip away.'

'Let's not pretend, neither of us was ever invited.'

'We were never her favourites.' Constance sulked acting like a spoilt child.

They both sat back down; exhausted with the realisation that perhaps they were on their own.

Hartright was unwilling to confess that every time he thought of Shem, he felt his knees buckle. He was petrified and no matter how much she tried to boost his confidence he was not about to kill Shem. He had deluded himself that he was such a big man and so brave, now he wanted to run and hide, he felt like a weak fool.

'Please Hartright, you need to do something. Do not disappoint me. You really would not wish to disappoint me.' She had adopted her little girl lost routine.

'Jesus my love. As if!' he did not sound convincing even to himself.

'So, he hasn't got you yet, so that gives you time, I suggest you really start thinking of an attack strategy.' He forced a grin 'That's settled then. And my love, not a word to my precious William.'

'As if?'

They both chuckled together. Neither filled with any real confidence at this stage.


'My mum can fish.' The young boy said in his babyish way.

'Can she now?'

'Yes and she can swim and ride and she can fight. And she can dance at the fairs, and ....'

'Can she fly?'

'NOOO, ...... silly.' Seb curled his shoulders up giggling.

'Yeah, silly me.' Shem tried not to sound too hurt. 'Girls can't fly.'

'My mum can fling a dagger, she can sword fight, and she can use a bow and that thing.' He made a motion with his hands and Shem nodded.

'Arrow.' Shem offered. 'Your mum's clever.' Shem thought he had best let Seb win the battle of the words just to shut him up. The boy could talk and talk forever. He never recalled being that vocal as a child.

'Can you fight?'

'Not as good as your mum.' He retorted.

'What did you say?'

'I certainly can.' He grinned back giving the young boy his full attention.

'Do you have a pistol?' Shem knew where Seb was going.

'I am not showing you how to use a pistol, you are far too young.'

'When will you show me?'

'I did not say I would.'

'When I am bigger?'

'No!'

'Why?'

'Because, I am not.'

'Why?'

'Because, I do not want to.'

'That's not nice'

'Pistols are dangerous and when you come to wish to learn how to use one, I may not be here to teach you.'

'Where will you be?'

'I don't know.'

'I going to tell my mum about you.' Shem stopped, he put his hands on his hips and took a breath and watched from the corner of his eyes as his brother Rafe witnessed the exchange, knowing he dare not look his way. He could see that Rafe was suppressing a laugh. He thought he would never see the day when a toddler could clearly best him. He too tried to contain himself and did his usual shake of his head to rid himself of the giggles.

'You got your hands full there boy.' Was all Bob kept saying before he would have to be off, doing things, and not hanging around playing nursemaid? He had had his share of bringing up children.

'Have you seen Nanny Rosamund today?' Shem found himself uttering.

'Nanny Rosamund brings me sweets?'

'And she'll tan ya arse if ya naughty.' Rafe offered.

'You said a bad word.'

'Yeah tell him off Seb, he should know better.' Shem fond that entertaining children was indeed hard work. They stopped as Paully greeted them at the foot of the barn.

'Yeah, Rafe you should know better, no tea for you, you been so naughty, you bad, bad boy.' Paully added his halfpence worth. Seb started to laugh and as he did, he always curled his shoulders forward. He liked to see grownups make fun of each other. Paully indicated for them all to make their way into the barn and motioned for them all to be quiet, and was met by a growling Earl guarding his new family.

Phoebe was also on guard duty by the stalls and kneeling down. Rafe knelled down beside her and gave her a big kiss and cuddle while Seb sat next to her and grinned wildly. The two had hit it off straight away and it was as if the two had always been together.

In the middle of one of the stalls, amongst the hay, lay one of the farm dog's great hounds surrounded by her new litter. They were all in slumber and looked heavenly.

'Now Seb,' Paully lowered himself to Seb and Phoebe's level. 'Phoebe here has chosen that mutt over there, the one with no ears, eyes and generally should be taken out and drowned.' Both children looked at him in mock horror, already at such a young age realising when he was messing about. Phoebe pointed to her new puppy. 'So as you been goodish too, you can have a puppy also.' Paully laughed. 'Auntie Rosamund will be over the moon to look after you, ya mum, and your new puppy.'

Both Shem and Rafe looked at each other and pulled faces, Rosamund would be livid about the pup. Earl came and rested against Shem's leg overlooking his new family and now comfortable that the young one's offered no threat to his new family. Shem patted him proudly.

'I can really have a puppy, all of my own?' Seb's eyes nearly shot out of his eye sockets.

'Yes, but only if you promise to be good.' Paully was laughing openly at the boy's enthusiasm.

'I'm always good!' Even Phoebe nudged him at that.

'Now, now Seb, you're talking to me, I know that ain't the case. You can be a right little shit at times.'

'Paully.' Shem warned and again they watched as Seb curled his shoulders up and laughed. Phoebe lent her head down trying to hide her grin, Rafe laughed at her.

'You're being naughty now.' Seb laughed.

'Yeah, no tea for you too.' Rafe added.

They all then returned to look at the litter.

'I don't think any of them want to leave their mummy yet. I wouldn't.'

'That's a fair point lad, and a good one, but we all have to leave home at some stage and you can't have all of them, but maybe, we can pretend just for now.' Paully sounded very wise at that moment.

Hours later Paully, Phoebe, and Seb could be found still chatting away and stroking all the pups in the barn. They had tried to pick names for all the dogs, and then had discounted them, but still up until teatime, Seb had still not chosen one puppy to call his own. He was still arguing that it was best if he had all of them, so they could all still stay together as a family.


'If you ask me deary, I think you're being abit silly.'

'Well I didn't, did I?'

'After all he has done for you!' Chrissy continued ignoring her patient. 'Night after night, he has tended to you. Washed, cleaned, fed, changed your dressings, oiled your face and back. He treasures you.'

'He is a regular saint, ain't he?'

Chrissy stopped and looked down at her disapprovingly. Rosie felt at that moment it was like being told off by Nana. She lowered her eyes in shame. 'As well you should. You ungrateful moo.'

'Moo?' Rosie mocked trying not to laugh at Chrissy's use of language. The woman annoyed her!

'Yes, moo. I'd rather not say anything more, as it would be out of character, but consider this deary, you bring me to nearly swear!'

'We can't have that!'

'Now that is enough. You are acting like a spoilt child.'

'Oh for fucks sake, just piss off and leave me alone. I don't need you. I don't want ya. And I certainly don't need a fucking lecture about that two timing womanising whore bag. - Who you all seem to forget, or did he not say? Tried to kill me!' Rosie had worked herself up into a frenzy.

'Never!' Chrissy leaped to Shem's defence.

'Chrissy would you mind?' Neither had noticed Rosamund's sudden arrival. Chrissy sighed in relief, made a quick exit, and felt the air go very cold, be it that she was feeling rather flushed at the whole episode.

Rosamund waited for the door to shut and as Chrissy descended the stairs she heard Rosamund volley her. There was no holding back, and as Rosie tried to defend herself, she heard Rosamund put her down and then one almighty smack.

As she got to the bottom of the stairs, Shem poked his head around and looked up considering whether to go up and help Rosamund.

'Oh my word! Oh my word!' Chrissy felt herself becoming even more agitated, hearing the screaming of Rosamund.

'Don't worry Chrissy. Rosamund knows how to handle her and a good ear bashing and smack is the least of her problems.'

'That is what I'm worried about, everyone going for her when all we want is to get her better. Except perhaps that saucy Valentina's getting all uppity and me piggy in the middle. Oh dear! You seem to forget Rosie has been through such a time. What did she mean?'

She reached the last step. Shem looked in question at her, he didn't like the thought of Valentina interfering and that Rosie had mentioned about when he had found her after her attack. She looked around and over his shoulder to make sure no one was in earshot.

'Rosie said something up there, which left me a little concerned!' She began to whisper.

'It's alright. Tell me!' Chrissy nodded to herself, she trusted him to say.

'She obviously is getting better. Quite vocal isn't she?' She stopped and then continued. 'She insists she doesn't have to be grateful to you as you tried to kill her!'

'Oh that!' Shem looked down. Chrissy's mouth fell open.

'Oh my dear! Oh my dear!' She found herself in a dilemma. She was drowning in quick sand.

'It wasn't like that Chrissy.' Shem's voice was so sincere. Chrissy decided she needed to get away from him. She was feeling very awkward realising it was all too much.

'It wasn't like that. Believe me.'

'If you say so, deary.' He knew he hadn't won her over. If she could have run, she would have but her motherly instinct stopped her.

'Listen Chrissy.' He sighed, thinking of how he was going to explain, not really knowing how to express any of it, but she rescued him again. She placed her hand on his arm and patted it.

'We'll say no more about it. You love her, I can see, she is mad as hell, feeling useless and hates not being independent. She'll be fine later!'

'Thank you.' Shem whispered and pulled the women towards him and kissed her on the forehead.

'Oh what are you like?' She cooed flapping her hands at him; she made to pass him and both their eyes went to the top of the stairs.

'I don't think it wise right now.' At that point, she knew that Shem trusted her completely and maybe he should not venture up there at this point.

'No you're right.'

'Oh dear, I've just witnessed the great Shem Smith bow out of danger.' She felt brave.

'Yes, you've witnessed me being a complete coward!'

'You slap me again, I swear. I'll get up and I'll go. I'll fuck off out of here and none of ya will ever see me again.'

'Well you tried that already and where did it get ya? Not far. What are ya? Not even ten miles from home. I could not believe that your brothers couldn't be bothered, but then I see this nasty, horrible bitch and I see why.'

Rosamund had known the girl since she was a small girl. Every year when the fair was on, Rosamund knew that Rosie would pop up and she wouldn't be able to get rid of her or shut her up. The lass did not stop talking and many a time, Rosamund would just answer with a really, is that so, yes, yes. Of Course, I am listening!

'You talk so much shit.' Rosie sulked. Now Rosamund could hardly get anything out of her.

'You're a nasty little slut that doesn't know when to shut it. You unclean gorgio, none of us should give you the time of day.'

'Did I ask you to come? Do I need ya insults? Do I need ya?'

'That's gratitude. I carry meself half across the country and that's the welcome?'

'From the fucking New Forest.' Rosie barked back. 'There's the door.' Rosie pointed and stood waiting for her to leave. Rosamund just stood there in limbo.

'What is it? What has got into ya?' Rosamund almost whispered. She sat on the bed in defeat. She watched as Rosie looked out of the window with such a stern expression on her face.

'Oh hello, have you not heard, have you looked at me? I'm sorry I ain't in any welcoming mood but I've had alot on me plate lately.' Her tone had not altered and Rosamund could see that the sickness was deep. Her girl was bitter, twisted and in no position to want to trust and confide in anyone at this stage. She needed a remedy and Rosamund needed time to digest and work out some medicines that would help the girl's state of mind. She could not continue on the laudanum. She also needed a potion for her back. Rosie had not yet trusted her enough to share.

'I'll come back when you are in a better mood.' She was tired and slowly got to her feet, looking at Rosie's back and wanted to just go, grab her, and cuddle her all up in a big hug.

'I wouldn't bother, you've said enough. You're nothing to me anyway. Who are ya? Some old bird I chat and see every now and again? You ain't family, you ain't me friend. You're only here for him. Well fuck him, fuck you and fuck this shit.'

Rosamund felt like she had been stabbed with the ferocity of the hatred that spilled from her mouth. She lowered her head and slowly left the girl. She would pray for her. This was going to be harder than she thought.

'Don't ever do that to me again.' Paully moaned

'What?' Shem looked up innocently.

'Make me babysit.' Paully lay his head down exhausted on the tavern table. 'He doesn't stop; he just doesn't shut up, asks question after question, and has the cheek to tell you when he thinks you are making it up.' He groaned and Chrissy put his drink down. He couldn't even lift his head to wink at her. 'That Rosie must be a saint to put up with that.' He grabbed his drink and took a great mouthful. 'Phoebe's a joy, no trouble, such a lovely thing, but that Seb, has he knocked his head as a kid?' He asked no one in particular. 'Maybe we should give him a daily dose of laudanum to chill him out abit.'

'All too much for you, old man?' Rafe laughed and feeling rather proud that Phoebe had made such a good impression.

'Yes it is. I have to say I am knackered.'

'He's a good kid.' Rafe tried to defend Sebastian. Shem liked that and smiled at the support.

'You say that cos he's left you alone. He asks you a question and you say. I don't know.'

'That's generally because I don't know.' Rafe confessed.

'What like, where does milk come from? How do they get it out? What are tits?'

'Shut the fuck up, cave man.'

'Oh, here we go, resort to offensive language. You're just sooooo jealous that I am better at this than you.' Paully tried to be serious; he did have a few nieces and nephews to practise on. He laid his head back on the table.

'Better at what?' Rafe questioned.

'Being liked!'

William Devereux had ridden to the beach at Cuckmere as if his life had depended on it. Like a man drunk with the effort, he had nearly collapsed off his horse and deserted it as he made his way to the surf. His feet crunched on the huge pebbles until he met the water. To his left he had the tall white cliffs and to his right rolling hills to the cliffs which formed Burling Gap.

The sea was in a temper. Rolling and spitting, while the wind hissed around Williams feet. It wasn't overly cold, just fresh with the wind.

Again and again, his mind kept repeating that he could not believe she was dead. He had only just received the news having been away. His heart seemed to crash and twist and he found he could not breathe. He closed his eyes and the image of Rosie stood before him. She was giggling wildly and leaning over holding her stomach, trying desperately to stop and then starting all over again, this would then always set him off, he would have to look away, she would claw at him to turn back, and they would end up on their knees. She had been so much fun and so mischievous and getting him into all sorts. He just loved being around her.

Then he started to grow up and look beyond his limited horizon, and yearn for more. He had enjoyed getting involved with the Cavendish's and Shaun Cavendish taking him under his wing to help with their little side ventures of smuggling contraband through the marshes into London. He had enjoyed the thrill of transporting goods in the middle of the night. He remembered the first thrill of the mist circling his feet and every sound putting him on edge. He enjoyed the many different characters he had met, and the mystery of some, amongst them Shaun and his past, as well as Bob, Larry, and Harry Hawkins, Gideon and the legendary Mr. H, who he wondered if he really was real. He also wondered after the new gang leader and who really was this Shem?

He knew he partly escaped to the Cavendish's in Alfriston to get away from his over bearing family. He had never fitted in and was always at odds with his mother. He knew his family looked forward to the time when he would settle down and return to the fold, but why should he when he had a gorgeous playmate, two great friends and every day at the Manor house was an adventure?

He had really missed Rosie when she had gone to stay with one of Nana's relatives, things had not been right between them for ages but still that did not stop how he felt. He had constantly had it on his mind that he would go and visit her, but he had been too caught up in other pursuits. He had continued to visit his foxy lady friend Elsa, who worked out of the Star Inn at Alfriston and had also started to flirt outrageously with the new Riding officer's sister, Constance Mordesan, who had been visiting his own sister. That had started to become serious until that little voice in his head told him to just be careful. He had taken a step back to clear his thoughts and found he really did not like what he had become.

Rosie would not even have given Constance a second look. Rosie had always been dismissive of highborn women. She would say they are all dolled up to walk down the street. They did not know how to get their hands dirty. They all looked like white plaster and all fluffy and pink, pink and more pink. Rosie and William had been so used to each other for those many years and when he had been hit by this lust for other women, he just could not contain himself.

He'd shared so much with Rosie; he could talk complete rubbish with her and not feel stupid about anything that came out of his mouth. He had always been comfortable with her, much like her brothers. At one time, they had all been inseparable. Now he knew he was growing up, be it rather later than most. There was a whole new world out there, not just this narrow-minded community. Other people had other fresh, exciting ideas, who was he not to run and try to grasp just a little of that fun?

Shaun had said, you grow up when death is near and you are faced with it on every turn. He had said that it just hits you hard. Shaun in his wisdom had said when you are young, you are dismissive of time, and you have no emotional attachment to those who pass away around you. They are just people you knew, without really knowing them at all. Then slowly time creeps by, and you have experiences, you get wiser and deeper and then it is upon you, your own morality! It hits home. Rosie's death could not have hit him any harder.

Now William had this ache in his heart, a desperate longing to hear that chuckle, that outrageous laugh and his girl making fun of him. He would give anything in the world to see her one last time. Why did he feel so guilty? Why did he feel so alone? Why hadn't she been enough for him? He closed his eyes savouring her vision, her laughing, and her running away from him, with all her hair flying everywhere. His Rosie. His first and real only love. Why had he let it go? The others were nothing in comparison. Why did it hurt so much?

The beach was littered with little pockets of sand banks amongst the pebbles and he leant down and scoped up a handful. He looked towards the horizon and let the tears stream down his face. He slowly opened his hand and let the wind blow his love away.

If Shem needed to leave Rosie, he would explain that he had to go, how long he would be and who would be there to look after her. Slowly she had got used to the comings and goings. She resided herself to the fact that she was a burden to him. She allowed her paranoia to get the better of everything. Shem's life was driven and busy. She was not naive as to what he did, and whereas her brothers played at smuggling, Shem and his gang were totally absorbed in every aspect of the trade and the set up was well organised. She allowed herself to belief that the local community liked and respected him; she refused to look at the other side of this and that people feared him.

Shem's gang seemed to control a huge area and Pevensey village was located on a ridge of land, which jutted out onto marshland and along the high street stood the courthouse, with the Mint house, various flint cottages and just as the High Street turned towards Pevensey Castle entrance laid the Castle Inn.

There were constant meetings, discussions and parties and most of the villagers were involved in some shape or form with the main smuggling trade. The traffic through the village was constant and all the surrounding fields were managed successfully with stables, outbuildings, and horses. The gangs influence was wide spread and behind Pevensey village was a smaller village called Pevensey Bay, which lay, on the shingle beach. The local fisherman who also helped with loading and unloading shipments mainly inhabited this. Further along from Pevensey Bay was a small settlement called Norman's Bay and a most popular Inn called The Star of Bethlehem. Rafe especially liked that Inn and the barmaid. The Inn lay on original marshland, which the Romans had reclaimed and alongside the Inn, a small river made its way inland. This small inlet allowed the smaller cutters to ferry their cargoes up further into the belly of the land and easier to off load and move on towards London. Here at any one time were about twenty of Shem's men working constantly with the stream of transport in and off land.

Rosie was free to come and go as she pleased and spent many hours exploring and tried to steer clear of the Mint House at all costs, knowing that the black haired woman was there and she would only have to swing for her if she came too near.

Her life took on a slow pace through this period. She was looked after and protected with someone always watching out for her. She ended up helping Chrissy with her many jobs and the rest of her time chasing after Seb. He was a terror and never stopped until he lay down exhausted. Everyone had taken to him and if in any doubt about where he was, she was sure to find him with either Shem or Rafe in the stables. She immersed herself in keeping going, not stopping for a break so she did not have to dwell on the pain of her ordeal. She could live with the numbness of it. The Laudanum was still to hand and Rosamund had made her some more soothing oil lotion for her back. Made mainly of sandalwood, geranium, and rosewood.

Rosie liked Shem's younger brother Rafe, who she saw as the light to Shem's darkness. He was the cheekiest man she had ever known. He seemed to bring the sunshine back into her life and when he and Shem were together it was like magic, they rubbed off on each other and were so comfortable, it reminded her of her own family.

Rosie observed first hand Shem's determination and his need to keep in control and not allow the smouldering blackness to all consume him. She could see the passion run through him, the need to have revenge now and satisfy his blood lust, and she also admitted that when he succumb to the blackness he petrified her to the core.

He was a contradiction, as he had become her rock; he was always there, and he always had someone looking out for her, but still they had not spoken about what had happened. She had put a shield up, not let him back in, and the tension was killing both of them.

Shem had thought it prudent to move Rosie and Seb to protect them from speculation. Already there was talk and he needed to keep her existence secret from Hartright and her brothers until his purpose was served, but he had only moved them into the Coach House, which made Rosie slightly more nervous being so near to that vile woman in the Mint House!

They were a stone's throw away from each other, Valentina made no secret of how smug she felt, and it was only a matter of time before Shem came back to her. Rosie also smiled to herself, the woman had no idea what she was capable of, and oh by God, she would learn soon enough!

She knew it was wearing thin keeping Shem at arm's length and every day she realised she loved him more and more. She would not deal with her own jealousy; she just could not let it go. Then she decided she hated him for making her feel so weak and feeble and being in love, when it was obvious he wanted shot of both of her and Sebastian.

It was warm and humid; she had walked for ages and on becoming aware of where she was found herself outside of Hattie's cottage. How had she allowed herself to walk this far? Was Bob still with her? Wherever she went, she had a chaperone. Shem insisted that she needed to be protected at all times.

She stood in front of the ruined cottage. There was hardly anything left. She wondered if at any time her brothers had made a pilgrimage to see where she had supposedly died. The house had completely been burnt away. It was wet from rain and black with the fire. It was woeful. Her vegetable patch was over grown and she could see pathways through the growth where the foxes had burrowed through. It was all so wild and desolate. But there was a resistance to continue which flourished everywhere. Even though the earth was torched and wounded, there was hope and rebirth. She hoped the same for herself. There were lovely memories to savour from this once beautiful home.

She closed her eyes and found herself kneeling on the ground. Slowly the tears that had been waiting to shed crept down her face. She wanted so much to hear Hattie's soft voice call out to her. The sun heated her face and a soft wind ruffled her hair. It had turned out to be a fine day but not so in her heart. She let the tears flow, not having the strength to hold them back. Before her, her mind's eye brought Hattie to life, clapping her hands to get the Black Crows of the fields; picking up the chicken eggs, and milking the cow. She recalled Hattie trying desperately to chop wood and laughing at herself. She had such a way and every now and then would let her hair down, especially at the fair when she had a few too many to drink. She'd give anything to be back in that loving house, nestled up against the fire and

Hattie reading her a story. She even thought of her own mother. How her mother would wrap her arms tightly round her and they would rock back and forth. She had such a great childhood, they were always doing things as a family, always laughing, being happy, loved, and cherished. Where had that all gone? She found that she was on all fours punching the floor pathetically and letting herself just cry and cry. She collapsed on the floor and curled up in a ball; and found that it was just all black, swirling madness that she could not control. She abandoned herself to the depths of it.

Bob sat down amongst the trees and looked away as he witnessed her compete meltdown. She had been walking around like a lost soul. He remembered when first they had brought her back after her attack, she had hardly spoken. Then to those in her circle she had let rip in anger and frustration. On Rosamund's arrival, she had virtually forced some herbal remedies onto the girl and within weeks, she had seemed to calm down. He remembered Chrissy being in similar state years ago. He now remembered her from the fairs. He confessed he had never paid her much attention; she was just this small little thing who popped up. She had been a funny little thing, full of life and fire. He could see why Shem had fallen head over heels. Love was rough and he should know. It played funny games. He wanted so much for this all to be over so that Shem and Rosie could have some life together without any more pain.

## Chapter Eight

They watched as the baggage carriage drew away, along with the last of the servants for the previous inhabitant of the Hall and only then did Shem casually walk to the front of the Elizabethan house, nestled in the heart of Cornwall.

Its Grandeur never ceased to amaze him. Rafe held back slightly, not believing that they were here. Both feeling very intimated and overpowered by the house.

The Elizabethan oak front door was massive and had the biggest key that either of them had ever seen. The door was permanently shut, locked, and so never used. They automatically followed the well-worn paved way round the E shaped building to the library. Their hearts sunk as they observed that the whole grounds were calling out to be loved once again. The house was surrounded by both formal and natural gardens, with former glorious flowerbeds and woodland. Shem and Rafe started to pick up the old plant pots outside the library windows looking for a key and again felt saddened at how the once lush plants had long since died and the earth within had turned to a grey dusty matter. Wisteria and roses climbed the walls and were diseased and needed cutting right back. Rafe laughed when he found the key and flung it to Shem.

The French patio door creaked as Shem opened the door. They desperately needed attention and a good oil. The brothers found themselves in the library, which had seen better days. There was still a musky male smell present and Shem run his fingers along the beautiful walnut desk. Some shelves were empty of books, long since sold. The luxurious red velvet curtains were faded and worn. The solid oak internal floor had lost its lustre and the candelabrum had old candle stubs caked in dust. Dust was everywhere. It looked like the whole place had not been thoroughly cleaned for years. Mouse droppings were evident everywhere.

From outside, the brothers begun to hear their hired men start to arrive. There was much to do, but they had now the time and money to do it. Both could not believe this day had arrived!

The Lady Lydia Mordesan, who until that morning had resided at the Mordesan Hall, had received word that her allowance would be greatly reduced due to her brother in laws expensive tastes. The letter had just arrived being over four weeks old and having to make its way across Europe to her. This meant that she would no longer afford to live there, even in the few rooms she still kept open. She had taken it upon herself over the last few years to sell whatever treasure remained in the house that she could. However, that had been limited. On her return many years ago from a London trip, to see her daughter, she had returned to see that the old Dowager had gained entry to her old home, and taken all the remaining family heirlooms with her. The Silver, paintings, even the Family seal of arms and there was nothing Lydia could do.

Over the years, as well as selling of what she could from inside, she had started to sell off some of the outside stock. She had sold of the sheep, the horses and tried to rent out parts of the land. However, was stopped from doing this, as she had no power of attorney and authority to do so. Her income had been reduced to a pittance and her own family had turned their back on her long since. She had originally come to her first marriage with a large dowry and in a short space of time had spent it all on high living, entertaining, and her wardrobe. Her husband's family had also been extremely rich, and once the heir had died, she understood that the next heir, Mestor, her brother in law, would keep her in the custom she was used to until she could secure a further marriage. How wrong she had been.

Now she had gone and left the once great home in a complete mess and Shem felt crestfallen at it all. Both brothers' emotions were in turmoil.

After a fashion, they came to the drawing room, where the family porcelain collection had once been displayed but not anymore. The room was very dark but in its glory had been magnificent. The walls were covered in panelled walnut, with the ceilings vaulted and painted white for effect. To the left of the fireplace, there stood a striking carving of Queen Elizabeth I in all her glory.

'Never noticed before how fit she was.' Rafe grinned and Shem pretended to go for him in jest. Neither could believe that this house was now in their possession.

The current owner, Lord Mestor Mordesan had forfeited on a loan and Meir Plancey, a Jewish Money Lender in London had offered him terms to take the grand Mordesan Hall of his hands at a reasonable price. This would allow Mestor to keep his Italian paradise. This had all been done with complete discretion, but everyone knew everything that went on and soon word had spread that the Lord had hoodwinked his mother who held an interest in Mordesan and long since managed to legally remove her name from the deeds.

Mestor Mordesan had not been a great Lord and had failed to develop the family's potential land resources and the possibility exploring the mining of coal from his land. This promised to open up all new areas but to Mestor it could quiet easily fail and he needed the money for himself and not to invest in possibilities. God, he could hardly stomach the fact that people thought he could go into business! God forbid that was so beneath him and his standing. To many, it just confirmed that Mestor was lazy. Meir had then sold the house on and Mr. Saltdean had been instructed to return the house to its rightful owner.

Now the brothers looked over a lost world that had been full of so much warmth, love, and fun. Now it was cold, neglected, and forgotten.

'How the mighty fall.' Shem observed.

'Quite.' They heard from behind and both men turned to see the familiar tall stern figure of Gunthorpe standing there. He stood in his usual stance with his hands behind his back, looking down at them as if they were mere insects that he could step upon and crush. As always, he was immaculately dressed and if you did not know he was the Butler to Lady Theia Mordesan of Croxley Green, you would have assumed he was of high birth and the lord of the manor.

Both found themselves jumping in fright and then swallowed, but neither of them surprised at him showing up here and now. Why did he always have that effect on them?

'Hello.' Rafe smiled and went forward to shake his hand. Gunthorpe wasn't one to show emotion or smile, but he did and the atmosphere relaxed.

'Nathaniel, Rafe, whatever, my precious child, go and play, let the men talk.' Gunthorpe commanded in his dry flat tone.

Rafe would never argue with him and nodded, then went off to investigate, sighing in relief that Gunthorpe had not told him off as was the usual case. He loved and respected the old boy with a passion, but he was not the type you would ever demonstrate this too. He was held in high esteem and in turn, you acted within the boundaries of what was expected when you were in his presence.

Shem smiled fondly at the older man who never seemed to age. Shem knew he must be at least seventy. Rosamund was his younger sister and she claimed to be nearing that age soon. The two could not be further apart in life styles. Gunthorpe had chosen a life of service to a family he adored and his sister and his family continued the life of Romani.

The two men walked through the hall of the house each remembering different times and events that had brought them back together.

Gunthorpe had been a constant in his life and the glue that kept the whole smuggling outfit together. He was the man confident to Mr. H. A very dear old friend to Bob Hawkins and Shaun Cavendish on the South Coast. He had connections everywhere, in all walks of life and a huge family in the gypsies. Shem could not believe the suggestion that it was Gunthorpe plotting against him.

'You have surpassed my wildest expectations young man.'

'Thank you.' To be acknowledged by Gunthorpe was high praise indeed and Shem knew he had his seal of approval.

'Your recent success had threatened Mr. H into acting rash.' Shem nodded, acknowledging the confirmation that it was indeed Mr. H who had been responsible for setting fire to his warehouse in France.

'He knows my plans!'

'It does seem unusual for him to be so concerned now for the welfare of Hartright and his wonderful sister Constance. He hardly cared for them when they were small.'

'You know he gave your name as a decoy when Hartright first attacked Rafe.' Shem offered.

'Yes. Not the first and will not be the last. He has alot to answer for! I like his divide and conquer routine.'

'So I can be assured that you are not playing us against each other for some sick game?' Shem then flung at him. Gunthorpe choked with laughter.

'Dear boy, you have developed a sense of humour. I had assumed it had missed you completely in favour of your brother. Theia would love that! No. Mr. H is needless to say, apprehensive for the future and what you can now achieve.' Shem walked a few yards ahead of him in thought. For a moment, he pictured her face when she returned to her home but quickly returned his focus on the discussion to hand.

'He worries all this power will go to your head and you will challenge him.'

'I'm not a threat.' Shem lied.

'Oh come, come, pretending to be so naive? It's what you chose to do about that. You have had your revenge on the pathetic imbecile, Hartright. Torture is so not you Shem. Moving into new territory. Slightly over the top. Any way I digress, Mr. H knows that it's only a matter of time before you go to sort out that fat buffoon. You are ready now?' He asked raising his eyebrow.

'He will not interfere on that score? That book needs to be closed.' Shem found himself asking and not stating. Gunthorpe dismissed the whole episode with a wave of his elegant hand. He was a man of little movement but when he did, it was like watching a dancer. Every action was smooth, thought of, and leisured. 'You have shown that you are a master player, a great technician, a good financial investment and to add, your men respect you.'

'I'm a mini state!' Shem mocked throwing Gunthorpe a wonderful smile.

'Yes, you are.' He liked that and found himself smiling again. 'With a mind, for the political arena, perhaps?'

'That would be taking it too far.'

'Not at all, many Lord's have those in opposition removed without trace and you have had a thoroughly good apprenticeship and at a click, resources. You could go far.' They both stopped as they came to one of the older rooms of the house, long since shut up and not seen for an age. It had been the original Lord Mordesan's rooms, and long ago given up to his son, Troy who had been so viciously killed and then Mestor had succeeded. Mestor Mordesan could not abide entering the rooms and so had discarded them completely, and when his mother had been banished from the house, no one had entered the rooms at all.

Shem's hand hesitated on the doorknob. He closed his eyes as the memories swiped through him. He heard the laughter, the giggling, and the hearty singing of his father. He found himself leaning forward and resting his head on the huge oak door.

He felt Gunthorpe's hand on his shoulder and softly he was made to step aside. Gunthorpe opened the door slowly and he let Shem enter the room. He too was washed over with emotion and felt himself well up inside. He had prided himself in being able to remain focused and to never let his true emotions show, but this was proving to be too hard.

Shem felt tears prick his eyes, and from behind Gunthorpe gently whispered, 'Into the arms of those you love Master Samuel.'

She banged on the front door, having been extremely annoyed that no one had greeted her accordingly, as her status would suggest, having just arrived at the beautiful home.

She had previously looked to her driver who had jumped down from the carriage and proceeded to knock at the door. But no one answered. She was red with humiliation and found herself disembarking from the coach to hammer on the front door like a commoner.

She banged again and was quite flush with the effort. She was mad as hell and stepped back to wait crossing her arms, observing with envy that Lascelles House was built with huge block borders. The design was mock castle with stone cream pillars bordering the window and doorframes. The grounds were lovely and lush with mostly evergreens and shrubs wrapping the hall in a cocoon of wonderment. Off to the left and south facing, lay a walled fruit tree garden. Lydia imagined that there would be an abundance of roses in the back garden and most likely looking gorgeous and well cared for. She ached to have such a home again and was even more jealous of Lady Theia.

The door opened and she stepped back and tried to compose herself.

'Gunthorpe! How dare you keep me waiting? How dare you not have the door open on my arrival? I shall have you sacked for this. Do you hear?' She had soon recovered and shrieked at him.

Gunthorpe looked down his hawk nose at Lydia Mordesan, the late Mr. Hector Mordesan wife. She had arrived from Cornwall, giving no indication that she was on route and that she required an interview with her mother in law. It was just as well he knew everything; he had just got back himself that morning. He was rather tired and if he was true to himself, the journey had taken alot out of him both physically and mentally, but duty called, even if the bitch from hell stood at the doorway! God she had a cheek!

The years had been kind to her, and even though she too had travelled a long distance to get to Hertfordshire so quickly, her toilet was immaculate. She had always been a striking woman who liked to look after herself. She was conceited, vein and selfish and Gunthorpe had rather hoped never to lay eyes on her ever again. She was of medium height with dark blond hair rolled in the latest fashion. Her eyes were dark brown and masked with lovely long lushes. She was very attractive and oozed authority.

When he and the Dowager had spotted the carriage coming up the drive, they could not quite make out who it was, neither of them possessing good eye sight at their age. They had laughed and elbowed each other as they had squinted through the glass to see, then roared with laughter when the woman had been in sight and they could make out who indeed it was. It was good to share a joke or two. The Lady Theia had not been well recently and was just getting back to normal. Her illness had weakened her and she had spent many hours in bed, with her mind wandering and her youth springing back as if it were yesterday.

It was a turn up for the book that Lydia would dare show her face. The Dowager told Gunthorpe to relish the moment. The cheek of the women, they had expected her to drive straight to her daughter Constance's house in London on hearing her news and were puzzled that she had decided to visit the one lady she was most jealous of and who she had deliberately hurt the most.

Unbeknown to Lydia, the Dowager had walked to the front door with Gunthorpe and had positioned herself behind it so she could hear everything.

Martha the old Cook, had also been sent for, to watch the situation unfold and made her way slowly to the hall. She had hugged up to her dearest oldest childhood friend, the Dowager, having been told who was at the door and like giggling silly girls they both tried to behave keeping one hand over their mouths and the other squeezing each other's hands in anticipation.

Gunthorpe was going to love every minute of this and he remarked in his dry hard voice.

'The dowagers' is not home to you; she has given me permission to add that she will never be home to you. You are to leave this instance before she sets the hounds on you.' Unbeknown to Lydia, they had a Foxhound that was as docile as anything or as Theia had giggled; they had Martha with a broom!

'How dare you speak to me so?' Lydia spat. 'Let me through.' She started to edge forward and tried to shove him out of the way.

Firmly he grabbed her by the shoulders and pushed her back, she wobbled as she tried to find her balance. She jumped forward again; however, Gunthorpe was ready and casually stepped back and slammed the door shut in her face.

She screamed in disbelief, started to jump up and down in temper, thudded the door like a lunatic, and was even more incensed when she was sure she heard what sounded like little girls giggling in glee at her!

Whilst Rosamund was in residence, most nights were spent, subject to the weather, outside enjoying an evening meal, with a roaring fire and music in the background. At every available opportunity, Rosamund or one of her Gypsy family would delight everyone with some sort of entertainment, which they just loved to do. Rosamund had a fondness for music and dancing. As a young woman, Rosamund had danced and sang for money at local fairs and horse races. She remembered the sound of tambourines as she and her sisters would swirl about in their colourful skirts performing to whoever threw coins for them.

After eating and drinking, with many dozing lightly, Marcel had started to sing and was accompanied by Ziggi on the guitar. He had a beautiful blessed mellow voice that was very warm and created an atmosphere that was magical.

Phoebe and Seb were cuddled up to Rosamund and she was constantly making them laugh. They all had blankets wrapped round them for extra warmth. It was wonderful.

'Oh I think I am pregnant.' Rosamund cried as she had another bout of pain wrench through her body. She was getting wind more and more, and tried to make light of it.

Shem spat his tea out all over and Rafe, nearly choked, and the children fell about laughing. Rosamund rocked back letting the wind flow freely and covered her month in both shame and laughter.

'You smelly cow.' Her old friend Bob remarked. She went to smack him, but knew he was too far away to reach.

'Nanny you stink.' Seb giggled shaking his head.

'What, don't you fart?' She asked him.

'You said a bad word.' He cried.

'Oh will someone control the woman.' Bob moaned.

Seb suppressed a giggle. 'Nanny, it was just abit loud.'

'Can we change the subject?' Bob was struggling.

'What your shit don't stink?'

'It's abit off, we have just eaten.'

They continued with their banter until Daisy decided it was way past the children's bedtime.

Rosie had watched as Rafe had got up and given Daisy a warm goodnight kiss and a tender cuddle, which was so sweet. He had whispered in her ear, which had made her smile dreamily. Rosie also smiled, imagining the implication and laughed as Rafe then shuffled across to her and winked. She grinned at him and whacked him playfully with her hand. She sat cross-legged wrapped in a wool blanket and he lay on the floor next to her.

'Do that again!' He pleaded.

Shem looked across at them and shook his head at his brother, not being able to hear the conversation but guess at what Rafe was about.

'He is so jealous. Look at him checking me out. What's he think I'm gonna do run away with ya? I've got two on the go as it is, I couldn't manage three, well I can, you're up for it?'

He had rested himself on his elbow and crossed his legs. He looked up longingly at her with his sad eyes with that mischievous grin just surfacing. God, Rosie thought, this man is a vision, like one of those beautiful angels you see on the glass in the churches.

'Make out ya loving it and I bet he starts to get agitated. You know when he does, he starts to snarl, and these horns came out the top of his head and his eyes go red.' Rafe teased.

'Stop, being so wicked!' She was openly laughing and it felt good, she had missed them when they had been away for an age.

'Go on, let's wind him up, lean down as if I am whispering sweet nothings.' What she did was smack him again. 'Oh do it harder, I say I don't like it rough, but I love it coming from you.'

Both looked across like naughty children waiting to be scolded. Shem was having an in depth conversation with Bob, and he had not sprouted horns, however Rosie did catch his eye.

'God, you've got him wrapped round your little finger ain't ya?'

'I wouldn't say that.' She was still laughing. His magic was working.

'I would, I should know.'

She looked away in embarrassment; her cheeks were already red with warmth from the fire, now her whole face was alight.

'Stop pretending to be so timid. I hear you got a right mouth on ya.'

'Who told ya that?' She watched him shrug and then laugh at her.

'I have heard you give it off.' He confessed.

'Rubbish!' He looked at her knowingly and saying, who are you trying to kid?

'So, pray tell, why haven't you given it off to Valentina?' Obviously, Daisy had been filling him in on the goings on and his tone was mocking in jest.

'Because that's what she wants.' Rosie's gaze went back to Shem. She wanted to add, *I want more than to have words, I want to beat her senseless!*

'So you know she used to share Shem's bed.' Would she be shocked at his frankness?

'I know now.' Rafe laughed at that. He knew better.

'Women and their jealousy!' Rosie blushed again.

'She's just been fishing for information on me and not exactly been directly horrible, but just pushing it. I'm the one who has been a cow.'

'How, so?'

'It doesn't matter.'

'No, you can't start something and then bow out.'

He was right. He sat up and nudged her for encouragement. Why was she telling him all this? He certainly had a way about him. She found she was opening up to him and she wanted to off load it all. She carried too much and it was becoming too heavy a burden.

'When I was ill in bed, she came in and tried to flirt with him.'

'Oh, it all makes sense now. He's been banging his head against a brick wall, trying to fathom out what he has done wrong. He told me that she'd visited him and he was pissed as hell about that.' Rafe became serious now. 'So that's also why you've been giving him a hard time?' She felt like a fool.

'I was hardly a saint me self.' She offered. 'Well, I used to be with William Devereux.'

'I had heard. But come on, you were a one-man girl.' He winked at her.

'Yeah, one man at a time.' They both burst out laughing at her implication and innuendo. She covered her face with her hands in embarrassment at her forwardness.

'God, you're as bad as me, you whore.' He mocked and tried to avoid the smack. This time Shem stared right at them.

'No one can be as bad as you.' She giggled.

'You don't know the half of it!' She looked lovely when she smiled and Rafe was glad he had encouraged that. 'But seriously you need to make that man over there happy.' He could see why Shem called her his pixie.

'It's not that easy.' She looked down into her lap and unconsciously stroked her scar.

'I know, but promise me you'll try.' He encouraged being serious.

'I can't, I just want to smack him one.' She whispered sweetly at which Rafe roared again. He really liked her and could see why she and Shem would be so good together again if only they would both stop being so silly.

'You do have violent issues, my arms killing me. Saucy mare!'

'Could you flirt anymore?' Shem was right on him when Rosie had retired for the night.

'Jealous are ya?'

'Fuck off plep!'

'Ohhh Shemmy is jealous, your girlfriend prefers me.' Rafe sung. Rosamund looked cross and warned him to stop.

'Say another word, prat.' Rafe laughed at him.

'God, you are so similar, that's twice tonight I've been abused. Do you see the bruises your woman's given me?' He held out his arm, which was a mistake; Shem grabbed it and pinched him.

'You bastard, you're such a bully. Do ya see what he has done?' He looked across to Rosamund for help.

'I'll do more than that, prat, you keep on. What did she say?'

'Why?' Rafe was going to milk it.

'What do you mean why, because I want to know?'

'She said you were a dirty scum bag idiot, who snores, has smelly feet and the manners of an alley cat.' Shem gave out a heavy sigh and Rafe was very surprised that he hadn't swung for him. Rosamund sucked in her cheeks and wanted to laugh.

'I am trying to have an adult conversation.' Shem groaned through gritted teeth.

'Then stop acting like a love sick fool and confront the woman then.' Rafe waited for the comeback.

'You're right, I will.' Rafe and Rosamund looked in surprise at each other. Shem had

lowered his head to his chest in defeat. The whole thing was so out of character. Rafe waited to see what his brother would do. As Shem made to get up, so did he.

'Not now, it's too late, there all be asleep?' He held his arms out to stop Shem from going in.

'Alright plep, I wasn't gonna do it straight away.'

'Well, I'll make sure to keep clear in the morning, bound to get messy.' Rafe warned still not convinced that Shem was genuine.

'I won't do it first thing.' Shem seemed to cob out; he went and stood by the fire with Rosamund to watch the flames fizzle away. 'Then when?' Rafe wanted to know and knew as soon as the words left his mouth that he should have kept quiet.

'Stop pressuring me for God's sake.' Shem shouted at him. Rosamund looked from one to the other. They were both acting like young teenagers and at that point, Shem decided he had had enough and was making for bed hoping that Rosie and

Seb would have already settled for the night.

'You chicken shit!' again the words just seemed to spill out.

Shem turned back to him and in his low voice warned. 'Say another word, go on.'

At which Rafe proceeded to act like a chicken and start to flap his arms like wings, mocking him. Shem did not move an inch; he just looked at Rafe as if he was a simpleton. Rafe continued to dance around, others started to take heed, and Rosamund was suppressing a chuckle. Shem could not take it and went to dart after Rafe, but one yell from Rosamund was enough to stop them in their tracks.

'Both of you, to bed now.' She warned. Shem obliged and Rafe stayed to grovel.


It had been raining; she had run for cover, laughing as she did. She had only a few hundred yards to go to get to the Coach House along the lane when the heavens had opened and a downpour had made its entrance.

The rain pounded heavily against the ground, bouncing back up and splattering everywhere. She framed herself under a huge oak and smiled as trickles of rain managed to find their way through the thick canopy and land on her face.

Not two minutes before the sun had been out, now a horrendous black cloud glided past in all its glory. The sun was peaking through and promising to emerge any minute now. When it did, she looked up for a rainbow and at the same time continued her journey down the high street, passing the Old Mint House.

It was a beautiful large half-timbered country house with apparently over twenty rooms, all rich in oak beams in an excellent state of preservation. She remembered the long nights of her recovery and Shem speaking to her long into the night and telling her all the old stories associated with the place. He said that Edward IV stayed here in the 1540's for the benefit of his health. He relayed the story about the Mint House Ghost. All she could think about was how many whores worked in that place. It was massive!

She laughed when Shem had told her the story about the ghost hoping it was true and scared Valentina senseless. Apparently, over a hundred years ago a certain London merchant had rented the Old Mint House from its then owner, and came to live in Pevensey with his mistress. All went well until one night he returned unexpectedly, to find the woman in the arms of her lover. Furious with jealousy, he had them both seized, and then cut out the woman's tongue, (Rosie liked that idea for Valentina). He hung the lover in chains from the ceiling and then made a fire underneath him, and made his Mistress watch her lover's death and his agony, as he died slowly from the smoke and heat. Then, the London Merchant left the woman with hands and feet tied, to die a lingering death of starvation. Again, Rosie could see herself doing just that to the Spanish Whore.

She was still daydreaming when the great oak door was flung open and Valentina walked out of the Mint House and smiled mischievously at her.

That's all she needed!

Valentina tutted in utter disgust at her and with her face displaying such at Rosie, she looked her up and down. It did not help that Valentina looked gorgeous, whereas her hair and clothes all clung to her and she knew she looked a state. Valentina wore beautiful pale blue silk Mantua dress with hand stitched silver patterns of fantastic fruits and leaves all over. Rosie felt her back go up and hated the woman more and more.

'He must have to close his eyes.' Valentina purred as she stood and crossed her arms and laughed in Rosie's face. Every fibre of Rosie wanted to smack her right then at that insult but she knew that is exactly what the woman wanted, she tried hard not to give her the satisfaction. But she was already lost.

'You may think that you have him, but it's only a matter of time before he understands that he needs a proper woman, not some haggard old scarred up monster, that he feels sorry for.' Valentina spat at her, 'He'll be back in my bed before you know it.' She swaggered in confidence.

'Glad for ya, when's the wedding?' Rosie remembered they were just words, where was the opening so she could just smash her one. Who was this woman to start mouthing off at her? She wasn't doing well with trying to control her anger.

'You may mock, but you know it's true. I mean look at you.' She felt Valentina's eyes all over her and was conscious that compared to her she really was not looking quite so good. 'You are a disfigured ugly, scarred up mare!'

'And you are a cruel, bitter, flea infested rank whore.' Rosie wasn't helping herself and knew she needed to walk away right that minute.

'Yet beautiful,' she purred. 'I am an expert in the arts of love and I can seduce whoever I desire. Who would wish to wake up to that face each morning? Jesus the very thought makes me want to heave and let's be honest, the Laudanum did not really block out your nightmares, I swear I can still hear you still scream in torment about the little rape. Or are they the screams of ecstasy at what you have been missing all these years? Oh go on, admit it, you liked it rough.'

'Talking from experience ya sick smelly minged simpleton.' Rosie started to move forward. Valentina should have known better!

'Tut, tut. Shame on you. You have a vulgar mouth. If you can't take it, don't dish it out. You will not go to heaven.' Valentina laughed again in her face.

Rosie found that her first punch collided into the woman's left ear without her thinking about it. As Valentina lost her balance, (as Rosie knew she would), she followed through with a left hook up to her chin. The woman fell on her backside and Rosie found herself stamping and kicking her. She laughed as Valentina had fallen bum first into a puddle and her dress was caked in mud. It was a shame, it was a lovely dress, but the whore who wore it, was wicked, and needed to be taught a lesson.

Rosie's brothers had taught her how to fight well and with no regard for her own health, having not completely healed yet, she just let rip. She revelled in the moment. She was like a mad woman possessed.

Valentina was screaming in terror, not believing that the invalid as she believed, was ever capable of physically retaliating. It was just like her to pick on the weak and feeble and assume she would triumph.

From nowhere, there was a sudden roar of voices and dogs barking, pure strength grabbed Rosie from behind and literally hauled her up, and she found Paully shoving her away. She lost her balance and fell to her knees growling and getting quickly back on her feet to attack again. Paully had swung back round, hearing her and waited for her to pounce. He could not believe the strength of the little mite and started to laugh at the wild cat as she started to kick and lay punches on him. Earl was barking insanely.

'Now, now Rosie that isn't fair. Behave or I'll have to chin ya myself. Enough!' He could not believe that this little one had just recovered from a near death experience and was dishing out some serious beatings. 'Get that fucking whore outta here?' He called over his shoulder whilst still trying to control Rosie as gently as he could.

Jesus had also appeared and proceeded to manhandle Valentina, who now turned and spat verbal abuse at him. The look on his face was enough to convey how much he detested the woman, whose morals, he so deposed. In touching and breathing the same air as such evil, he would have to clean himself in holy water and rid the stench of the devils spawn.

Paully found himself shouting towards the Castle Inn, and after a fashion Gideon come out having been alerted to the commotion.

He was huffing and buffing as he made his way through the puddles and pretended to be more annoyed than he really felt at Jesus holding his wife in locked arms. She was trying to turn and spit at Jesus and across the way he mused that Paully was being whirled around and round with Rosie who was giving him such a hard time, screaming that she would kill them all unless he let her go. She had punched, kicked, tried to knee him between the legs, and even stamped his foot twice. She was a wild cat.

The commotion had caught the attention of the occupants of the Mint House and heads could be seen peering out to be nosey. Men were pouring out of the Inn when they heard an almighty scream from Daisy, who had also come to see what was going on, she fell to her knees clutching her stomach.

Gideon turned back and covered his eyes with his hands, having just witnessed all too clearly that poor Daisy's waters had broken. He backed away feeling quite ill and then focused his full attention on Jesus trying to throw Valentina back into her front door of the Mint House. He did not like the way Jesus' hands seem to be roaming all over her!

'Oi, get your hands off her.' Jesus did exactly that and Valentina fell again to the floor with a thud.

'You wanna keep this dog on a lead, she is one spiteful evil piece of work, and if I ever have to sort her out again, I will have no hesitation in just carving the bitch up. You need to keep your whore in tow and pray for this wretched soul's forgiveness. She'll go to Hell, mark my words.' Jesus then proceeded to spit in her face. Gideon could not believe that his old friend would embarrass him so but then he had done that to himself a long time ago, by marrying a woman half his age, who clearly had just wanted his money. She had been a whore then and he thought that he could change her. But he could not give her what she wanted, so he just let her get on with it. He was a spineless fool and now she had further embarrassed him.

'What have you done now you stupid bitch?' Jesus heard Gideon moaning as he walloped Valentina and slumped shut the front door as he physically pulled her to the Mint House. Jesus proceeded to the Coach house where Daisy had been carried back into.

The Coach house was in chaos. It was bedlam. Paully was walking backward and forward and Daisy was screaming on the floor. He wanted to be given permission to just run away and leave the women to it. Rosie was now busy comforting Daisy who was curled up.

'Paully, my love, would you be so good as to take Daisy up stairs to her room. Oh, there you are Jesus, could you take over, the lunch time coach is due any minute.' He nodded at Chrissy.

Paully lifted Daisy up as if she was no weight at all, he was desperately trying not to look at her and pretend he was anywhere else than there. He could not wait to get her in her room, make sure she was comfortable, and then run!

Jesus had never heard Daisy with a raised voice and to hear her now scream the house down was just too much. It just couldn't be done! He needed to escape and by overseeing the coach that was due any minute now was a God send. The relief on his face was a picture.


'Why are you siding with that whore?'

'I was not.' Shem knew this was not the right time; he should have ignored Rafe's advice and just confronted Rosie the previous evening when he didn't feel so vulnerable. Rosie managed to make him just want to either throttle her or just cuddle her up and say anything to make her happy. He had already started on the wrong foot and he knew it would not end well. He had caught her just after Daisy had given birth to a boy and Rafe was allowed in to visit. Rosie had closed the door and found Shem waiting for her. She looked exhausted and blood had soaked through to her under dress. Her hair was everywhere and she needed a good hot bath. She wanted to melt into his arms, but he gestured for her to follow him down the small hallway.

They had manoeuvred into their room, both just seemed to stare into space for an age, and then he had asked her to tell him what had happened.

They could hear that everyone else was in high spirits and a celebration was just starting down at The Castle Inn. They should be celebrating too and putting all this behind them. However, he had broken the spell and had annoyed her straight away.

'Looks like it to me.' They were facing each other now.

'Will you let me get a word in woman?' His voice was that low menacing tone.

'She starts on me, I plant one on her, and I'm the one in the wrong.' He had always been proud of her being feisty but sometimes, she took it too far.

'You still haven't told me why you hit her.' It was becoming harder to not loss it with her when she was like this!

'Fuck you; I dunno who you think you are?' She flung at him and then Shem checked himself and the whole episode was absurd and he realised he wanted to laugh.

'I'm trying to be patient here.' He knew if he laughed at her then, she would have no hesitation, so he suppressed his grin.

'No, what you are doing is trying to keep your whore sweet.' She fired at him standing before him with her hands on her hips.

'She ain't my whore. For Gods sakes woman, can't we just get over this?' He flung his head back and his eyes to the sky in frustration. How was it that this woman could get so under his skin that he did not know whether to laugh or cry?

'Over what?'

'All of this.' She knew exactly what he referred to but she was not going to give in that easily. She deliberated avoided that conversation.

'Side with her, go on then. You are a fucking joke. I hate you.' She had lost it now and he knew he would not be able to contain himself. 'Do you hear? I fucking hate you.' She just had to have another dig and found that she had really worked herself up now and was screaming at the top of her voice. His mood soon changed back.

'Then fuck off then.' He thought that would do it, he was at the end of his tether and if she was fit enough now to be lording it about and flinging punches, then she would get as good as she got. There would be no more walking on tiptoe around her now. Over the last few days, she didn't appear to be too ill, she looked like she was having too much fun and she certainly had got her voice back. He would not let anyone say he had gone soft for a woman, but wasn't that the truth of the matter?

'I will.'

'Go now; go on, there's the door.' *That would show her*, he thought. He moved away from the door to give her room to pass and actually bowed to the door mocking her.

'I will.' She went to leave but could not resist just having one last dig at him and she knew she would have him. 'You think you'll see me or my son again, you got another thing coming.' He looked up to the sky for help and shook his head at her in disappointment. His foul mood returned. His glare would have frozen most. Would she use that argument again when she come off worse?

'You will not take my son.' He groaned. She knew she had taken it too far she stepped back.

'Who said he was yours?' She could be so spiteful when she wanted to.

'Don't.' He warned and stepped towards her in threat.

'Don't, don't.' She mocked him. 'What you gonna do? Hit me? Well, you have already tried to kill me and put me out of me misery, so bring it on.' She actually then swaggered forward facing him. She then thought better of it and started to move back when she read his face. His eyes were now no more than slits and wholly black and his face had taken on that sternness. He could not believe that she could go that low.

'Is this what all this is about?' He barked. She made to move. He came towards her. She stopped.

At one moment he was quite proud of her for being so brave and standing up to him, the next he did not yet know whether he'd just knock her one or not. She made him so mad. He was agitated.

'I ain't got time for this. I need to leave.' She felt her insides start to panic. She knew she had pushed it too far.

'You ain't going anywhere until we have this out.'

'Over my dead body! Just piss off and let me pass.' She wanted to just run now.

'I'm warning you. Don't push ya luck.'

'You can't make me do anything; I ain't one of your luggies.' She just had to have the last word. She pushed towards him and he grabbed her arm. Her whole arm was alight with fire. His hold was firm and there was no way he would let go.

'Don't you dare touch me?' She roared more in anger at herself than him. She had worked herself up and was frightened of the intensity of his touch on her skin. He always made her tingle with such delight, but this time, it was more, it was hot! Smouldering. She felt her whole body start to burn. He let her go. She jumped away from him and looked away in embarrassment.

Both of them did not quite know what to do. She felt his presence behind her and his breath on her neck. This time there was no touch, just the nearness. She would not turn. She could not. Then he backed away and she felt him leave.

She let her shoulders drop and almost crumbled to the floor. She listened as he descended the stairs just hoping he would stop and come back.

She stood for a while just looking into space catching her breath.

She felt a lump in her throat. She could not cope. She was going mad. He had cared for her and looked after her and she had treated him so badly.

It was all that dreadful woman's fault. The woman had made her feel like a fool and deliberately had wound her up. Why had the woman been so cruel? She nodded knowing full well, that it was herself that was the problem. She had nothing to offer him. Valentina was beautiful and made her feel ugly. She was jealous and resentful. She placed her hand over her scar and then sat on the bed and twisted her skirt in her hands. So this was what she was to expect? Was everyone looking at her in pity? Was that all he had left for her? She was feeling sorry for herself and should have known better.

She needed to clear the air, and she needed to do it now. She raced from the room, half falling down the stairs and did not hear when Chrissy called after her.

Chrissy had heard everything and knew exactly how the argument had started with Valentina. Rosie needed to be reined in and if she caused a further row with Shem, she dreaded to think what would happen. Shem only had so much patience.

She flew out of the door and run around the courtyard to the front, she had to explain why she had the courage otherwise the self-hate would fester and she had to make it go away. In that, she needed his help.

'Jesus, Mary, and Christ! It's him!' Shem stopped in his tracks. 'Is he taking the piss?' Shem had been mad when he had left Rosie, but now the newcomer had further fuelled his anger. He went to walk forward to confront the man looking as if he lorded it over the whole county. Bob then appeared, grabbed his arm, and yanked him back. He hated it when Shem went off on one.

'Shem leave it.' Bob hissed.

He stopped then and watched as William Devereux got off his horse outside The Castle Inn, which stood a few hundred yards down the road from the Coach House. Shem turned back to the Coach House and looked to check and make sure Rosie wasn't planning to come down and finish their conversation and thump him, if she was playing to form.

He and Bob skirted around the side of the Alehouse, where Shem signalled Paully to stay there and watch where the man was going.

'She can't see him.' Shem whispered in annoyance.

'I know.' Bob agreed. He watched Shem calculate and then advise what was to be done, but it was all in vain, Rosie walked out of the back door of the Coach House and soon would be in William's vision if he turned, but as Shem walked to divert her, she froze. Next minute she was physically picked up and carted off by Shem. He could not believe that he had read her so correctly. He heard from behind as Paully headed towards William, outside The Castle Inn.

'What do you want here young Master William?'

'Just stay put.' Shem snarled. He had thrown her back onto the bed where they had just come from and followed her. It had all happened in a few seconds. She had not stopped wriggling and fighting him all the way up the stairs and he would make her stop moving if it was the last thing he did. She needed to know who the boss was. He grabbed both her hands and spread them out. She was powerless under all his weight

She froze, and closed her eyes to it all. She could not believe that William was there. She could not believe that Shem had physically grabbed her and thrown her on the bed. Then she started to panic.

'You're hurting me.' She half whispered not knowing whether still to be angry or grateful that he had rescued her from seeing William at this stage but also afraid as to the memories that were creeping in. Her insides started to cramp.

*I'll will hurt you in a minute if you don't just shut up.* Was what he wanted to say but then he adjusted his weight but found this made matters worse. *No, that's my prick getting hard woman.* He had managed to get himself well and truly tangled up now.

'Oh my God.' He let out and she felt him catch his breath. He tried to get up and started to, but then just froze in mid air. He could not look at her.

She could not open her eyes and tried to control her breathing. This was turning from bad to worse! Her whole body was on fire.

He just did not want to get up and let her go.

Her insides screamed.

'Just please don't move' He found himself whispering. He could feel every bone in her body shake, her breathing becoming erratic and he was sure that she was about to have a fit. She was holding on in sheer panic. What was he thinking? He remembered and felt completely stupid. She must be so frightened. He wanted so much to just crush her to him and make all the madness go away.

'Rosie, you know I would never hurt you.' Everything seemed to disappear, it was just them. William's appearance faded in the distance. It really did not matter. She felt his breath against her chin and she started to count out her own breathing.

They both seemed to relax in time.

She slowly opened her eyes and met his gaze. They had turned that smouldering green. His breathing too had become erratic and both just heard and felt each other's every movement. It was getting warm, so warm.

She licked her lips and let out a long breath closing her eyes again. She had to regain her composure. She could not endure looking at him. She could not feel this way after all that had happened to her. It was wrong. It was so wrong! She concentrated on just focusing on him.

He groaned when she licked her lips and felt his whole body just mould into hers. Like a gentle breeze flattering at her face, he lowered his lips. She opened her eyes and his loving face astounded her.

'I've been a cow.' She whispered letting the tears prickle her eyes. He shook his head at her smiling in reassurance.

'Nothing new there then?' And with that, he kissed her

'Hello William. What are you doing here?'

'I heard Shem wanted to see me.' William had his hands on his hips looking all about him and he really did look like the lord of the manor. He wore a practical knee length coat, which was of dark navy wool with just some black embroidery around the cuffs and back of the neck. His waistcoat and trousers matched and his hair was matted and everywhere from riding.

'You took ya fucking time.' He laughed at him, and then remarked, 'he ain't here.'

'I want to see him.' William said definitely.

'Then you've come along way for nothing. Bye then.' Paully headed into the pub. He thought William had the cheek of the devil.

'Is Bob here?' William conceded and followed him in.

'How's ya Dad holding up?' Paully asked. Claude raised his eyes knowing what was coming. He had joined them and they all sat down. Gideon brought over some drinks. Claude thanked him.

'He is well, thank you for asking.' William's attention was slightly diverted to the merriment about, there appeared to be a celebration going on. He did not want them to know how bad his relationship with his father had become. 'Not getting too stressed with it all then?'

'God man, with what?' William should have known by now what Paully was like. They had never got on and all too quickly, he lost patience with him.

'The debts?'

'What debts?'

'Your Dad has mortgaged the Hall to the hilt. So it won't be home for too long. Did ya Dad not tell ya he has a bad gambling habit? Oh and who holds the loan? Could it be my father? No could it be Meir the Jew, or, oh let me think. Could it possibly be me?'

'You liar!'

'Paully behave.' Claude warned suppressing a grin at his friend's antics. Shaking his head and thinking to himself that Paully was an idiot!

'You do know that I am richer than Midas. I have more money than you ever will, in fact I'm richer than my father. In fact everyone is. Does it grate me that I am his only son, and that I will not ever have the title? Couldn't give a fuck! But you, 'ole Willy you. Grates you, don't it? What are you third in line? Had to get work somehow didn't ya? You always wanted to be a gentleman. Not a vile peasant hey? Not low born like me. Did I say my mother is a Parsons daughter, seventh son to old Cromwell's third daughter? Or is that second?'

William just looked at Paully in bewilderment. He never knew how to take him, but he did know that with a flick of a coin Paully's mood could change and whereby one minute he could be making fun of you, the next he could be kicking you to death. He tried desperately not to show how much Paully affected him.

'Oh let me kill him.' Paully mocked at Claude bringing his hands up in a prayer. Claude glared at him for having far too much fun.

'What is going on?' William was not happy and fighting for control. All he wanted to do, was just run now, his bravado at coming to the lion's den was fading fast. It perhaps had not been one of his best ideas to come on his own. His impulsiveness would kill him one day!

'William, William, you been a naughty boy. But we are prepared to let it slide if you play ball.' Bob joined them and sat down frowning. The men exchanged nods of greeting. Why was everyone talking to him as if he was a naughty child?

'What are you talking about?'

'You been doing the dirty behind our backs. Bringing in shipments that haven't been agreed, you been mugging us and your friends off, boy. Been bragging about getting one over on us also ain't ya? You know what I mean?' William sat back and sighed, they knew everything, and he was trapped. Gideon brought over Bob a drink and watched as he had a sip and nodded his appreciation.

'Listen, I ...'

'Shut the fuck up. You're lucky you ain't dead already; it's only out of respect for

Shaun you're not. Now, tell us, have you spoken to your new friend Hartright shithead lately?' Paully spat impatiently.

William was astounded at the way the conversation was going. They had been playing him. It all seemed to fall into place now. What was the point in denying any of it? He had one thing up his sleeve, and that was luck. He was lucky to still be breathing, if they had wanted him dead, he would be. They needed him for something and there it was!

'If you mean Hartright. He is in London. He is being re deployed or something.' The truth came easy. If it meant him being spared, he'd give them everything back. He let them all see how defeated he was and his shoulders slumped.

'We know that, you not heard from him lately, you must know that his sister is with him? He not tell ya that Shem went to see him and introduced him to his pal, Luca. Nice, big man, liked Hartright's bum, if you know what I mean.'

'You heard that Clay and Hartright's men have gone missing, dead?' Claude flung into the mix.

'Like's his sister too I hear.' Paully added in a rather suggestive voice.

'What did you just say?' William found his attention being drawn from one to the other. Too much going on and only now was he digesting what they had flung at him. Reality dawned on what Paully had implied. 'That's disgusting, take that back.' William automatically shouted, forgetting he was scared, in the lion's den and perhaps on the brink of getting his balls cut off. He rose to his feet.

'Sit down.' Bob ordered in a bored expression. He found he had no real time for the pup after all.

'Like the rape and murder that Hartright has just committed in the name of duty.' Paully continued.

'What are you talking about? Hartright has been working on some tip offs just recently.'

'So that's a no to knowing about the rape and murder? Do your servants not talk?'

'How can you defend him?' Claude queried disgustedly. Their double act worked to perfection in bombarding William with questions. 'You're an idiot.'

'What are you talking about?' William kept looking from one to the other.

'Did you not put two and two together or is that too hard for your pretty head?

Even I sussed it and that's saying something'

'What?'

'Aunt Hattie and Rosie Cavendish's death? Is that a coincidence?'

'What?'

'Where you been boy? Too, wrapped up in shagging that whore to notice anything? Where you been for your friends? You have completely fucked up and been made to look a fool.' He roared at him.

William could not believe what he was hearing. He could not comprehend what their purpose was. One minute he was angry, then frightened. What was going on?

'You're saying that Hartright raped and killed Rosie. That he killed the other lady, Nana's sister? It was a fire, an accident?' He looked at Bob for confirmation. This was all too much. He sat back in his chair and wiped his hand across his face. He could not believe what they were saying.

'You've been warned William and I'm telling you, you breathe a word of this to anyone and I will kill you.' Paully smiled in pure pleasure at the thought.

'Now you go home and we'll be in touch. Don't do anything like let silly bollocks know.' Claude added.

'Hartright's been mugging you off severely. You may wanna watch Constance and her lovely room, bribe her lovely maid. Maisy is it? Because believe me when I tell ya, they do shag when you're not there. They have been, since they were kids. It's also rumoured that Constance got her Uncle to help her kill her first husband as he caught them also in bed. Well dodgy family, mate! So watch ya back. My sister Bella knows someone in service up London and her sister was once Constance's maid. But she was let go, when the old man was killed off.' William should never have come, he should have just run and got on a boat and gone to the new world.

'You're in league with a woman who swings both ways and assists with rapist and murdering .......Oh and by the way we know it was you who grassed on Rafe.' William could not hold any more information in and found his head swimming. 'We told the Cavendish's it was a fire that killed the ladies, to save them any further stress.' William heard and tried to reason with himself, and slowly he started to see the picture. 'Hartright had beaten, tortured, and repeatedly raped Rosie. They hung her up like a piece of meat. Then they set fire to the cottage because someone had told them that Hattie was a supporter.' Paully moved closer to William for full affect. 'That poor old cow, Hattie's cargo had long since been moved, so Hartright was a bit pissed at that so needed to take his revenge on someone!' Paully snapped and William felt like his head was going to explode. He could have been half way across the ocean by now.

'You should have stayed with those who loved and cared for you. You took the wrong turning, what you gonna do now boy?' Bob asked quietly.

William just sat there. His mouth aghast. He felt cold all over. He shivered in fear. What had he done? Hartright had persuaded him to join forces, explore new territories, and leave his friends behind. Now he had been made to look like a deserter, even Paully said people were saying it was him who had got Rafe attacked and kidnapped. That was a lie. Paully was winding him up, and by God, he had. He had let people down, he had let himself down. His mind was a whirl of questions. Had he helped get Rosie killed? He could not face that guilt. What was he going to do?

'I'll kill him.' He whispered. How dare Hartright touch her! That's what they wanted wasn't it? He had come looking for a way out and that would be the price he would have to pay. He was their weapon. He had played into their hands.

'No, William.' He heard Bob say softly as if he was talking to a child. William's eyes were closed to it all. 'You will go home, speak to Shaun. You will hand over a percentage of your mark up to us from now and bring the Cavendish brother's in on the deal, you need them more than ever boy, as well as the extra protection. Later we will discuss when you can start a new life in the Americas.' How did Bob know that that was what he wanted more than anything in the world? He opened his eyes and looked at Bob dumbfounded. Who did he believe?

What were they hoping to achieve?

What had he got himself into?

Would they really let him leave?

Hartright had touched her, and he would kill him.

What must Ned and Ray really think of him now? They must know? Surely, they had a right to know everything?

What was Shem's game?

How could they say such bad things about Constance?

He had been a fool to think he could ever have bested any of them. He needed to talk with Shaun.

'Sir, sir, sir, you can't just barge in there.' Maisy shrieked as she chased after him up the flight of stairs. Mr. Devereux knew exactly where he was going.

'I am not waiting around.' He barked at the girl. She jumped back in astonishment at his tone. Tears pricked her eyes. He blotted through the door.

'Well, well, what do we have here?' Constance smirked sarcastically as she rose from the bed where she had been laying with Hartright. Hartright looked terrible and had the sheets and blankets up high over his chest. Constance was fully clothed and above the bed but had been lying across his chest with his arms wrapped around her. She gave Maisy a menacing look as she bent forward and grabbed the door handle to shut the door.

'William! William, so delightful to see you.' Hartright called feebly even though William had the cheek to come gatecrashing into his private rooms.

'What are you doing in your brother's bedroom?' He totally ignored Hartright and looked directly at Constance. His heart was pounding in fury. She was a bitch and laughing at him along with everyone else.

'Perhaps we can discuss this down stairs?' Constance's tone was very calm and almost dismissive of his feelings. She always made him feel that he had to try that bit harder. He hated her.

'William, William, you must help me,' Hartright started and seemed to totally ignore his question to Constance, 'Shem is after me, he's killed Clay and the men have gone missing. He thinks I killed that old woman and my troop raped the other one!'

'Did you?' His full attention was on him now and William did not like what he saw or how he felt. He wanted to kill this man. He had been made to look a fool by this imbecile who was curled up with his sister, like some sad puppy dog looking for affection and love. He really was quite pathetic. How could he not believe what he had been told, and these two here would spin any lie to save themselves? In a rage, he had made straight for London looking for answers.

'God how stupid do you think I am?' Hartright acted all hurt and wounded. 'I know my limitations and yes, I have been a little over zealous and gone abit overboard but all the call of duty. Come on, if I had been that bad Lord Lennard would have booted me out long ago.' He dare not mention that Lennard was gunning for him and his dear Uncle Secomb was fighting for his reputation.

'I think you need to leave my brother alone now, you can see he is not well, and you barge in here, with all sorts of accusations, showing no respect. I say William, it is not on.'

'No! No, Constance, please, he is my friend. It is understandable how he must be feeling, with everyone flinging accusations. It was so kind of you to come.' Hartright rested back on the pillows, the effort of talking making him weak. William thought he would be sick.

'We will leave you my love.' Constance manoeuvred William out of the room.

William had no idea what was happening. His mind whirled. He did not want this woman to touch him.

They had retired to the drawing room of the London home and were not impressed that the maid had still not yet offered him tea. The fire was slowly dying and there was no wood in the basket to re kindle the flames. He was exhausted from the trip and with his mind running rings. He needed time to get his facts straight and confront her, but he was too mad and seeing Hartright's little performance had made him wish to vomit.

The house looked in disarray but as ever Constance had made a special effect with her toilet. She smelled so good that he could have almost forgotten his purpose and just lost himself in that wonderful aroma. He was so tired of it all. He would not look directly at her.

'As you quite clearly saw for yourself, he is ill,' Constance spat at him, she was not best pleased. 'He has suffered a savage attack and what with that business with Clay.' She looked long into the fire. 'The Magistrates are after him for questioning. Your father has written for an explanation, as well as Lord Essex. Everyone is gunning for him. I daren't tell him that his men have also been murdered. My God William, he needs me.'

'To be at his beck and call, every hour and every day?' William spat, he was mad at being so humiliated. Hartright must have brought this all on himself. Constance did not like this William; it would not appear to be that easy this time to win him over with her charms. He had no idea of what she referred to about Clay and really did not care, he was just so livid.

'Would you not do the same for your brothers and sisters?'

'There are Doctors for that!' He replied flippantly.

'Perhaps that answers why you are not so close to any of your brothers and sisters.'

'Please do not insult me any more Constance or try to twist matters.' He looked away through the window, hoping to catch something resembling normality.

'My love, sit down relax, you have travelled far and we have not even greeted each other properly yet. My God man, we are to be married.' Constance was trying very hard to contain herself. He had burst into her brother's room, suggesting indecency and flung at her that she had been rude!

William physically shuddered at her suggestion that they were to be married and remembered everything that had happened. Why had he come? He should have stayed put until he could make sense of it all, but no, he had rushed off, and been impulsive. Why had he just not listened to Shaun's advice?

Constance looked longingly at him and decided she was not about to lose him. He was a Devereux, although not the next heir, his name, and family statue could not be surpassed. She needed this. She casually sat down and looked towards the fire that desperately needed attention. Whatever it took to save her relationship with William, she would try. 'What do you want from me?' She decided to act demure.

'I want the truth.'

'He needed comfort.' She laughed dismissively at him as if he were mad and had seen nothing that was wrong. She gave it one last shot. 'He has been attacked by that mad man.'

'You expect me to believe that?' Yet he knew it was true but she deliberately flung it out there to deflect from the truth.

'Darling, please, I love you.' He stepped back at that, as if he had been slapped in the face. He could not believe the lies that spilled from her mouth. He heard her approach and she caught his hand, he flicked it away, feeling bile rise in his throat.

'God, I detest you. I have to leave. The sight of you disgusts me.' He could not contain himself anymore. This was madness. He was backing away.

'My love, what has got into you? How can you say such horrid things?' She tried to come to him again. 'I am not ashamed to say that I love Hartright. He is my brother.'

'I love my brothers and sisters, but you don't see me coupling with them.' He spat and just could not look at her. He had said it and he wanted to be sick. 'You have disgraced me, humiliated me. I don't know how I will go on.' Constance stopped in her tracks. So there it was. They both stood for a while lost in their own thoughts. She had lost him. What was the point in enduring anymore of this farce?

'Oh I'm sure you will.' She drawled and her mood turned in an instance. 'Look at you William.' Her voice had become stronger, not so pleading. She swaggered towards her drinks cabinet and poured herself a huge brandy, a gift from Hartright, with a smug look on her evil face.

'Oh don't worry. You will soon have someone else swooning at your side, or indulge with some low base trollop. Let's face it; you are such a pretty little thing.' She snarled gulping her drink in one. He could not believe she could be so unladylike. 'I was good for you. I taught you things you could never imagine possible. And I warn you, you will not wish to make accusations about my character, unlike my brother, who needs to be pushed into doing anything; I will not have my reputation put into jeopardy by the likes of you.' He started to laugh then at that, the absurdity of the woman. She did not like that at all.

'How dare you stand there and assume you can threaten me. You have no idea.' He sighed with relief that the cloud he had hanging over him had finally dispersed. She was a manipulated, selfish incestuous whore! 'I can't stand the sight of you.' He barked at her. She had used him and now stood there threatening him. Her threats were hollow to him. He could not look at her and left only hearing the swish of her skirts as she turned to see his back disappear through the door.

He slammed the door as hard as he could, but felt no pleasure from the action. What had he got himself into? What had he done?

He could not let this ever get out; the humiliation would kill him and his family. On the way to London all he could think off, was how foolish he was. He had been better off with Ned and Ray. All three pulling together to make decisions and get things done. On breaking away from them, he had just made a complete mess of it all. He hated Paully and his gang for mocking him but mostly he hated himself. It was his entire fault. He should not have been so selfish.

He needed to get out of this house, and far away as possible from these people. It was sick and he felt dread to the core of his being. He composed himself and wanted to leave with his head held high. Although, inside he felt like he was losing everything!

Maisy had been standing in the hallway holding his tricorne ready and her face was full of sorrow for him. She had a large bruise on her cheek and had tried to hide it with her hair. She smiled weakly and handed him the hat and curtsied.

'Thank you Maisy, I wish you all the best.' Even though he now hated both Constance and Hartright, he had been wrong to take it out on the girl. She looked so pitiful and lost and went red when he looked again at the bruise. At least he could escape.

Constance stood at the window and watched him walk out of her life. She watched until his figure completely disappeared, she closed her eyes to savour his image and sighed in regret for what could have been. Oh well, there were plenty of others out there. If this silly man gave her any more trouble, she had only to call on dear old Uncle Secomb, her Uncle Mestor's ex lover. He rather had a soft spot for her, as they shared the same passions in life. She smiled to herself and felt a little better. She would return to her brother, work her magic on him, and make some new plans for their future, which was minus Mr. William Devereux and that annoying Shem Smith.

If only Hartright had come to her sooner. Perhaps none of this would have happened.

'I am not surprised. My God girl can you not hold a man? He was good for you, for the family. My God a Devereux! Do you know how old that family is? It goes right back to Norman times, William the bastard, I'll have you know. My God, I just can't believe it. What did you do?' Constance raised her eyes to the ceiling and dreaded letting the woman in. As she had watched William walk out of her life, her mother had come back in.

'Mother!' Hartright cried in his sister defence. He had joined them in the drawing room and was wrapped on the sofa in a warm blanket as close as he could get to the open fire.

'Oh let her waffle on, who cares what you think. You come here with all your high and mighty ways and just expect me to welcome you to my home and settle for that?' Constance argued defending herself bitterly.

'You forget Hartright asked for me when he was ill.' Lydia retorted.

'That was weeks ago and only now you pay a visit?' Constance raised her eyebrows.

'There are things a foot that I need to discuss with you.' Lydia confirmed rather awkwardly. Lydia dare not admit that she had headed to see Lady Theia in Croxley and when she had been sent backing, she had thrown herself on her family's mercy. Her brother held the family estates in Buckinghamshire and she had arrived uninvited and obviously not welcome. She had outstayed her welcome there and had nowhere else to go, other than her daughters. They were always at odds.

'Well?' Constance was giving no quarter.

'Mestor has ceased my allowance.' She advised flatly.

'What?' Hartright jumped from his seat in horror. Constance held out her hand to steady him.

'It would appear that Mestor felt his generosity had stretched far enough. He has every right and he advised that he would never return here. His life is in Italy and so should his money and wealth be too.' Lydia circled her hands and did not look up from them.

'What about the Hall?' Hartright started but was stopped in mid sentence when there was a knock at the door.

'There is a message my Lady.' Maisy entered and after bobbing added. 'It seems to have followed you from the Hall, your brothers man delivered it just now.' She almost run out of the room having received a back hander from Lady Constance earlier which had turned purple?

Lydia ripped open the letter not even giving the girl a second thought. 'It's a further letter from Mestor! Perhaps he has seen the error of his ways and wishes me to forgive his silly behaviour.' She took her time to digest the contents and found herself going red with rage.

'The fat buffoon!' She cried and flung the letter to the fire. She went red and felt herself begin to flush.

Hartright surprised himself by being quite so agile and retrieved the letter as it floated to the edge of the grate. He read it through.

'My God we are doomed. How could he?'

'Will someone tell me in God's name what has happened? He hasn't gone and got himself a wife and sired an off spring and kicked you while you're down has he?' Constance laughed at her own joke.

'He has sold the Hall!'

'I don't believe you.' She too now had risen. She looked from her mother to her brother. What would this mean for Hartright's inheritance and future title?

'Read for yourself.' She snatched the letter and read it through twice, not quite believing what he had done.

'Oh my God! This can't be happening.'

'It would appear that his debts have been called in by the lecherous Jew.' Lydia said spitefully.

'He has every right Mama.'

'Every right? Does he not know who we are? To have to leave the Hall due to a temporary relapse in finance is one thing, but to now lose the family ancestral home to selfish greed, well it's sickening.' She could not believe that her daughter would defend a loan shark!

'I did not see you holding out the hand of friendship to Grandmother when Mestor left you in charge of running the Estates when he went off gallivanting.'

'That was different.'

'How so?'

'I don't have to answer to you, do I?' Lydia did not wish to defend herself against her own children.

'You seem to forget all I have been through in the last few years to get some honour back to our name. Mestor has made us a laughing stock.' Hartright added. All his dreams of power and prestige were disappearing before him.

'And you have brought further shame to us and your goings on along the South Coast.' Constance tartly barked.

'What are your talking about?' Lydia asked looking from one to the other.

'Perhaps Hartright should bring you up to speed on all of his activities. Maybe you can talk some sense into him. He has been made to look a fool by a common thug. He needs to assert himself and be a man.'

'What nonsense does she talk?'

'It is nothing, Constance being over dramatic as normal.' Hartright tried to be dismissive.

'Really?'

'Really.'

'I need to write and plead with Mestor. The Jew will no doubt sell off the house. Who could he sell the house too? My God, this is ridiculous. I wonder if your grandmother knows?'

'Perhaps you should take a drive out to see her Mama?' Hartright suggested he wanted to get her out of the way; he needed to confirm his future.

'No no, no that best be Constance. She had a soft spot for you.' Lydia would never share her previous experience of paying court at Lascelles House.

'Me? You are joking; she's called me a Gorgon, Stheno, no less! And even when she was really annoyed and thought better of smearing me with one of her wonderful Greek myth Gods, she said I was Satan's little bitch.'

'You could be so boisterous in your youth.'

'She is an old hag, and I refuse to have anything to do with her.'

'Constance please?' Hartright begged.

'Just stop it, stop it all of you. This is too much to take.'

## Chapter Nine

'Has someone died?' Paully called as he entered The Castle and found the Inn lifeless, there was no atmosphere and all seemed to be crouched over their drinks, almost cuddling themselves. Outside it was bitterly cold and he had ridden hard to get back to Pevensey before the night drew in. He stamped his feet to get some life back into him, and cuddled himself, laughing at his own joke.

'Well actually Paully.....yes they have.'

'Well never mind.' He remarked dismissively looking across the old stand up bar for Gideon the Landlord. 'Landlord, a jug of your finest.' He called still quite merry. Daisy appeared and seemed to be crying. He looked questioningly at her, but she just shook her head and looked like a desperate angel. 'Paully, the landlord is dead!' She sniffled. He now lost his grin.

'What d'ya mean, Gideon is dead?' He looked at Daisy and back at the pub. He could not believe it. They were jesting. His mouth fell open.

'Aye dropped down dead about twenty minutes ago. Right on the other side of bar.' One of the old men remarked.

Paully proceeded to lean across the bar and shot back immediately, having seen that Gideon was still there, as dead as a door nail, on the floor!

'Has someone checked that he is dead?' He cried incredulously backing away from the bar.

'Course man! You think we're daft?'

Paully was flabbergasted. He checked again, looked down at the Landlord, and shook his head repeatedly. His whole world had just been tipped upside down. He was sure he felt tears welling up in his eyes! At that point, Rafe and Bob run through the door with half of the girls from the whorehouse in tow, having just discovered the news.

'Does he have an apprentice?' Paully choked, it was the only thing that sprung to his mind.

'Why do you think we are sitting here savouring the moment and ale you daft bugger? There's no fucking apprentice!'

The whole pub seemed to sob at the same time and then again fell silent in reflection of the damn loss!

He and his men rode into the back stables, having crossed the moat bridge, ducked through the drawbridge gate and having entered the gatehouse, swung left to skirt the castle and make for the back. The groomsman took his horse and welcomed him as an old and frequent visitor. He made his way to the back door and knocked on the kitchen door to gain entrance.

Bella and a few of her younger girls were there levering away. Bella looked at her girls and without a word, they all disappeared.

Bella looked at Shem with that expression of your presence only brings trouble. She tutted at him and gestured for him to take a seat. She grabbed the kettle, added water, and put it back on the fire to boil. Bella's movements were always sharp as though she was constantly annoyed. She took her tea tin from the welsh dresser and looked at him, indicating that her tin was near empty.

Shem smiled and from his pocket, he pulled out a bag and flung it to her.

'Better not be Borfa.' She warned as she reached for another tea tin, which held the cheaper tea.

'You'd think I'd insult you?'

'I think you'd try!' She smelled the tea and smiled in delight smelling the distinct aroma of Hyson, her favourite Chinese Tea. 'Well best put the Borfa away then.' There was no mistaking that Bella and Paully were brother and sister. They were both tall and hard looking. Bella had cheeky dimples when she smiled and the darkest brown hair that always shiny and spelt fresh. She could not abide untidiness and everything had a place and order. She was a passionate woman who took no prisoners and could give as well as she got. How she had ended up with a mouse like George English no one knew. They seemed to glow in each other's company and he worshipped her and she him. They were very happy and had been blessed with four children.

'You were going to give me crap?' He cried.

'Of course.' They both laughed.

'Hear you got alot on your plate!' She said as she made the tea. She handed him the bowl and saucer and separately gave him a plate with a slice of warm freshly baked bread smothered in honey.

He nodded whilst eating and looked deep into the fire.

'My babies alright?'

'You know they are.'

'You best be watching out for them.'

'I can't watch everyone. Anyway, they got their Uncle Paully!'

'That's why I am warning you.' He grinned at that. He would hate to let her down, she was his friend, and like Paully, she was relentless in her pursuits and would hold a grudge forever if she was ever wronged. When he had first met her he had immediately known she was a woman who he could trust and never ever mess with. Well if she could frighten Paully then that spoke volumes.

'I heard you had arrived. Typical hey? Always in the kitchen. What?' Both turned to the door to greet the new comer.

'I know where I will be looked after.'

'Certainly, certainly.' His Lordship came towards him and waved Shem down from getting up, they shock hands and then Shem watched as he went to his daughter and planted a fatherly kiss on her cheek. He looked longingly at the bread and honey and she waved him away to sit down and proceeded to cut him a slice of bread. They grinned at each other.

'I'll take some out to your men Shem, with some Ale.' She said tactfully to allow them some time to talk and he sent her a grateful smile.

'You've heard from London I take it.' Shem asked in between bites.

'My God man there's been a constant too and throwing of correspondence, you know, before the ink is dry, I have another letter.' Lennard mused. 'As you well know, Mr. Mordesan has been up in front of his seniors to report and they are not best pleased. Not pleased at all. Requested a deployment, what? Heard the reports and the gossip is of his failure. You see. But old Secomb has been rallying to his cause.' Shem shook his head in memory of the man. The Secomb's and Mordesan had been connected since the Civil war through marriage, friendship, and business. Lennard wasn't telling him anything he did not know already from his spies. Lennard knew this also, however Shem could bounce off Lennard, and he liked him immensely as well as he liked his council immensely.

'You're lucky the Lieutenant Colonel Wainwright hasn't sent the whole military to sort the area out, but you will be happy to hear that they are temporarily putting someone else in charge of the Riding Officers to shake them up a little bit.' Shem cocked his eyebrow, he knew it was a mad dream to believe that perhaps they would not deploy anyone and leave the south coast alone, and Lieutenant Colonel Wainwright had personal reasons for not wishing to get too personally involved. He loved his Geneva brandy and hated paying over the odds!

The military had to show that they were trying to tackle the smuggling problem and rumour had it that the government was planning to pass new bills on further restrictions.

'But be warned, someone will have to be a scapegoat at some stage.'

'Do they know who I am?' Shem mocked grinning. There were more than a few men who would jump into his shoes and pretend to be him, if it meant a new life abroad. He was never going to have anyone hang for him, and no authority would ever imprison him.

'Hardly. Although I can see you playing that card soon, hey sonny Jim?' Lennard laughed with his friend.

'Well, when needs must.' He referred to the future, which Lennard was privy to. Shem carried too many secrets, and Lennard did not know how he could sleep at night, but then he too had his secrets and sleep was a luxury that found him very rarely these days.

'Emm!' Lennard smiled at the younger man and then advised. 'I have already nominated my son in law, Charles for the post, he is keen. Keen. Barbara wants to return home and all in all, if this plays out, will be good news for all of us. Good news indeed.' Shem was not ready to wholly agree at this stage, his experience taught him not to be too complacent. Could Charles be moulded to suit all of their needs? From what he heard and saw of Charles, he too wanted to make a further name for himself, and equally make Barbara happy. Barbara was a lovely girl and in her youth had relied on Bella to steer her in the right direction, so it could work again for all of them. In any event, Charles and Barbara would have a rude awakening when they did come, Charles would soon learn that Herstmonceux's allure was not quite so shiny and what would he do to ensure that his beloved

Barbara could stay in the family home? They would have to keep it close to their chest and Lennard was loathe to think of what Shem, let alone Paully would do to Charles if he made waves. Shem was just happy to steer the subject away from Lennard telling him off over recent events.

Rosie had been for one of her long walks and like always had been followed by one of the men. She had been walking along the Watling Road heading back home when around the bend; a carriage had thundered by and hit a puddle, which had proceeded to spurt all over her. She knew who the carriage belonged too. She stood in the middle of the road with arms outstretched not knowing whether to laugh or cry. Then the heavens opened up once more and torrential rains started to hammer down on her. Just off to the right was an old farmstead that had been vacant for years. The old stable still had a roof, so it would be a good shelter to ride out the rain. She run across to it and wasn't making much head way, as the earth was caked in mud and with each step she felt herself being pulled down into the mud . Eventually she threw herself into the doorway. She knew her minder would be close to hand.

'You look as if you been through a hedge back ward.' He laughed. She jumped back in surprise seeing Shem sat with a few of his men around a small fire. It looked as if they had been abit more sensible and taken shelter before the rain had hit. Shem did not appear to be wet at all. All their horses were unsaddled and were resting in the corner.

They had been returning from seeing Lord Essex at Herstmonceux when they too had been caught out. His men decided to make their excuses, head out, and suffer the storm, it would ease off shortly, and they thought it would be better than staying. He nodded in appreciation.

Shem and Rosie had deliberately tried to avoid each other since their last intimate encounter, each still coming to terms with their own thoughts and how they were going to go forward. Shem never imagined it would ever have been this difficult with his pixie. He had given her space and she had savoured it. There was still so much to say and do.

'Don't start, just don't start.' She marched forward in a complete state. He could see she was in no mood. She stopped in her tracks. He could see she was fighting with herself for control and had turned a great shade of red in temper and humiliation at him seeing her in such a state. 'Are you fucking following me? You seem to be everywhere I don't want you to fucking be.' She accused him. 'If ya not rescuing me from fucking horses, you're trying to kill me. Then you fucking make out ya don't know me, to just piss me off and make me feel, yeah, yeah this small.' She put her thumb and finger together to show him how small he made her feel. 'Arse hole!' She was in no mood at all and found herself to be completely livid.

'You talking to me?' He pulled himself up and took a step towards her. Why did she always have to start? Especially after the other day?

She took a step back but she was still being brave. At least she was speaking to him! But it was a bit rich her blaming him for their current situation, she was the one who had started it.

'Do you see anyone else here? I am sick to death of you playing fucking God and lording it over me. Just fuck off, go on fuck off.' She had lost it now. She was wet, cold, and boiling with anger and shame.

'You finished?'

She put her hand to her head and turned away, exhausted with the effort. He thought he would hold his tongue, when she got going there had been nothing on earth to stop her. She would explode and let rip and then only after could he ever get a word in edge ways. Why he tried any other approach was beyond him. He knew her too well. If it had been anyone else speaking to him like that, they would be dead on the floor! However, she had already called out to him the other day. It had been a start. His presence had just startled her and she was unprepared. They needed to face facts and start to talk again. He would not allow her to get him angry again.

In a softer voice, he called.

'Just come over here and take ya clothes off.' As soon as he said it, he knew it was the wrong thing to say. She whirled round in anger. In time, he hid a smirk!

'You think I'm taking my clothes in front of you, you got another thing coming.' The look she gave him, was enough to drive him over the edge. That was it! Enough was enough. He was not walking on eggshells any more.

'What you think, every time I see you. I wanna shag ya? Oh behave. You're so fucking rigid; I might as well have a wank and let's be honest. I got enough pussy waiting for me at the Mint House without me ever having to think about you.' He turned away from her, deliberately wanting to hurt her and again knowing that perhaps it had been so wrong to say such crude and hurtful things. God how she made him so mad!

She just stood there, with her month open in shock. If she had felt awkward from before, now she felt awful. The other day had meant nothing to him.

'I can't believe you just said that to me..... You, -.... I, God!'

To himself, he could not believe the way the conversation was going.

'That's fucking rich, I offer me hospitality, and she thinks I just wanna shag her! There is no fucking pleasing you!' He spoke to himself but loud enough for her to hear; he bent down to the fire, then got up again from his crouched position in temper. 'And she wonders why I stay fucking clear.' He turned to face her. 'All you do is cause me fucking grief, grief, grief, and more grief.' He roared, pointing his finger at her. He snatched his coat firmly around him and made towards his horse, then turned back to the small fire he had made, then had second thoughts about putting it out, she may need it, he had been prepared to ride the storm, but now he just wanted to get away from her. He looked across at her, resting against the wall, looking out to the distant, her shoulders slumped. He stopped and took stock. He heard her sob and watched her move her body as if in disgust with herself for being so weak.

'So what was the other day? Did you use me?' She asked completely humiliated with the whole thing. He had not come to bed until she was fast asleep and again been up and out before she awoke.

'Jesus Christ.' He swore. 'Again you have got the wrong end of the stick.' He cried. 'Why do you always think too much?' She flinched and kept her eyes lowered. It had taken so much for her to come to him and he had just thrown it back in her face. 'That came out wrong.' He looked towards her but she hadn't turned round, she still looked to the distance. 'I should not have taken advantage of you. I was wrong....'

'So she was right all along...you just felt sorry for me?' Her bitterness choked him.

'You know that's not true. How can you ever say that?' She heard the raw emotion in his voice and heard him walk towards her.

He couldn't go and leave it like this. He stopped and tried to control himself. After a time, he stepped forward, wanting to say something, and then he heard her quietly start.

'That bitch deliberately made that coach go through that puddle to soak me just now. That tart you been shagging behind my back. I'm fucking livid, I'm livid with her. I'm mad at you. I am embarrassed and ashamed at myself. Yes and of course, I'm jealous. Who wouldn't be? Look at her.' She had worked herself up now. 'I wanna fucking squeeze the fucking life outta her, stab her through the eyes, cut her fucking stomach open and watch and see her guts fall out. I wanna skin her alive.' Jesus he could not believe how graphic she was. 'It's evil, evil, I know. Oh I am so angry, ohh, I could ......'As she spoke her voice raised higher and higher and at the same time, her arms were swinging around in motion with her anger and she had started to pace the floor, then she wrenched off her cloak and flung it to the ground. She then grabbed her hat and threw that to the ground and then went to it and started to stamp on it, time and time again. The mud from her boots flew off.

He stood frozen just watching this explosion of emotion engulf her whole being.

'I swear she won't do that again. I'll fucking have her. I don't care who she is. Fucking whore. I should have beat her senseless when I had the chance. Who does she think she is to try and mug me off? She can't be allowed to say those things to me. I won't have it. I wish I'd never come here. I wanna go home.'

He went to the horse, fetched his blanket, and flung it towards her. She caught it, continued to rant, turned away from him, and slowly removed her over- dress. She also flung that to the ground. She wrapped the blanket protectively around her. Every movement she made was abrupt, angry, and aggressive. He was quite enjoying seeing this show but was wise not to let her see that given it was emotionally charged and she had had a bad couple of years, he was seeing the old fire return to her and he wanted that back as much for him as her.

He knew she needed to rant, so he held back. He wasn't going to join in the conversation about any of his ex lovers. He wasn't that stupid!

'They must all be pretty stupid to think that can get one up on me. They know you'll have them.' She now turned to face him. 'She knew I was there. I know what will really piss her off. I'll get into her shit hole room that will smell well rank and I'll cut all her fucking hair off while she is asleep.' She shook her head in pure madness and tried to control her breathing.

'What do you mean, I will have them?' He grinned knowingly at her.

'What.' She looked up sharply and tried to appear innocent.

'That's what you just said.'

'No. You're mistaken. I didn't say that.' She shook her head trying to avoid eye contact. He made her look at him and she caught the slight twinkle in his eyes. 'Did I say that?' She asked coyly. He nodded. 'I said it out loud?' She asked again. Her secret was out. She had laid herself bear and he was milking it. She had declared that she knew he loved her and would do anything for her and so she was allowed to say and do whatever she wanted because in turn, no matter how annoyed she was at the whole situation, she loved him still.

'I have good hearing.' He watched her avert her eyes; he witnessed her blush from top to bottom. She lowered her head in complete shame. He wanted to laugh, but he held himself for her.

'I hate you.' She whispered in defiance. She looked like a lost soul, not knowing what to do with herself, realising that she had let him in, her defences were down. He slowly approached her and slowly raised his hands up to hers. She tried to back away.

'No you don't.' He whispered back, taking that chance. Hesitantly she put one of her hands in his.

'Yes I do.' She was trying to convince herself, she knew she was losing. They were just an arm apart, she raised her other hand into his. She could feel his power. He was waiting for her. Waiting for her to come to him. She breathed so heavily she thought her heart would burst. She so wanted to be hugged, but had not been able to let anyone get near. All she could see was him with a knife to her throat. She went to pull away. However, he held firm. He could feel her start to panic and then he let one of hands go and slowly he reached forward and put his hand under her chin. His touch burned her chin and the warmth oozed through her face and neck, counteracting with the raw fear that was trying to engulf her. She tried to hold the fear at bay, put it away. He did love her, how could she doubt that. She remembered all those nights when she had been recovering and he had been there. Always constant and then there was the other day. It had just happened because the trust had returned, be it that she so wanted to deny it. She loved him so.

'Look at me.' He whispered as a stern order. Every part of her body was screaming in pure fear of just letting go completely. He needed her to see she was not in any danger. His touch was like fire. 'Look at me Rosie.' She heard him command in a whisper again. She opened her eyes and looked into those deep green eyes. She could feel herself whirling up. She could not focus. She was petrified. She had to let go. She could not breathe. She was going to die, God help her!

'Seriously, you stink!' He winked and giggled at her to try and lighten the atmosphere. What he said slowly sunk in. He was making fun of her at this moment in time!

'You bloody bastard.' She whispered trying to control her breathing. 'You bastard.' She roared and then she put all her weight behind pushing him so hard, he did not even move. She tried again and he tried not to chuckle at her effort. She half wanted to laugh. It had dawned on her about his reference to their first meeting all that time ago when she had nearly been run over by horses and both of them had ended up stepping in horse manure. All he had kept saying that great autumn afternoon was, 'God you stink!' He was so enjoying teasing her like he always had.

She started to slap him, while still trying to hold the blanket around her and he pretended to curl up to defend himself, and then moved back as she launched herself at him. She was trying not to giggle. She needed this. He had given her this moment. She was lost.

'Stop being stupid.' She called. He stuck his tongue out. Her legs nearly buckled with laughter.

'Try and stop me.' He called back. She then decided to play act and slouched her shoulders in defeat, and shovelled back to the warmth of the fire, seeing that the rain still had not subsided. She looked back over her shoulder to him with ever so sad eyes and he slowly made his way back to her. She shook her head and laughed at him. The flames of the fire and the warmth from him were both alluring. She felt him stand directly behind her. Her body became rigid with panic again. But she knew it would be fine.

'You can't make it all go away with fun!' She felt she needed to be serious. She found herself stiffening. She tried to tell her body to relax.

'But it helps.' He whispered into her ear. He was standing so close. She felt the dip of his chin move across the top of her hair. His chest slightly touched her back. She found her breathing start to change. Slowly she felt her body betray her, she relaxed, she breathed normally, and she leant back against him. His arms slowly wrapped themselves around her and she lifted her arms and wrapped them into his. She turned bravely to face him and then she remembered her face. She covered her scar with her hand and looked down in embarrassment. He pulled her hand away. He had her back at long last!

'I don't want your pity or guilt.' She whispered.

'I'm not given you that, I'm giving you me.' He smiled. She hit him knowing full well what he referred to and felt her whole body glow with the memory.

'It's too late now.' She did not sound convincing even to herself.

'Is it?' He made her look at him. 'You never left me Rosie. Not for a day.'

'You were going to kill me.' She was trying everything to make him pull away. 'Look what they have done to me. I can't......' She was offering him just one last chance for him to run away.

'You are mine, and I am not going anywhere!' She diverted her eyes again. Now was not the time for him to discuss that any further. She needed small steps.

'I need to go.' She was avoiding the issue. She tried to pull away. He pulled her further into his embrace. She felt his smile and it warmed her. She knew she wasn't going anywhere. 'Seb will want to know where I am.'

'You can't keep running and I can't keep avoiding.' He sighed and then he looked down at her. 'When were you going to tell me he is mine?' They had been there before.

'Who says he is?'

'Don't.' She looked away in shame. She knew it was time to be completely honest with him. She sighed.

'Can we speak about it later? It's not as if I'm going anywhere.' She looked at him longingly trying to pull away. 'Where am I gonna go? It's not as if I can hitch up me skirts, and do a runner across the fields is it? You're the one with the horse.' She tried to joke. He laughed with her and again planted a kiss on her forehead to try and ease her.

'Not from want of trying.' He gestured for her to sit with him by the fire. He stretched and yawned. 'God I am so tired.'

She sat and leant beside him and flung the blanket across both their backs. He eased himself softly next to her and ever so gently cradled into her. She was still so cold and he could feel she had become rigid again. He watched her face and read how she was thinking in her mind, all of the possible answers to his questions, the hurt, and the regret, the need to off load, the want, and desire. He let the time slip by.

He had known Seb was his the moment they had mentioned about the boy when they had first found Rosie after her ordeal. Then when he had first seen him, when he had been brought across, he knew. He had not spoken to him or been anywhere near him until the night when he had been fretting with Chrissy. He had deliberately avoided seeing Seb before, as he just knew he was his son and it was just too much. He smiled to himself, both he and Rafe's line's were secure, be it bastards and no children yet born in wedlock. Nevertheless, he would remedy that at some stage.

'Feeling better now?' He whispered. For all her bravado, she was still vulnerable. She was trying so hard to keep it together. She had suppressed things for too long. He felt her body relax and he felt her reach for his hand and hold it firm. It was like it had been before, so completely as one. Slowly they felt themselves drift into being comfortable with each other and that this was the time to start afresh. Then bravely she leant forward and kissed him ever so lightly on his lips. He felt her anxiety, her worry for being damaged and her nervousness. The kiss meant the world to him, it was simple and lovely, and as she pulled away, she whispered looking deep into his eyes. 'His name is Sebastian Samuel Troy, and the surname for now is Cavendish.' The smile he gave her was one that she would treasure for all her days.

'You remembered!' He choked back.

Jesus had been assigned to watch Rosie whilst Shem was out. He now crept up to the ruin on hearing voices and smiled as he heard the familiar tones; he backed off away and cuddled up in the arms of an old tree to see out the rain. He wrapped himself in his coat and cocooned himself well. He sighed to himself and prayed to the Lord to bring them and him both joy, peace and the love.

'What?' Shem and Jesus had just got back when they heard the news.

'He's dead!' Paully repeated.

'Does Valentina know?' Jesus asked. 'God rest his soul.'

'No, she left earlier for Rye Market, seems not expected back until late tomorrow.' Rafe advised. He came to Shem and they greeted each other.

'I don't believe this. Blessed be God!' Jesus was astounded; he and Gideon went way back.

'He just dropped down dead.'

'My God!' The atmosphere in the Castle Inn was slightly subdued and Daisy had been crying all day being too sensitive for her own good. Rafe had taken her back to the Coach House to look after her, she was still so weak after having Little Nat. Rafe was also worried, the baby fat she had put on with Little Nat, seemed to be disappearing too quickly and she had no milk for the boy. 'Does Valentine know about his first wife?' They all looked at Jesus in wonder.

'What first wife?' Shem enquired.

'Chrissy knows, she was her cousin.' Jesus hated being the centre of attention. He would have to answer too many awkward questions. Why had he spoken out loud? 'She died, after having Harry. God rest her soul.' He remembered her as plain as anything, she had been fun.

'Harry?'

'Yes, Harry.'

'Well?' Shem was losing his patience now.

'Gideon could not cope with the loss of his wife and raising a boy on his own, so he sent the boy to his sister. She lives in London somewhere. He sent her all his money and I should imagine, - Gideon would have left everything to her and the boy.' Jesus knew more than he was letting on. Gideon's sister had been Jesus' first true love and she had run off with a sailor, then the swine had left her and she had ended up penniless and living in slums in London. Gideon had gone to London to find her. Whilst he was away, Gideon had asked Jesus to watch over his wife. That ended up being a big mistake!

Gideon had set his sister up and bought her a boarding house and she made a reasonable living and was only too happy to take on the boy when Gideon's wife died.

'Not Valentina?' Claude would have expected Gideon to secure Valentina's future.

'You mean there is a recipe?' Paully interrupted. Only Jesus looked at him in wonder. He could not believe that Paully was that thick and had forgotten where the recipe was!

'Well he hated her, didn't he?'

They all laughed at that nodding their heads in agreement. Valentina and Gideon's relationship had more than diminished over the last few years to them hardly speaking. They only communicated as and when necessary about work and if Valentina felt the level of loathing she showed her husband was not going to affect any inheritance she may well be due, she was only fooling herself.

'We must go and get him.' Paully offered and they all ignored him and his motives.

'How old is this Harry?' Claude asked. He of all was trying to be good mannered and ask the relevant appropriate questions.

'Must be coming on for twelve, maybe thirteen. Bless him!'

'That's even better, he will have the recipe won't he and hand over with no problem?' Paully's eyes were alight with glee.

'For fucks sake Paully, do you think the boy will give a toss about the poxy recipe? Maybe the solicitor will have it with the papers; a kid is hardly going to care.' Claude declared.

'Then can you find out?'

'You're an idiot.'

Shem was not interested to know what personal provisions Gideon had made for his family, he knew about the business provisions and for that, he was pleased. He asked Claude to get word to Mr. Saltdean in London, who also dealt with Gideon's estate.

'Poor Valentina, do you really think he would have left her nothing?' Claude was genuinely concerned for her and his friends all looked oddly at him.

'Got a soft spot?' Paully sung.

'Please, the woman is a whore.' Claude batted it back.

'A good whore.' Paully laughed and winked at Shem, who chose to ignore him.

'I can't see that he would leave her penniless.' Claude said again to no one in particular.

'Well, let's place our bets now on the outcome. This is going to be so much fun!' Paully beamed.

'You sick bastard.' Claude could not believe Paully. He had no sympathy for the plight of the young orphan and was just anxious to know that his stake in the precious brewery would not be wasted and the business fold. He was relying on Gideon to have given the recipe details on to someone at least. Again, Jesus just could not belief how absolutely stupid Paully could be and he certainly was in no mood to put him out of his misery and tell him where the recipe was. If he had forgotten, then there was really no hope. He had bigger concerns to contend with if Gideon's sister and the boy returned!

'Roll up, roll up, odds on the boy.' Paully started to sing. 'Me and little Harry gonna be like that.' He turned back to his friends and had crossed his fingers.

'He is such a prat!' Claude moaned and again Jesus shook his head, and mouthed.

'Don't I know it? Forgive him Lord.' Surely, Paully had not forgotten everything?

'Well what do we have here? Lamiae's off spring how is the vampiric monster? Does her nose hurt? I'd say, hey Gunthorpe?' Lady Theia Mordesan started to laugh. She was a delightful looking woman. She was very petite with a regal air around her. She had sparkling young eyes and a mischievous grin. She could be quite short with you and was said to be very rude, however she referred to her manner as being direct and assertive and yes, not to everyone's taste, but that was their problem. Life was too short and she was not going to waste time being wishy-washy.

Constance had been allowed to enter the house without any ado. All the staff had been exceptionally hospitable and Constance was impressed with the efficiency of everything and how the house seemed to glow with warmth that was certainly lacking in any home she had since they had left the Hall.

'Oh I forgot to say, the carpenter has done a wonderful job of removing those small dents in the door. It is looking absolutely gorgeous, my lady.' Gunthorpe answered and joined in the joke. They had rather hoped that Lydia had broken her nose when she last visited, as the door had slammed straight on her face. Constance looked at the Lady and the butler and was disgusted at the banter and had no idea what they talking about. In her opinion, her grandmother had always been too over friendly with the staff. She could remember her Grandmother and the blessed cook, Martha, sitting in the main parlour at the old house, drinking tea, sharing a sofa, laughing, and joking like two silly little girls.

'You were right, I let my pride get the better of me, yes, and I should have sent her the bill! Oh and Gunthorpe please do not go, this little mix is a spiteful one, like her mother. My poor door. This thing here, she would pounce, if she doesn't like what I am saying. What has she done to my poor house, I should wonder? So bear witness. Stay.' Lady Theia then smiled sweetly at her visitor. Constance knew this was not going to be easy. Theia was thankful that she had regained some of her strength, she had been unwell, and that just wasn't on. At least her cheeks were rosy again.

'Grandmother please, you make me out to be quite the ogre!' She would try and be nice.

'Well aren't you?' Still, Lady Theia wore a truly lovely smile on her friendly face.

'I take offence.' Constance fidgeted in her seat.

'Good, now hurry up we haven't got all day. Say what you will, and then go.' Lady Theia continued to smile at her.

'I can't believe how rude you are being.'

'Can you not. Shall I be plainer?'

'What have I ever done to warrant such hostility?'

'My dear, dear Constance! Such a show? Gunthorpe, you see?' She turned in her seat, still looking at Constance, however her whole body facing her friend.

'Pitiful my Lady.' Gunthorpe had his eyes to the floor and was actually shaking his head in disappointment at Constance.

Constance wanted to leave at that instant, however as much as they subjected her to their rudeness, she would do as requested and present the facts. Rather smugly, she reported what she knew about Mordesan Hall being sold off, and thought she would relish the moment she got to the knitty gritty. Her Grandmother had loved that house so very much and to finally know it was lost to her would probably kill her.

'Emm.' Was all she heard from her Grandmother in response? 'Is that all?' She was being dismissed and was extremely put out that her words had no visual impact. She shook in anger as she rose to her feet and every movement was sharp and irritable. She held her head high and made for the door; she could not wait to leave, feeling her cheeks very flush with the humiliation of the whole episode. She was even madder that her intentions to upset and torment the old woman had been flung back in her face.

'Constance?' She turned as her Grandmother called after her. Every part of her body was on edge and she just wished she had something to fling at the old woman. 'You were not to know that I too had received word from Mestor. As you know, my son and I have not really been in correspondence since he allowed your mother to throw an old lady out of her ancestral home and subsequently due to lack of breeding and character, destroy everything that was once so cherished and loved. Your mother is a stupid woman and to come begging to me a few weeks ago, quite frankly was desperate and confirmed that your mother is without doubt one selfish and sad individual.' She watched as Constance's eye brows raised 'So she did not advise you she came here?' Came the sweet whisper of innocent disbelief. Constance did not make any eye contact. 'How the mighty fall. Your family have been very busy of late. First you, with the rumours around your first husband's death, then your brother and lastly your mother.'

Constance went to walk away again. 'Your father would be so proud!' Lady Theia mocked enjoying herself immensely at her Granddaughter's expense. 'So now, the leech's plight rests on your shoulders. I know a man who will give you favourable rates of interest should you need a loan!'

Constance went to open the door and did not wish to ever look back; the humiliation and scorn she wished to throw at this woman, had back fired onto her, and she did not like it one bit that this frail old woman, who she had always seen as a pathetic creature, had shown her out it was truly done.

If she had been of a clearer mind, she would have admired her grandmother, but that was one of her worst traits, Constance was far too selfish.

'One last thing, if I may?' Constance waited in annoyance. Theia did feel a little guilty but thought it would be one of the last times she would ever see her granddaughter. 'Pray humble an old woman, tell me, what did I ever do to you and yours to warrant such malice? The Hall had been my home all my life. It was your home and you had everything you ever wanted and needed given to you in love. We looked after you.' Theia sighed. It was a thin line to throw and Theia knew it made her look weak after all.

'You lie.' Came the spiteful retort. 'You did not give us anything; my mother had to beg for everything when my father died. You made life hell for her. You even accused her of having something to do with Uncle Troy's death. How dare you make out you were the victim.' Constance was red with anger and resentment.

'Oh child, do you believe everything your mother tells you.' Her grandmother looked at her now with such pity. 'Such a shame and you did show such promise. But now you are lost and just as evil and selfish as her. How different your life would have been if your father was still alive.'

'Well he is not, so get over it.'

'Such anger.' Lady Theia acted all hurt and miserable. She then shrugged her shoulders and then in her normal voice flung at her. 'You may wish to lose the attitude once you ask your mother who bailed her out time and time again, every time she went on one of her many trips to London. You conveniently forget your mother was a very wealthy woman in her own right at one time. Pray tell, what did she do with it? Oh I remember,' she raised her finger to the ceiling. 'She left you and your brother with me and my dear Sade, and went to London to find a husband, but ended up drinking, gambling, buying fabulous jewellery and falling in love with all and sundry, and giving all her money away.'

'You lie.'

'For years you have taken your anger out on me, a frail, weak old lady who did nothing but try to love and protect you. But to no avail.'

'You are the one who is evil. You washed out old hag. I hate you. I have always hated you.'

'Such a shame, hey Gunthorpe? Such bitterness to the world! Shame on you child.' Lady Theia was almost laughing at her. 'Shame on you for your misguided delusions, and for your judgments. Never assume and be lead, get your facts straight and then you can attack with conviction.' She seemed to dismiss her granddaughter away and in a lower tone said. 'It is good you love and defend your mother, but you are not stupid, I know it must pain you to know that one's mother is such a parasite!'

'I need no lessons from you, I think I done exceedingly well as it is.'

'Emm, yes, by seeking the comfort from her own brother, all these years. You see, I get my facts straight, and do not rely on gossip. You are quite very sick, wanton, and shameful.' Theia shook her head at the woman and turned away from her. 'Now get out of my house and do not ever think to come back again.'

'Don't worry I doubt you have long to live and in fact I wish you dead and rejoice you never see that stupid Hall again.'

'If I have any more fun like this, I think I'll die laughing.' Theia was very much enjoying herself. 'Gunthorpe, the door, mind her precious nose, and if she does not go now, you have my authority to take matters into your own hands, yes ...'

'I will not let a lady suggest such things.' Gunthorpe was opening laughing.

'Oh have I been bad? Well, you are no fun, no fun at all.' Theia giggled, enjoying how feisty Constance was. She had loved every minute of it.

Constance stood there horrified and was even more when Gunthorpe pushed her all the way from the drawing room, through the hall and out of the door. He pushed her so hard, she fell to the floor, and he physically kicked her across the threshold. She screamed in pain and found herself backing up on her bottom across the polished floors, keeping Gunthorpe at bay with her free hands. Her dress would be ruined. She had never ever been treated in so vile a fashion. She was degraded and felt like the scum of the earth. Her hair was falling out everywhere. She promised vengeance for her treatment.

'How dare you, I have a mind to fetch the local Magistrate and have you arrested for assault and for that witch threatening to have me killed!' She managed to roar through gritted teeth. She got to her feet, and straightened up, and Gunthorpe had opened the door and in a whirl, she found herself outside eating dirt.

'Hurry up then you silly cow, he has his tea at five and will be frightfully put out if you disturb him then. While you are there, tell him his Uncle said to say hello.'


Valentina had waited until Constance had left then she signalled for her driver to drop her off outside the back of the house. She quickly manoeuvred through the tradesman entrance wearing a large crushed deep blue cape, with black velvet trims. No one could see her face and she was confident she had been undetected. All had been prepared for her arrival. Her presence was not however undetected and a figure lurked in the background taking stock.

Hartright had been delighted by the surprise, looking for distractions having been waiting to hear from his old family friend Secomb about how his career would fair after the disappointment he had made of overseeing the South Coast.

Hartright's Uncle Secomb had made his case after it had been reported that Hartright had been severely beaten and all eyes had turned to the gangs as being responsible; but there was no real proof. Hartright hoped that after his medical condition had been discussed they would be lenient, possibly offer him somewhere else, and not leave him hanging on the shelf. However, in his heart he knew, his time was up, he needed to run and get away as he had planned before.

The appeal of being Mestor's sole heir wasn't so alluring, and with the way, that Mestor had messed up, would there be anything left, now that the Hall had been sold off? Constance had gone off to see his Grandmother and rub that in and he waited in anticipation at that outcome.

His dear mother had made her excuses also earlier and he had no doubt that she was reacquainting herself with some old lovers. She was a sorry creature and the more time he spent with her, the more he become conscious he really did not like her.

He wanted desperately to make something of himself, but, however hard he tried, he knew he just would not ever get there. His venture with William had brought him a good living, but that was all tied up and he was in no position to fund such a big purchase as buying back the Hall.

'So what is it you want from this?' Hartright asked as he looked down at the beautiful woman. She just purred and smiled seductively at him. They were curled up together wrapped in crisp clean sheets Valentina had been used to seeing men scared and beaten, and did not bat an eyelid at Hartright's injuries. He seemed to have lost his edge slightly and was trying to appear brave and in charge. Their previous encounters had always been very businesslike and very quick.

'I want to see Shem take a big fall. Look, I have told you, the girl is alive and Shem is going to use her to give evidence against you. He means to destroy both you and William.'

'How little you know.' He looked away from her in boredom. He was already doomed.

'You fool. He has Chater already and he knows all about your escapades. Even William's old friends know what you have been up to, Hartright.' He looked back at her then.

'What!'

'Your problem is that you have always underestimated Shem.'

'I take exception to that.'

'You English are fools. You think that because you are from a noble house, that makes you more intelligent than someone like Shem?'

'Of course!'

'Then there is your ignorance. Shem is twenty times the man you will ever be. How you thought you could best him is beyond me! You should make it your business to learn about this man.'

'Lady.' He let the sarcasm make a point. 'I don't like your tone. And rest assured Shem will get his come-uppance.' He grabbed her by the wrist and held her fast. The playing seemed to have come to an abrupt end. He had excelled himself after his previous embarrassment and had wanted to prove his worth. She had certainly seemed to have enjoyed their afternoon exercise, and just because he did not like what she said, the activities need not cease. 'Oh, but you smell soooo good.'

'Let me go or else.' Her tone suggested otherwise as he bent down and kissed her long and hard. He seemed to have forgotten all about what they had been discussing.

'What do you mean they know all about me and William?' He asked.

'They mean to totally destroy both of you and your families. They have been watching your every move. Don't say you have been naive to this?' He certainly had not, having been very happy to give information out when Shem's men had captured and tortured him. He unconsciously felt for the missing piece of his ear.

'So you have a plan to get me out of here without being observed.' There may be a flicker of hope yet!

'It can be arranged.'

'And where is the girl?'

'She is living at the Coach House under Shem's protection. I can get you close to her.'

'Again what is in this for you?

'I am sick of being used by men for their own gain.' She smiled at the irony of it all. 'You would have thought you would have learnt by now to accept the inevitable.' She smiled sarcastically at that. 'In another world, another time, my God, could you imagine what we would have achieved together?' He flirted. She indulged him and smiled encouragingly as he whirled her hair in his hands.

'I can be your Cleopatra.' She made his whole body tingle. Her skin was like silk. For an older woman she was remarkable and it was always a pleasure to bed a woman of knowing, to the quick tumbles he had to endure with the serving maids. God they never stopped crying and there was him doing them a great favour!

'I hardly want to be Anthony. The bloody fool got himself killed through his love of that silly whore!' He laughed at his own joke, smiled down at her, she had bought him new hope, and he had missed the feeling of excitement. 'I rather like the idea of being William the Conqueror. I'll conquer you again and ride you bloody hard this time you wanton slag, and then by God, I'll flush the deceitful bitch out. I'll have her again and see how she screams this time and then I'll skin her alive and cut of her bloody head, how dare she not bloody die the first time, the bloody nuisance?'

'Oh my Cherie be careful.' The girl collided into Claude's chest and bounced straight back off. 'Oh I am so sorry I did not mean to startle you.' He half laughed and watched as the girl balanced herself holding firmly onto his arm.

'No, sorry, I wasn't looking where I was going.' She looked into his eyes and smiled at him, and he grinned warmly at her and had no malice or intent at all on his face. Both stepped apart from each other. It was especially early and the city was not fully awake. The air was crisp and the sky grey. Claude bowed and she curtsied.

'Do you work there?' He casually asked looking up at Constance's new style huge town house in the heart of the city of London. This gave Maisy time to compose herself. They both turned to look back at the house. Maisy more in apprehension.

'Yes.' She nodded and thought that she did not wish to go; he had the most adorable blue eyes and such a lovely voice. She reluctantly turned to face the way she was going.

'Is it your day off?'

'Yes.' Was all she could say, she felt all giddy with excitement and really did not wish to drag herself away from his friendly face. She felt self-conscious that he would see the bruise on her chin. As one bruise faded, another took its place!

'Same here.' He offered and again gave her a nod and smile.

'Well I'd best be off, I am catching the stage to me Mum's.' She dragged her feet.

'Well have a good day. You look as if you need it from what I been hearing about the goings on in that place.' He joked and then noticed her stroke her chin.

'Yes I would say.' She agreed nodding her head and thinking if only he knew the half of it. She felt herself blush all over. Well gossip got around and although she had not said a word herself, news was bound to travel.

'Well, goodbye.' He waved and she knew he had seen her bruise, she felt she needed to explain in some weird way, however before she gathered her thoughts he had walked off leaving her standing watching after him. She found herself skipping off with a huge grin and glow in her heart and as she turned the corner, she giggled and dared herself to take a sneaky peek back. She did and watched the back of the tall man and laughed, he looked so nice, and she hoped to God she bumped into him again and soon.

'Did she look back Jesus?' Claude was anxious to know as Jesus caught up with him.

'Course she did.' Jesus grinned. Shem had decided to send his men to see Mr. Saltdean in London and while they were at it, to catch up with all their local spies and the going on's with Hartright and co.

'She loves me.' Claude mocked.

'She's only just met ya.'

'It's not just Rafe whose got it.' Claude said full of himself rocking back and forth on his heels.

'Now who is the idiot?' Jesus flung back at Claude. 'She must have shit in her eyes.' At which Claude playfully whacked him for swearing. 'Now now, violence never solved anything, I'll have you know. Forgive him Lord.' Jesus play-acted and spoke like his brother when giving a sermon and looked all about him righteously as if speaking to his flock.

'And hold back on forgiving me, the day's not yet finished.' At which both of them burst out laughing.


'You alright Jesus, you look abit nervous?' Rafe sat with Jesus while they waited for the coach to arrive. Jesus had been on edge since Chrissy had received word that Gwen, Gideon's sister, was returning to Pevensey with Gideon's son, Harry Moseley. Rafe had tried to question him over the last few weeks about why he was so itchy whenever Gwen or the boy's name was mentioned, but he had just kept quiet. He knew she was his old sweetheart but there must have been more to the story.

Jesus kept looking at the Grandfather clock and looking out the window, as they waited at the Coach House. Then he would wring his hands together nervously and then clasp them in prayer.

'Any minute now.' Jesus repeatedly whispered. Paully joined them and looked at Rafe in question. 'Any minute now.' Jesus said again to himself, and then he heard a sound and leaped to his feet, knocking the table. Rafe steadied the table and he and Paully chased after him as he entered the courtyard, knowing that reuniting with his old sweetheart had been playing on his mind and if it did not go well, then he would need some sort of support.

'Will she recognise ya?' Paully joked standing next to him.

'Course she will.'

'True, you haven't changed much. Still a piece of long stringed piss!' Paully joked.

'You could have washed and combed ya rat's tail's.' He nudged his friend.

'What if she looks like a bag of bollocks?' Rafe added to the mix.

'Oi.' Jesus moaned in defence. He subconsciously stroked his hair, he had made an effort that day and had actually been to the river and washed all over and even plaited his hair.

The coach pulled up on time and the normal hub of array surrounded it. Chrissy greeted the passengers and directing them accordingly. She too was anxious about the meeting and her face lit up like a picture when finally, everyone had been herded out of the coach and Gwen was the last to disembark. She helped her from the coach and Gwen looked about taking in the scene and the feeling ever so happy at being home, she sighed in relief. She wondered if old man Mole was still alive.

She was a small skinny woman whose face was gaunt with tiredness. She had light brown hair, which in places was turning gray. It was pulled into a simple bun and had small ringlets falling here and there. She had such sad brown eyes, however she looked like a woman who was doing well out of life but was not too showy. Chrissy immediately started to think of what she could feed her with, to get some meat on her bones. Gwen hugged her heartily and knew that the motherly Chrissy would look after them. She then called for her nephew to hurry up.

He was still in the back of the coach, wiping his eyes of sleep, being one of those lucky individuals that could sleep anywhere and anytime. He climbed down from the coach, hitched up his pants, and smiled at his Aunt awkwardly as she introduced him to Chrissy. He was a boy just coming out of puppy fat. He had sharp blue piercing eyes and dimples in his cheeks. His hair was jet black, cut to his shoulders, and lanky. He looked like a cheeky chap.

As they turned to enter the coach house, Gwen caught the eye of Jesus. They seemed to stare at each other for an eternity. Her heart missed a beat and he felt like he was going to die. God had placed her in front of him and he was going to make Jesus suffer for all eternity. Then his eyes moved and caught sight of the boy and he staggered back! It was true after all!

'Oh my God! It all makes sense now, don't it, Paully you seen this?' Rafe chuckled, and then he turned to Jesus. 'You dirty bastard.' Rafe could not help it and then fell about laughing and watched as Jesus' eyes followed the party into the Coach House, in longing. 'No wonder you're forever in that church! You'd best get your arse back up there now and really give it some.' Paully followed through with and Jesus just stood there in shock. The boy was his spitting image. If he had any doubts years ago, the proof was standing in front of him. There was going to be trouble and Gideon's Will had not yet even been read!

'You're a dark horse ain't ya? Surely, we can't call Shem Old Roger now. It's clearly you.'

'No wonder your family don't have anything to do with ya! No wonder Gideon hated ya! No wonder, Gwen can't look at ya!'

'Just leave it Paully.'

'Oh Jesus, Jesus. What have you done? No wonder, you pray to the Lord all the time, my God, what a naughty boy you were and all these years! I didn't have a clue. Now it's all falling into place.' Paully was ecstatic at the term of events and loving every minute of being able to take the Michael out of one of his oldest friends.

Jesus and Gwen had been childhood sweethearts and it was expected that they would marry as soon as Jesus had got enough money together to build up a home. But in between Gwen had got familiar with a new fisherman. He had swept her of her feet and before anyone knew it, she had opted, married him, and moved to London.

Gideon had never discussed Gwen with anyone and only when his wife had died a few months after giving birth to their son, Gideon had sent the boy to his childless sister to bring up. Her husband, by then, had left her for better climates and was last heard of on the merchant ships around the Caribbean.

So little Harry had been brought up by his Auntie Gwen, who had been beside herself at hearing of her brother's death and having received such a wonderful letter of invite from Chrissy, decided to return home.

'Do ya think he has bought the recipe with him?' Paully pondered.

'Is that all you can think about?' Rafe barked.

'Yes!'

'Not the well fare of the child or anything like that?'

'No!'


It had only taken a few days for matters to be sorted and as Lord Lennard had been one of the main witnesses to Gideon's Will, it could hardly be contested. Valentina had gone into a fit and decided to escape again to acquaintances in London to review her options and also to do some more shopping. Unbeknown, she was trailed again.

Gideon had left only the Mint House to her, and the rest of his asset had been left in equal shares to his sister Gwen and Harry. Everyone assumed that the shrewd Valentina would have had a tidy sum put by. She had not been overly kind to Gwen when she had arrived and made it more than clear that she had expected everything to be left to her and why the woman had made the effort to come all this way was beyond her.

Valentina had not attempted to have anything to do with Harry who just looked at her with contempt. He had immediately taken with Chrissy and started to make friends with the local children.

The whole episode had left Valentina more bitter and she had become more and more isolated. She had hated her husband and was glad he had died. She had the freedom now to do as she pleased, and the blood lust consumed her. She would make them all suffer and especially Rosie who had taken her lover away.

She knew she needed an exit strategy and already had started to make plans to return home to Spain. She knew she could easily be a Bawd back home, there was nothing here now. She reasoned that she could just go now and be done with them all, however to have one last stab at Shem blinkered her reality.


After their initial meeting, Maisy and Claude had bumped into each other again and before they knew it, they were regularly meeting up. After a fashion, Maisy found it easy to open up to Claude as he really listened to her. Claude had her wrapped round his little finger, ad she craved for his company, and even though she was a little trying at times, he started to really feel sorry for her. For years, she had had to put up with Constance's ways, Maisy felt undervalued, and if she were to make one mistake, that's it, she would be out on her ear. She had seen and heard too much and every day she lived on her nerves. She was a small girl with thick long light brown hair, which was always plaited and held, in her maids cap. She had an eager look about her and lived on her nerves. Her eyes constantly darted from one place to the other and reminded Claude of a frightened mouse.

She had a new true friend in Claude and found it easy to confide in someone, having never had any friends or acquaintance outside of the house. He was like a breath of fresh air; he actually listened and never asked her about any bruises or scratches that he noticed on her. She was very aware that he did not mention them and was thankful that her loyalties to the house were never tested, although in hindsight she realised that she had offered, in her chatter, perhaps far too much information. Nevertheless, none of that mattered; her head was full of a young woman's dreams of being in love and finding the perfect man to share all her hopes and aspirations with. He was a little older than she would have liked. He was taller than most men she knew, and she could see how strong and lean he was. He treated her like she was a princess.

He had not taken any liberties and she had become impatient with his lack of forthrightness. She had been bold and rather than accept the small peck on the cheek, she had been very wanton and actually kissed him full on the lips. Well he had certainly been taken by surprise and she had loved the liberation it gave her!

He had promised to take her away from all of this and if all went to plan, it would not be too long before she would be free and they could think about a possible future. When he had gained her full trust, he then had started to ask her about her Mistress and she had given the information more freely and could not wait for the day when she rode off into the sunset with this man. Claude had been a blessing to her, and to the gang, she was everything they wanted.

He had no qualms about the dishonesty in his motives and if this girl served her purpose, then that was all well and good, she would be rewarded, he would see to it that she would be looked after and never have to suffer ever again.

## Chapter Ten

'What have you done?' Shem appeared in the stables. Rafe had been rubbing the horses down and humming whilst he worked. It had been spitting outside and Rafe had left the stable doors open to listen to the rain as is hit the yard floor and splash everywhere. Shem shook his coat and whipped back his hair, which had fallen all across his face. The sky was grey, with no promise of turning.

'What are you talking about?' Rafe did not stop what he was doing. His eyes concentrated on the horse to ensure its well-being.

'Look, guilt all over your face.'

'Well, if you know, why you asking me? Rafe laughed, after each brush he run his hand over the area knowing this also soothed the horse. His brother stood there and placed his hands on his hips. Oh, God, now he was in for it. Rafe braced himself.

'Couldn't keep it in your pants could you?' At this point Earl appeared and proceeded to shake all the rain away whilst standing guard at the doorway.

'Oh fuck it!' Rafe sighed, he nervously tucked his lose hair behind his ears. The horse jittered uneasily. Shem had obviously found out. 'Look, it was...'

'Oh I know what it was. You are one tart, I swear! What is it your mission to bed every woman in the world?'

'Oh you do tend to exaggerate!'

'Exaggerate! Fucking hell! I've got old Harry over there, at best he's like a fucking animal; he's got Theo with him!' The penny dropped and Rafe was half relieved it wasn't the other thing. This then was about his little rendezvous with his lovely Amelia.

'It was just a one off.' Rafe lied. He tried to concentrate again on the task in hand and returned to his loving motion of brushing the horse down.

'A one off! You've had it away with his daughter!'

'Look! Amelia loves me and I just couldn't contain myself. Are they at the Castle?'

'You've got Daisy.' Shem said in disbelief at his brother's dismissive attitude.

'Well Daisy was indisposed and I.....'

'She was just about to drop!'

'Well, I have needs?' Rafe looked with that sad face of innocence that he had perfected over the years. The horse turned his head and Rafe nibbled at his face. Man and horse both loving the affection shared.

'When we were on the beach ages ago now, you thought that there may be another child, that you had heard of! For fucks sake Rafe! How many do you have?' Rafe raised his shoulders. He had heard that he may have fathered a boy over Rye way, but he could not be sure. He was hardly going to go back and ask! He gave his brother that heart wrenching innocent look of, - *Look at me, I am too cute for you to chastise.*

'He is insisting you marry her.' Shem crossed his arms and waited. He was shaking his head trying not to look at his brother and his fantastic performance of him being the victim in all of this. Earl had now curled himself up getting comfortable.

'Oh behave!' Rafe fell about laughing. His horse snorted also. He went back to continue to work on the horse and whisper sweet nothings in his ear.

'Nathaniel!' Shem was being very serious. Earl raised his head.

'Oh look? Have you told them I am here?' Rafe turned back knowing when Shem used his real name he was in bother. His whole body looked annoyed at Shem for disturbing him and his beloved animal more than the threat of Harry and his boys coming across to potentially give him a wallop. Shem shook his head. Rafe sighed and then sprung on him. 'Let me get away for a few days, let it all settle and then ...'

'At one time you said you would stay put and support me and now you bring this to our door Nathaniel, it will not go away. You think I can bribe him some money and it will be an end of it?' When Shem's voice turned into his clipped natural tones and every word was pronounced, he knew he was really in trouble. Rafe felt all his insides start to churn and he felt quite faint. He lent on the horse and hid his face. The horse snorted again.

'Daisy didn't hear any of this did she?' Shem again shook his head; perhaps Rafe did have a heart? What was he saying? Rafe started to stroke the horse again.

'Good, then I'll be off.' Rafe had made up his mind to run! Daisy's health had seemed to improve and she was with child again.

'Oh no, you will not. Amelia is pregnant.' Rafe stopped in his tracks; he slowly turned back to Shem with the biggest grin on his face. He licked his lips.

'You're kidding?' He was over the moon.

'It is not anything to be happy about.'

'Can you imagine, he'll be lovely? Is Amelia alright?' He had already assumed it would be a boy. He was giddy with excitement. He had Phoebe, Little Nat and soon they would have another one, no two, to add to the mix. He completely ignored Shem's statement.

'You are such a prat.' Shem declared. 'What am I going to do with you?'

'Look give it a couple of days.' Rafe now put on his serious mature voice.

'You have two children with Daisy, another on the way and you've got another lovely girl pregnant. If you think I'm mad with you, you haven't seen them. Remember her Grandfather, her father and Uncle are here.' Rafe seemed to shrug as if they were not important in the scheme of things. 'And you are forgetting one big thing?'

'The tension is killing me.' Rafe said dryly. Shem went for him and Rafe backed off laughing holding his arms out in defence, with his horses brush as a weapon. The dog barked.

'Kebo!' Shem watched as Rafe's started to comprehend what he was saying. Kebo was his Uncle and a man he would never ever dare to defy, Kebo would eat him for dinner.

'Kebo!' Rafe shrugged it off trying to be brave. 'Kebo loves me.' Rafe hated being in his Uncles bad books, and would avoid at all costs him being told if he had misbehaved or done anything wrong. Kebo would say he had no respect and treated everyone with disdain. He would preach that he had no honour and dignity. 'You forget yourself you moron, Amelia is his niece by blood.'

Rafe stopped and lent back against the horse for comfort. How could he ever forget? However, it was so easy when you had a new name, a new identity and half your original family was lost to you. Only a few were privy and Kebo would kill him, regardless of whether he was his nephew or not. He lowered his head.

'I know. I just chose to forget for a brief moment.' He closed his eyes and thought of times long ago. 'Fuckin' hell! No, you are right; I'll have to face them all. Come on let's get it over with.' He pretended to go forward, knowing full well that Shem would not feed him to the lions. He stopped deliberately in front of Shem and gestured for him to lead the way. Shem whacked him round the head. 'Ouch.' Rafe cried like a girl. 'God, you're so rough all the time, just tell me what the bloody hell I am supposed to do?'

'That's the most sensible thing you've said.' Shem sighed, it would be best for Rafe to lay low again for a while, he'd send him with some horse stock to Marcel, and perhaps bring the planned visit to the Hall forward. He would then plan to join him shortly thereafter.

'Will you miss me?'

'No, you are a pain up the backside. What am I going to do with you?'

'You love me.' Rafe winked and punched Shem playfully, at which Shem got his head in a headlock and started to knuckle his head spitefully. The horse moaned his irritation at the pair. Earl barked once and gave up, having seen this too many times before. Shem flung Rafe into a free stall and then went to throw himself on him. Rafe held out his hands in defence, warding him off screaming: 'No, you're hurting me, you such a bully!'

'Good! You are such a girl!' Shem landed straight on him and both proceeded to wrestle. 'You deserve a beating  you, silly tart! The sooner we hear back from Saltdean, the better, and then you'll be on your way and spend the time reflecting on your bad habits. I've had enough of bailing you out.'

'Next you will make me go back to church.'

'Yeah, where is Jesus?'


'Have you cooled down now so that we can talk sensibly?' Shem taunted. He knew that they had just returned from visiting the Mint House and it had given him time to have a word with Rafe and decide how he was going to play this. In any event, he had to keep everyone happy and the threatening face of his Uncle Kebo kept haunting him.

'Don't patronise us you fucking bastard. Your brother is a whore.' Theo Hawkins flung out the insult.

'Do you do wanna die?'

'Who the fuck are you?' Harry Hawkins, Theo's father, groaned.

'Do I look in any mood to take your shit?' They should have seen that Shem's eyes were black.

'My daughter is pregnant with your brother's bastard and you stand there like it's a business deal. I am that mad.' Theo could not contain his hate at that point.

'So you said.' Shem snarled. He sighed in boredom and started to rub his thighs and look out the window. At that, Theo lost patience and launched himself at him in anger but Shem was too quick and in a flash had pounced and had Theo sprawled out onto of the table with his hand around his throat squeezing. 'Say another word and I'll crush your wind pipe.' Shem's menacing voice threatened. Theo understood he had gone too far. The others were all on their feet and Shem felt hands across his shoulders urging him to let Theo go. 'I allowed you to have your say earlier but do not think that gives you licence to continue to disrespect me?' Shem pushed himself off Theo and turned to face the party.

'You give me what? You seem to forget boy, we made you.' Harry spat as Idris helped Theo off the table. Theo was soothing his wounded neck.

'You made me? You Harry?' Shem sneered leaning forward.

'Yes me, my brother's, and all the other buggers that Gunthorpe has mugged off.'

'Just remind me for a minute, where you would be now without me? Potless and shitless you fucking plep. You forget you had ploughed all your money into the forge and was only sailing the Three Brothers for fun?' Shem shook his head in disgust at the older man. 'You'd pissed most of your earnings up the wall and as I seem to recall made Theo give you half of his wives dowry to pay off what you owed to Meir the Jew. So don't fucking come here giving it large. You wanna shut ya mouth and behave.'

'Don't talk to my father like that.' Kish Hawkins piped up.

'Or what?'

'We came here to talk but we don't want you rubbing our faces in shit.' Kish was the quieter brother and Shem had never taken much notice of him.

'What, you want me to give my brother over to you, then what? You string him up by his balls? You forget she spread her legs on more than one occasion.'

'Don't you dare try and say she is .....' Theo could not say the word.

'What, she is a slapper?' Shem played them.

'I'll have you.' Harry stepped forward and was held back by his sons. Shem laughed at him.

'Look old man, shit happens; it's what we do now.'

'You want us to just ignore this?'

'Rafe won't and can't marry her.' Shem sat down and smiled.

'He fucking will.' Harry pointed hard at him and so Shem just sighed.

'He is married already.' He said in a very low voice. If only they knew the half of it?

'You fucking liar.' Harry moaned.

'You'd do anything to protect him.' Idris laughed shaking his head disbelievingly.

'That boy needs stringing up.' Harry ripped.

'What a cunt!'

'I don't believe you.' Came back the retorts. Claude at this point came forward, he could see that Shem was mad, mad, as hell, and they did not know the signs like he did. One of them would die at any minute if they pushed him too far, so he suggested;-

'Rather than rushing into decisions, have any of you actually spoken to Rafe and Amelia. What is it that they want? What does your wife have to say on the matter?'

'What the fuck has my wife got to do with this?' Theo growled. Shem looked at Theo incredulously. 'My wife will do whatever she is told.'

'Good marriage is it then?' Shem smirked. He hated Theo so much.

'Who do you think you fucking are, you know nothing, and you hardly set a good example with your fucking whore in tow? Heard you got a bastard as well. Seems to be a family trait! Fuck them and leave them to stew.' Shem sat completely still, engulfed in rage and blackness. 'Heard she's right carved up and a right minger. Shame you can't get rid quite so easily of her, as you would my girl.'

Theo hit the floor unconscious before he knew what had happened. The next minute Kish smacked a chair over Shem's shoulders, coming to his brother's aid. Shem roared in anger and pain, he flung his elbow back and it hit Kish square in the chin. He rounded on him and kicked his legs from under him. As he found his balance, Harry then roared towards him. Idris pulled Harry away, knowing he was no match. Shem then rounded back on Kish and locked his head in his arms.

'NOOOO.' Harry screamed in terror.

'Shem stop, your killing them.' Idris roared. Shem held fast. 'Look what your family have done Shem? How is this right?' Shem's eyes were on fire, he grinned maliciously at them all and their weakness. Claude was keeping everyone off him and willing Shem to look at him. Shem looked at Theo sprawled out on the floor and spat at him, not letting Kish go at all. He added extra pressure. In the next second, he flung Kish hard across the floor. Kish knew he had a lucky escape. He lay where he fell and tried to control his breathing.

'Any of you speak of my woman again and I will kill you. Do you understand?' His words were low and menacing. Idris backed up watching as Kish crawled to Theo. 'I will do all I can to help Amelia, you have my word. Her child will be my blood and both I, and my brother will not turn our backs on family. Is that understood?' They all knew then that they had pushed it too far and were lucky to be alive.

They were thankful that their humiliation had not been witnessed by a whole room of patrons at the Inn, yet the frustration and embarrassment of the incident spread through to their every core. What was it about these brothers that held so much mystic? Why were they so protected?

This was not over. They would leave with their tails between their legs but Shem saw the defiance there. The knowing looks between families. He inwardly sighed. He would give anything for this situation to disappear, but he could not control everything. He would have to watch them now. The trust was gone and there would be penance to pay. He would hold out the hand of friendship and give them some extra runs and perhaps a share in the galley business. He would do that for Amelia and the child she carried.

The party got themselves together, agreed the new term through gritted teeth, and left still in anger. Claude looked across at Shem as he watched their backs and then Shem looked at him and conveyed a message that he clearly understood. Give it time for them to brag about how they had got one over him, how they had supposedly mugged him off, and won this battle. When they were complacent and had let their guard down, he would kill them all. Shem's grin was evil and from outside in the dark, Harry had looked back one last time into the light of the Inn. It looked aflame with Hells fire with Satan and his minions guarding the entrance. He witnessed the unspoken exchange between Shem and Claude and felt a shiver up his spine. He become very very scared at that point knowing he was looking at a man who had completely played them.

He saw Shem in a whole new light and realised all too quickly that they had under estimated the power of Shem and had played this whole incident wrongly. He would have to talk to Bob to sort matters out, the fear of what Shem would do, would not leave his mind. The blood lust and humiliation was too much for some men and they were blinded by hate, and so Harry's sons and Idris would not listen to reason. They believed that had won a major battle and that Shem had seemingly bowed down and had given them more than they ever wanted. They felt empowered that they had got one over on Shem and were smug, choosing to concentrate on their glory and did not dwell on the fact that they had let their guard down and when that happened they would be vulnerable. Harry knew the Devil was Shem and he would play merry hell with all their souls.

'What?' The young Harry seemed to follow Shem around. If he wasn't with his father Jesus, he could be found following Shem. Gwen was still on tender hooks about her boy, whilst Jesus guided the boy as and when he needed it. It would take a long time for him to accept him and Jesus would not let anything jeopardise that. He loved the boy from the moment he first set eyes on him. God, had set him a new challenge and he would pride himself on being a better father than he ever had. Harry was naturally inquisitive and Jesus would answer every question as best he could. Both Jesus and Shem laughed about his ways, yet both saw no harm in nurturing him for his future, he just needed to lose the chip on his shoulder.

Harry was quite amiable when he lost his attitude and had made friends easily and seemed to have settled in with the local children, but Shem would not allow him to disrespect him, or to show off in front of his friends.

'What yaself.'

Shem just laughed at the boy. 'Abit lairy, ain't ya?'

'You got a problem with that?' The boy was so cocky and playing up, however with no one to witness.

'You'd best fuck off before I stab ya.' Shem warned, even though inside the boy intrigued him. He was a mini version of Jesus and seemed just as forth coming, be it that his Dad was vicious, he looked both clever and cunning. Shem looked around and Earl trotted behind.

'I ain't scared of you. Who are you, some dodgy no body? I know people and I'll get you sorted right enough.'

'You know people, do ya?' The dog was catching up.

'You can laugh mate, you're soon see.' Shem just looked at the boy in awe and then just smiled at him.

'Come here.' Earl thought he meant him and leant up against his master for his ears to be caressed.

'Why?' The boy did not even flinch.

'So I can smack ya one?' Shem laughed.

'Don't laugh at me.' The boy warned Shem.

'I'll tell ya what, big boy. Get your friends to come, tell them my name, then come back and grovel, ya little shit. Now fuck off.'

'You can't.....'

'Harry, who are you shouting at?' Gwen appeared from the kitchens having heard her nephew, dragged, and hugged him to her, seeing who he had been talking to. She was petrified. She had been drinking tea with Chrissy and seeking advice on buying one of the smaller cottages down the lane.

'I'm sorry Mr. Smith, if he was...' Shem waved his hand for her to stop. He found that he very much liked the woman. She had come to him a few days after Gideon's Will had been read, understanding the business partnership that he and Gideon had and wasn't naive to his position. She knew if he wanted to, he could just take it all away. He scared her so, she trembled from head to toe every time he came anywhere near and when she spoke to him, and her voice portrayed her nerves. Harry started to protest and wriggled away from his Aunt.

'Don't apologise to him. Who does he think he is? He ain't no one!' Harry was clearly embarrassed.

'My God Harry! Can't you just shut up for a moment and think, why do you always have to go off on one? You are too much! Too much! I can't cope anymore! Why do you think I brought you back here? I'm hoping that someone will help me. This is too much.' Gwen let all her feelings spill out and tears sprung and flew freely down her face. Chrissy grabbed her and cuddled her. The poor woman was at her wits end after making the journey, finding it frosty with Valentina and now this with Harry acting up, whenever he felt like it. She had lost her brother and was feeling lost. She was awash with embarrassment and humiliated at letting her guard down. She felt foolish, weak and worst the audience was one of the most powerful men she had ever met.

Shem felt sorry for the woman, understanding completely where she was coming from. He looked at the boy and knew what he had to do. He could not get away with hurting the woman who had done everything for him. He knew the boy was just hitting out and had taken it too far. He was just too spoilt and needed taking down a peg or two.

Before he knew it, Shem had grabbed Harry's ear and was pressing down hard. Harry was screaming in pain and Shem made him sink to his knees. Earl, by this time had moved well away.

'Apologise to ya Aunt now.' He whispered into his ear and the boy was very frightened at how things had turned out.

In the meantime, the commotion was bringing the scene to the attention of the Inn and Shem was loath to continue with an audience.

'I will not.' With that, Shem dragged the boy by the ear through the kitchen door and he flung him across the floor with a kick to the behind.

'You will apologise to your Aunt, and after, if ya know what's good for ya, you will go the Castle, see ya Dad, and tell him I said to get you working now!'

'You can't order me around.' His protest had lost their previous anger.

'Oh for Fucks sake Harry, ya lucky I like ya, and you know you were out of order. Now do as I say.' The boy needed a direction, a purpose.

'He ain't me Dad.' Harry flung back. Shem knew then that he had him. He folded his arms and just stared at him.

'If you are going to work for me, Harry Boy, you are gonna have to learn to keep that shut and take orders with no questions asked.' Shem proceeded in a less threatening tone.

'What if I don't wanna work for ya?'

'Then, I'll have to kill ya.' Shem went to walk forward and the boy tried to get up on his legs. He stumbled and then was up and backing away. 'Go and see ya Dad now or I will slice of ya ear, then I will.....'

'He's threatening me, do something.' Harry interrupted seeing Jesus out of the corner of his eyes. Jesus had heard that Harry had been playing up all day and to see him mouthing off at Shem, could only spell real trouble and he did not want Gwen to get even more upset. The boy could be a handful at times and sometimes he just got a bee in his bonnet and needed reigning in. Shem seemed to be enjoying himself.

Jesus merely folded his arms and leant against the door opening. 'That gob will get you killed, now curb it boy or I too will have ya tongue. God forgive me.'

'You would not dare?'

'Shem, grab him, while I...' The boy pushed through him and darted away. Earl trotted out too see where he was going.

Shem and Jesus smiled at each other and went outside to watch Harry plough through the fields, looking back occasionally to see if they were after him. Both men just seemed to have folded their arms and weren't really paying him any attention, just chatting and laughing.

'His is a right one.' Jesus said proudly. Shem agreed and added.

'He is going to have a great future, that boy; he is bright, not like you.' Jesus just grinned at the jest. 'But he needs to be taught some respect and first and foremost to his Aunt.'

'You're not wrong there.' Jesus looked back over his shoulder to catch a glimpse of Gwen.

'She seems to have had it hard.' Shem tried to open the conversation, which Jesus appeared reluctant to start.

'I am afraid the hate she had for what I did has been driven into him.' He said awkwardly.

'I heard she run off and left you.' Shem pressed. He remembered when he and Rafe had been rescued and for a time he had been especially cocky and pushing his luck.

'I don't blame her now Shem. The sailor had the advantage at the time.'

'And you just had to add fuel to the fire?'

'I was angry and look what I did. I messed up and still do not feel worthy of any.....'
He had sinned and would have to repent for the rest of his days. He had bedded
another man's wife and gotten her with child.

'Jesus, you are too hard on yourself.'

'Time gives you hindsight.'

'*Let every man be master of his time!*' Shem quoted. 'God I wish that was so! I wait and
wait and wait to make my move. Being patient kills me when I have made all these
plans. The anger and frustration builds and builds until sometimes the blackness is
all consuming.' He looked to the sky for the Black Crows to hover above and
mock him. 'I live for the day that I can rest and find peace.' He murmured more to
himself. 'Will I ever?' He sighed. 'What is peace?' He rubbed his head and closed
his eyes. Jesus let his head fall to his chest daring not to look into the eyes of his
leader who for one small moment had let his guard down. Jesus knew very little
about Shem and Rafe's former life but knew they were really of high birth, having
heard Shem's normal voice on more than one occasion and was amazed at the ease
he could just transform back into a hard gang leader. He knew he was tormented
by events from his previous life and looking for solutions. He worried that the
blackness and Lucifer himself would engulf him for eternity unless he and his
friends watched and helped him along the way. Shem's rages into blackness were
becoming ever more frequent and he did not like it one bit.

'I pray you find what you are looking for my friend.' They both looked at each
other and nodded in mutual respect for each other. Since they had originally met all
those years ago, they had immediately got on. Shem had not judged Jesus, as many
did; he had just accepted him as the eccentric religious lunatic that he was. They
both turned back to try and spot Harry in the fields, but he had long since gone.

'He'll be back for his tea.' Jesus mused and Shem turned to see his friend's look of
concern for both the boy and then Gwen at the Coach House.

'Go and talk to her, you can't keep avoiding her.' Shem advised as Jesus shuffled
from foot to foot. Confronting Gwen was going to be one of the hardest things
Jesus ever had to do. It consumed him, and God forbid try as he might, there was
no denying the pull she had on him. It had been so long, but his heart could not
stop pounding at the thought of her being just a space away. God help him for he

still loved her so.

Did she feel the same? The torture of not seeing her ever again had killed him. Now she was back and he had become a coward. He found he would make his excuses and go if she was anywhere near, rather than face that awkward conversation. But he wanted her, he needed a good woman and she needed help with the wayward lad. He did not blame the lad for being up in arms. It was all so new and he had left his home and friends. It wasn't going to be easy, but Harry had spirit and Jesus smiled at that. If he was half as clever as he expected, he would be a great lad.

'You are right, there is no time. I'll go and ask her to marry me now. I have earned God's blessing.' Shem was slightly taken back and watched as Jesus smiled yet again at his reaction and decision. He seemed to be overcome with happiness and not lost in paying penance. The weight of the world fell off his shoulders.

'You are just going to go straight in and ask?' Shem asked shocked.

'Yes! It's about time! I must be master of me own time, whether He wishes it or not, this is what I want!'


Old Man Mole had eventually succumbed and asked Shem to take the rest of the Coach House off his hand. They had struck a deal and Old Man Mole had moved to the old cottage by the side of the Coach House and made it quite cosy and warm. He was watered and fed and was still around to offer help and assistance, and respected for calling time when he knew it was all too much. Every one adored him and everywhere he went there was always laughter. He was a landlord who knew how to be discreet and the Coach House had a good reputation and welcomed all walks of life and the news they brought with them. The gossip was rife and served Shem well, both with information coming in and what he wanted going out.

To the side of the coach house, Shem had added some extra rooms; He had especially wanted a study and somewhere he could just go, relax, and be quiet. He had his study decorated with beautiful panelled walnut wood and carvings. It was a soothing room and although it had seemed to have taken an age to get finished, his carpenters had done a superb job and he had rewarded them well. As it was so lovely, he would not let the children into it. Paully had laughed that Shem was playing up to his Dad and if he wanted, he could get him a globe, as his father had in his own room. Then Shem had pointed out that Paully would want to play with it and the room was for Shem and not for Paully to hide from Bella!

Shem had received a letter that morning from London and had been anxious to open and take time to read and reflect on its contents and after Mole had left, he had sat and mused over the contents. It had become a regular morning feature for Old Man Mole and Shem to meet up, share tea and news and both enjoyed the banter greatly. Shem had surrounded himself with older men of wisdom and experience. He had much yet still to learn and thrived on their council.

Shem's smile widened and he felt like everything was at last going his way. He re read the letter and sat for a long while planning his next move. With a heavy heart, his mind's eye took him to Rosie. She would hate part of his plans but then he would make her understand the bigger picture. They were finally getting somewhere and she had taken to the life style with ease. They were comfortable with each other and he smiled at this morning's activities and the woman's cheek.

'Quick.' Rosie had suddenly said.

'What?' He sat up in panic. His hair was a mess and he shook himself out of sleep.

'Get up.' She had flung the sheets back and jumped up with a grin on her face.

'Why, what's happened?' He stood up still half asleep and looked for his trousers, scratching his privates.

'The suns out and there is a small breeze, if we get them sheets out quickly, they will all be dry and smell lovely, it will save Chrissy a job.' He stopped dead.

'You having a laugh?' He collapsed back on the bed, struggling to get the blankets from under him and over him.

'Don't get back in bed.' She turned with her hands on her hips.

'I can think of better things to do, than hang out washing.' He grabbed her and wrestled her back to the bed. She shoved him and motioned for him to keep the noise down, as Seb still was asleep across the way.

'Come on. Let's get back under the sheets.' He raised his eyebrows in anticipation.

'I'll tell you what. If you help me, I will......' She smooched to him seductively, he grinned at her teasing smile. Her hair was all lose and fell over her shoulders in an abundance of large curls. He sunk back into the bed and she crawled up over him and gave him a small peck on his nose. He closed his eyes and smiled. They rubbed noses and ever so lightly, he whispered.

'Cross ya heart and hope to die.'

'Oh yes.'

He lightly pushed her back to the bed and quick as a flush was up putting his trousers on and as he run through the door loudly whispered over his shoulder. 'What you waiting for, come on then.' His eyes were alight with fire and mischief.

The sheets kept blowing all over the place and every time Shem thought he had one end, and tried to match up with the other corner, the wind would take it. The small breeze had turned into a gust of wind. Rosie could not stop laughing at him. The day before had seen wet and drizzling and so nothing had been able to dry and Chrissy hated being behind with the washing.

'If anyone sees me Rose, then that's it, you know then you must die.' He threw at her between giggles.

'Need a hand there Shem?' Shem could have died and looked to see Chrissy leaning up against the kitchen doorway sipping tea and laughing at him. God knows how long she had been there!

He gave her the filthiest of looks; she coughed back a laugh, but just could not help herself. 'Next, God forbid, you'll be emptying your own piss pot!'

Rosie gave her a warning look and shooed her away, but to Shem she winked and he laughed with her at the whole situation. What did he look like?

'Just pour me a cup of tea witch.' He called to Chrissy. 'And you.' He pointed at Rosie. 'You better be following me up the stairs, as soon as you're finished.'

'Or what?' She teased.

'Oh you're brave.' He laughed mocking her. 'Or what? She says.' He shook his head at her nerve. 'You know wench, you'll be up them stairs like lighting. I have your promise.'

'Don't flatter yourself.'

'Oh, hark at her; be singing a different song soon.' He cried being really saucy.

'Shem!' She exclaimed and he stuck out his tongue and run off into the kitchen where Chrissy was chuckling away. He gave Chrissy a thankful kiss, and with tea in hand, he run back up stairs humming to himself and sure enough Rosie wasn't too far behind.

Shem patted the letter and almost felt like jumping in joy. He needed to find Rafe and share the news. He calmly made for the kitchens to find Rosie folding some of the dry sheets from earlier. She made his insides somersault.

'Where's Seb?' He asked as an afterthought seeing she was all alone.

'Following Harry.'

'Where's Harry?' He prompted.

'Following Jesus and before you ask, they have all been at the Brewery. Jesus has let Rafe in on his secret.' He laughed and strolled forward opening his arms for a cuddle.

'You mean Jesus' got another secret?' She grinned at him, played with his shirt, and looked into his eyes with mischief on her mind. 'You obviously know what it is?' He quizzed.

'And you too will, if you go to the brewery.' She gave him a quick peck on the cheek and pushed him away but her smile was so suggestive he grabbed her to him and gave her a big kiss. He then slapped her behind and winked as he left, both with knowing smiles on their faces.

'Now, now, none of that hanky panky.' Bob laughed entering the kitchen with Chrissy. They seemed to be spending so much time together just lately and both Shem and Rosie shared the thought.

As Shem entered the back of the Castle Inn to make his way to the brewery, he heard loads of laughing and jeering. Harry was leaning up against the doorway with Seb saddled around him. As he approached, Harry gave him a look.

'What?' Shem warned him mockingly, he came forward and kissed Seb on the head and ruffled Harry's hair.

'What yaself.' Harry smirked back; it had now become a game with them.

'You lairy bastard, I'll do ya.' Shem laughed at Harry while at the same time he raised his eyebrows at Seb in play.

'You're all talk.'

'Don't I know it?' He winked at Harry. 'Here Rafe?' He called. Rafe looked across from the barrels and could see the excitement on Shem's face.

'Do you see this?' Rafe was too excited and wanted to share his news first.

'What?'

'Look.'

As Shem came forward, he realised that the brewery was actually in the process of making more Ale. Paully had nearly had a fit previously thinking that as soon as the last batches of ale went, there would be no further Ale to follow, with the recipe dying with Gideon. They had a large stockpile, but needed to start the ball rolling again to meet the various orders that the Castle Inn had received. It was still proving to be very popular.

'Oh my God, you've got the recipe?' Shem half asked and stated.

'Always had it.' Jesus piped up and laughed. God since he had asked Gwen to marry him, he seemed to be a changed man and actually had learned to have a little bit more fun without it being quite a sin. The fact that he and Gwen could not wed had not deterred him. Gwen was none the wiser as to whether her current husband was dead or alive, and so they had agreed that even though it was a mortal sin and Jesus had to wrestle with his beliefs, life was far too short and so they had agreed to be together no matter what.

This had not gone down well with Jesus' brother Jordan, who had said that God would not ever forgive him, however Jesus was adamant and even though Jordan preached against it, he was secretly overjoyed that at last his brother was happy.

'You mean you never brought it Harry?' Shem looked directly at the boy.

'No,' Harry handed him Seb who had been fighting to get Shem's attention once more. Shem took him from Harry, he too saddled him around his side, and they rubbed noses.

'You weren't to know, but that great lump Paully should have remembered that me and Gideon served as apprentices here.' Jesus cried. Rafe and Shem looked at each other and shook their heads. Jesus had known all along!

'And the great idiot should have remembered that Gideon's dad did write it on the wall over there, with one secret ingredient missing, mind though. Paully was here enough times! He used to come across when he had wound up his Dad and thought we'd be able to go off on an adventure.' Jesus actually grinned. 'Oh he'd hang about making a nuisance of himself. Gideon's dad thought he would learn something. However it never happened.' Jesus pointed at the back of the workshop and Shem looked across and nearly wet himself laughing as he could make out long since faded writing on the white washed walls. The recipe was clearly laid out in all its glory.

'That bloody idiot has been causing no end of grief about that poxy recipe and all the time......'

'He gets worse as he gets older. God bless him.' Jesus was shaking his head laughing at his old friend. 'When's he due back?'

'Any time now,' Shem could not wait to hear back from him on his latest escapade to the big city. 'Anyway, Rafe, a word? '

The brothers with Seb in tow moved out of earshot of Jesus and Harry.

'Our cousin Oliver has made it back safely. He'll send word when he can meet up.'

'You're joking? Oh my God!' Rafe mopped his hair back and looked at wonder to his brother. His eyes nearly popped out of their sockets. This news meant so much to them.

'No fucker can ever tell us what to do now.' Seb looked at him in surprise and Shem mouthed sorry to his son.

'Does that mean I still have to go away?' Rafe looked pleadingly at his brother. Seb chuckled at Rafe's face, who played on it to impress his nephew. Seb was laughing at Rafe who kept pocking out his tongue.

'Yes you plep.'

'Rafe's been naughty.'

'That's right, you tell him Seb.'

'What did you do?' He asked innocently and both looked at him and suppressed grins.


The carriage pulled up and Lady Theia Mordesan let the tears full down her face. She did not care who saw, she was so overcome, and she was home where she belonged.

It had been a slow pace to get from Croxley to Cornwall and one that had exhausted her. Throughout the journey, she had drifted in and out of sleep and then had been woken by Martha or Gunthorpe and she had stated that she was not asleep just resting her eyes. Unlike the Greek Goddess she had been named after, she knew she was not immortal and time was precious and she wanted to savour this time.

Her heart swelled and even before she was helped off the carriage, she knew that there was no way that she would ever leave again. Lady Theia grabbed Martha's hand for comfort.

They had arrived at Mordesan Hall and the day could not be any better. The sun was smiling and the heat was comfortable, and there was a small light breeze. She was still surprised how she had got the house back, but she would muse on that later. She was home!

She looked over her old home and her mind swam with all the memories. Her heart swelled. Tears trickled down her face. She absorbed every inch of this fabulous house and her eyes rested on the great door and the memory of its enormous key. The house had a lovely stone facade, which was heavily hidden now by the evergreens. A row of red lush roses were in full bloom however completely overgrown and needed to be pruned as soon as possible. She could see that attempts had started to be made to rectify the years of neglect.

She remembered how she had loved to sit and just be in her mother's flower garden around the back of the house, just off to the left where the formal gardens were. She had no delusion that this probably too had been totally neglected and was overgrown; however with a little hard work, it could all be restored. She was overcome with emotion.

Unceremoniously Gunthorpe came to her and grabbed her elbow for support. She looked up at him with love and respect. They had shared so much, this was a moment she wished to savour forever, and it was only fitting that he was there to share it with her along with Martha. Gunthorpe returned the look of love with warmth. 'We are finally home Gunthorpe.' She could hardly speak and her voice was a mere whisper.

'Yes,' His voice was also full of emotion.

'You'll have to carry me out in a box before I leave again.' She smiled wickedly at herself.

'Shh, such talk!' He patted her hand and just at that moment, they heard a commotion and Theia stopped in her tracks as a man came running from the back of the house at full speed. Martha put both her hands over her mouth in shock and wonder at seeing him and not comprehending that it could actually be.........

Theia stepped back in wonder and found again the reassurance of Gunthorpe so close to hand. The young man stopped not six feet in front of her, he lent back to catch his breath, and then lent forward with his hair waving all over. His white shirt was rolled to the elbows and his once clean trousers were caked in dirt. He still held a horse brush in his hand and looked at it and with his usual cockiness, flung it over his shoulder and then rested his hands on his hips. He adopted a natural pose and laughed at her informally. He was so cheeky!

'Where have you been, I have really missed you?' He grinned in that boyish way and Gunthorpe found himself laughing in joy at the rascal. This man was full of surprises and their last conversation had certainly opened his eyes.

Theia blinked back tears, not believing it was him; she was holding her breath and looked from Gunthorpe to him in shock. Was it truly him? There was no doubt. God, how was this possible? Her baby! Her beloved angel was standing in front of her. But he was no longer a baby, but a man. A beautiful man! 'We're not going to stand on ceremony and be formal are we? Because I know deep down you want to smother me with pinches, kisses and loads of lovely hugs, oh come on, get over here.' The young man laughed and joked waving her towards him, at the same time, he made towards her, and she crumbled into him, in complete happiness. He held her so tightly, rocking her from side to side, both exchanging kisses and greetings, and sharing in a love, that had long since been lost. He had answered her prayers and had been restored. He surely must have had something to do with her getting the Hall back.

'Tell me you both survived for the love of God, and I'll die now in complete and utter bliss.' Theia cried in joy and thought she was in the arms of Apollo!

Rafe, Little Paully and some of Marcel and Ziggi's men waited in the thick of the trees patiently. If the information had been correct, the carriage was due at any time.

They had been returning to the South Coast with a good stock of horses and Shem would be pleased. Rosamund had been over the moon to see Rafe and he had enjoyed his visit with his gypsy cousins after he had returned from Cornwall and the Hall. He felt all warm and contented at the reunion with his family. He smiled recalling Rosamund warning him to behave and had done rather well considering. He had flirted outrageously with all the women at the camp and they absolutely loved him for it, whilst the men just shook their heads at him, knowing he was harmless.

Rafe loved where they stayed in the New forest, it was a mini paradise with abundance of with wild flowers, herbs and other medicinal plants. There was wild game and springs of fresh water. The forest was a magical place and Rafe loved the sense of protection from the outside world. The area served as a barrier to the local people, and Rafe had witnessed firsthand how some of the local peoples despised those he loved. He could not hold his hand on heart and say in some cases it was indeed warranted. He chuckled in memory at more than one of his joint exploits with Marcel and Ziggi Vargas.

He hated to leave but he had orders to move the stock back to Shem, and thought maybe one day, when he and Shem had sorted matters out he could chose a life roaming the countryside and meeting all types of wonderful women. However, duty called and soon he would have some extra mouths to feed. He laughed to himself at that. He wanted to be a good father, but he certainly wasn't making life easy for himself! He could change, but not quite yet, in any event, he had more women to charm, and he found his mind wondering to Felicity, the vixen at the Mint House. She had become a good friend and she had many hidden talents.

On key, the carriage seemed too stop and the baggage went flying. The driver had jumped off and discovered that one of the horse's bridles had snapped.

Rafe and co were hidden at least 30 yards away and observed a woman in all her finery, climb down and start sorting out the baggage's in temper, her body language evidently showing how inconvenient this all was and she could certainly be heard screaming in anger in her native tongue.

'Do you want us to help? If we all stay we can get her sorted and out of here in no time at all.' Little Paully asked in a whisper teasing Rafe.

'What part of the plan did you miss at the Inn you wally?' Rafe spat back. The others in the party started to laugh. 'Unless you have some sick fantasy about a threesome, I suggest you piss off and when I am done with the lovely Valentina, I'll ask her for special lessons for you, cos I am worried about you.' Little Paully proceeded to go a particular shade of red at being so chastised whilst still laughing at the whole thing.

'Tut tut young Paully, you know better.' Rafe just had to chastise him even more.

'We'll be off then.' Little Paully laughed looking at the scene and the rascal Rafe. He could not believe how Rafe continued to get away with it? He loved him to death and could not believe his sister Amelia had fallen for his charms. He was a rascal and caused all those he loved no end of trouble. Little Paully's parents were having kittens and pulling him from all sides.

'That would be sooo wise and thoughtful of you. Ta, ta.' Rafe was also laughing.

'Will you even attempt at pretending to be of some use and help the driver?' Rafe looked at Little Paully like he was mad. Little Paully answered his own question. 'Hard labour and you just do not go.'

'True.' They grinned knowingly at each other. There only seemed to be the lady and her driver.

'So see you in a few hours then. That should give you enough time to get re-acquainted ..........'

'Slowly you are learning my boy.' Little Paully laughed and with a fond wave, he rode off too leave Rafe to his pleasures.

Rafe had no doubt that Little Paully would spin a yarn or two for his friends and loved one's waiting his return.

When Rafe and company had pulled up at the local coach house at Hands Cross, Rafe had immediately noticed Valentina's carriage. He had made some enquiries and found from the driver that she was returning from a shopping trip from London and was all alone. Rafe thought he would hatch a plan to have some time with the Spanish temptress and so persuaded the driver of the coach to indulge him. If he was going home to a life of trying to be faithful and loyal to one woman, he had wanted to go out with a bang at least! Who was he kidding, since Annatasia, there could be no one to compare or hold him down!

Rafe's companions had read his mind and knew exactly what would happen. He shouldn't have wasted his breath.

'Well, well, what do we have here?' Rafe rode up and grinned.

'Rafe what a surprise!' Valentina cried. She turned to see him and he grinned at her and all the piles of baggages. She always returned from a shopping trip with an abundance of clothes for her and the girls, but she did not seem particularly pleased to see him. He would remedy that!

'Hello Master Smith.' Hartright appeared from nowhere. His confidence oozed from every pore.

'What the f....' At that point, the butt of the pistol knocked Rafe sideward's. Hartright smiled in satisfaction. Constance was right; he could do anything if he had the mind to.

'Hey you, what's your game. Do you know who that is?' The driver called.

'Certainly,' and with that Hartright levelled the pistol and fired. The driver did not stand a chance. Valentina screamed and Hartright looked at her with loathing whilst backing up wanting some distance from Rafe. Hartright was shaking from head to toe but also he found he felt quite detached.

In the distance, Little Paully and party stopped in their tracks, without hesitation they turned back.

'My dear, such dramatics at a time like this.' Hartright replaced his pistol and went to retrieve the other from his belt. 'If one wants to be a lady, one has to act like one.' The next minute, he flew off his feet as Rafe steamed into him. Rafe landed on top of him and the gun went flying. Hartright was winded and was subjected to a horrific beating, with Rafe even resulting to biting him. Rafe was going to make this man pay and by God, he did.

Hartright lay on the floor semi unconscious and was a bloody mess. How could he think he could best anyone? He wanted to curl up and die; this whole thing had been a big joke.

Rafe stood over him staggering with the effort and mopped back his hair. He kicked Hartright again for measure and backed away breathing heavily.

Valentina was laying just to the side of Hartright in shock at the events and looked at Rafe with a new kind of respect and admiration.

'Oh Rafe! Rafe! Thank God you came!' He looked at her in question. 'He got in the coach at Forest Row. I could not stop him; He held a gun to my head. I tried to alert the driver, but could not. I was petrified. He said he was going to kill Shem. He was going mad.' She started to whimper hoping that Rafe would believe every word.

'It's alright, really Valentina you are safe now, I'll tie him up, and we will get him to the court house. It will be fine.' He averted his eyes and started to look about for something to bind Hartright with, when he heard Hartright snarl.

'You lying bitch.' Hartright grabbed her wrist and pulled her to him in temper. She scratched at his face and dug her nails in deep. He punched her across the face and she landed on her backside. 'You'd do anything to clear your name.'

Rafe stormed forward. 'Harry, leave her alone now.' He yelled. Valentina saw the pistol not two feet away, she grabbed and cocked it. Her hands could not stop shaking.

'Put that down you deceitful bitch.' Hartright warned and turned towards her. He was in her firing line. His face was full of vile and hatred for her. She felt like her heart was going to explode. 'You just dare.' He lurched forward and as he did, the gun went off.

Rafe fell to the floor.

'What have you done you stupid woman?' Hartright and Valentina froze.

'Oh my God. Oh my God. Rafe. Rafe!' She flung the gun away and crawled towards Rafe, oblivious to the dirt on her hands and skirts.

'You've killed him! You killed him!' Hartright murmured as he managed to get to his feet and wobbled with the effort. His vision was blurred as blood dripped down his face. What had happened? By God, this was not supposed to happen? But then he had been planning to do exactly the same to Shem. It was all her stupid fault. With his shoulders slumped and breathing hard with the pain, he made his way to Rafe's horse. He screamed at the effort to mount the horse and without a backward look, kicked the horse, and fled. It had all gone so horribly wrong.

'Oh my God, Rafe, Rafe. Please, please. Oh my God!' Valentina cradled Rafe in her arms, allowing his blood to cover her completely.

---

**Act Three**

**Chapter Eleven**

There was stillness in the room. The wind blew through the only glassed window, and the heavens opened as an August down pour, showed its hand. Paully stood blocking the entrance to the room at the Barley Mow Inn, at Hand Cross, where they had taken Rafe. Claude and the rest of the crew were picketed all around the small village.

It seemed like an age before their Guvnor showed up and now Paully would not let him through. Paully looked at him warning him with his expression of what he was to see and Shem looked into his eyes and then shouldered him out of the way. Paully followed him up to the small bedroom where they had placed Rafe and then watched as Shem just stood in complete shock. He fell to his knees, hitting a sick bowl whose contents went flying everywhere. He did not seem to notice. He sobbed, losing his breath and almost choked, Rafe had been shot!

Paully just stood there lost. Dr. Fox had previously been called for and met them at the Inn, and Claude had organised everything. He had also sent word to the rest of the gangs to meet on the morrow, as well as alerting the Magistrate and Military. He also had sent word across to Mr. H.

Claude went to Shem who was still on his knees just looking at his brother. 'Shem. Fox needs a word.' He whispered.

'No one touches him. No one.' Shem hissed and glared at Claude to defy him. He got up from his knees and slowly covered his face with his hands, but knew that he would never forget this and his heart pounded so strongly he was amazed that no one else heard it. He walked towards his brother who lay in the bed deathly pale. Shem leant down, stroked Rafe's forehead, and kissed him tenderly. Rafe was hot to the touch and sweating in fever. 'I'm here you little prick. I'll speak to Fox, and then maybe we can take you home.' He whispered as his voice choked. The air was thick with foreboding. Rafe's eyelids moved and Shem moved nearer to him.

'Samuel?'

'I'm here.' He placed his hand on his cheek and with his other hand squeezed his brother's hand. Paully heard Rafe call him Samuel.

'Good.' Rafe managed a half smile. He opened his eyes slightly. 'God you look rough.'

'Look at ya self you dick head. What you playing at giving it large hey? Have I ever said you can be a right prat sometimes?' Rafe was far too weak and smiled, he wanted to say more, but his eyelids were closing. 'Keep that big gob shut and get some sleep you idiot. I need you to return to me in one piece.'

'Nice.' Rafe mouthed through a small grin; he forced his eyes open and looked at the tears in his brothers eyes. 'Love you too, fool.' He fell back to sleep with a bigger grin on his face. Shem padded his hand and looked at the bruises across his knuckles. He grinned weakly thinking that Rafe had indeed given it out. He would not leave his side now until he was better.

There was a knock at the door and Doctor Fox came in again to speak to Shem.

Outside most of the villagers had heard what had happened and slowly made their way along the long lane to the old stone house asking;-

'Who's died?'

'What's happened?'

'Who did you say it was?'

'Is Rafe dead?'

'Oh, he's alive, just, oh my God.'


Shem had finally been coaxed out of the tiny room; having not moved from Rafe's side. He had not said a word to anyone, not even Rosie when she had arrived. He would not even look at her. He had withdrawn into himself. He hadn't eaten anything, and it was as if his whole body had shut down.

It was nearly morning, the sun was just trying to push through and call out, I'm here! They were both up and met each other on the stairs and Rosie felt so awkward, she just touched his hand and caressed it. He looked down at it and did not move. It was all too familiar to her, how he had been when she had been ill. He was focusing everything on his brother and praying for him to get better. She felt him turn her hand and he squeezed it slightly. They then looked at each other long and hard at that point, conveying so much without having to speak, and then he walked away. She entered the room and closed the door behind her and leant against it, breathing heavy, she had not heard him descend the stairs. The tension for Rafe was suffocating. She could not breathe. She then heard his slow footsteps on the stairs. She went to the window knowing he would emerge from the back door at any minute and watched for him. He felt and looked up at her, she did not move and just stared at him. He nodded and she found herself waving in acknowledgement. What could words do at this time? She moved away, and felt flush; she could not control her breathing. Then she restored herself and set to Rafe. Life had begun to get so good, now it had all come crushing down. She prayed to God that Rafe would recover.

Shem had mastered his emotions and controlled his anger at the man who had attacked her and had wanted to kill Hartright on many occasions, however there were things working in the background, which deterred him from doing it. Now Shem was re living a nightmare and she could see him fight and try to keep the devil at bay. She prayed with all her heart for both Shem and Rafe.


Doctor Fox shook his head as he examined Rafe and as he put back the sheet to cover his patient, he patted the young man. Doctor Fox had always liked the two boys who his cousin Bob had brought to the area.

'No, no,no.' Rosie said pleadingly as Doctor Fox shrugged his shoulders in sorrow. 'His breathing is shallow, I'm afraid there is nothing more I can do....' He left the sentence hanging in the air. At that very moment, Shem burst into the room; having been outside and told that Fox was examining Rafe again. He rushed to the bed and witnessed the anguish in Rosie's eyes as she withdrew her gaze from Fox to him.

She lay atop the bed with Rafe's head cradled in her arms. This could not be happening.

The room was excessively hot from the fire and sweat poured from Fox's brow, Rosie hair was damp with the heat, she held back her tears.

Shem moved forward and Rosie let him replace her and cuddled his brother to him, he begun to softly rock back and forth with him in his arms. He was numb. Fox indicated to Rosie that he would be outside, she nodded.

Every breath that Rafe took, Shem and Rosie took with him; they waited for every breath to come and go. As time slipped by, so did Rafe's breathing, each breath a grasp for life? In her mind, Rosie started to count the seconds between each breath. Shem was soothing him and saying words of encouragement. He found he could not focus. He thought it must be a dream.

Time slipped by. They urged Rafe on with all their hearts. He breathed hard. Then breathed hard again. Then again. Shem cried with the effort.

Then came one last attempt at holding on, one last hold. One last long........breath, then nothing. No breath. No sound. Emptiness. Silence. Silence!

Rosie counted the seconds rather than face the horrid reality.

Shem sat astonished. He knew in his mind that Rafe had gone, but he could not let him go. He wiped back his damp blond hair and cuddled him further into himself. He was still warm to his touch. He kissed him all over his face and whispered endearments, all the time rocking back and forth. No one else mattered, just him and Rafe. As it had always been.

Rosie sat in shock at the grief of it all. She was numb. She went to the door and tried to call out, but her throat was dry, it was just a croak, but nevertheless, was heard from below.

Doctor Fox went to Shem and tried to guide him away so that he could examine Rafe. But Shem just held him firm. He held him tighter. Fox tried again to unclasp Shem's hands and was conscious that this was not a man to make an enemy of, but from his eyes, he could see he was lost. Still Shem refused to let go.

Fox looked to Rosie for help, he felt useless, and no matter how many times he had witnessed death, it never failed to tear at his insides. Slowly Rosie leant across to try to cradle, and at the same time, steer Shem away from Rafe, but Shem just glared at her.

'He's just sleeping,' he hissed as he nodded his head to try to convince himself. Rosie backed off and understood that Shem needed more time. He lay beside his brother and cuddled up to him. 'He will want me to be here when he awakes.' He whispered to himself. 'Come on you prat!' A tear trickled down his nose. Again, he caressed his brother's cheek. He looked back to Rosie for reassurance that everything was going to be alright. She shook her head at him and he reached out and took her hand. She squeezed his hand tightly, and kissed it. Shem then lifted her hand to cup his face. The tears streamed freely down his face as he looked back at his brother. 'Silly twat, you are not waking up are ya?' He started to moan and slowly the hurt made his insides churn. 'He must return to me.' He lifted himself from the bed and started to pace the room. Fox and Rosie backed away from him. As quickly as he had started he stopped, he looked again at his brother lying dead on the bed. They backed out of the door. Shem closed his eyes and without any warning, he started to trash the room. Both Rosie and Fox cleared the doorway before they heard the thud of the side cabinet in the room smash against the door. They then heard him kick and kick and kick the door, until it gave way. He grabbed the door and yanked like a mad man at the hinges.

Fox fled down the stairs; and stopped anyone else going up. His older cousin Bob and he shared a moment of understanding and this made Paully and Claude hold back, however ready at any minute to go to Shem. They all took in without being told what had happened. Paully sobbed uncontrollably, Claude let the tears just roll of his cheeks, and Bob bent his head to his chest and cried without any shame or embarrassed to do so.

Rosie remained and sat at the top of the stairs. She was empty of any emotion.

After a while, it went quiet and she ebbed her way forward. She looked down the stairs and motioned for them to stay put. She rested her head against the now open doorway and peeped around to see Shem at the foot of the bed, with tears streaming down his face, his hands wringing through the sheets and then she watched as he started to moan like a lost animal. He rocked back and forth, and then his anguish intensified to a roar. More and more followed this and the rawness of the emotion tore into everyone in that Inn.

The howling consumed his being, his every core. He felt ripped apart and was eternally dammed, and everyone was going to pay, there would be pain, suffering, blood, gore and he did not delude himself, he had nothing to lose now and he wanted everyone to die a horrible death.

Everyone downstairs in the Inn felt the sheer enormity of what that sound meant. That raw emotion of so much hurt, so much pain, so much longing that for a few minutes it astounded them. They were all lost in a whirlwind of emotion and crying with the sheer intensity of the moment, there was no shame amongst these men for

289

what they did, for what they felt. Rafe was lost to them and Shem; their leader had lost his brother. Everyone in the Inn knew this was a bad day and drowned their sorrows in their ale. They cried into each other's arms, some held each other, some curled up on their own, but none choked back the tears. Rafe was a good bloke, a diamond who had had his fair share of it lately. Now he had paid the final price. There would be a reckoning and the devil upstairs was on fire.

Bob was anxious as he had sent word to both Mr. H and Rosamund and wondered who would be sent to break the news to poor Daisy. Daisy had been desperate to come to Rafe after hearing about his accident. She had missed him so much and just needed to see his cheery face to make the world a better place. After Rafe had gone on his trip, Daisy had a small fever, then Phoebe had caught it and then Little Nat had it and so she could not leave him. Now she would never see Rafe ever again!

Bob also wondered how the news would be received across at Burwash. No doubt Amelia would be distraught and be comforted by her mother Sade. However, Amelia's father would probably be over-joyed and Bob's brother Harry would sigh with relief that while Shem had this to deal with, he would not be so interested in him and his gang. Bob and Harry had disagreed about Shem's motives and Bob could not see how Harry could still be wary of Shem. Both knew that Bob was deluding himself and being naive. They both knew that Shem had men watching Burwash all the time. Shem was trying to intimidate the Burwash gang and it was working. Harry would never ask Bob to get Shem to let up and Bob would not confess he knew about everything that was going on. The paranoia was rife and Bob knew it was just a matter of time before Shem would screw them over. Shem never let anything lie. If they thought Shem would forget over Rafe's death, they had another thing coming.

No one could forget the other person involved in all of this and Valentina had been placed in a room as far away from Rafe as possible. She had been completely distraught and had to have laudanum to calm her from her hysterics. She was so scared and paranoid and found herself jumping at shadows. She had heard all the commotion and then that roar. She had jumped out of her skin and would swear at that point that she had seen Rafe standing in the corner of the room laughing at her. Laughing at what was coming. He would be avenged. She cuddled her knees to her chest and rocked back and forth with tears streaming down her face. She would not open her eyes again.

'Oh my God, oh my God.' Was all she cried.


Hartright had lost himself when he panicked and had to back track and double back, knowing that they would be hunting him. He had tried to hide and keep to the shadows. It had been late when he had reached Firle village and he found himself falling in exhaustion. Only to recover and then wrench. Nothing lay in his stomach so he just retched and retched in pain.

A dog barked and he spurred his horse on and heard metal swinging in the night breeze; he looked and found where the noise had come from. A gibbet hung from the local courthouse with a decaying body held fast. He sat motionless. There wasn't a soul about, just voices in his head, the dead mocking him. The wind had taken up and the dead men swayed in the wind again. Black Crows circled their foe and waited for him to pass in order to return to feast on the dead man's corpse. They mocked him with their cheers. The clouds took up speed and curled in anger and he felt the power of death engulf him. He needed to get to safety.

He had just one focus, to get to William. William would help and protect him and get him out of there. Surely, their friendship still meant something?

This whole thing had all been a big mistake. He was under no illusion that Valentina would say he did it. Shem had been taunting him, and playing with him rather than bring down justice immediately. His eye for an eye tactic had been laboured. How much more was he to endure? He had been abused and disfigured. Shem would hound him for the death of the driver by the authorities and the death of Rafe.

He would be hung like a common criminal at Tyburn Tree in London. He tried not to ponder on the images, which constantly frightened him of the rowdy crowds at his hanging. He pictured the crowds arriving early to secure their places and jeer him, as he would be led to his death. He could see Constance howling for him. He could see them all, the men, women, children, gentry and paupers alike, all attended the execution in the hope of witnessing a particularly dramatic declaration, or a courageous, applause-worthy farewell from him. He was doomed. Would anyone come to his rescue? He laughed to himself that his mother would never dare be witness to it. His mind was in turmoil, screaming at him. Where was his beloved Constance, why was she not here? Would she come to his aid again? He could not bear it. This could not be the end. He would escape, he had to escape. Shem could not win. It just could not end like this!

Shem slowly opened his eyes and looked to the open latticed window. The sun was just rising, a strong wind blew the massive clouds away, and he watched the trees dance back and forth. It was not cold in the room, just fresh. His eyes were sore. His whole body ached. How long ago had it been? Rosie lay by him, with her arm across him in protection and comfort. It was far too late for that. On his other side lay Earl, who rested his head on his master's chest and just looked lovingly at him. He stroked his head.

He did not know what day it was, far too many nights seemed to have gone by while he lay there hearing murmurs, and whispered conversations. The long nights had looked into emptiness. Rosie had tried to rouse him, but he had just turned over. He just wanted the numbness to go away. It was just too black. The crows cawed.

He listened to the soft breathing of Rosie. She was still fully dressed and he felt her warmness, her breath against his throat, that wonderful morning softness. Her face was smooth from sleep and she looked so rested. Her hair was everywhere like a thick blanket of cover. It looked as if she had just collapsed in exhaustion. She had just recovered from her own ordeal and he did not wish for her to be brought down again. On his return to the Coach House, he had not been able to speak to any one and it was left to Rosie, to let everyone know what had happened. He had left her to cope with Daisy. He had heard the telling scream and then Daisy collapsing. He had curled himself in a ball trying desperately to shut out her grief. He wished with all his heart that his father was there to comfort him. He had succumb to a panic attack and blacked out.

He needed Rosamund and knew that she would be there soon and help Rosie who was being pulled in all directions. Rosie had tried to stay with him, but found that she had to explain to both Seb and Phoebe what was happening. He heard the children cry, the dogs whine.

At one time, Earl had managed to squeeze past Rosie and had jumped up to his master and after licking Shem's face, curled up to his stomach and would not budge. He had heard Chrissy giving Rosie comfort and both of them consoling Daisy. He heard all his men's voices on a regular basis and even Jesus' brother, Jordan the Vicar, came across from Hankham to offer comfort.

He heard Bella and Lord Lennard and was touched by that. He remembered hearing that Lord Lennard had received word that extra Riding Officers were on the way to oversee the area believing that there would be further bloodshed.

Shem was struck by how so many cared and how in addition, so many relied on him. He just did not know how he would go on. He had protected Rafe for years, looked after him and they were at the last legs to get everything back. He had even sent him home in preparation for their return there. Now he was all alone. What had it all been for? He should not have listened to anyone and killed that bastard Hartright when he had the chance. He would never make that mistake again.

Rosie had resided herself to the numbness. A way of getting through the pain. If she did not feel, then she could cope and so come to terms with her life, her disfigurement and how her world would be with this great tower of strength, her Shem. Now their roles were reversed. She had become his rock and nursed him.

When Shem had woken, he reached out his hand to her in comfort. There was no need for words, her presence had been enough. He had been in a dream state, not willing to come back to reality, not quite yet. The loss was too much to confront.

Rosie and Chrissy and held him firm, all his men and companions had come from miles. There was a sense of foreboding and counting the days when the whole world would erupt. This was a bad business, Shem had become a force of nature, someone not to be messed with, but now, now, it was like waiting for Lucifer to show his hand once and for all, and everyone was waiting to let out their breath.

When Rosamund had eventually arrived, she had immediately taken charge. She had told Shem that many of the clans were on their way to him to show their respect and that Marcel and Ziggi, her sons, would do whatever he wished them to do, as would the rest of the clan's men. They would all pull together.

When Rosamund and Shem were alone, he had pressed himself against her so tightly; she had rocked him back and forth. He looked like death warmed up. His hair all greasy and lank. He had not shaven for ages and he was rank with sweat and dirt. She held his hand and silently made him stand up. She put his coat on and then led him bear foot out of the house, gathering up blankets. Paully and Claude held guard and she took him across the small backfield to the river, which run adjacent to the sea.

He just stood there in a trance and allowed her to slowly remove all his clothing and then she walked him into the water. She was fully clothed and she made him sink into the water and let the waters lap all over him. He did not need any more bad luck, so as per the clan's tradition, he had to bath in pure moving water. The water was cool, the current soft, and relaxing. All around the river, life continued as normal.

Shem let Rosamund wash him all over. She washed his hair and promised she would sort out his beard later, all the while singing a lovely Romani lullaby. She knew she had to be strong now for Shem and put him back on his path, but by God, she would give anything to turn back time.

Rosamund loved her boys so very much but her sunshine was her favourite. Her baby! Whenever he came to see her, he would creep up to her and whistle. She would laugh and beam with joy when he popped his head into view.

'I'll have tea if you are brewing one.' He'd say and then they would hug and talk for hours and hours on end.

Her brother Gunthorpe had brought the two boys to her whilst her clan had been travelling through Andalucía. He had given the boys new names and never discussed who they were or what business he and Bob Hawkins had with them. She was just told to look and watch over them. She had been asked to emerge the boys into their culture, teach them all they could and then they arrived in England to send word to Gunthorpe.

Rosamund could see that both children had suffered greatly but more so for the younger boy. She saw the torture in his eyes. The older boy was built of sterner stuff and straight away, her husband had seen a strength and leadership about him. Shem was able to lock things away and control his emotions, until he almost appeared cold, but his main aim was to protect his brother at all costs and Martinez Vargas was impressed by the boys' passion and loyalty. He joined him and his son's on many scraps whilst Rafe was allowed to be a little more relaxed and so had exiled in entertaining himself, but when the Vargas's observed how natural Rafe was with horses, he had a new apprentice.

They worked him hard and he exiled and when he was allowed to play, all just sat back as the boy run riot. He sought both fun and adventure. He loved life and God forbid, he loved the ladies!

It had been made very clear to both the Gorgios that all the girls were totally out of bounds for them and it would be punishable by death if either were to touch one of the Gypsy girls. They did not mingle or marry outsiders and be it that the two were adopted; they had no claim on any of the women.

But everyone loved Rafe and knew he was completely harmless and so he was allowed to flirt outrageously with all of the women, be they young or old. He loved to watch, talk, and learn from all the women, regardless of age and regardless of what they looked like, who their brothers and fathers were, and what they would do if he ever was that stupid to try!

When they were at a fair or camped outside of some village or town, he was allowed to go and run free with the local girls, and by God, - he had. He had learned a thing or two and had many a fine story to share.

Shem in the meantime had spent a great deal of time with Martinez and learned from him how to conduct himself, how to hold court or Kris as he called it. They taught him how to wrestle, how to look after himself and use a dagger in hand-to-hand combat. Shem loved all the training, having been taught how to sword fence and box by his father from a very young age.

Every now and again either Gunthorpe or Bob Hawkins would show up to see how the boys faired, and Rosamund knew it was only a matter of time before the boys would be whisked away to another life and be protected from God knew what? They were a part of her family and she loved them dearly.

How was Shem going to cope? The light had been taken away. Life was so unfair, after all the boys had gone through, for Rafe to be taken so suddenly and so badly. Shem had seemed to lose half himself. She, like her clansman believed that a person might return from the dead to seek vengeance on those who had wronged them during life. It was only a matter of time before Rafe showed himself and then she knew without a shadow of a doubt, that Shem would bring it to pass that he would rest in peace.

It had seemed like an age, but the time had come for the laying out of Rafe. Rosie had tried to get Daisy to help, however the woman was too distraught and mindful that she carried Rafe's unborn baby, it was best not to put too much pressure on her already fragile state. Rosie was even more concerned as she seemed to have put on no weight during the pregnancy and now was worried that she hardly ate anything.

Rosie had helped and when they had finished, she had left Rosamund to spend some time alone with Rafe. Rosamund had been fasting after the loss of a loved one, she felt weak, sad, and at a loss as to how God and the spirits, could not have warned her. She stood over him, holding his lifeless hands in hers, fighting for control. She felt old and felt her knees give way and she crumbled to the floor and cried into her hands.

'Oh my sunshine.' She kept moaning.

Shem must have heard her fall and he appeared right by her side. He had gathered her up and both cuddled each other again so tightly. She should have been comforting him. She just could not hold it in any longer. She looked straight into his eyes and took his head in her hands trying to get back some control.

'Look at me.' She ordered. He blinked back more tears. 'We bury my boy now; you take as much time as you need to moan my precious baby. Then you, Marcel, Ziggi, and all of your most loyal, must finish this. I know you were held back before, but not now. You have much power now, you are strong, and your business is mighty now. You can cope. You have to deal with this now. I will speak to Gunthorpe.' She kissed his forehead. 'Samuel, kill them. You kill them all; you make them pay each and every one of them for this now, for my sunshine, for Rosie and Seb, and for Troy!' Her fingers held his face firmly. Her stare tore into his very soul. He nodded to her, and she stroked his face with all the love she could muster, then they both silently cried in each other's arms.

After a time she went to leave him to be alone, one last time with his brother. She hesitated and kept looking back as she retreated.

He looked at Rafe and again experienced that all consuming fear that he could not breathe. Rafe looked so content and Shem was sure he was mocking him even from the grave. He caught his breath and felt the whole world run in on him. He fell to his knees. 'You fucking selfish prat.' He cried. 'I told you not to leave me.' He moaned. 'I'm lost without you. Come back, you plep.' He covered his face with his hands. 'It's just black without you.' He cried again. He felt weak, alone and vulnerable. Slowly he pulled himself together. He rose to his feet like a man who had been so ill and was so weak, who was careful of every movement. He looked again at his brother's face. He hesitantly leant forward knowing this was the last time he would ever see him. He looked at peace, and again Shem swore he saw that expression on his face, almost making fun of him. He felt a small smile creep onto his face. He cupped his brother's face and was taken back at the coldness. This was not the image he would hold. He stroked his brother's long curly hair and pulled his dagger out and softly, trying not to hurt his dead brother, he cut off a long strand of his hair. He curled it around his hand and smiled at his brother. He then retrieved a beautiful white laced handkerchief from his pocket. It was one of Rafe's most precious possessions and from someone they had lost along the way. Shem stroked the embroidery and looked at the stitched red A, on the beautiful work and placed it in his brother's hand. *You are together now.* He thought, and then he whispered aloud. 'Soon.' He let his tears fall on Rafe's face; he then kissed him softly one last time. 'I love you.'

The day had turned out to be wonderful, with a fresh breeze that cooled it down to comfortable. The willows danced in the light breeze and Shem watched the tree tops swayed. They had buried Rafe at the back of the church, where the land slowly tilted off to the fields that lead to the beach. It was an area cocooned with tress and Rafe had loved this place. He would explore the old church; the old castle, follows, and dare to jump across the winding stream. The place was alive with wildlife, birds singing, and the humming of insects.

There was a tree just inside the castle grounds, which had grown over a build up verge and nestled over the mounted old cannon, which had been used previously to guard for any attacks by sea along the bay. Someone had fastened a robe around one of the branches of the tree, so that you could launch off from the side and swing across to the other side, with a slight bowl beneath. Many a time, Shem and Rafe had lurked about there, trying to get back some lost youth. Swinging and swinging, then doubling up and laughing nervously to see if the great tree would hold both their weight. How many times had they lost their hold and fell, crashing to the ground? It did not matter what the weather had been, nothing deterred them. It was their special larking about space. The place they felt they could let their hair down.

As he stood there lost in thought, he promised his brother that he would commission the biggest and greatest headstone that would ever be set in the graveyard. He wanted to proudly show the world his brother's name when all of this was finished.

He could hear Rafe laughing and winding him up saying, that it was so over the top and gaudy! However, he knew he would love it all the same, anything to remain the centre of attention!

It was dusk when he felt the hands on his sleeve; he tried to look through tear soaked eyes, and heard the murmurs of his friends and Rosie, who had stayed all this time to watch over him. Earl had never left his side and he circled the dog's ear in affection.

Everything was a blur to Shem. The graveyard was silent and the only noise was the chirping of the birds and the cawing of the crows. The wind whistled through the trees and his friends' lead him away, their feet crunched against the grass as they walked and all seemed to look up at the sky at the same time. They all slowed down and took in the sunset. Shem's vision cleared all at once.

The sky was shades of pink, mingled with orange and reds. The sun burnt a scorching orange, and as far as the eye could see, just glowed. They all absorbed the wonder of the skies glory. It was magnificent. The swallows danced through the small pink clouds, seemingly also basking in the joy of it and slowly the sun set to bed.

'I think that was the best tribute that Him upstairs could have possibly given my mate.' Paully choked through tears streaming down his face. Claude patted him on the back in comfort. Rosie moved away knowing they all needed a moment. Shem nodded and warmly smiled as she slipped away and caught a glimpse of Jesus in amongst the trees.

'You were a right pain up the arse, but I did love you,' Paully choked back the tears. 'I haven't ever experienced pain like this before and I am telling you fuckers here and now, if you ever, ever, go and do something, like get yourself killed, I just couldn't cope.' Paully knew know how much Shem had suffered and felt even more in awe at the man for containing it.

'Oh you big softy, come here.' Claude took his big giant of a friend into his embrace. Then Paully grabbed Shem's arm and roughly brought him into the fold. All three held each other tight, then Paully called Jesus over and then Shem looked at Rosie. She floated into the big embrace and all of them shared the experience together and cried into the night.


Jesus had crept through the undergrowth with Ned and Ray to the edge of the estates. With clear whistle signals, they heard that their path was clear to venture forward. Like ghosts in the night, the three glided towards the old ruins. The original entrance to the estates had been blocked up years ago, and the original gatehouse left to rot. The air was moist and silent, there was no wind, and any sound would carry. It was black. Here, Hartright had been lying low.

They were that close to hear every word.

'You seem a little on edge William.' William was indeed.

'Pardon me for being off Hartright; however I'm not happy with this.' He wanted to remain calm and give nothing away. Every nerve in his body was on edge. He could not make a wrong move and alert Hartright. Every part of William's body shook with fear and drink. He found he could not get through a day now without a drink or two and looking at this man, all he wanted to do was throttle him.

'I'm hardly happy with this either. You aren't the one who has been constantly bullied by Shem and his gang, beaten senseless, abused, and then again left for dead on groundless accusations.'

'Really, really, Hartright?' William cried in disbelief. 'I am beginning to suspect you know a little bit more than you let on.' William wanted to kill him now and have it all finished with. He had never killed anyone before and had started to believe that maybe what Paully had said was all-true, that his man was poison! He had wanted adventure and thought that his little schemes with Hartright would satisfy that need, but all it had brought was pain and suffering. He had been wallowing in drink, his purpose lost.

'And what does that mean?' Hartright looked across and wondered how much he really knew about that Pevensey Burning. Hartright had told William that he had burnt out the cottage when he had not found the contraband that he had been tipped off about. He never mentioned anything else and it was only later that Hartright had learnt that the girl he had raped and supposedly killed had been related to the Cavendish's. He understood that Shem had not wished to upset the locals with details and he was amazed that the rape had been concealed. He wanted people to know how bad he could be and when he had raped that other sweet little whore, he thought his reputation would improve. But no! He had not heard a flutter.

Either William was very stupid or he generally was that selfish he did not care. He rather thought it was the latter if he knew his sister! Two peas in a pod.

'Look I don't have to answer to you. As soon as you are gone, I'll be glad.' The gang was waiting and he had done his part in alerting them.

'Well, you've hardly put yourself out to help me.'

'Your gratitude is unbelievable! You really haven't given me much choice have you? I am getting abit peeved at being played.' William had not happy to collaborate with Hartright and immediately had sent word to Shem's gang via a trusted aid, rather than Constance, who Hartright had wished to assist him. He had received word straight back, that a carriage would be across to pick Hartright up under the guise that it was from Constance. The carriage was arranged for that night and William could not believe how relieved he had felt at the double cross. Hartright deserved everything that was coming to him. He was annoyed at himself for being so pulled in by this man and wished with all his heart he could turn back time and not now be in a position where he had to make amends with those who could quite easily have finished him off. How many times would the gang call on his services to right the wrong?

'I would have thought you would have been used to it.'

'There really is no need for your sarcasm.'

'You haven't said anything about our business venture William.'

'Well Hartright you are hardly in a position to dictate. You have more pressing matters in hand to address, would you not agree?'

'You think you'll be able to continue your little games without your boys finding out.' William was astounded that Hartright appeared to completely ignore him and his current predicament.

'That's hardly your problem.' What Hartright did not know would not hurt him. The runs were Shem's now. It was all lies now. 'I am more concerned that Shem will find out that I helped you, when all I want to do is to be away from you and all this madness.' It amazed William that Hartright had not thought that he would ever betray him and had he forgotten that Shem knew everything anyway.

'And there was me thinking you were a friend. You proved not so.'

'Quite frankly Hartright I don't need any more friends. I've already lost the people I love, and what do you seriously think Shem will do to me? He has been playing you for fun these last few years, with a snap of his fingers he can destroy you and yours. My God man, do you know what he has done to me and my family? Do you not remember Clay being dumped at the bottom of your stairs? Your men butchered and gibbeted? Rumour has it; he has already had poor Chater killed, as a consequence of your cock-ups. My God, everyone is relieved to see the back of you and wants your just deserts. Some have a mind, that Shem should not have just cut a piece of your ear off, but lunged a dagger into your heart. And what with the latest! I honestly wish I had never met you.' All he kept thinking was how he could kill him right there and then, regardless of the gangs instructions. Someone else had obviously tried as Hartright had a huge scar on his face. How he hated this man. He was standing there in the dead of night pretending to save a man who had raped Rosie, for God's sake, what would he say when they met again? Would he ever see her again? God he hoped so.

'You have made your position very clear, thank you William.' Hartright was getting angry and trying to keep an even tone.

'Really, I can't say seeing the back of you is not coming soon enough. The sense of relief I have that you are going tonight cannot be comprehended. This conversation is finished. I hope I never ever see you again.' He moved away and Hartright looked on at him with disgust. The man had no stamina and had proved to be weak. He could not wait for the carriage.

Hartright jumped straight into the carriage and could not contain the glee he felt that Constance had come to his rescue.

'You made this all too easy Harry!' He jumped back into the seat and looked hard into the face of the man opposite. He recognised him from somewhere, but he could not quite place it. The man smiled sweetly at him from across the way. Hartright then swallowed hard as a cocked pistol was aimed at his head. The man voice was strong and hearty.

'Who are you?' Had he walked into a trap after all? He wanted to appear brave, but that sinking feeling returned. He tried to control his breathing and not show the fear.

'Your saviour!' The man smirked.

'Hardly.' He tutted. 'What of my sister?' He tried in the darkness to make more of the man out. He was obviously very rich with his clothes being of the finest cloth and he smelt very fresh and actually quite lovely. He was a handsome older man with laughter lines around his eyes. His hair had been fairer and was now pulled back into a ponytail. He was clean-shaven and had two moles on his cheek. He had dark eyes that twinkled. Hartright did not feel so threatened.

'She has been told all she needs to know.'

'Who do your work for? Secomb? How do I know you are not Shem's man?' He swallowed hard. It was a trap after all.

'Who is Shem?' The man grinned back putting away the pistol. Hartright immediately relaxed, raising his eyes to the ceiling, thinking the man before him was a complete buffoon. Hartright chuckled at that and sighed with such relief. He leant back and controlled his breathing. The panic was over. What had life in store now? Surely, he thought life could not get any better. This was brilliant. He slapped his thighs in glee.

'Please do not get too complacent, secrecy and keeping a low profile is paramount to the success of this little adventure. And you are hardly the best candidate for keeping a low profile.'

Two cloaked men ensuring that no one was watching and to deliver Hartright safely back to London and the safe house arranged were following the carriage.

What the occupants of the coach and the riders were not aware of was that the whole thing was a set up by Shem. The messenger to Constance was one of Shem's men and at every point Shem's contact's in London reported all the comings and goings through Luca in Covent Garden. Constance had immediately sent a messenger and within hours had been visited by an old family friend. Soon after a carriage had been dispatched with a chaperon and two armed guards to rescue Hartright and following were gang members sending back reports at all times. Shem needed to find the source of who in high places was really pulling the strings. As soon as Shem found out the names involved, he took a trip to the city.


The fog crept around their ankles and the soft sway of the tide could be heard in the silence. It was late in the evening and they could hear the muffled tones of revellers along the riverbank chatting and singing in the Alehouses along the river Thames.

The air reeked of stale water and the wharfs of urine. Everywhere was filth and slime. It was deadly dark and the only light was the torches they carried along the banks. Along the embankments at certain points, some street torches could also be seen. A soft orange glow haloed them. Cats and foxes could be heard calling out. Dogs barked in the distance, threatening to be let loose and have a field day with the smaller animals.

The man they had sought was not too hard to find on one of the many barges moored.

He had taken a beating by them and as he leaned over, Paully followed through with a left hook, into the man's stomach. The man lifted into the air then thunderously crashed to the boat floor. Paully stood over him like a big black cloud and the grim reaper. The man was unable to move as the fear had made him paralysed. Paully slowly lowered his foot onto the man's neck.

'Waiting!' Shem drawled from behind. Shem had decided to stay on shore, which was a few feet away. He hated boats!

'I just got me orders from Jo.' The man choked. It had been established that if Constance ever needed help, she was to contact this man, who in turn would contact the next up the ladder, but from the off this man had been lairy and not wanted to give anything away. He had been cocky and Paully had immediately taken a dislike to him.

'Jo who?'

'Jo from the Cats Whiskers?'

'Jo Bravio?' Claude looked surprised and moved forward.

'Yes.' Paully released the pressure slightly in the man's neck and watched as the man sighed in relief. From being completely terrified he moved to near ecstatic hysteria at being released. He got up and laughed to himself in relief.

'What did ya say?' Paully leaned forward.

'Nothing mate.'

'No, what did ya say?'

'Upon my soul, nothing.'

'Then what you grinning at?'

'Mate, behave, I told ya what ya wanted, I am relived I can be of service. I'll be on me way.' The man knew he was still on a knife-edge and he needed to go.

'No, no you won't.'

He then looked to Shem who waved his hand and watched as Paully grabbed the man's throat, and then physically lifted him off the floor, he slapped him back down to the deck, at which point the man was winded. The man's hands went straight to his windpipe, at which point Paully then kicked him hard in his privates. The man bent forward and as he did, Paully manoeuvred around his back and as quick as a flash broke the man's neck. The crunch of the neck breaking sent shivers down Paully's back.

'Fucking prick, laughing at me!' He growled in frustration and kicked the dead man in the head.

At that point, Shem coughed and Paully held his gaze. Paully nodded knowing without words what Shem was conveying. It was a gentle nudge to calm down. Both men shared a rage that on many occasions could quite easily get out of hand. Both equalled each other in strength and when the devil possessed either of them, but all it needed was a look and Paully was back. The blackness slowly disappeared from his eyes.

Claude gathered the dead man up, threw him into the thick of the water, and watched as the Thames engulfed the body. 'Idiot.'

Jo Bravio was Luca's younger brother and they were very similar in appearance, with Jo being slightly smaller and leaner. Both Luca and Jo shaved their heads clear, and whereas Luca was clean-shaven on his face, Jo had a long plaited black beard and moustache. He also wore gold earrings. He looked like a man who had been ill and lost too much weight too quickly. He was a man who could be bought at any price. He had no loyalty to any gang and was a freelancer to the highest bidder. He asked no questions and as long as he was paid, he was happy.

He was not interested in who he offended and was a selfish man on a mission to make as much money as possible. It would only be a matter of time before he was found. Jo Bravio was scum, he was a show off and liked to hold court and after a few too many, then gloat.

It had not taken Claude and Paully much to persuade him to come back to his brothers for a drink and he was now quite settled in Luca's back bar.

They had learnt that Jo had been paid to handle getting Hartright back to London by an anonymous source, after he had left a message as pre arranged at the Coffee house at Ludgate. It had been arranged that should he receive further instruction then a message would be left for him the next day at 9 o'clock in the morning. He had been instructed to rent a carriage with a good man and collect a passenger at the club later that day. He was very forthcoming on the description of the man, as he had taken the liberty of having his man wait outside the club and report who got in. Jo had also arranged for the carriage to be followed, knowing that the man in the carriage also had his heavies guarding him and following in their own transport.

Jo was chuffed to pieces that he held all the cards and confirmed what they already knew about where the returned carriage had alighted its cargo.

Shem was also happy to hear that his suspicions were founded and that Benedict Hunter had recently returned from the Caribbean and needed friends, and it would appear that he and Felix Secomb was best pals now.

They had been drinking all evening and Luca had become increasingly irritated at his brother and his lack of morals. He could not believe that his brother could not remember Shem and Rafe from their youth. Luca could see that Jo was so self centred that no one else was important, other than his next scam and being paid handsomely for some job and hired at times to commit murder. It was business and he had to make a living.

Long ago, Jo had worked for Luca, but he was a man with his own agenda and so Luca had let him go his separate way, but with the understanding that he was never to interfere with any of his business ventures. It had worked, but Jo had a reputation as a grass, a low life leech who would sell his own mother. Well he had tried to sell one of his children already and when the mother of the child had dared to make a stand, he had flung her in the Thames. That's when Luca had stepped in and had all of Jo's many children, by various different women, rounded up and given a home with him at the Inn. The mothers were all welcome too and although slightly unconventional, Luca had a huge family and there was never a dull moment.

'Shall I kill him?' Paully had joked at one point as the evening had worn on and Luca had been very tempted to let him. Shem had again given him the evil eye.

'Luca, Luca it is business.' As drink took its toll, Jo had started to annoy his older brother. Jo had seen his brother's expression and the look of disgust he had given him. He knew that Luca despised him and knew there was no love lost between the two. 'You do what you have to and I do what I have to.' Luca did not like anyone ridiculing him and Jo was deliberately winding him up, knowing that he could get away with murder. Jo believed that as his brother he was immune from ever being held to task. However, sometimes people pushed it just abit too far.

Luca downed his drink and made to get up and leave the party. His brother embarrassed him.

'Old man tired, need ya bed. No young man to keep ya company tonight?' Jo laughed at him lurching back and stretching. Luca smiled at his brother but there was no light in his eyes and he seemed to sigh to himself about a decision having to be made. He nodded to himself. 'Yes tired of this.' He rested his head on his chest for a moment, then without warning he produced a dagger from behind, tucked in his back belt and in the next second, he had been flung and it went straight into Jo's windpipe.

Paully, Claude, and Shem jumped from their chairs as the blood smothered the table and the dead man.

Jo's body fell back in the chair lifeless; his eyes still open in surprise at the turn of events! Luca casually looked down at his dead brother, showing no remorse. One of his women handed him a further bottle of brandy and glasses and it was as if nothing had happened. The silence in the bar was deafening. Luca made for another table, which was currently occupied, however within seconds, the party had moved away to allow him to take their seats.

Shem, Paully, and Claude just stood in shock and watched as Luca casually sat down and poured more drinks. He motioned for everyone to be offered a glass, then saluted his brother, and again downed his drink in one. He gestured for everyone to continue with their conversations, and slowly the hush turned to whispers. 'I hated that bastard.' He groaned. Shem shivered and Paully and Claude shared an expression that said that they couldn't wait to get out of there. 'I've just found out, he has managed to get another of my girls up the duff and as well as keep them while they're indisposed and lose good money, I have to feed the fucking rest of them in the nursery. All his bastards. You know he tried to sell one of kids to some fucking pervert and I suppose you were told about flinging one of the mother's in the river to shut her up. Disgusting.' He shook his head as he relayed the information. He poured out another drink. He was going nowhere and was going to drown his sorrows. Jo's remained where he had died. 'My poor mother would be mortified.'

'You got alot on ya plate; we'll leave you to it.' Paully was desperate to get away.

Shem had to say something and he tried to make sense of what had happened. He had lost his own brother through violence and revenge, yet Luca had taken the life of his own brother with no remorse, just relief that it was all now over! The man never ceased to amaze him. 'Luca.' Shem almost whispered and the huge man looked into his eyes.

'I know my friend.' He sighed and looked about him in sorrow, he had many demons. 'The lure of home pulls at my heart Samuel, but I need to find positions for some of these fucking orphans. God I'm tired.' He lowered his eyes. 'I see Annatasia in all of them.' He choked. 'Maybe we will talk later about going home.' He whispered and let his emotion show just slightly with a tear forming. It was the third time in so many months recently that Shem had recalled the image of Annatasia. As children, they had all played together and she and Rafe had been inseparable.

'Will they be Luca trained?' Paully laughed trying to lighten the atmosphere. They certainly did not wish to inherit any mini psychopaths! He looked at Claude in question to see if he had also registered the reference to home and the drop of the name again!

'No, no no.' Luca shook his head and smiled weakly knowing what he was trying to do under the circumstances. He wiped his eyes. 'They deserve so much better than this life, it's not their fault. I want good lives for the little shits. Each of them gives me a headache, especially Marcus, he'll be swinging soon. But God, I love them all so very much.' They all witnessed softness from the giant of a man. Every time he mentioned one of them, his eyes lit up.

'How many are there?' Paully queried, making conversation but really wanting to finish his drink and run.

'Eight. Five girls and three stupid boys.' He smiled in pride. Shem could identify with that. Both their brothers had left their off spring and now both he and Luca would do whatever it took to protect them all. God, both Rafe and Jo had left their mark! While they spoke, Claude had been peering out of the back door to make sure the coast was clear and advised that it was after one of their men patrolling gave the nod, he could not wait to get home.

He had earlier met up with his little maid Maisy to see if there was any news from that front, and learnt that it would appear that Constance was frantic to hear from her brother and had vented her anger on Maisy more than once. Maisy had confirmed that Secomb had indeed visited and she had tried to listen in, but she had got too frightened.

Claude had been livid at the way she had been treated and had to calm her down and make promises he really did not wish to keep. She was a lovely girl but not one he wanted to spend the rest of his life with.

Shem had finished his drink and held out his hand to his old friend. 'I'm sorry it had to come to this.' Some of Luca's men were now coming forward to clear away the mess. Luca waved his hand for them to continue. He closed his eyes as his brothers corpse was carried by. He poured another drink. He drunk it in one hit and then stood up.

'My decision, Shem, this is my world.' He almost whispered in regret at the outcome. They shook hands and Shem did not feel the need any more to understand the man's motives.

'God bless old friend.' He flung out his arms and they hugged. Luca lowered his head as they parted and Shem whispered in French for him only. 'I will contact you soon; we may be going home sooner rather than later.' Luca nodded in understanding. 'We will talk then about the Mint House?' Claude overheard and looked at Paully in knowing and a suggestion that they would talk later. There were too many hidden messages, which Luca and Shem exchanged.

They slithered into the night and groaned at Paully as he moaned. 'We ain't coming here again; it's a dirty, murdering, fucking shit hole!'

Valentina brushed her hair as she looked out of the window. If she looked from her bedroom window, she could see The Castle Inn and all the goings on. She had bathed in lavender oil, knowing this was a favourite of Shem's and tried to catch a further glimpse of him. Each and every day she waited to see him and knew he would come to her at some stage.

The village had been packed with people from every part of the south coast visiting and paying their respects to Shem. The area had been well protected and everyone coming in and going were watched and noted. Every day Shem's informants came and went, and amongst all that, the patrons to the Coach House were fed with information and gave news freely.

No one could get near Shem, an army of men surrounded him, and his women folk kept themselves to themselves.

Every night she had said to herself that he would come to her to hear her tell him herself what had happened. He had then disappeared and she had then dreaded his return. She had had to repeat the story so many times for Bob and Claude and actually started to belief in her own deceit. She knew in time he would come to her and then he had. She had smiled deluding herself that he cared and that he just could not keep away. She had worked herself up and the thought of him filled her with hope and longing.

She thought he would come in the dead of the night but he had come as the sun had set and it was not too late. He was clearly seen coming across and that is exactly what he wanted. She was annoyed by this. That bitch had him!

She had withdrawn to her room and started to pace up and down, her nerves getting the better of her. She knew she would say something wrong and he would slit her throat then and there and there would be no one in the world to care. How could she make him see that she loved him so?

She heard him knock below and listened as he was let in. Her heart thumped with every step he took up the stairs. She clutched her throat in panic. Her knees gave way and she sat on the bed to steady herself. He must have some feelings for her and he would understand. He knocked and slowly he opened the door.

His tall figure engulfed the whole doorframe and for a second she was taken back to those nights when she would go to him and he would love only her. Now that time was long gone.

Shem was not patient and he wanted answers. He wanted to know exactly what had happened and listened to her as she whispered the events. She cried and cried, looking for comfort but he just stood there cold and aloft. She could not bear that he would never touch her again. She needed him. He was cold to her stare. He was a man lost. A light had gone out of him. She could re kindle that. He could never find out what she had done. However, what if he did, he may understand. After all, it was all Hartright fault. Shem would eventually kill him and it all would be over. She could then rest easy.

She had played a dangerous game in aiding Hartright before and look where it had got her? She would keep herself to herself, not meddle anymore, and just keep her head down. She had made plans to return to Spain and make a fresh start. However, she could do whatever she wanted; maybe go to the new world! She would make a definite decision and plans; she would sell up or maybe not. Perhaps after a time, Shem would come back to her. How could she have ever thought to go along with Hartright and kill this man? God she loved him so!

She would bide her time. This Rosie was a passing fashion, she was beneath him, he would come to see that, and slowly he would see what he had lost. She would be a jewel. She had come from a good family. She knew how to behave. She would exceed everyone's expectations and be a much better person. She could do it. After he had left, she plaited her hair and looked at herself in the mirror. She smiled at her reflection. If she could make it this far then the rest would be a breeze.

'You know that Paully had the nerve to ask me if you had lost it, well he's like a pig in shit when he tells you how he tortures people. If anyone is sick, it's him. You know what I mean? No it was concern.' Bob had been drinking quite heavily of late and his conversation was very picky. It was no wonder he was feeling stressed. 'No wonder he gets on so well with Luca. By God what is the world coming to?' Bob lost himself in his drink and motioned for Chrissy to give him a refill. 'You alright love?' He asked her.

'Good, thank you Bob. How are you?' She poured his drink and smiled warmly at him.

'Abit tired.' He confessed. He just wanted her to sit down and take the weight off her feet. They both needed a break from it all and to sit down and chat with the woman would have been lovely.

'Same here, I've been chasing after them two little ones.' She laughed and looked at Shem who also smiled.

'Keep's all of us on our toes.'

'They're two terrible terrors, that's what they are. But oh so funny, the things they say and do. And the baby! Well....' She shook her head laughing and wandered off to serve and socialise amongst the regulars. Both men watched after her and Bob grinned.

'My, my what a turn up hey?' Bob mused. 'Look at her laugh, haven't seen her like that for years, know what I mean? Pissy Chrissy, what a fucking cheek!' He drunk more, feeling people had been cruel to call her such things. 'Well since Arthur........ God silly sod, went and got himself killed! I still miss the silly git.' Bob seemed to get lost in his nostalgia. Shem watched Chrissy circle the room and had to admit that life never cease to amaze him. 'And I miss her company and chatting to her. We all used to be such good mates. You know what I mean? Just used to chew the fat.'

Shem reflected that as Bob would put it, he had a diamond amongst the rough there. Once she had sobered up, people begun to discover what a nice woman she was. She had a comely aura about her. Chrissy always asked after people and their family. She always remembered your name and made you feel welcome and special. She had time for everyone and people found they could identify with her. She had been a wreck and now appeared to be getting her life together. She had people to look after now, a purpose and Shem knew he had to show his appreciation; he casually averted his eyes to Bob and grinned, seeing that Bob had not taken his eyes off her!

He then checked himself, he could not afford to get too sentimental, he may have loved Bob to pieces, but Bob's loyalty was to Mr. H. As much as it pained him, the thought had occurred that perhaps Bob had told Mr. H when Shem had got too near to take the bugger, Hartright, but that still could have happened, even if Shem knew now to watch both Mr H and Secomb.

He also had been put in a difficult position now that Bob's brother had made his feelings clear on the Amelia and Rafe previous situation. He was annoyed with himself, but he had been taught to look at situations from all angles and never rule anything out, and never be too surprised, people always let you down.

His mind then went to Daisy, trying to think of better things. She had coped extremely well, and like Chrissy, she was a part of his life now. She had held herself with dignity and he was proud of her. He had told her that he would always look after her and the children and she had cried and cried in gratitude. This had left him feeling a little embarrassed! Shem was in awe of his brother and knew that be it that he had lost him forever his legacy would continue and surprise him for a long time to come. He was very much still there and it helped greatly. His family meant everything to him and when he was away on business, he needed to ensure that they were fully protected.

He just hoped that Rosie did not feel rejected and get too hurt by his constantly having to go, and that she was not made to suffer over Daisy being pregnant again. They had not discussed any of those issues yet, he knew she would be feeling a little vulnerable and some subjects were just held back on as they were still trying to find each other. However, he had deluded himself; he was setting her up for a big fall. It was inevitable. But what could he do? The pain of it was too much for him to dwell on. If only they had more time, but now he had the power and money to accomplish anything he wanted. He was influential and no one was ever going to get in his way again.


Lord Lennard and Shem had been sitting and drinking brandy in the day room. From the windows, you could see all the way across the flat fields, to the sea beyond. To Shem's left the South Downs crept inland to the coast at Beachy Head. There was a fierce wind outside and this blew the clouds over the Downs towards them in a constant hurry.

Shem always thought that the Earl of Sussex had been very lucky with the location of the family home. It was truly beautiful with an abundance of lush evergreens.

'There is a warrant out for your arrest dear boy.'

'On what grounds?' Shem wasn't surprised at the turn of events.

'Murder.' Lennard said dryly. He had a knack of making bad news sound so boring and tedious. Shem did not seem taken back. They both knew the charge was unreasonable. Lennard did not wish to mention his brother and he was thankful.

'Hartright and me, both.' Shem laughed but there was no joy in it.

'They are sending Dragoons down as well to get you, as they do not trust the new Riding officers, what with Hartright missing.' Shem did not offer the fact that he knew where Hartright was and that it was only a matter of time before his plans were put in motion. He would not give him up to the authorities to hang in public. He had plans.

'So I had best get packing. Tie up some loose ends as it were.' He was thankful that Wainwrght had not been set the task.

'That would be good.'

'Oh, who am I supposed to have killed?' Shem asked cheekily. Lennard raised his eyebrow and tutted at him.

'Chater?'

'Oh I did not do it. They got the wrong man, so that will be thrown out easily.' Shem waved his hand dismissively and continued to lose himself in the view, Chater wasn't dead just missing in France, he wasn't even going to reflect on who else he had killed.

'Shem, you are talking to me now.'

'If he is dead. Honestly, it wasn't me.' He looked at Lennard with such innocent eyes, and Lennard tried to suppress a grin. All of them knowing this was no real laughing matter.

'Your friend is mocking me, Paully.' Lennard called over his shoulder.

Paully had been playing with the globe in the study again. He had always loved to play with it and the second Mrs. Lennard had no hesitation in whacking him when she caught him in there. He remembered her saying that he was the stupidest child that she had ever met. Whenever he was in mischief, which was every day! He would go and hide, and then nip into the kitchen and pinch some food that his mother Nelly Rose, had conveniently left on the table. He would then lose himself in the house, but always end up in the study. He would twirl the globe around and around then find the Atlas and co ordinate all the places and memorise the trade routes and then pick a country and explore their history and culture. Paully had never been stupid, far from it, he was just lazy and liked to play the fool.

'Paully!' Lennard barked. Paully jumped out of it and stood to attention in front of his father.

'What?' He said like a petulant child. His father raised his eyes in wonder at how he had ever produced him. Shem suppressed a grin and winking at Paully added.

'You killed him didn't you?' Lennard shook his head, not surprised at all!

'Hello, can I come in?'

Rosie looked over her shoulder and saw one of the young women from Valentina's at her kitchen door. Rosie rose to her feet and looked at the young girl. She knew her name was Felicity and she was a pretty little thing. She had a round button face with sparkly dark brown eyes and dark freckles; she was a soft brown colour with long blond afro hair that seemed to have a life of its own. Under her arm, she carried what looked like sheets and sheets of paper.

She beckoned her to come in. They had always just said hello in passing.

'I hope you don't mind me just coming across, it's just the girls are feeling a little lost at the minute.' Rosie could hear the nerves in her voice.

'Really?' Rosie automatically answered, and then she laughed. 'Sorry, come in, make yourself at home, and sit down.' Both made a curtsy and laughed at their play-acting.

'Do you want some tea?' Felicity smiled and was slightly in awe that Rosie had not judged her and shunned her away and was making her at ease and being quite funny into the bargain.

They drunk the tea and chatted about this and that and then Felicity approached the reason for her call.

'I was going to come across and ask to see the Guvnor, but I lost me nerve abit. So we all agreed you'd be the next best thing, having his ear and all that.' Rosie smiled encouragement and found that she really liked her, she reminded her of when she was younger, so cock sure and full of life.

'Well, you have probably heard that Valentina is, - well one minute thinking of going then she ain't, and well, we wanted to know what would happen to us.'

'Oh, I see.' Rosie had visions of her own on what to do with the lovely Valentina. One included flinging her off a boat, way out at sea! Rosie hoped that it would annoy Valentina to hear that Felicity had come to see her on behalf of the girls rather than straight to Shem.

'Well, we hear things and Claude has assured us that it would be alright, but well.'

'I am sure that there is always a need of a whore...' Rosie stopped in mid sentence and chewed her lip mimicking slightly.

'A good, whore house.' Felicity laughed and Rosie joined her, feeling relieved that she hadn't completely put her foot in it.

'Yes. You know Shem probably has something in mind already, but what's that?' Felicity smiled at her and slowly she unwrapped her tube of papers.

As the pages unwrapped, Rosie found herself covering her mouth and felt the tears start to pour down her face. She was completely overcome.

'I'm sorry, I did not mean to ...'

'No, please its fine, it's just such a wonderful surprise...' before her were pages of drawings and portraits.

At the top, was a fantastic portrait capturing Rafe at his best. It was just a drawing of him from his shoulders upwards, with his hair all long and curly, with that knowing cocky smile.

'Did you do these?' Rosie whispered full of emotion.

'Yes. I have many.'

'These are beautiful Felicity.' Rosie was in awe and thought that she had never seen anything quite so wonderful.

'I have loads and could afford to share.' She explained that whenever she was free she spent her time watching and observing the locals and drawing them in their every day poses. Her drawings captured their world exactly.

She had a few drawings of Rafe on the beach, with his children and explained she had a few more private ones at which Rosie laughed knowingly. Rafe had been a complete rascal.

'Best keep that to yourself. ' Rosie knew she did not need to explain. It was not in anyone's best interest to let Daisy know ever about the more intimate pictures. They flicked through the pile, and she stopped at an image of herself. She did not wish to dwell on it but found she kept going back to the one image that captured her on the beach looking out to sea. Her hair was everywhere and Felicity had captured it dancing in the wind so beautifully. Her hands were clenched holding fast her cloak around her body and her stare was far, far away.

'I look sad in that.' Rosie offered feeling quite exposed not taking her eyes off the drawing.

'No.' Felicity looked at her in question. 'No, you don't. You were just day dreaming on that day.' Rosie smiled weakly, she thought Felicity was trying not to hurt her feelings and then she added. 'Best keep you on side because you'll more than likely batter me otherwise.' Rosie's smile widened at Felicity being quite bold and referring to her previous fight with Valentina.

'I thought Shem would especially like this one and he could keep it close to hand.' She handed Rosie back the beautiful image of Rafe.

Rosie nodded in agreement and Felicity could see that she was trying to control her emotions. Her eyes were glistening with unshed tears.

'Rafe always encouraged me to draw at every opportunity; he brought me paper and pencils back from his travels.' She shared.

'You could do something with this talent.' Rosie voice was so choked.

'That's what Rafe said. He wanted me to move on.' Felicity's voice seemed to lower as she spoke. Rafe although a complete cad, seem to fill all the women in his life with a smile and encouragement for the future.

'Why have you waited so long to share this?'

'Grief and the letting go.' She answered softly. Rosie nodded and found herself holding the girls hand. Both had only really known Rafe for really such a short time; however, his absence was a void that no one would easily fill.

Felicity started to inform her that this wasn't the life she had wanted. She had been one of six. Her father was a sailor across at Hastings way, his father had been from Africa, and his mother had been from the Netherlands. She recalled that she and only one of her sisters made it past the age of ten. Her mother had died, and then her father died in grief. Both girls had managed to get a place at the local manor house, however when Felicity had become pregnant she had been out on her ear. She did not expand on who the father was and Rosie thought it rude to pursue. She had hardly wanted anyone knowing her own business! The baby had died and she had to leave her sister. She hadn't seen her sister in years.

'I used to draw as a child and my dad said I was good. I drew Laila at every opportunity. She was born too early.' Felicity looked away, started to chew at her fingernails, and tried to control herself. It had taken guts for her to come across and Rosie was glad she had.

Felicity smiled at her and tried to control her composure. Felicity did not intend to spill her life story, but felt somehow relieved and comfortable with Rosie. 'Come here ya silly cow.' Rosie grabbed the girl to her and let her cry into her shoulder.

She was not the only one in the world to ever suffer and she needed to remind herself of that. She could be so selfish.

'Ya know that soppy bastard George hung on for dear life. Well, me and Claude were pissing ourselves.'

'We blindfolded him, and we had scarves on and tried to disguise our voices,' Claude took up the story of that evening's adventures while they were out on patrol. Shem expected all his men to still do and make patrols and get involved in the transferring of goods as he still did, no matter how big they were in the scheme of things. They had just got back to The Castle and could not stop laughing.

'And we had his legs bound.' Paully added. He nodded at the gang that they were listening, 'Well we held him at each end and counted, one, two three and chucked the bugger over a cliff.'

The gang did a combined Ohhh and then burst out laughing seeing from Paully's expression that there was more to follow and that George was his brother in law!

Paully rubbed his belly with the pressure of laughing. 'He is screaming like a banshee and the fool manages to cling on to tufts of grass as he fell and he's hanging and hanging, calling out, I know it's you, I know it's you, Paully, I'm gonna tell, ...' Claude was doubled over and Shem was shaking his head, trying not to giggle. 'Well his legs are dangling, oh God, for ages and ages.'

'Well I'm looking at Paully thinking, your brother in law is not that stupid? Surely, he knows where we flung him. God is he such an idiot?' The gang looked at each other in wonder now.

'Well the winds blowing, the rains coming down, the poor boys struggling and God, he can hear us pissing ourselves. Well give him his due; he is still hanging on for dear life.' Paully sipped his drink and held his hand up telling them he to wait. 'Well, gradually his blindfold slipped down and in his panic he started to jerk about and he nearly fell again.....Ohh I can't go on.' Paully doubled over and Claude whacked him on the back to continue.

'Did he fall and splatter all over?' Little Paul eagerly asked.

Paully was shaking his head and looking directly at Claude who was literally crying now, he added, 'the silly fucker realised his feet were a matter of inches above the ground.' Everyone just keeled over 'The cliff was only seven feet high.' Realisation of the cliff spread and the pub was in up roar. It was a section of Beachy Head that was like a ridge which was indeed only seven foot high and around twenty feet wide, and around five feet deep.

'Ya lucky we got back, cos we nearly killed ourselves from trying to stop laughing, oh God, I'm gonna die of laughing, it fucking hurts.' They were always making a fool of George and one day they would take it too far.

'That poor fucker George, you mug him off every time.' Bob laughed.

'Well, we did leave him his horse, some brandy, and tea at the top of the cliff.' How George put up with Paully no one understood. However, he always seemed to be in the wrong place at the wrong time. He was supposed to be having a day off, and not guarding the coastline, east of Beachy Head, along the South Coast.

'Here Paully, you best be doing a runner?' Paully heard Shem call. He turned to Shem questioning and found his eyes following and looking out through one of the pub's small windows. 'Cos Bella's just coming up the lane.' All eyes darted to look outside.

'No, you're joking.' But just in case, Paully grabbed his coat and run like a mad man to the back door. All the men moved to the side of the Inn and looked out the small windows, to see that Paully's sister was indeed jumping down from their father's coach and tearing up the road, they could see she heard the back door bang, she grinned in knowing and darted to the back of the Inn. Everyone tried to pile out and from the back of the Inn they watched as Paully run like a mad man, jumping over the hedgerow and darting through the fields.

He heard their voices call out encouragement and fade away, he dared a look behind and there she was, as bold as brass making straight for him. He gave a little nervous grin both in awe at her and in fright, she would give him a good thrashing and he would never ever dare raise a finger to her. God he loved his sister, and although he could see she was gaining ground and calling him all the names under the sun, he knew he needed to make haste and run!

'She's gonna do him severely.' Bob could not stop laughing.

'Don't you think you'd best go and help ya mate?' Shem teased Claude as they all returned inside and Claude sat back down and shook his head.

'No.' He continued with his drink and smiled.

'No, you're bang out of order.'

'No, just not stupid, did you see what she did to us both last time, no, no I can't go through that emotional turmoil again. I'm not an idiot!' At that point, the door to the tavern opened and all looked at the new comer. Claude sighed in relief that it was not Bella.

George English waltzed in like the Lord of the manor and seeing an empty chair by Bob, took a seat. Bob handed him a tankard and Daisy quickly came over to fill it. He thanked her and asked after her health. All eyes were on him and he slowly sipped his ale. He wiped his mouth and looked at Bob then Claude. 'Well you have truly gone and done it now. I can't take anymore. I will be sacked.'

'Oh come on George it's not that bad.' It was the first time in his life, that George had ever held court and be it that he was nervous, but he had enough and knew it was time he stood his ground.

'No Mr. Bob it is, we had an accord, I've given you the best years of my life, turning a blind eye, you giving me the wink on discovering a small hoard every now and again. Well, no more.' It was the first time they had ever seen George be assertive, although they could hear the nerves in his voice. 'I have to say Mr. Shem that I have been grateful to you and you have shown me consideration when you have worked with me; I thought I had come out of the previous commandment under Mr. High and Mighty Mr. Mordesan, who, I have to say, was a complete nightmare, such a horrid man. I hate to be ill about anyone and try and find the good. However, sorry I digress, any new management will wish to disassociate with any remaining officers, so they will look at any excuse to get rid of me, and today I rather had the impression that my own brother in law did too.'

'It was just a bit of fun!' Claude piped up trying to defend their play.

'Fun to you yes, but I was the one that had a near death experience.' At this, they all burst out laughing again. George was starting to be heckled about nearly dying!

'Well, we can see Bella's going after Paully, it was all his idea.' Claude offered. Shem looked at him disgustedly and the crowd jeered Claude for his cowardliness. He mocked them all by sticking his middle finger up at them.

'Yes, I just could not stop myself from getting my own back, I am not apologising, and ....' George sipped more of his ale. 'I hope she catches the bugger and beats seven shades of shit out of him. I do, I most certainly do.' At which George actually grinned in merriment rocking back and forth in his chair with glee and felt very liberated at swearing so freely. He just did not care and felt unburdened. Jesus made the sign of the cross and tutted at him but still had a smile on his face.

'Not like you George to blaspheme?' Bob was shocked. George smiled again at Bob and his smile rested on everyone, at which point the whole pub started to laugh with George.

'You clever bastard!' Bob got up and whacked him on the back in appreciation. He waved for Daisy to give him another drink. 'So you'll be looking for work now then George?'

'Mr. Bob, with all due respect, please behave.' George was lapping it up being assertive and Bob knew it was the Ale.

'Bella will make Paully pay in more ways than one and I'm going to enjoy every moment of it.' He sipped his drink. 'But God forbid, I can't stay at home with her. Why do you think I have endured this line of work before now?' The implication of his words hit home, and again the pub crowd roared with appreciation. George was a pure joy! He would make Paully fund his holiday and when he was ready he would have to return to do some form of work, else the torture of being with his wife would kill him!

'But I know that will not last forever. And well, a man has his limits and pride!' The crowd liked that and watched as George continued to rock having so much fun, 'and don't think you are off the hook Mr. Claude. Oh no, when my Bella has finished with Paully, she'll be coming after you regardless of whose idea it was!' George was enjoying the moment and the audience, he also felt a little dizzy.

Claude rose to his feet with an expression of what have I done, but thought he too should make haste, he glared at George who merely waved Goodbye rather sarcastically to him, and then Claude fled!

'Oh this is gonna be a long night.' Shem burst out laughing and patted Bob on the back, then called, 'Daisy, please be so kind as to serve drinks all round and George, let's toast George, welcome to the fold and well done you sly dog!'

It was very late when he staggered in. He had really let his hair down and was glowing with drink. The kitchen fire was alight and although dying slowly, gave him enough light to find his way. As he went by the kitchen table, his eyes caught attention to a pile of drawings. He stopped intrigued at how wonderful they were and captured the subject so well. He went to the fire and taking a light, lit some of the candles. He sat at the kitchen table and made himself comfortable.

He thought the picture of Rosie was outstanding and captured her deep in thought. Those who did not know would have said their looked a tinge of sadness around her eyes, but he knew all of her expressions so well, and this was one of dreams and consideration. Whoever drew this picture was a true wonder! He had quickly scanned at all of the pictures of Rafe and did not wish to dwell on them as he felt his heart swell and about to explode with emotion.

After a time looking through the many, he managed to calm himself down and allow his eyes to just set on and really look at the portrait of Rafe. Rafe's smile beamed across the page and Shem smiled lovingly back at the drawing.

He heard a creek on the stairs and the dogs descending, obviously having heard him coming in. They pushed open the kitchen door and both Earl and Jester padded towards him with tails wagging slowly and tiredly. He welcomed both of them and allowed them to sit almost atop of his feet. He then looked back at the doorway and watched as the sleepy figure of Seb followed in the dogs' footsteps.

He shuffled forward and ducked under Shem's arms and nestled his body between Shem's legs, he placed his hands on Shem's legs and rested back. Rosie leant against the door. He looked back over his shoulder and saw the sadness in Shem's face. They both looked again at the picture in Shem's hands. Seb smiled seeing Rafe looking back at him.

'He is cheeky, ain't he?' The boy laughed.

'He certainly is.' Shem swallowed hard. Seb turned and kissed Shem on the cheek.

'He is always with us, but he said to remind you that he is always here.' Seb pointed to his own heart, and then his head and then he touched Shem's heart and head. 'Just close your eyes and there he is.' Shem was taken back and found himself choking back tears. 'He is with me and Phoebe all the time. We talk to him and when he isn't here; you too can look at this and see him smiling back all the time.' The boy chuckled to himself and smiled sweetly at Shem. 'Don't be sad Dad.'

Shem cuddled him up to him and found himself laughing and next minute the two were tickling and chuckling in glee however, Shem was slightly unnerved. Shem had lost his brother but now he had all of his son. However, all too soon that too would be missed as his plans were a foot and he would have to leave them for a time. It left a bittersweet taste in his mouth. He had Hartright and soon all his plans would be fulfilled.

## Chapter Twelve

He smelled the air and smiled in satisfaction. He had been running, and he had overstepped the mark, but knew he was free. The wind hit his face and he sighed and closed his eyes. He could start a new life. Make a fresh start. Make new friends and put this whole thing behind him.

At one point, he thought the game was up. Good old William had decided to help him in the end, only then he was unceremoniously snatched and thought that Shem had discovered him again. Only he found that he was placed in a beautiful house, lavished with beautiful clothes and given instructions on what was to happen, who was to come for him and when he would leave. He nearly jumped with joy at his good fortune and knew that it must all have been the work of Secomb.

He had tried to identify the other benefactor in the coach and had given up after a fashion. He was just glad to be protected. The gentleman had left him clear instructions that he was to remain in the house and not try to escape or bribe the staff to get a message to anyone. The staff was loyal to their master and Hartright would never discover who that was.

A passage had been arranged for him and he was to be ferried away in secrecy to start a completely new life to the new world. He was a lucky man to have such friends and it would not do for him to ask too many questions. His every need had been catered for and he could not believe his good fortune. He had a new identity and money to carry forward in the new world.

A Waterman had picked him up from London Bridge. The boat ebbed away into the night and Hartright thought it was rather ironic that he was being ferried away in the depths of night to elude his capture by the gangs when for the past few years he had been trying to capture them in the act of smuggling contraband. How the tide had turned? He was now being ferried towards the Thames estuary to pick up a further boat, heading for Portsmouth

He had got in too deep and in his arrogance had not appreciated how easily he could have drowned. They all thought he had killed Rafe, be it that he had intended to kill Shem and that bitch, Rosie. Now he had a warrant out for his arrest and he had to escape and now had the means to start a new life. He visualised Shem's face and laughed in glee at it. Shem would be livid that he had disappeared without a trace, hunted for a crime he did not commit. He dismissed the death of the driver completely and deluded himself about his guilt. He just kept thinking that the bitch Valentina, had alot to answer for and he could imagine her pitiful face, spilling out all manner of lies to frame him and have him wanted for Rafe's murder! He wished he had never entertained that evil whore. Oh, she would get her come-uppance! He did not know how, or when, but she would get it.

Nevertheless, he had got away. He had won in any event.

However, that was in the past now. He curled his lips. Shem was a powerful man, and at one time Hartright believed his power did indeed stretch to London and beyond however someone was helping him, and therefore was more powerful than Shem and his small time smuggling racket. Hartright still had friends in high places and they would cover his tracks. He was free, and would only have to keep low until he was confident the coast was clear, and then the world was his oyster.

He knocked at the door and waited.

'Who is it?'

'Felicity, its Shem.'

She raised herself from her bed and felt the blood drain from her face. She looked about her room and thought that this was so unreal. Why was she worried if the room was tidy? If he was going to kill her, he'd hardly worry! Why was he here? Why had she panicked, of course he wasn't going to kill her, what for? Well, Paully did say before she was lucky to still be breathing. God she was in a flurry! She stood for a full minute trying to calm herself.

'Can I come in?' He did not sound impatient just curious as to why he was still waiting like a fool at the door.

The door was flung open and Felicity stood in front of him, dressed all in beautiful lace lingerie, which at one time he would have been quite happy to take a step back and admire. Her hair was loose and she looked fresh and lovely. She seemed to have blossomed since he had last noticed her.

He had been assured that she was not working at the moment and hence been allowed to climb the stairs to her little room which was found in the eves of the old house.

The girls had their own little rooms and then worked out of the special rooms on the first floor. They had all been recently decorated after Gideon's death for a more up market feel and apparently so Shem had been lead to believe, looked quite elegant, rather like the London gentleman's clubs.

Shem smiled to himself, this was only the second time he had been face to face with this girl, and the first time, she had got in his way. This time she moved aside to allow him in.

The room was very small, with one small wooden bed, which was covered in white cotton sheets and lush covers of purple and reds. All looked to be of Arabic origin and she seemed to be a girl who had taste and must have been doing considerably well to afford such things from overseas. The small room just had one dresser and one wardrobe, and on every surface, against the walls, over the dresser and on top of the wardrobe, all he could see was drawing after drawing.

He moved forward and stopped before the dresser seeing that Felicity had indeed more drawings of Rafe in various poses. In some Felicity had captured him while he slept, in some, he was posing, and some were moments of him sketched in memory but captured so very well. It was obvious that the drawings showed a couple who were comfortable with each other and who had spent a considerable amount of time together and she had managed to bring to life the man, his gestures and his cheeky charm. She really had captured the true nature of him.

Felicity had sat down on the bed and watched as Shem looked at each and every picture. She was becoming very apprehensive as to why he was here and knew that Valentina would be at the door shortly fishing for information. She was fully alert and found her neck muscles straining with her anxiety.

Slowly he turned to face her and gave her a beautiful natural smile. This unnerved her as usual she would avoid him at any cost, he made her very frightened. She refused to relax.

'Jesus, is this a fucking shrine or what?' He shook his head at the wonder of it all. If she had been less nervous, she would have laughed.

'What do you want me to say?' He knew she had to tread very carefully with this man. Every fibre of her was shaking in fear.

'The truth would be nice. This is a social call, and I should not have to explain that I am not a paying customer!' Felicity felt every part of her scream in fear at his tone.

'Yes but if I upset you, ya more than likely to cut off all my limbs and tear out me tongue!' Could he hear how scared she was? She certainly could.

'That's a bit harsh.' He tried to sound hurt and failed due to the big grin on his face. Up close and now in a better light, there was a certain something about this man. Whereas Rafe was just drop dead gorgeous, Shem had an all-together different attraction going on. She knew she could like him, if she wasn't so damn scared. 'I am a little more subtle, maybe just your ears and eyelids?' He wasn't looking at her as he spoke and was lost looking at a picture of his brother.

'Nice!' She laughed, he looked over his shoulder, and laughed with her, she felt her tension start to ease.

'I hear you are a good whore.' He actually complimented her and this took her back. Although on reflection, it really wasn't the greatest thing she ever wanted to be told.

'Nice way to start the conversation.' She felt more and more comfortable now and found that he was indeed growing on her. Rafe always said that if she ever got to speak to Shem, she would be surprised. How anyone thought Shem was a complete maniac, Rafe could never quite understand.

'You loved him?' He asked softly.

'Of course!' She held his gaze. An age seemed to pass as he examined and was lost in his own thoughts over the drawings.

'How would you like to work for me?' This took her back.

'Depends in what capacity?' He liked her quickness. His mind was made up.

'I see you have such an eye for detail. Can you draw houses, estates, roads, markings, maps, mines?'

'I can draw anything to whatever scale, just tell me what you need.'

'How do you feel about moving to Cornwall and becoming a whole new person?' He watched her intently.

'To the Hall?' She offered. He looked long and hard at her. 'Nathaniel told me his story.' She offered in a whisper.

He did not answer. She got up and looked seriously at the man who was about to change her whole future. She felt overawed and a feeling of freedom and promise engulfed her. If she had a chance, just a small chance at escaping this existence and going somewhere, she would jump right now. She wrapped her arms around herself. He was offering her hope. Why would he do that? It was wonderful and she felt extremely overwhelmed with emotion.

'You are offering me an opportunity to get out of this way of life, and go to a very special place and I promise you with all my heart, that I have never ever said or will say anything unless you tell me otherwise about you or Rafe.' She felt all choked and allowed a tear to slip away. 'Rafe, Nathaniel whatever his name. He was my best friend and we loved each other, but not in that, - I'll spend the rest of my life with you. My God, you know your brother. He was a right player.' She breathed heavily and let go of a little sob. 'God, how I miss the silly so and so, more than words can say. I see his children and it breaks my heart.' She tried to compose herself. How could her grief even compare to his brothers after all they had gone through. Shem was his brother and the pain must have been insufferable, and there she was expressing her feelings. How selfish was she? 'I sometimes dream that he hasn't really gone, he is just playing and will be back soon.' She choked back her tears. 'I am sorry, I am being so selfish.' The tears flowed freely now down her face. She looked so young and vulnerable.

He could not allow her sorrow to touch him. He needed to keep the door shut to his emotions. He needed to maintain control, an even head in all matters. 'It is sorted then, you will leave tomorrow with my instructions and the necessaries. You will be going first via London to see my acquaintance and he will also provide you with your contract, allowance, and new identity.' He was offering her hope, escape, a whole new life, and world. She tried to wipe the tears from her eyes, but to no avail as a fresh lot piled up, however this time in joy. She gave thanks for having such talent and thanks to the dear friend and lover, she had lost.

'Thank you.' She whispered. The brothers had given her so much and she given really so little. She grabbed Shem's hands and squeezed them tightly. 'Thank you. I won't ever let you down.' She was not a fool to comprehend what would happen if she did.

It was late, it was cold, and the only noise was the surf. There was a full moon, which lit the whole bay up. Around the bay, you could make a few lights from people's homes, but mostly the coast was black. Very clearly, you could see and hear small rowing boats float towards the surf.

The small boat skimmed the surf and then crunched against the shingle and rode the waves coming to a smooth stop.

On top of the beach, Shem had posted pickets to keep an eye out just in case this was witnessed.

'Already for the off?'' Shem was asked and nodded. Shem turned back to Bob and held out his hand. Bob took it heartfully and then pulled the man forward for an embrace. They had been arguing earlier and this had left a bad taste with each of them. Neither could leave it like that, as they genuinely loved each other like father and son.

Shem knew that Bob had not been comfortable with events, but destiny had a way of handling matters that perhaps did not always sit well. There was a natural law of action and this had not been followed through to fulfil Shem's revenge on what had happened to his family. He had had a clear-cut view of what should happen, but it had not come to that and now he waited to be taken away to fulfil at least one part. He felt just apprehension.

'How many more people will have to die or get hurt before this is over Shem?' Bob had questioned.

'I did not start this!' Shem had retaliated.

'But you can finish it!' Shem knew that Bob did not want him to go at this moment; He wanted him to stay and sort things out at home. However, Shem was impatient.

'His lies caused all of this heartache.' Shem had answered defensively.

'It's Mestor you really want.' Bob almost said to himself.

'No, what I want is Rafe sitting where you are now and I want my father back too. But that isn't going to happen!'

'He will come after you if you kill his family.' They both knew of who Bob referred.

'What did he seriously think; I had been planning over the last few years, a family reunion? And anyway, I gotta find the fucker first. Any ideas, Bob?' Shem finished flippantly. Bob chose to ignore the remark. It was a low blow he felt, but he did not know that Shem knew exactly where Hartright was.

'He saved your arse. He rescued you remember!' Shem seemed to recall that this had been constantly thrown in his path how Mr. H had been his saviour.

'And I am grateful, but he knows what comes next.' He felt like he had said this a hundred times.

'He ordered you to back down.' Bob tried to word it as softly as possible. He knew before he even spoke it that there was no way that Shem would stop his plan of action.

'And you Bob?'

They both looked at each other for a long time. Bob was the first to look away, look into the swirling sea, and watch how it almost carried his anger at the whole injustice of it all. The sea spray reached them as they stood on the beach. Bob picked a pebble and with no real enthusiasm threw it at the sea in frustration. There was no impact. What had Bob expected? He was lost. He hated that it had come to this; He could see it from both sides. He was torn.

'I'll not watch the two of you destroy each other.' Shem looked up at the older man and nodded. They walked towards the waiting boat.

'Look after yourself Samuel. You know I will do anything to protect Seb, and all off Nathaniel's off spring. You should wed that Lass when you get back. Don't let her go on any account.' And with that, Shem watched as his friend slowly made his way back up the beach, fighting against the pebbles and the hurried wind. An image of his pixie entered his mind. God she would be livid!

Bob stopped as two hooded figures emerged from the dark. Both were covered from head to toe in black, and if there had not been pebbles underfoot, Bob would never have seen them.

'Evening Bob.' One of them greeted him and Bob immediately recognised the deep voice of Pasha Mordesan. So he knew without being told that the other fellow was Kebo Mordesan.

They were Mr. H and Gunthorpe's sidekicks and here they were, in the middle of the night escorting the young Master. This could only mean trouble. Shem was full of surprises.

All three were secure in the boat now and Bob watched as they drifted away with the tide. He stood there for an age, just watching as he had done with many of his many other friends. There were always goodbyes, long departures, long periods of no news, uncertainties, until they met again, but this time all Bob felt was sorrow. He raised his hand in a salute, not sure, if they could still see him, and was surprised to see all three wave goodbye. He swallowed down the lump in his throat.


The bed was empty! Where was he, his side was cold?

No, he had gone. Gone! She scrabbled out of the bed. Her heart raced. She had been dreading this! He'd left her in the middle of the night, gone! Jester, the young puppy, groaned at being flung of the bed and having just woken from a great sleep was not impressed that his owner was acting weird.

'Shem!'

He may have just been outside; she rushed down the stairs to the front of the Coach House, and found the door unlocked, she threw open the heavy wooden door and rushed out into the night air. Jester trotted behind, curious as to what the fuss was all about. The cool October freshness hit her; she looked from left to right, but knew she'd find nothing. What was she to do? He may just be out here! She knew she was trying to kid herself.

'Shem!' She called into the silence, waiting, knowing there would be no response. She run to the stables and knew before she got there that his horse's stall was empty. His horse was gone. She stood there frozen, oblivious to her wet feet and the grass tingling between her toes. Her mind was ticking over what to do? *He's left me, had he not left in the middle of the night before? Of course he had.* She argued with herself.

But never without saying goodbye! *Why did he not wake me?* This was different this time, she felt dread. He had deliberately kept her up late knowing that she would be so very tired. So tired she would not hear a thing. He was gone! She knew it was coming had he not told her that it was only a matter of time?

*Just don't panic. Don't panic.* She thought to herself. *There is a reason for this. Now think.* She returned to the house, the dog trotted behind, not a care in the world. Perhaps Chrissy knew what was happening?

'What's going on?' Came the familiar voice. Chrissy was standing in the doorway.

'Thank God you're here! Shem's gone, gone Chrissy?'

'Gone where, Darling?' She was wiping her eyes of sleep.

'He didn't say anything to you, you did not hear anything?' This could not be the big trip away he had been planning?

Chrissy just stood there looking lost. Shem usually told her if he was going away and what to get ready, but not this time. 'Look after Seb.' Rosie called over her shoulder. She climbed back up the stairs. She grabbed at her cloak, swung it round herself, and looked for her old boots. She found them back downstairs. She tried to put her boots on and found them heavy with dried mud left on them. Within seconds she was outside again and racing past Little Paully who had heard all of the commotion. Chrissy shortly followed cursing.

'Rosie darling, stop, Rosie, look!' But she was already gone. 'You were supposed to be protecting her, now get after her for God's sake. I'll alert Claude and Paully.'

All Rosie kept thinking was that she must find him. *Run Rosie,* she told herself, *Run, run for him!*

Jester started after her, thinking this was a game, he rushed around her leg. Well he was up for it; a walk at any time, it was out wasn't it?

'He'd be at the beach.' The dread engulfed her. She then thought she hadn't seen Earl either.

The night was a lot colder than she thought, and her anxiety intensified her dread. She raced towards the beach, it was a good way off, and she rushed through the fields at all speed. Her mind racing with the black thoughts, towards an uncertain future, her man gone! The night, grey with mist and she knowing exactly what direction to take. She come towards the fields end and worked her way to the edge of the field, where the flinted wall barrier had crumbled away. Jester jumped after and crossing the small trodden cart way, they descended onto the beach lands. Pockets of mist floated here and there.

She stopped at the foot of the decline to the beach to catch her breath; the air was still, as if the whole world had gone to sleep. She tried to listen but could not hear a thing! It was eerie. She had never been frightened of the dark; however the not knowing, was giving her goose pimples.

*Shem?* Her heart called, the dog was circling her legs, 'Move Jester, just move!' she pleaded.

She was shaking now, shaking with fright. Her body was tense and cold. She appreciated that this was not wise being out in the dead of night. Why did this feel so bad?

Her heart was bursting; she trotted down the narrow tread to the beach, anxious not to slip on the now wet path. She tried to control her breathing, the sweat trickled down her back. The back of her legs were tightening up and her face was red with the exertion. She hadn't time to fully get dressed, and her shift kept getting caught between her legs, and she was struggling to keep her balance and untangle the cotton with her other hand, as well as have the dog making enough noise to raise an army. She felt her hair whip against her face, and with a sob, she put the memory to one side of him plaiting her hair that very morning. She then heard a dog bark.

'What the hell!' Hissed a familiar voice, at the foot of the beach path. She heard Earl bound towards her and Jester yelp in glee. For a moment, she felt relief. He must be near if Earl was here!

Slowly the stout figure of Bob Hawkins moved towards her. She pulled herself together and heard her breath echo in the still of the night. She heard her steps crunch onto a pocket of the pebbles from the top of the beach.

Bob stopped and waited for her to meet him. He had evil black eyes that disappeared into the depths of his sockets. His small lips pursed up in anger.

'What you doing here making all that fucking racket?' His whisper was sure to be heard in the pits of hell for its intensity. He eyed again the area, all night he had been watching. He was in two minds as to whether to belt her one to knock her out, for the noise she was making. He looked over her shoulder and tutted. Earl had stopped his excitement now was at the seas edge looking out to sea.

'He's gone hasn't he?' She cried looking beyond him for a sight of anything. This was it; it wasn't supposed to be for ages. Shem had hinted that a long journey was coming up but she had never perused it. The pain of it was too much to bear.

Bob grabbed her arm thinking; *I should have just smacked her one,* he thought as he headed her back up the small hillside to the top of the beach. She tried to protest and kept trying to turn back down, however the powerful man dragged her along with ease.

'Dog, here.' He groaned and Jester obediently walked behind, frightened to hear such authority from anyone other than his master. Earl needed no commands. He followed Bob.

She tried to fight him off but the man's strength was legendary. He just applied enough pressure on her arm to make it numb.

At the top of the verge, he scanned the area and turned back towards the beach. Still the mist screened the sea, and the only noise was the soft splurged of the surf as it broke and then withered away, to come back again, and again. He whistled to his men, satisfied all was well, he then turned towards her.

'They left ages ago; I was scouted to make sure the authorities hadn't got wind. Know what I mean?'

'Left?'

'Do I have to repeat myself?' He groaned, still looking around, expecting to be surprised.

'He's left;' she dropped her head to her chin. What was she to do? He had abandoned her. Her whole world crashed around her. She knew, knew from the moment she opened her eyes. He had left without a word. No words of comfort. She had known something was a foot. She could feel it. Everyone had seemed to sense that something was happening. They had all been vague about this job, which would take Shem away.

Bob rested both his hands on her upper arms and slowly rubbed her shoulders to give her some sort of comfort. This was a bad night, a bad night all round. He hated to see her like this. He had a fondness for the lass. He felt a lump form in his throat and he was Bob Hawkins, he could not allow anyone to see him acting like a soppy poof. However, seeing a woman in distress left him feeling awkward.

It was the middle of the night, one of the first few nights of winter, telling you to wrap up, but you never did, thinking it was still warm enough for a smaller coat, but knowing that it could freeze the tits off a witch. And here he was giving comfort to the main man's woman. Shem had not intended to depart any time before Christmas, but what with the developments with Hartright, Shem decided now was as good a time as any. The few who knew, the better. There were no comebacks then. Therefore, with everyone tucked up in bed, waiting for the new day to begin and not having a clue as to what was happening on their doorsteps, Shem had arranged everything. He knew the agony Rosie would face and go through and no words of comfort were going to make this one better. How do you let go? How do you cut those ties, how do you not hurt the one's you love the most? Shem had decided to go now and leave the flack to Bob it would seem. Bob could not believe that a man like that could be scared shitless of this little piece Rosie.

'Let's get you home love; he said you would go mad.' He tried to sound comforting but found it ended in anger when Little Paully run towards them. 'You were supposed to be watching her. Anything could have happened. You know what I mean?' He roared through gritted teeth.

'I'm sorry Bob. She just rushed out. I tried.....'

'Oh give it a rest. I've heard it all before.' Little Paully knew this was not the end for him; Bob would deal with him later. He seemed to let everyone down and it was still raw how he felt about leaving Rafe for him to get shot and then die. His family had ordered him home, and still he had not gone. Bob indicated to the horses that were off away and then he turned back to Rosie, who kept looking back towards the sea. Tears streamed down her face.

'He will be back before you know it.' Bob offered, but it was of no comfort at all. None at all. Rosie felt her heart break with rejection.

'Cousins.'

'It is good to see you.' They spook in French. After the formal welcome and permission to board the ship, the group of men all took turns in hugging the Captain of the ship. Shem indicated to his cousin's face and a fresh scar across his right eye. Oliver Levaseur waved it away.

'Stupid accident, casualty of war, hey?' Oliver Levaseur was as tall and lean as his cousin but with shoulder length wavy black hair. He had full bread with a whisper of a moustache and dark skin, showing his Spanish descent. His features were sharp and suggested he should not be trusted. He laughed at Shem who made for the edge of the ship and placed his hand on the side to keep his balance.

'I can't believe you can't stomach the sea, where you make most of your profit, but hey ho.' Oliver was a loud man. Shem merely smiled at this trying desperately not to look at the sea.

'You know this is killing me!' They all laughed at him and Kebo smacked him on the back in jest. Shem looked at him in mock anger and mouthed. 'Don't!'

Oliver Levaseur was lucky to have a Letter of Marque and Reprisal from the French Government and having initially some years previously approached Kebo and Pasha to do business, they all agreed to bring Shem into their partnership as he was making a name for himself and had the land transport and connections all in place. Oliver had recently returned from the Indian Ocean and now with the new cargo was ready to set sail again, for Madagascar.

'Well, let's go below and talk.' His expression more serious now. 'We salute and drink for Nathaniel, my cousin, then we drink some more, then we go and meet up with Eddy yes?'

'When is the rendezvous?' Shem asked trying to hold his ground and feeling very wobbly already.

'My God man, already you are turning green.' Pasha mocked.

'We set sail, first thing with tide, then you should be back here maximum three days turn around, then we are off.'

'Excellent.' Shem rolled his eyes and his voice was flat with emotion.

'Relax, it will be a breeze.' His cousin was always too casual about everything. Shem looked back out at the sea and raised his eyebrows. It was the wrong thing to do. He felt his stomach groan.

'Well, maybe a little patchy.' Oliver agreed shrugging his shoulders.

'A little patchy, that's roaring down there.' Oliver waved his hand dismissively and looked at Shem as if he were a great wimp.

'Stop showing us up and get below.' Pasha groaned at him, and like a child that had been told off, he did what his Uncle ordered.

Hartright had been in his quarters enjoying an afternoon doze when he noticed a change in the ships rhythm; they had been heading into Portsmouth and come along the Thames estuary and round the coast. He had been so happy and had a permanent smile on his face. He heard whistles and commands up top and took a glance out of the window. He noticed a frigate approaching and signally with flags to his Merchant ship, 'The Lady Luck.'

He sighed and rested back on his bed, laying his head on his hands and crossing his feet for comfort, knowing that it was not unusual for Captain's to relay news and take on board letters and cargo on route. No matter, within 24 hours the 'Neptune' would be heading him to the Americas and his whole new life. He heard the Captain give permission for someone or something to board his ship and Hartright closed his eyes to rest, listening to the wave's splash up against the ship. Someone's voice triggered a memory to him, but he could not put his finger or what it was. He heard someone on the ships stairs and they stopped outside of his small room. There was the lightest tap on the door. He tutted, not wanting to be disturbed.

'Enter.' He drawled in a rather bored manner.

'Hello Harry.' Shem spoke in his normal voice and was clean-shaven. He was dressed as a gentleman and his wealth was evident. He oozed confidence and determination, but Hartright could see the blackness in the knowing eyes. He shot up in panic, recognition, horror, and fear. His legs almost gave way seeing familiar faces before him.

'Oh my God. What is this?' He sounded like a little girl lost and all alone.

'Pay back.' He watched as Pasha and Kebo stood ready to come forward.

'What in hell's name is.....' He walked back as far as he could, then stopped, and slumped in panic. 'My God, my God, all this time you.....' He looked in memory now at his Uncles and reality started to dawn. It was a family reunion!

'Your treachery and sick pleasures have caused no end of suffering for all of us pup.' Kebo growled at him. Hartright hadn't seen Kebo or Pasha in years, however he immediately felt like a small boy again in their presence. They had always looked down at him, as if he were a fool and Kebo had always scared him so.

'You've always been a selfish prick, but you just had to push it too far?' Shem smiled sweetly and Hartright knew he had been playing with the devil all this while. The man had been setting him up for a fall. How could he have not seen it? Not known him for who he really was? He had thought he had recognised him, and now it was all dawning on him who he had been sparring with over the last few years and who Rafe really was!

'This is your fault. I haven't done anything!' Hartright screamed in sheer panic.

'Not from where I am standing, you prick?' Shem stepped forward, bending his head through the small doorway and spat at him. Kebo moved into the little room, grabbed his arm, and pulled him away.

'You've got it all wrong; for once just listen to me.' Hartright begged.

'Shut up.' Kebo leant forward and warned. Hartright could not mistake that look of pure hatred from Kebo, who had always managed to frighten the life out of him. He had hoped to never see either of his adopted Uncles ever again.

'You are a disgrace to our family. Why did you have to do it? Nathaniel was a good man. A gem amongst us.'

'I never knew. I never knew.' He looked at all of them in turn. 'It wasn't me! I never killed him!' He had to convince them; they thought he had killed his own cousin.

'Shut your mouth you fucking prat. You deserve everything that is coming to you. An eye for an eye!'

'No. No. Shem, no Samuel, Pasha. You don't understand. You can't do this!' He looked from one to the other, sweat pouring from his brow. He held his hands up to defend himself. This was not supposed to happen like this. He had a new life planned. He was pleading for his life!

'Oh, but Harry we can.' Kebo had grabbed him by the collar and with such ease brought his nephew into the corridor. Hartright deliberately made himself limp, so he fell to the floor. Kebo threw him round like he was a rag doll and bound his hands. Hartright continued to whine, being too weak and pitiful in his unmanly behaviour to fight. He was begging them to listen to him.

'You have to listen, it was that bitch.' He had again fallen to his knees and tears were streaming down his face. 'I can't hang, I won't not for that. It was not me.

She pulled the trigger. Ask that dreadful Spanish.....' He received a swipe around the mouth and blood trickled down his mouth. His knees buckled and he thought he would faint and somehow managed to lurch back slightly when his cousin roared;-

'I'll cut out his tongue.' All at once, Shem was upon him again with such force that Pasha lost his footing and Shem managed to bring his knife up to Hartright's face in one swoop. The ferocity had completely engulfed him.

'You can't be serious.' Pasha managed to wrestle his arm away and both men glared at each other.

'I'm waiting.' Shem warned as he sized up to him, Pasha was no match for this madness.

'Get your control back now.' The atmosphere had intensified.

'Get out of my way. You know where the exit is?'

'Don't do this.' Pasha hissed in warning.

'You still here?'

'Back off boy!' Pasha pushed him back, Shem immediately stepped back towards him, and in the next minute, he had grabbed Pasha by the collar and flung him across the room. In an instance Kebo was at Shem and yanked him back with ease, he turned his nephew towards him and Shem felt the power of him vibrant from every pore. Shem always thought that he was a fair height and weight but no match for Kebo. He was enormous. They both glared at each other and Shem was the first to step back from the massive man. Kebo would pull him apart.

'That's rich, what part of, I want him to suffer for eternity did you not get?' Shem was livid and the blackness had engulfed him into pure utter rage.

'He will do. If you allow us to finish what we have started. Now calm down.' Pasha moaned trying to get up whilst rubbing his neck. Shem had never ever attacked him like that before and both his Uncles were disgusted at him.

Hartright whimpered as he moved further and further into the corner watching as his family quarrelled amongst themselves. Shem paced back and forth, as his adrenalin hit its peak.

'Shut the fuck up you pathetic poof.' Kebo snarled in irritation to Hartright. He dragged him back up and Hartright played dumb and feeble. Shem came forward and Hartright flung himself to him pitifully and rested his head against him. 'Samuel, listen to me, please listen....' He begged as snot and dribble mixed.

'No you listen, prick!' Shem whispered pulling his head back by his hair. 'Every day for the rest of your pitiful life, will be in such pain, agony, sick, piss, and shit? Just like you had a mind for me and Nathaniel.' The two men looked deep into each other's eyes. So much was communicated within that look. What they had shared as children, growing up, their unknown reunion and what had befallen both in adulthood. 'I hope you live a long, long life in complete misery and you suffer for an eternity.'

Hartright gasped in pure fright at the utter venom and evil that was his cousin. He had under estimated Shem as an enemy and now would pay. However, he had also under estimated who his cousin really was. How could he have deluded himself that his Uncles would allow for their brother and his son's all to be lost at sea, presumed all dead, without doing some investigations?

He had never really taken the time to think about what he had heard on the quiet about his Uncles and their many goings on. Now it all fell into place. They had obviously rescued Samuel and Nathaniel and given them a new identity so that they could gain strength and power to come back at him and those in his family who had wronged them. How naive and a fool he had been. Samuel Mordesan had always been resourceful and always loved. That love had saved him and moulded him into something unique. A man who had lived by many aliases and who had clearly hoodwinked him. Samuel was a powerhouse, and he had that special Mordesan trait. Pure evil running through his veins. Hartright always knew he was himself bad, or misunderstood and enjoyed it immensely, but his cousin had that insane mad out of control black madness.

Both knew it was useless. The evil had taken their Grandfather Harold Mordesan, and what made Samuel think that he could contain that inherited family streak? Moreover, in saying that, what gave Samuel the right to think he was any better than him?

Hartright decided his cousin was insane and was indeed worse, and he had the scars to prove it. However, added to that, Shem or Samuel had managed to put the fear of the devil on him and he could not imagine what fate had in store, but he would suffer for an eternity he knew.

From behind, Shem felt Pashas strong arms pull him away. He turned and closed his eyes, fighting to hold back his tears of temper. His Uncle loosened his hold and softly rubbed his arms in comfort. He nodded his head feeling ashamed at his earlier outburst and attack on them. He tried so hard to lose the blackness. He clutched his necklace to calm himself and let his Uncle lead him up top.

Hartright was now screaming to be let go, and trying everything to get away from his Uncle Kebo who was carrying him up the stairs on his shoulder to the deck. God what fate did they have in store? This was déjà vu! Surely, they did not intend to serve him the same fortune he had helped to serve against his younger cousins all that time ago? He was deluding himself. Of course they were! He was doomed. He knew his fate now and it wasn' pretty. He was to suffer the same that they had planned for the brothers, a live sold into slavery. It all fell into place.

A small subtle cough from the Captain and all hands turned and looked away as Kebo stepped onto the top deck. The small party all nodded at the Captain in respect.

Kebo and Pasha made to leave and climb down to the small boat, which would take them back to their own ship, however before they preceded a young man came up the ladder to stand by their side. He was dressed as a gentleman and looked ill suited in his new clothes; however, the grin on his face was a picture. He was to replace Hartright and he had been given a new life to look forward to in the Americas. His Uncle Luca had told him he was a lucky lad and if he kept his wits about him, he would not swing as quickly as he would have if he had been allowed to stay in London. Marcus Luca Bravio was made up and had a new job with the backing of both the Mordesans' and his Uncle. He would be a fool to blow it.

Unceremoniously, Kebo and Pasha flung their new charge Hartright into the boat; he landed with a huge thud.

Shem came forward and with hand outstretched thanked the Captain wholeheartedly.

'I am in your debt. This will never be forgotten Edward.' Shem assured the man he had known as a young boy. The older man smiled at him and he patted the younger man on his back as he made to disembark.

'God bless you Master Samuel, and do not fear all is in hand.' At that point, Marcus came and stood beside him. He had a cheeky grin on his face and mockingly saluted Shem in thanks and all of them laughed at the gesture. He saw Edward nudge Marcus with a twinkle in his eye and was glad the feeling of blackness was subsiding. Luca was right, Marcus reminded Shem of Annatasia.

Hartright was now their prisoner, lying battered and bruised at the bottom of the boat, his mind played tricks with him, while the stagnant water at the foot of the boat lapped up against him. He would be rescued again. This would not be allowed to happen. Secomb and that man would find him. He was a Mordesan, no one took him prisoner. He was not a man to be sold into slavery. He went all warm and found he had wet himself in panic. He could not open his eyes and just whined and cried and cried, as the boat pulled away and his life was left in limbo. He received a few choice kicks and thumps but knew this was noting to what was to come. Why had Shem just not had his men kill him all that time ago when he had first attacked Rafe? He felt pathetic and swore he would wish himself to death; he was lost to where he was heading and what lay in store. He was doomed for eternity. It was too much for him.

'You're not listening to me, it was all her fault.' Then there was silence as Kebo punched him into oblivion.

---

**Act Four**

**Chapter Thirteen**

It was hot! Hotter than it had been this time last year and the locals were worrying already about the lakes and streams and not having enough water to keep them going through the summer. What could be done! They needed some rain. The land was grey with dryness and it needed some rain to soak through and re vitalise the spring bloom. The roses were just coming through and the spring pink blossoms were awash and in the winds providing confetti of dancing rain.

Rosie sat beside the stream with her chin on her knees and one hand resting in the coolest of the water, as it slowly glided by. The day was slowly ending. She watched and sighed as the clear water trickled through her hands as the current slowly made its way down stream carrying small lost leaves in its path. Across in the woodland, she watched as the boys from the camp played their wrestling game, huffing, puffing, and promoting the male pride.

Rosie let her vision wonder along the lines of the stream, up above the tree tops and looked at the soft white clouds slowly flutter by against a backdrop of the richest blue sky she had seen in a long while. She found it hard to relax. She concentrated on the beauty of her natural surroundings, and the feel of the whistle and song of the cool evening breeze, making the leaves sing in tune against the slow trickle of the stream. Underfoot the Autumn leaves where fading and the new life of spring was making its mark, fox gloves just about to burst, snowdrops dainty and flowing back and forth. Spring buds on the trees. This was bliss.

Then her mind's eye wondered and that face slowly took form, his confident slow swagger, oozing with strength and authority. His smile that would make her catch her breath and her insides somersault a million times over. The way he would cock his head to one side and for her, wink and slowly let his smile light up his whole face. She held her breath as his image glided towards her, grinning like the cat that had the cream, seductively creep up her body on all fours. She could feel his warm breath on her neck and him slowly nuzzle her neck. He would always then lie beside her and cradle her in so much strength and love that she could burst. She could smell him. She leisurely raised her arm and found her hand rising to stroke his face.

'Mum!' Screamed the excited boy running gleefully to her whilst his friend dug his heels in behind him with his fists tightly wrapped around the younger boys shirttails and was pulling him back to play. Other children amongst them followed them, Seb's Cousin Phoebe and as ever were all guarded by their loyal dogs, Jester and Earl. 'Mum help me, please.'

Rosie shook her head of the dream and coming too and laughed at her son as he tried to fight free. He laughed at her and then turned swiftly to confront his friend and bump into him. They both hit the floor, wrestling, laughing, and choking at the same time. Jester kept circling and circling, with his tail constantly wagging while Earl strolled towards Phoebe who circled his ear, he wagged his tail.

Rosie sighed so deeply coming back to reality and felt her heart strings pull and fought the unshed tears behind her eyes from being let lose. It was becoming ever so hard to blame. Ever so hard to keep the boiled hate raging in her heart, when time went by and as always the good memories kept coming back to comfort in days of solitude and loneliness. She missed Hattie, she missed her old home, her brothers, and she missed that feeling of being so in love, so wanted, so cherished that together with Shem, they would right the world, and all they needed was each other. He would help banish all her demons, her nightmares and stroke away her pains. She remembered that the end of the day would bring them to each other, best friends, and lovers. His smell, his touch, his voice, just him. A single tear set itself free and then she let her eyes focus on the next best thing she had to him, Sebastian.

She picked herself up and roughly smoothed down her long skirts and shook at the hem to clear them of any dried leaves and earth. She was irritated with herself and covered her eyes with both her hands. She would never see any of them again. Some lost, some betrayed her, one left and deserted her and filled her with some insecurity that she felt discarded and used. What was she now? An unmarried young woman with no money of her own and people protecting her from what?

She rubbed her forehead and as normal stroked her scar, which run from her left ear to under her chin, and then with another sigh, she turned to face the children, wiping all the hurt from her face, and slowly producing a warming smile. She wrapped her shawl tightly over her bosom. How easy it was to shut it away and return to the real world. She was angry and miserable. She needed to focus to keep the memories at bay and having Sebastian stood there laughing and joking having so much fun, it brought her so much joy.

She headed back to Rosamund and the campfire. It was dusk and always a time to reflect on the day. Rosamund and her family were seated out in the open, with a fire for comfort, the night was new. All around her, she heard soft singing and people enjoying each other's conversations. They spoke about the children, the anticipated fair and remarked on how warm it was this evening, however knowing that the weather would probably turn, in hope that rain would come.

Rosamund poked at the fire with no real purpose. She raised her eyes to look directly at Rosie with such intensity that the younger woman had to look away first. Rosie sat with Jester the dog's head in her lap, and she curled his ear around her hand, while the dog's father Earl, stood watching out for both his charges, Sebastian and Phoebe.

They had had a row earlier and its aftermath was still hanging in the air. Rosamund had moaned again, at her being so miserable, and for being frightened of the future and not off loading her concerns. 'Let people in Rosie; let them in before you become too bitter and twisted in this game.'

'It is not a game. This is my life, so just let me be.' Rosie had answered earlier. Her thoughts were broken when she caught the cuddly figure of Chrissy come out from the back of the Coach Inn and make her way towards them. It was getting late and marked the children's bedtime.

Both Sebastian and Phoebe charged forward and run into a huge cuddle. The children adored her so. Rosamund and Rosie then shared a smile. Chrissy had been a Godsend and Rosamund was pleased Rosie had found such a good friend.

'I'm not tired.' Phoebe had protested and sighed as she rubbed her eyes. She was the image of her father. Her hair was a mass of tight curls and she was just losing her puppy fat. She was a gentle child, who was no trouble. She looked after herself and was one of those rare children who could entertain herself and others. She and Seb had bonded straight away and both Shem and Rafe had been astounded at how natural it was between the pair. It was as if it had always been. Seb was like a whirlwind and Phoebe a quite gentle mouse.

'Oh I think you are my love, we all are.' She managed to raise herself with the child now being held in her arms, with her legs wrapped round her waist.

Rosamund watched from the fire and smiled warmly. Rosie was a good mother, it was a shame she had not been blessed with more children. However, it looked as if that was going to be unlikely. 'Say good night to Nana Rosa.' She bent down and let Rosamund kiss her charge. Rosie held out her hand and Rosamund held it firmly. They shared a smile.

'I'm just restless and frustrated.' She whispered and to herself she said, *and I miss him so.*


The morning air was fresh with dew and the sky above was orange with hope. Rosie stood in the doorway of the Coach House and looked across the back fields at the array of tents, the gypsies had erected in the field. Their visit had seemed to last an age and she knew that Marcel and Bob had been working more closely. Rosamund had hitched her tent at the furthest point, and she could see her in conversation with her son Marcel and Bob. She would not admit that having Rosamund around had been of great comfort, but the woman also annoyed and challenged her so, and sometimes she just wanted to wring her neck. She sipped at her fresh tea, and felt slightly less anxious and blessed the shipment. A good cup of tea always made her feel that everything would appear nice and rosy; it blew the cobwebs away and allowed you to see things afresh. Her mind wandered to a faraway place. It had been a beautiful day, the sun had been burning all day, and they had all been down on the beach. Her brothers were all playing on the sandy beach, each running towards the receding surf and being caught out by the bubbles of the swash as it burst towards them, trying to catch them un-aware and trickle through their bare feet. Bobby was the youngest and was screaming in delight, while his older brothers tried to grab his hand for protection and end up laughing at each other as each dared the other to hold fast and then........for it all to start again. From behind, Rosie had turned her head when she heard the crunch of the pebbles and the pebbles cascading down the mounds of Cuckmere beach and rolling then on to the under sand. Her mother was trying not to run down the beach in glee as the depth of the mounds speeded up her descent. She looked up from her footing and laughed at her children.

'Look at you all, you'll feel the cold soon enough in those wet pants. Come on make yourself lively, your Dad will be back soon and we want to get his tea ready.' Her voice was like velvet, always warm and just made you melt with the love it generated.

'Just a little more Mum, come on join us.' She shook her head and just laughed as the wind caught her hair and it flipped across her face. Who was to know that within months she would be dead?

'Bob said there was no news.' Rosamund said and Rosie let out her breath. Each week, the same, as she had suspected from earlier. Why could they not see that it was useless? He had gone!

'Just stop it, stop it, for fuck's sake. He is dead. Please just let me get on with it.' Rosamund was determined to get through to the girl. 'If he is dead as you keep saying, then you need to get back in contact with your family. Because you're penniless and at the moment being kept by the man you are thinking ill of.'

'I don't need family. I have Bob, Paully, Claude and all the men looking out for me. I have no need of them.'

'But you do Rosie. You need someone to help, because you're not letting me help you.'

'Oh for God's sake. Here we go again.' She argued. 'That's because you believe he is still alive. So that hardly helps me, does it? My God, you are a wicked cow.' Rosie groaned inwardly. She watched as Sebastian moved off with his friends and turn and given her a small wave. She smiled back and then turned to Rosamund who did not hide the grin quickly enough.

'Well for being a witch you can make your own Tea.' Why was Rosamund always trying to wind her up?

'Do you know they have a bet on how long I will tolerate you before I strangle you to death?'

'You have had plenty of opportunity, you know where your bread is buttered, now I will say one more thing then I will not say anymore until well, next time.'

Rosie raised her brows and shook her head. She sighed and crossing her arms waiting for Rosamund to off load her font of all wisdom.

'You are restless, impatient, and you need to do something. Put these nightmares to bed. You need to see and make amends with your family.' Rosie went to interrupt, but Rosamund held her hand up. Slowly the old woman shifted her weight into a better position; she then turned and looked intensely at Rosie. Rosie relaxed and waited. She nodded for the old woman to continue. 'I have arranged with Bob and Marcel for you to go home for a time.'

'Who are you to order me around.....?'

'Bob will take you; he has agreed that you can tell them everything. They are better acquainted with the gang now. '

'And if I am gone and he comes back?'

'So now you think he is alive?'

'I don't know. Stop playing with me.'

'You know he is alive.'

'No, he is a selfish prick who left me. He always fucking leaves me. I feel like a fool.'

'Why my love, why do you feel like a fool?'

'Because he did not trust me to tell me. He just left. He uses me. I sometimes feel he just pities me, and if it were not for Seb, I'd have been put out to pasture.'

'You know that is not so.'

'Then why does it always have to feel like this so empty? So lost of hope?'

'I can't promise you that your visit to your family will be of benefit, it may heal some old wounds. You are so restless. Believe me when I say the future for you is warm.'

She opened her eyes and looked intently at Rosie.

'I can't let go, I just can't. I don't think I ever will. I am tired of this misery and guilt, and riding these emotions all the time. I just want peace. Is that too much to ask? Perhaps I did not want to tell and share with you, I wanted you to love me for me and not because you felt sorry for me.'

'Rosie, I have known you since you were a small child.' Rosamund grabbed hold of the young woman's hand and squeezed, 'have shared all of your joys and woes. You have so much to give, so much love, you deserve happiness, and I want that for you. Enough hiding! Please Rosie, start to live again, and don't keep hiding behind your son. You know you have to return to your brothers, they have been through enough my love, do they deserve this? Do you? You all need comfort.'

Rain had come and drenched the land. The skies threatened to break with sunshine, and the slow wind persisted and kept the clouds clustered together to warm a sky of grey. The locals had sung a song of joy at the change in weather.

Rosie sighed, looking at the greyness, *that's how my heart is, grey with dread.* Rosamund had unchained her. She tightened her grip on Seb's hand and looked down at him as they hid under the arches of the tree branches. They were both well protected against the weather in thick wool coats and Seb had a red nose from the cold. His blond hair was matted to his head and hung in ringlets at its end's. As always, Jester was leaning against his legs for comfort. Unconsciously Seb stroked the dog. Earl held back watching and smelling.

The rain beat down on the surrounding fields, however only trickles filtered through the canopy of trees. Rhododendrons, as high as trees, crept through and the beautiful pinks and purples made the sheltered walk less intimidating.

Rosie recalled walking along this as a young girl in the thick of winter when dusk was looming, and she swore those trees were eyeing her up to eat her for dinner. All the boys at various times had tried to frighten each over along the lane. Moreover, she had been near to wetting herself with the fright of it all. Rosie pulled Sebastian off the road through a well-trodden path and they skirted around the farmers fields. She remembered that ripe was grown there and smelt was vile. She and Seb started to trot as the rain came down heavier.

They stopped under a cob of trees and Rosie leant down and slowly pointed across a few fields into a small valley. She smiled encouragingly at her boy. Jester stopped and kept looking at them as if to say; 'And what now?'

The view was misty; however, you could see the picturesque view of an inviting stone Manor house that had been extended many times over the years with the affluence of each new generation. There were numerous outbuildings and on the fringes of the land, you could make out other homesteads. To the east lay the Great Oak Tree and further afield, the woodlands lurked. You could make out a flicker of light from within the large manor house and see the smoke from the chimneys of the extended buildings from each side of the original building. Seb looked up to his mother and beamed with delight. The prospect of getting out of the rain was a welcome. 'Is that Nana's?'

'Yes that's Nana's.'

'Looks nice and warm in there.' Seb smiled at his mother. Even though he was cold and tired form the walk where Marcel and his men had left them, he was optimistic that there was warmth and a pot of gold at the end of the rainbow. 'Will she like me?'

'Oh yes, she and Uncle Ned an Uncle Ray will like you and when she sees you walk through that door, she cuddle you up like Rosa, Daisy and Chrissy do, rustle your hair and then immediately feed you up so you have a fat belly.'

He laughed. No matter how much he ate, he never put on weight; he was like a string bean. She looked over her shoulder to find Marcel a few yards away. He had kept his distance, and nodded to her and she smiled back and watched as he disappeared from view. Jester skipped about eager to be off.

They had left very early that morning and pulled up long one of the main roads, Rosie had wanted to walk the last few miles and compile her thoughts and re familiarize herself with the area.

'But will she whack me round the ear if I forget to take me boots off.' He nodded confirmation to himself, trying to recall the instructions his mother had been trying to tell him on the way. 'I have to be good and remember me pleases and ta's.' He nodded again and this time he took her hand. 'Come then.'

He had no idea what was to come. Rosie reluctantly pulled back behind; he looked up at her in question and tugged at her arm. He called to the dogs and let him lead. He was so brave, so young, and naive, and he set a good example, all he wanted was comfort, food and the knowledge that everyone he ever met liked him and he always made people smile. Oh, if only life would be that simple, she thought! She just felt disappointed with it all and resented those who always had love in their hearts and those who smiled through whatever the almighty threw at them.

*Now or never,* she thought. *Never, never!* However, there was no turning back, she had been bullied into this, and it needed to be done. She was out of the fire but had been pulled into the Devil's den. She laughed to herself at that. That was hardy right, Shem was the devil, and none of those people down there had a patch on him!

She hated the deception to Nana, but Rosie hoped that both Nana and her Grandfather Shaun would understand everything. Her brothers were sure to kill her, but she hated them and she would let them know and give as good as she got. They had deserted her, left her when she needed them. They had just not considered her in any of their schemes, and where did that leave her?

It was right to come back now. Shem would have forbidden it until he knew that everything was safe and sorted. However, Bob would protect her and even now, she knew she was being watched if not by Marcel then one of his men. Rosamund had been right; it was time to face her demons.

Bob hadn't been happy about the arrangements for her to visit, he wanted to keep her secret still, but Rosamund had persuaded him and worn him down. The gang would not let anything happen to her, and especially not Seb. She also knew without a shadow of a doubt that once Paully and Claude returned from their latest assignment, they would go ballistic at the turn of events. She managed to smile to herself, as she half expected to see Paully ride across the field, pull up, jump off his horse, bow mischievously, and then point his finger at her. He would deliberately look glum, then smile delightfully in that boyish rogue fashion and say: 'Get on the bloody horse, you stupid cow and stop playing silly beggars.'

She hoped that her brothers would eventually forgive her, take her back. There would be tensions for a long time and perhaps they would realise how bad they had treated her.

Rosie, Seb and the dogs, descended the hill into the homestead of Shaun and Nana Cavendish. Rosie was full of apprehension and regret that it had come to this, but she held her head up high. It would be a battle of wills ahead, alot of give and take, but she would make them pay. Regardless of the love, they each had for one another. She walked around the great Oak tree that loomed a few hundred yards away from the home and did not look at the Tombstones of relatives at peace laying and surveying their lands. She walked straight by the latest Tombstone which read;-

Our Rosie Cavendish.

Taken before her time.

Loved, cherished, and missed by all.

'Someone's coming.' She put her hand across the table and patted Seb's hand in anticipation, he kicked his socked feet under the table and smiled back at his mother and took another bite of the delicious fresh loaf that had been cooked that morning.

'It will be alright Mum.' Earl had heard someone approaching and stood to attention, while Jester was happy by the fire, minding his own business. Earl had previously gone around every nock and cranny smelling out for the other dogs and snorted at disgust at Jesters lack of help.

Rosie swallowed some tea and found her heart racing. She looked over the brim of the cup with anticipation. She stood up. No one had been home when they had first entered.

'Shem will be here soon.' Seb whispered and she looked at him in question. He had a habit of saying random things and if the wrong person heard, there would be hell to pay. Too many people were still too suspicious of witch talk. Earl backed away to the fire. Rosie's attention then was drawn to the door and she watched as the old woman entered the kitchen with thoughts on her mind and went straight to the fire and muttering to herself, sat on the edge and picking up the poker went to stoke the fire, however found that it was already primed and had been refuelled. She could not remember doing that, then laughed at herself, remembering that she was losing her mind.

Rosie felt her heart swell with love for this woman, no matter how hard she had wanted to hate, one look at Nana, and she was lost. Nana was small like Hattie. She glowed in good health and was always kind and gentle to everyone. She had soft wispier snow-white hair that she let lose to the middle of her neck. It was far too fine to hold back. She had small sparkling eyes and delicate features.

'You want tea Nana?' Rosie found herself saying automatically. Nana heard Rosie ask from behind her. 'Just brewed?'

'That will be lovely lass.' Nana answered not looking back, Seb looked at his Mum and put his hand over his mouth when he went to laugh and she gave him that look to keep it shut.

Nana sighed as the fire warmed her and she found herself stroking Jester and cooing to the dog. She closed her eyes and thought she'd just have five minutes and that was great that Rosie had read her mind and had tea waiting. She was so tired and then laughed at herself; her mind was playing with her. She swiped the air laughing at herself. 'As I live and breathe, I am losing it.' She shook her head and sighed. She then laughed at herself and then got choked as she thought of her lost girl. 'Look at me, hearing ghosts, oh my love.' She felt tears prick her eyes. Then she looked again at the dog at her feet. Then she saw the other dog. Whose dogs were they?

'Nana, where do you want your tea?' Nana stiffened. Was she losing her mind? Was that a voice? She straightened her back. Where was Meriska? Was she hearing things? *You daft cow!* She thought to herself, however with trepidation she slowly moved around.

Her hand came straight up to her mouth to stop her from screaming. She breathed heavy. She quickly shot up. She closed her eyes and backed out of the room. She did not look again, it would go away. She had lost it. 'Oh my God, what would Shaun think?' Her back hit the doorframe. Jester had followed her and was wagging his tail, while Earl just watched.

'Nana, open your eyes and look at me.' Nana shook her head as she heard the soothing voice she knew so well; she hadn't taken her hand from her mouth and now found herself biting her hand. It wasn't so. She had looked at the dead, with a child in tow. She was going mad.

'Is Nanny mad Mum?' The boy whispered across the table, it carried to Nana. Nana quickly opened her eyes to take in the view then shut them again.

Then from nowhere a big bouncing dog bunged threw the kitchen door way, she skirted around Nana and nearly took her legs from under her, the big wolf, hurled its way and took flight to the young lady and as she jumped up, she felt her impact on her arm. Seb cried in horror and darted under the table. Earl and Jester started to bark in warning. Rosie just roared assertively. 'Meriska, sit, sit down, Meriska, no, do as I say, for God's sake, dog!'

The dog had made her sit back in the chair, her front paws where now on her lap and she was trying desperately to lick her face as she fought to fend her off. Jester was barking like a dog gone mad and wagging his tail in excitement. Seb relaxed seeing his mum was laughing and slowly, at first still abit unsure he started to chuckle. Earl stopped barking and sat on his hind legs, knowing that the dog was not a threat.

Nana opened her eyes to the scene and saw Meriska mauling Rosie at the kitchen table, a young mutt was running around, and round, and a young boy, with butter round his mouth, was laughing and kicking his feet in delight under the table.

'For the love of God!' She moaned. 'For the love of God!'

'Nana, get him off me, please, please?'


'So you pissed someone else off and have the scars to show it, and we have to pick up the pieces.' There was no point in trying to talk to Ray when he was in one of his moods. He was like a dog with a bone, a man possessed. 'So who did you piss off this time?'

'What?'

'You heard.'

'What you talking about?' Rosie was trying desperately to get away from him, but he had blocked her exit from the kitchen door, to the passageway. The day had turned out to be very tiring and not over yet. Rosie had been sitting with her two brothers and knew they were looking for answers. She never imagined the reunion would be quite so nerve raking.

'The scar!' Rosie automatically covered her scar and turned away from him.

'So, again you obviously have pushed it too far this time, and thought, you know what, them mugs will have me back.' He stood behind her deliberately goading her. The dog's begun to bark. 'Mugs, that's what you think of us. Right mugs! You fucking whore. You're a fuck! Not a word for how long? We think ya dead and you swan back in here as large as life, given it a big'un, thinking it's all going to be sorted.' Rosie tried to back off him. However, Ray was virtually over her. Ned got up from his seat at the kitchen table.

'Leave it Ray!' Ned warned.

'Leave it, leave it? Look at her, lairy fucking bitch, she as the audacity to look at me like that. I'll wipe that smirk off ya face.' He went to swipe his arm back, she tried to dart away. The dogs were growling now.

'Like to see ya try, you fat bastard.' He lurched forward and backhanded her across the face. She went down with the force of the blow and hit the floor hard. She looked up in horror and felt a slit trickle of blood from her slit lip. Ned was livid and screaming at Ray to get out, he helped his sister off the floor, and as she found her footing, he was too slow to catch her as she went for Ray.

Ray stepped back as she aimed, but she managed to follow through with a kick that smacked into his shin, Ned pushed Rosie away getting in between them and ignoring Rosie's rant, he grabbed his brother by the scruff of his neck. The dog's were circling Ray now and snarling, looking ready to bounce on him.

'You dare touch her again and I'll do ya. You understand, now back off.' Ned screamed in his face. The dogs pulled back.

'Once a fucking trollop, always a trollop! I'll tell you what, let's just do us all a favour and give her over to Jeremiah at the Heron, she can be a whore for the ones who ain't got any taste, cos when they see that, there'll wanna be sick before they shag it!' Ray had no let up and Ned pushed him back again and punched him around the ear. Ray squared up to him but then thought better of it. Rosie recalled another saying exactly the same thing not long ago! 'I've finished with her, I can't bring me self to look at it. And as for the boy, he's another mouth to feed, a fucking bastard! For fucks sake, I wash me hands of the lot of ya. I don't want to see her. You hear me bitch, you're dead to me, ya nothing, you hear, you're nothing.' And with that, he left, banging the door behind him. Ray had inherited their father's temper. Ned let out a sigh, although the atmosphere was still tense.

'Come here lass.' He whispered and held his arms out. She shook her head and held up her arms in defiance.

'I only came back cos I had no money and nowhere to go, but you give me some money and I'll go. Forget this ever happened, forget you know me, I don't need you.' Words spilled from her mouth, she had no idea what she said, but it was all in spite. Ned did not believe one word and knew she lying and hurting.

'So it's just about the money?' He put his hands on his hips and shook his head at her in disappointment, why could she not just be honest for once?

'Oh yeah, what else?' She would not look at him.

'Tell me what has happened, I can help, you're obviously in trouble.' He tried to be sympathetic. There were too many holes in her story.

'Oh please!' She mocked. 'I seem to recall I needed you years ago. You couldn't be bothered.'

'But ya here now, so fucking behave Rosie.' He was losing his patience and sat back down mentally exhausted.

'None of you cared for me and you sighed with relieve when I went off.' She found herself back where she had promised not to be again, feeling extremely sorry for herself.

'That ain't true and you know it.' He was trying to calm his nerves. 'Is this what all this about, you running off like a spoilt child cos you thought we were ignoring you? Have you not grown up, because from where I am standing it doesn't look like it?'

'Oh I grew up, don't you worry. So, the money or what?' She was losing the battle and did not like it.

'You made your bed, you lie in it. You think you can come in here demanding money cos it hasn't gone your way, run off again, and hide? Well that tells me you need a good lesson girl. You don't need money. You need help. You came back for us!'

'Oh, I knew this wasn't going to be easy, but I thought you may give me a little support.'

'Well think again, all I see is a spoilt brat who can't get her own way and is having a sissy fit. My God woman, we have been mourning you.'

'Mourning me, my arse! Well I am certainly alive, have you looked at me, do I look as if I have been spoilt, you have no idea? ' She pointed to her face bending in defiance towards him.

'Shut the fuck up, you ain't getting any money, you ain't going anywhere. You ain't staying here with Nana, you get over to mine. When we've calmed down we'll have a little chat, but don't you think I have forgiven you.' He warned.

'I ain't no Joey for you and I certainly did not come here for forgiveness from the likes of you.'

'You'll be and do whatever I say until I see fit. Now shut the fuck up, get ya stuff and get walking.'

'Piss off.' She screamed.

'For fucks sake Rosie, shut it.' He got up and came towards her fiercely. He was the image then of their father and she backed off. She thought she'd start doing what he said as she very rarely ever saw him lose his temper and it did not suit well. In that department, he was more like their mother. She hated it when she upset Ned. Whereas with Ray, she had always loved to wind him up. This time she had taken it too far. She sighed to herself. She had been adamant that she would make them pay for their neglect of her and there she was feeling guilty. Why did everyone she love let her down?

Her mother had gone and died on her.

Their father had then apparently died, - God knows where?

Bobby had died.

Ned and Ray had abandoned her.

William had used her.

Shem had not trusted her.

Her heart was breaking all over again and she felt powerless. She wanted to be in control of her destiny, but she always failed to grasp it tight and hold on. 'I am leaving in the morning. And you can't stop me from doing anything.'

'What do we do?' Ned was at his wits end with both his siblings constant squabbling. He knew it was going to be rough but he never thought he'd see the day when Ray was that venomous about his sister.

'Do I look as if I give a fuck?' Ray sat down at the kitchen table next to his brother and watched as his wife Sharon took another cup to pour him tea. Sharon always managed to calm him down. She was Nana's oldest daughter and looked very much like a younger version. She had always been plump, but very pretty with a face that always smiled. She had stringy light brown hair and dark brown eyes.

'You can't just shut her out.' She offered.

'Watch me.'

'Ray, she's your sister.' Sharon pleaded.

'Was, as I said, she is dead.'

'Have you ever sat and wandered what the fuck led her to just stay away, she must have known that we would believe she was dead, or did she, what has been going on?' Ned's head hurt with all the worrying.

'From what I can see, whatever happened didn't stop her gob. Still a fucking lairy little cow!'

'She has changed.' Sharon wanted Ray to sympathize. Ray snorted, from where he sat, she was still a spoilt little bitch, and the only thing that had changed was her face.

'You can see it in her eyes. She's not the same, she's weary, looking over her shoulder. Ray, she's frightened, can you not see that?' Sharon asked.

'Her frightened, behave? We left her and Bobby on their own many a time in the dark, did she piss herself. Like fuck! If she knew it was on top, that girl could run, and she did. She run outta trouble loads of time, a little bit of darkness, scary monsters, ghosts in the cemetery. Bosh, she was gone.' Ray clapped his hand. 'Look at the last time, little thief stole and put it on top, what was it Ned...?' Ray turned to his brother for help.

'That ladies handkerchief.' Ray pointed at Ned and then looked at his wife nodding his head.

'Stole it blatantly, although she said, she found it on the floor, run like a hare and nearly smacks straight into a approaching horse, hadn't been for that tall blond lad, been dead as a donkey.' Ray said remembering one particular day when she had been playing up.

'So she could worm herself out of trouble, but she is back now, and she needs all our help.' Sharon advised. She patted her husband's hand; he shifted in his seat in awkwardness.

'Yeah but it never stops, remember after that, that day,' Ray went back to the tale. 'We catch up with her, and she then swears blind she ain't done a thing, we search her, no hanky, and then bold as you want, she fucks off for the rest of the day without a bye your leave. Gone, little minx shows up later, as bold as brass, tipsy!

Fucking drunk! God knows what she got up to, and can you believe, the bitch had planted the hanky on me. While I was telling her off, she had planted it on me, and then run off. Run off and went playing with that tall blond lad from earlier. Can you believe it? What if they had clocked me, I'd have swung.'

'He's gonna have a fit if he carries on......' Ned tried to make light of the situation.

'You were always too soft with her.' Ray moaned.

'Perhaps...' Ned mused.

'What! No come back, not defending her. God, this is a first.'

'I'm just tired Ray. Tired of it all.' Ned closed his eyes and tried to remember better times, but just lately, that seemed too hard to do. He rubbed his head again and sighed. Oh, she was a little minx, always was, and always would be. Then he chuckled. Both Sharon and Ray looked across at him. 'I'd rather have that pain up the arse any day, than having to walk past that fucking gravestone and wonder whether she died instantly of the fire or suffered. She has got alot to answer for, alot she ain't telling us and I will get it out of her. You know that, she always comes to me in the end. She can't keep a secret. Never has been able to. Two minutes ago, I had two dead siblings, now I have one, and I can live with that.'

'Said it, you should have let me whip her, smack her about a bit more when she was growing up, but you've always been soft with her. She runs rings round you, you soppy bastard.'

'He is a fine boy.' Nana smiled across at Seb who was playing with the dogs. They could see he was a contented child and could easily amuse himself. They both looked into the fire.

'Thank you.'

'You look so tired.'

'I am.' Rosie closed her eyes to the world and Shem's image just played havoc with her.

'Do you really have to go?' Rosie looked at her long and sadly. Nana patted her on the arm and smiled warmly. Having Rosie back was like a breath of fresh air. Rosie was like a whirlwind, you never knew whether she was in a foul mood or in the clouds. God, she had missed her so much! 'If you go, you can always come back. I told you before time is a great healer.' Rosie thought that Nana sounded so condescending.

'Has the time been of comfort to you, did me going bring you what you hoped?'

'That is low Rosie.' Shaun observed from behind. He had returned after finishing his chores outside and was ready to settle as the evening drew in. Rosie referred to her leaving and making it easier for them all, having all really known without saying that she had been supposedly carrying William's baby, and to remove her from the scene for a while would make life easier for all. She lowered her head in shame, for a small moment she had wanted to make them pay as their kindness choked her.

'You are mad with the world for so many reasons, some we understand or think we do, but Rosie you are so bitter, so distant. We have always loved you and only meant the best.' Nana offered.

'Perhaps we were misguided from before.' Shaun offered. Both had not changed at all during her time away. Shaun was a huge man who looked strong and powerful. He was deeply tanned and his skin was leathery. His hair was grey and long and held back in a ponytail. He had a huge beard and moustache. His eyes were bright and blue. Shaun had an authority that could not be dismissed. He was highly respected throughout and everyone sought his council on various matters.

Their home was the main Farm house. It had originally been part of a huge estate. However, on Shaun's father's death, the land had been divided between him and his brothers. His oldest brother having the title and he inherited the main manor house. The rest of the lands had been shared between the brothers. Their father had never believed that all his worth should just go his eldest and had the misfortune of breeding three children of which the eldest, if he had inherited everything, was perhaps the less capable of ever running anything other than into the ground. This had proved to be the case and within a few years of inheriting, Shaun's eldest brother had indeed approached him for financial help. Two years later, he was dead and his children inherited a mortgaged land. The Earl's widow then backed her family up to return to the remaining London house along with title. Shaun had bought the house back into the fold and had since rented the Manor house out. He had been a shrewd man and along with the Hawkins Brothers had made a good living. As young men, Shaun and Bob had gone off pirating and returned rich. However, boredom and the frill of adventure lured them back in and they all had a hand in the smuggling of wool across the channel and in doing so they could make a profit on both legs of their cross-channel journey. Ships that went out loaded with wool and came back groaning with foreign luxuries.

Shaun was in his winter years now and looking back on his life with both good memories and deeds done and shared with a woman he adored. He did not have too many regrets and one was standing in front of him, and this one needed a good slap.

'You always meant well, I have no issue with you, it's just I.....' She was not ready yet to share any of what had happened to anyone but knew she owed them an apology for her poor manners.

'Rosie, my love,' Nana was always first to offer a hand and to see away to heal things. They all grew silent, there was no rush. Rosie circled her hands into Nana's. Her shoulders dropped and they knew then that she was sorry for her behaviour. She could never be too angry with Nana for too long. No one could.

'Hattie did not suffer, she had fled the fire, she died of a stroke, it all had become too much. She lost consciousness.'

'I know. Larry came across and explained.' Nana stroked her chin and smiled lovingly at her. Rosie melted. She had not known that, however she knew he would have kept to the agreed script. Shem had been right to throw caution to the wind and Bob had been right to be mindful of what Rosie said and did. Bob had bombarded her with precautions and Shaun and Nana were trying. They had always loved her, even when she was a right madam. She just wanted to run away and hide, however she had no more arms to run too.

**Chapter Fourteen**

Shem approached the castle from the west wing, and having walked up the small incline and was taken aback by the magnificence of the sight that befell him. It was still early, however the sun had burned off the dampness to the earth, and the grass was dry to the touch. Only the shaded areas still glistened.

The ruined castle stood before him, wonderful in all its morning glory. The old trees to the right side of the castle seemed to stand guard and protect the wonder of the place and no matter how many times he took this path, he smiled with such joy that he felt his heart would explode. It was one of his favourite places. The birds chirped and made merry and he could imagine the dogs running around chasing long gone rabbits.

There was a perfect silence and he felt soothed after such a long time away. He headed up the slight hill and looked towards the sea, which fell around half a mile away having etched away from the side of the castle since those dreaded Normans had invaded. He sighed in pleasure and savoured the mood, smelling the morning air, he was home! He then looked to his right and descended the small incline to enter from the backfield, to St. Mary's Church, which wasn't as old as its neighbour was, Pevensey Castle. He smiled at all the ghost stories they had heard over the years. He made his way through the settled wood and overgrown bramble bushes and found the graveyard circled in the cradle of the trees. He was cocooned and there was an eerie wondrous feel about him. The light flickered through the trees, and the leaves danced whilst the gnats flattered about over his head.

He silently walked through the graves, trying not to step on any, knowing that he had been brought up to respect the dead in their slumber. He slowed down as he approached the area he had waited so long to return to. He swallowed and whispered, 'I miss you every day.' He found Rafe's headstone and patted it as he leant against it. He sighed as he made himself comfortable and smiled seeing Rosamund had planted a rose bush at Rafe's grave to prevent the ghost from rising. The rose bush was just about to bud and he could see soft shades of pink. Rafe would have loved that!

He tore at some of the surrounding long grass, closed his eyes, and leant his head back against the headstone. The birds cooed around him and crows cawed in the distance, overshadowing their domain. He nodded in respect at their wisdom.

He let his mind wonder and take up a conversation with Rafe and out aloud he remarked. 'You would like Italy.' In his mind, he waffled on, sharing memories about the trip and found himself laughing and smiling, at the better parts. He was making believe that Rafe was there and this was one of their special times together away from everyone. Time slipped by and Shem sighed and relaxed, watching the many different birds circle above. The Black Crows still watched and still waited.

He had been so tired, so travel weary and now to be back, was a joy. He could go home now, slip into bed, and cuddle up to the woman whose hold he craved. He sighed and felt a glimmer of hope for the future.

'Mestor's gardens were beautiful; maybe we can do something similar in the gardens at the back of the Coach house!' He smiled remembering the pitiful man's death at his hands and then his smile widened at the suffering poor Hartright was enduring also at his hands. His cousin Oliver would have been well on his way, to selling Hartright to one of the slave galleys. 'We may have the Hall back now, however this is our home now. What do ya think?' He laughed knowing what Rafe would say.

'Gardens, flowers, trees, you gone soft?'


She stood before her Gravestone and read again and again the inscription. A memorial made in her honour. A symbol for them to see and look at and know they had let her down. It represented to her their guilt. Her brothers had more or less left her to her own devices as they had grown up. They had both gone off, got married, were throwing out children like no one's business, and had left her at the Farm with Nana and Shaun. They had set their own agenda and she had become lost.

She had missed them all so much. She had been jealous of all of them and she always run away when it got just that little bit too tough. She was a coward.

She had festered with hate for all of them and now that she had to come back, it made her blood boil, made her wish she had died. However where would that have left Seb? She could not do that, no matter what, he was her one salvation. She had to pick up the pieces again!

She looked back at the Farm House, and moved her eyes across the horizon so that she could just make out the Tavern roof. She further scanned the landscape and knew that one of Shem's gang would be out there watching her.

This was her home, her life. She remembered running from the farm to the tavern, then back again, in all weathers, for both silly and important things. They had been wondrous times, when she had not a care in the world. She believed that William, her childhood sweetheart, loved her no matter what, however now, through her eyes, William had abandoned her when she had needed him the most. She had tried to talk to him at that time, however he never wanted to talk, and he just wanted to have fun. Then she had discovered she was with child and knew it was not going to ever be a subject that she could talk to him about. Reality had hit her; she had no one to talk to. Nana and Shaun had hinted at that time that perhaps she look to marry a local lad, but she could not see that ever happening.

It was all her own doing; she had wanted love from two separate men, who both were unobtainable. Shem was a mystery, a soul mate, a delight, who she expected nothing from. The other, William, a man ready to leap back into his real life at any time and leave her wanting.

Would her brothers have understood? She had been rebellious, taking chances, flirting with the future. God it wasn't as if they did not know what she and William had been doing, however as Rosamund had said, you do not rub peoples noses in it. Perhaps if she had just tried to talk to her brother Ned about her pregnancy! She remembered thinking that by leaving she would spite them all. Ned would have been mortified, and Ray would want to have beaten seven shades of muck out of her. Given time, Ned would have sorted it all out; however, in her panic at the time, she needed to make decisions fast and quick. However, what had happened, the boys had gone off on a big job and left her yet again. Then Nana had came up with an off the cuff suggestion for her to go and spend some time with her widowed sister along the coast.

Rosie remembered the feeling of relief that she had been offered a lifeline of sorts for a while. She convinced herself that Nana had put her mopping around and depression down to missing William. All around people had made the decision that the relationship had run its course and a break from each other was on the cards. There was no way that William Devereux would take her hand. Nana had decided that she needed a bit of a colour in her cheeks, and thought that time well spent with her sister would be what the Doctor ordered. Therefore, she had been farmed off to Hattie.

Hattie was a widower, lived on her own, and had so for years. She had four sons and none of them ever visited. They all had their own lives. They sent her money and wrote all the time, but none ever asked her to visit or ever made any excuses as to why they did not visit. This wasn't to say that Hattie had been lonely, far from it; she had her friends in the area and had been looked after by Larry Hawkins. She had been self-sufficient and had a little money set aside for her old age. She had her large garden, a small orchard and grew all she needed. She had pigs, chickens, goats, geese, and all sorts. She had gone to church regularly and was known as a local healer and her lotions and potions were always popular.

On meeting, they had immediately fallen in with each other and it was as if they had never been apart. Hattie had been kind, warm, and loving. They had agreed the less revealed about her true identity was best and so had embellished a tall story about Rosie being a distant relative of her late husband's. They kept their fingers crossed that no one from Rosie's neighbourhood would venture this far from home. They both had agreed not to confide in Nana or the boys about her pregnancy and just take each day as it came.

Hattie believed in providence and no matter of planning was ever going to make matters better. They would ride the tide and see what lay ahead. This situation had not always made Rosie feel great. She imagined that William would somehow hear about her fate and come charging to her on a big White horse. Her Knight, in shining armour. William would make her all his, they would marry and set up home and live happy ever after. She was deluding herself, nothing had changed, and she lived in a fantasy world and wished to forget that they had previously parted on bad terms. She remembered him as someone he was not. She would have to face reality and that would mean making her and Seb secure and if that marriage to someone else, then she had better start accepting that fact.

Looking back, she realised William was no angel, and it was a secondary love, to what she knew was out there! Was it fair to expect him to love her when her heart really belonged elsewhere? She could not even bring herself to think or dream about the elusive Shem. Each time she opened her mind's eye to him, she knew that it would cause more pain than she could muster. Their love was a once in a lifetime, yet their lives were so very far apart. She knew Shem's real name, however had no idea where he lived and what he did. However, she knew from her very first meeting with him, that she loved him and would till the day she died.

Hattie and Rosie's life fell into a familiar pattern. Rosie found such joy in just being with Hattie, who slowly started to share all of her knowledge with Rosie on the garden plants. She knew that Rosie had had no real schooling and so she encouraged her and helped her to read and write.

She smiled as she remembered those lovely times. Hattie sitting by the fire reading wonderful stories and poems that took her to new worlds and places whilst her baby was growing inside her.

Then Hattie had let her into her secret, which was not too much of a surprise bearing in mind her family association with smuggling. Every so often, Rosie had been disturbed in her sleep and one night she looked out of her window to see what was going on. It was all too familiar. It was as if that part of her previous life had followed her there! It had been raining badly, and Rosie watched as Hattie had gone out to meet her friends and had watched her go up and down the track where the men must have carried their load through. Hattie was making other footprints, to deflect the evidence of any one other than someone walking, of being down her lane. However, Hattie had to keep stopping and wiping her boots clean with a stick, as the mud had congealed into a thick layer and she was having a hard time walking. Rosie had got up, wrapped herself against the rain, and joined her friend. She had just started to walk up and down, without a word just a nod and a smile, the secret was shared.

Then the baby had decided to come. He was so small and pink. He curled right into Rosie and was contented. She knew without a shadow of a doubt who the father was, and so she called him Sebastian Samuel Troy Cavendish. However since she had arrived at Hattie's she had gone by the name of Rosie Smith, so he became

Sebastian Smith. He had brought a new joy to the household but also for Rosie the fear that she would not see home any time soon.

Seb was so contented and just lay without a care in the world. He stretched, smiled and pulled silly faces and was only put out when he was disturbed for changing and he was hungry. His presence also brought more welcome visitors to the cottage.

As each month had ebbed by, she waited for news from home; Nana was a frequent letter writer. Initially there had been a few letters, which contained messages from her brothers, however not once did her brothers ask when she was coming home nor had she received any word from William.

She knew the baby would be a shock and there would be murder, and each day that come and went, her ache for home grew and a seed of anger started to grow. She grew to believe that she really did not mean anything to them. They had their own lives to lead; they had their own growing families. Slowly she had learnt to surround herself with a barrier. She was not going home.


She remembered the time so well, and eagerness of Hattie to keep her going. It could not have been easy for her. She had been landed with a young woman so full of life who was a little angry at the world, whose light had started to fade, and only ignite at the sight of that beautiful baby boy. With all her heart, she hoped that Hattie did really love her right up until that bad, bad last day. The sights smells, fears anxiety were never far and as always, when she started to get nervous, she rubbed the side of her legs.

She let her mind move to William. He had at one time, taken her breath away, she had been in awe of him, and not sure, what she felt now for him. Before she had left, he had been horrible, vicious, and spiteful. She had been equally horrible. Neither willing to give an inch. Neither willing to say what was happening in their relationship, which both knew deep down was doomed to failure. Sometimes, she dreamed and longed to be loved again by him, and then she remembered she hated him. She remembered that if he had wanted to marry her, he would have. However, he had never asked. It was unsaid that he thought she was beneath him. He wanted something better, to be accepted into the society that rumoured he was a bastard. Her mind whirled with emotions over him and then she rested on how

William wanted to be accepted. He wanted to be a success and had proved to be that. He had a good team, loyal friends, so why did he still feel he needed some seal of approval? Rosamund had said that what she had with William was lust, not love. As wisdom sets in and you look at your life, slowly these things make sense. William had killed time, been a good friend, a good lover, but had she been in love with him, or the idea of love?

With Shem, it had been a wonderful moment in time when you are with someone, your whole world revolves around them, and there are no judgments, no rivalries, no contest, just the joy of being together and having that most wonderful feeling of utter contentment envelope you in so much warmth and fulfilment. She knew that that time had been her heaven. However, her beloved had gone. He had been away too long, She missed him so. He was dead!

She became annoyed with herself, she found herself constantly looking back now, with regrets, at bad judgments, and love's lost. She looked to the sky and thought how God had punished her, and how he had continued to do so. She cuddled herself and shook her head, now looking up and laughing at the stars, who had appeared while she had been wallowing, she believed they were mocking her as always, as she had pondered her future.

She would leave in the morning, return to Pevensey, and start a life there with her new friends and family. It was her home, and if Shem never ever came back, she now accepted that she and Daisy would be looked after. She had worked herself up into a silly state and run off on one. She would go home, Seb kept asking in whispers when they were going home; he really missed his cousins and Harry.

She stroked her scared cheek in nervousness and then patted softly her sore from Ray's back hander. They doubtless would be going mad even now as to where she was, Ned having ordered her to help out in the Inn and pay her way or not eat. She found herself laughing to the stars; she'd get Ray back soon and pour a whole junk of ale over his big fathead. That would show him, and then she'd run like hell to Nana's and jump in bed with Seb and just hide!

It was late. Shem felt empty and disappointed. He had expected so much and now he lay with coldness. He touched her side of the bed, having spent a few minutes before settling to sleep cuddling and smelling both Rosie and Seb's clothes. He should have gone straight away and got her. He could imagine her on seeing him now. She'd pretend to be as mad as hell, but he'd see that twinkle in her eye and he knew he could twirl her round his little finger. He would promise with all his heart that he would never ever be away for that long again.

He could imagine that her brothers would give her hell and not understand what had been at stake. She should have waited so that they could have gone together. She had panicked and ran. He would have to put her on a short lead. He smiled at that. His pixie on a lead! No, it would never happen. He could only imagine the grief he would succumb to forever and a day.

He had missed Seb so much, they had bonded, and leaving him had broken his heart. He could just imagine how his father had felt when he had to leave him and his brother all those times. Shem then laughed to himself at the wonderful welcome he had received from one little cracker though, his little niece, Phoebe. She had not known or realised that her Uncle had returned. There was always a commotion of some sort or other going on, and she had ignored the rumpus. She had been in the back garden to the Coach House making circles with ribbon, and in doing so, making herself so dizzy in the process. Every now and again, she would look up, see her mother through the kitchen window, and hear little Nat cooing to her and Aunt Chrissy encouraging her. She was surrounded by a wonderful amount of warm and happy family and friends and all the men made a great fuss of her. She missed Seb desperately however knew he'd be back soon.

Her Uncle Claude always came by and only spoke French to her. She grinned and smiled through it. She did not wish to displease him when she did not have a clue what he said, and he rewarded her with little almond sweets that her mother said were very special.

Big Uncle Paully was all together different. He would roar as he saw her or any of the young ones and she would chuckle in delight and know to run and hide, as that was part of the fun. The dogs would always give them away, or so they thought. Paully could always hear them giggle and so find them, grab them and lift them high into the sky and whirl around and around, and fly with them across the court yard and gardens. He would sit her or Seb across his shoulders in turn and they would go for long walks and adventures, picking apples, pears, damsels and spend hours lying on the ground watching the wild life and trying to be quiet, which was always hard when Uncle Paully would do something silly like start to tickle them.

Shem remembered when Phoebe had seen him peeking his head around the kitchen door at her, she flustered and shook in joy and screamed in delight, her whole body went wooden and tense. She then had jumped up and down and her tight curls had bobbed up and down. Shem had flown out with arms outstretched, she had run herself at him, and he had flung her up high and gave her kisses and hugs galore, while whirling her around and around.

Chrissy was laughing in delight and relief while Daisy was crying in happiness, being still too over sensitive, but also laughing a little at the joy for her daughter.

Phoebe's Uncle was her Hero and for the next few hours, be it that Shem so wanted to retrieve his own family, he wasn't allowed to leave her side. She showed him all her drawings, all her new games, where the snails were and where all the new ants' nests were. She showed him little Nat and explained what he had been up to and Shem was choked at how much of his growing up he had missed. The little mite Nat had no idea who he was, kept hiding his face in his mothers shoulder and secretly peeping out every so often, and would find Shem smiling at him. He looked more like Daisy, however he had his father's expressions, and Shem promised, he would look after his niece and nephew whatever happened. He had been away far too long righting wrongs when he needed to concentrate on his own family and their needs. Daisy did not look so gaunt now and was well into her pregnancy. He was glad that she had a purpose in her children. She was a good mother, and he knew that the children could never ask for a sweeter person to raise them.

Eventually Phoebe had worn herself out and only when she was asleep on her feet was he allowed to leave her. 'I'll bring Seb back tomorrow.' He had promised and only then did she allow him to let go of her hand.

He closed his eyes searching for sleep, however his mind's eye crept to Rafe, and how proud he was of Phoebe and his son and how his brother could be such a fool sometimes. He remembered Rafe sitting astride the cannon, which was found in the grounds of Pevensey castle when they had first come to the area. He remembered that Rafe was pretending the cannon was a giant penis between his legs and every couple of seconds he would thrust and then make explosive noises and raise his hands in salute. Shem had been rolling around on the floor, calling him as usual a prat, and Rafe had been mocking him again, on how he was jealous of Rafe's luck with the ladies. He missed his brother so much. He touched the locket around his neck, which held Rafe' hair and stroked it and whispered. 'Plep!'

Just then, he heard a creak on the stairs and as quick as lightning he had grabbed his dagger and swung the door open before the person could reach the top. Had Chrissy not locked up? No one would get in who was not known.

Valentina stood there in the blackness. She was slightly taken aback, but recovered quickly seeing him just in his lose trousers with hair all tussled. She swayed forward.

'I've missed you.' She whispered seductively. She had waited so long to have him all to herself, and her confidence had slowly started to return. She had nothing to lose now. He thought she was innocent in the death of Rafe, and no one, not even her priest would ever know.

'I can't say the same.' He yawned in her face. She moved towards him and softly moaned.

'Shem, that's so not nice.' She pressed her leg against his and slowly raised and rubbed up against him. He could not believe the woman's cheek! But, that was Valentina, if there was an opportunity, she would grab it.

'No, I can't say I care. Why don't you just go away?' He was so tired and backed into the room away from her. She was the last person he wanted to see right now! He put the dagger down.

'We both like a challenge and you are mine tonight.' She smiled back at him, slowly swinging her hips towards him again. She was looking so full of herself. She wore her beautiful silk robe and beneath a sheer cotton chemise. She smelt of Egyptian Lotus. It was a wonderful smell.

'So, I suppose you are feeling a little pleased with yourself, thinking your ranting, made Rosie disappear.' He crossed his arms.

'If Rosie decided to go that's not my doing. The girl was a mystery. It would not be the first time she run off when it got too much.' She placed her hands on his hips and started to make small seductive circles.

'Know her business well then do you?'

'Look Shem, you had a little fling with the girl, you felt sorry for her. She touched what is left of your sensitive side.' She raised her hand to cup his face. 'But now you know you need a real woman who can match your vigour.' She leant forward to whisper in his ear. He had closed his eyes. 'You know this is so. You need me. I want you.' Her voice was husky with passion. 'Let me do this for you. You have been away too long.' Her hands moved to circle his back and she eased him forward to her. She rose to her tiptoes and he let her kiss him. She purred in triumph. He allowed her to cuddle into him and get lost in the passion. She had him. He believed her! His hands rounded her buttocks and he lifted her and she wrapped her legs around him grinning in triumph.

'Oh I missed you so.' She purred in excitement, her heart pounding. He was hers again and he would never regret this moment. She would do whatever it took.

'Oh I bet.' She kept her eyes closed and wallowed in all her glory. He felt him walk with her. She believed that they could make this work. She would ease his pain. She deliberately locked that away. It was of her making. He would never find out!

'You know Valentina?' He was going to declare himself. Oh the joy of it! Shem her love was back, he was her life! Her beautiful Shem! 'I'm just so bored of you.' She opened her eyes and glared at him. Her world come tumbling down. His eyes were black as coal. She trembled in rejection. What was this?

He put his hands under her armpits and lifted her off him. He held her up in the air for a fraction of a second and winked at her. She froze.

In the next second, he threw her away from him and watched as she flew and crashed down the stairs. He wiped his hands and sighed, it was done! God he was so tired!

She never saw it coming!

The horrendous noise brought a thud from next door and in seconds, he heard Chrissy's bedroom door, at the end of the hall open. She popped her head around the door and he saw that her hair was unbound and quite thick and wavy, be it all over the place. She raised a candle above her head into the darkness. She looked down the stairs and felt sick with shock and then she looked back at him in horror.

'You surely aren't expecting me to clean that up after you?'

'God, what am I paying your for then woman? She wouldn't be in here, if you had locked the door!' Shem was tutting at her. 'Oh just leave it, I will sort it out in the morning, I'm tired.' He wiped his eyes like a babe and turned away to go back into his room, dismissing her with a wave of his hand.

'And in the morning there will be more questions.' He tutted at that again, knowing she was right. He lowered his head to his chest. 'God, you will be impulsive, it's going to get you in so much bother!' She glided towards him and reminded Shem of a clucking hen with all her nagging. Both looked at each other and realised what she had just said and the absurdity of the situation. They both started to laugh. Chrissy's was a little bit more nervous and she found herself pointing down at the dead body at the foot of the stairs and accepting that life was never normal around this man. 'What are you like?' He shrugged his shoulders and she shooed him to go before her down to clean up the mess. He hesitated and she gave him a mock angry look. He collapsed his shoulders in defeat, like a child that had been told off. Chrissy followed behind and he laughed at her, knowing she was deliberately keeping back, in case he decided to serve her the same fate!

'I would not dream of doing the same to you!' Shem laughed descending the stairs very slowly with every part of his body aching and calling to return to bed. She hit him playfully across the head.

'And I ain't mug enough to chance it! Look what you have turned me into. I was a good woman before.'

'If you say so.'


All eyes went to the Tavern door to see Shem and his gang stroll in as if they owned the place. They peaked their hats and move to be nearer the warmth of the welcoming fire. Word had already reached the pub of their impending arrival. Everyone started to whisper among themselves about all the rumours that surrounded Shem's recent disappearance from the area, for the last few months. Some had whispered that he was dead, he had been kidnapped, he was on the run, or that he decided to take a trip on one of his ships to the Far East. Some even said that he had killed Hartright.

Ned and Ray remembered the last time they had met this man after the Pevensey job and it was not a situation they had wanted to see revisited. They both began to panic. Why was he here now in their Tavern? They knew that something was afoot and they kept their nerves alert. God, as if they did not have enough on their plate as it was, what with William's betrayal and their sister's return.

Everyone was on edge and after a fashion, settled and drinks started to flow. The conversation resumed with eyes still peering across, curious to see what was happening.

Rosie had just been outside and had gathered from the noise and the dogs barking madly, that someone had entered the Tavern and caused abit of a commotion. There was never a dull moment with all the coming and goings. Ned needed her again to help out and it would keep her mind active and perhaps help them all to try and be in each other's company and not fight. She returned to the hub of the pub by the back entrance and really did not pay much heed and was oblivious to what was happening, being too lost in her own thoughts and how come rain or shine she was off in the morning. She mingled around and waited on one and all. She handed out tankards, topped up jugs, did not pay any attention to the gossip and nudging amongst the punters, and ignored the sly looks across the way. She returned to the bar for more drinks and headed towards her brothers at the main table, thinking how she would get Ray back, she had it all worked out, she would pour the drink all over his thick fat head, then run like hell. She could be brave, face him, and slap him so hard that he would have an heart attack!

Ned nodded his head to invite her forward; she looked at him in question and only then took stock. Shem turned round and looked up at her as she handed him a tankard. She started to feel that eyes were on her and then her stomach begun to tinkle. Was it really him?

He smiled sweetly at her and she automatically grinned back but then dropped everything, as she looked straight into the eyes of him. Green eyes! He was back! She was mad as hell then.

He had just left her to stew after what had happened to her, hadn't even bothered to tell her what was happening and now here he was as large as life, smiling sweetly at her as of nothing had happened. He was a ghost. An angel reincarnated.

Shem! She could kill him!

'What the fuck, Rosie!' Ray roared. She jumped and immediately came out of it and felt herself going red from head to toe. Everyone was looking at her. She wished the ground would swallow her up.

'I have that effect on people. It's fine.' Shem tried to make light of the situation having concluded on his arrival that Rosie had not made any mention of him, as his reception would have been alot more frosted. She was in shock and made a show of herself and he knew she hated that.

Ray was mortified with embarrassment at his sister showing them up. Ale covered everything and she just stood there in shock. Ned was concerned with the mess, and Shem's men snickered at the insaneness of it all. Shem and Rosie kept staring at each other with not a care in the world, as if they were the only ones in the room. It seemed like an age, and then she came too. Nerves set in, she shook all over, she felt the blood rush out of her, and then she looked at her brothers and back at Shem. He wasn't dead! He watched the relief loosen in her shoulders. Then she checked herself, as she looked straight into his large green eyes. He saw the slight hesitation, and then she composed herself and sharply looked away. He laughed to himself knowing she did not find this situation at all funny and perhaps he had misjudged how much his absence had affected her. She would need all his support to explain to her family. He watched her and saw that in her nervousness, she rubbed her legs, and then she pushed her loose hair away from her face and put it back behind her ears. She turned her face slightly and then he spotted the bruise towards her ear.

'Who fucking hit you?' He growled through gritted teeth. He slowly got to his feet and she saw the rage begin to take shape in every pore of his being. His eyes slowly begun to set to black, and the whole world around him just zoned in on her.

'No one, no one.' She looked pleadingly at him, and then her eyes flickered to her brothers. She made towards Shem and saw that Ray and Ned had both risen from their seats. Something was amiss here and they did not like it one bit. The tension was rife and was becoming unbearable.

'What's going on...?' Ray started nervously. Like an animal stalking its prey, Shem slowly turned to Ray. Paully, Claude and Bob were also on their feet knowing the tell tale signs.

'Did you hit her?' Shem snarled stepping towards him accusingly; Bob came forward and stood between the two. He knew his boy well and could see the reason disappear and the darkness engulf him. 'Shem, Shem, please I walked into a door, come on sit down, have your drink, really.' Rosie had positioned herself against him and he felt her touch send sparks all over him.

When she touched him, she felt fire. She looked into his eyes but she had lost him. She knew when they were as black as coal there was no pay back. Shem stepped away from her and shoved Bob aside.

'Shem look at me; look at me it's nothing.' She could not afford for him to go mad, she tried to step back in front of him.

Both Ray and Ned wondered how she knew him so well. They looked to each other for answers and found none. Ned looked back at Shem, while Ray looked for the exit.

Shem was looking through her and before she knew it, he had thrashed her aside and as quick as lighting powered straight into Ray. Ray was driven back through the Tavern with such velocity that he burst through tables, chairs and everything in the way went flying. Ray hit the floor hard and Shem was on top of him, pounding him with solid punches. He would kill the bastard.

As suddenly as it had started, it was finished, as Shem's men grabbed him and physically dragged him away. He was fighting them like a complete mad man and they were trying desperately to get him out of the Tavern into the fresh air. Everyone was screaming and roaring. The dogs were all going ballistic. It was bedlam.

Rosie had been hit to the floor, and felt the strong arms of Bob pull her towards him. She was shaking all over. The Tavern then stood in silent amazement at the sheer intensity and ferocity of the man's rage, the violence, and consequence of his anger.

Ray sat up on the floor, knew he had been lucky, he had never ever been attacked like that before, and found himself shaking in shock and then looking away from his sister in shame. A wild savage animal had attacked him. Sharon had appeared and was crying over him and at the same time trying to wipe his wounds. He felt humiliated and made to look like a complete fool. This was the second time Shem had done it. Where did this leave them now? How was he to know that Shem knew his sister? He had not spoken to Rosie at all in disgust and now he just did not know what to think. Shem could and would have quite easily killed him because he rightly guessed that he had hit his sister. Ned helped him up and they both turned to their sister for some sort of explanation, as Shem wasn't known for being chivalrous to women. They had definitely missed something.

All eyes were on her and she wanted to be swallowed up. The man she loved and hated at this time had attacked her brother, who she very much hated at this time, but looked at him in concern. Shem could have killed him. He was the devil!

Half of her wanted to rush out and comfort Shem, make him see sense, the other half just wanted to grab Seb and run as far away from this mad man as she could. However, her heart told her she needed to see Shem. He was back, alive and her heart couldn't stop bumping, and she couldn't breathe for the intensity of it all. Had he come for her after all this time? It was too much, he was a mad man! She crumpled in the arms of Bob. How could she be so stupid? What should she do?

Ned went to her and with all the love he could muster, he pulled her from Bob and cuddled her up into his arms and took her outside. Relief flowed through her at her brother's love.

Shem's men had controlled him by now and he was pacing back and forth like a stalking beast. The men had formed a line between him and the Tavern and when they saw Ned leading Rosie out, they all turned. Shem snorted indicating to his men that he was in control. He waved them away and his men slowly, although reluctantly, walked down the street. All but Bob, who kept a safe distance. Shem gave him a filthy look, but he ignored it. He just watched as his leader paced up and down, ready to pounce.

Rosie just stood there waiting. Her heart raced so and she looking longingly at Shem for something. She dreaded to think of what demons he had unleashed on all his enemies and how he made Hartright suffer. She shook with fear, he was a cold bastard, who had held it all together and now would appear to have no restraints and act so spontaneously? Her mind run a riot. She really did not know him at all; he was a monster, an animal. He could turn on anyone and that included both her and Seb.

Ned knew that all the many things would be sorted this night and hopefully the intensity of the whole situation would wane.

'Ned, it will be alright.' She said trying to sound confident and looked back at Shem for some sort of assurance, not sure, she really wanted any of this.

'I'll kill you if you touch her.' Ned warned. Shem stopped and looked at him with such venom. Rosie put her arms out to Ned and to stop him from saying anything further.

'Oh you're brave and that's just fucking rich, you prick. You're lucky; I haven't torn your fucking tongue out!' Shem spat at him. Ned lowered his head, he could not look at the man; the hate was just too much. He believed at that time that Satan, no less, was holding court. He could not let his sister near this animal.

Shem looked away to try and calm himself further. He knew Ned was only protecting his sister and his feelings were everywhere having watched him attack his brother. Who would not be angry and weary of doing the wrong thing? Ned was a good man and Shem had put him in a very awkward position. He motioned for Bob.

Ned and Rosie waited and saw Jesus interrupted them; he seemed to slither from the shadows. After an age, Bob came to them. 'Will you meet him in the Church Yard in five minutes? Me and Jesus will be around.' He smiled reassuringly and Rosie looked to Ned for guidance.

'Do you mind telling me what is going on?' Ned asked whilst Rosie watched Shem move away. She nodded her head, knowing that this had to end, all the lies and secrecy.

'You deserve to know, and I know I've been a right cow. But I have to go to him now Ned.'

'You really have fucked it right up now haven't ya?' Ned roared at Ray. Bob had just filled them in and left them in the back room to let off steam. Ray was trying to soothe his wounds.

'Well how were any of us supposed to know, that for the last couple of years she has been shagging Shem behind our backs. And he's a one, swooning it over here, giving it large, not once saying that, oh by the way! We are now brother-in-laws.'

'That's why he has been so fucking nice to us.' Ned put two and two together.

'Nice, nice, what did you say? Are you for real? What has he done for us?'

'He left us alone when William fucked us off. He could have easily swallowed us up and given us to Paully or Claude or whoever, but no he left alone.' Ned tried to reason. 'Well, look what happened after the Pevensey job. He could have gone ballistic at us. But he did not touch us did he? He fed us information to watch William and now look where we are.'

'Licking his arse!'

'Better that, than dead Ray! Think on, we've done alright seeing how we ourselves have been fucked over just a few times, you may recall.'

'Fucking cock sucking wanker.' Ray just could not let it go how he hated Shem.

'We are bloody lucky to be alive. He could quite easily have made us pay for William's disrespect. William is one lucky bugger. We have his run now and will keep Shem sweet and off our back. My God! Don't say that you begrudge the benefits of what we now have?'

'Oh I ain't sucking up to that wanker. Taken us for right mugs, he has! Fucks her, gets her pregnant, she runs off! God knows what happened, but all we knew was she was dead! Kept that quiet about the boy! Fuck me, now when you look at him, you know, he is a ringer for his two dead Uncles, Bobby, and Rafe. Jesus Christ! Why did I not see it before? He is a fucking wanker.'

'He is the father of our nephew. He is the one who gives the orders around here and he came here tonight for his woman.'

'And look at what that bitch has done since she's been here. Fed us alot of dog shit. They are made for each other. She wasn't mad at us, more at him. Thought he'd done a runner and left the ugly scar faced whore. Well if I had been him, I wouldn't touch it.'

'Now that's enough.'

'What you gonna hit me too, go on, like to see you try you fucking tosser? All talk!' At that, Ned lashed out and threw him a right hander. Ray found himself back on the floor, only this time he laughed at his brother. Although Ned could see he was in alot of pain. Ned stood over him waiting to see what would happen next.

'That actually hurt!' Ray whinged. 'You are getting quite good at it.'

'God! I'm glad, but fuck me! I think I have broken my fucking hand.' Ned grinned through gritted teeth and then proceeded to jump up and down in pain, cuddling his hand under his armpit.

The grass crunched beneath and tickles of water sprayed the air as her footsteps crashed into the grass below and let a crescendo of water spray through the air. She was oblivious as the water slowly sipped into her shoes, just at the tips of her toes. She was cuddled up against the cool evening air and the mist whirling around her. The sun had leisurely glided to sleep, a little slow off the mark. Another day done. Her heart pounded; she felt her stomach jump in somersaults and her breathing catching. Her mind was awash with images, things to say and fear was still engulfing ever part of her body.

She looked around as she found herself near the entrance to the old Church of St Andrew's. In the stillness, she could hear the call of the black birds, birched up high at the very tops of the beautiful trees that lined the east side of the church. She heard the cooing of the pigeons that had nested on the old walls. She stopped to admire the spectacular night views as she made across the village green to the church. There were just small flickers of lights from the homesteads and then she saw him walk towards her.

'*He's gonna kill me!*' She exclaimed to herself.

His long blond wavy hair bounced as he made towards her. He was unshaven and looked unkept. He carried his bulk with ease and was sun burnt a dark brown, from too much exposure to the elements and she knew that his green eyes would be frighteningly intense. He wore his favourite long fur lined overcoat, and she could see that his riding boots were muddy. He looked tired and he needed to be taken care off.

He did not make eye contact once and had no emotion on his face.

*God, how I love him so*! She felt sweat build up on the top of her neck. God! If only she knew what was going through his head. She felt like she could not breathe. She was waiting cuddled up against the cold, and he knew she was petrified. He had prided himself on watching people's bodies to identify what was really going on.

She was standing proud, did not want to let him see that she was scared; however they knew each other well.

He looked at her through his lashes, and he had taken in the dark circles around her eyes, through lack of sleep, and that her hair was just gathered back loosely into a long ponytail, not plaited with ribbons running through it. When he had left her, she had returned to her cheeky smiley face. She had put on weight and looked healthy but now she looked weak and feeble.

Her cloak was creased and dirty, and just thrown around her, with no broach to hold in place and he could see her shoes were covered in grass and wet with the dew. She should have wrapped up warmer. He inwardly signed at himself. He'd get her a new cloak.

She was always so soft to the touch. She would say he was always so hot to the touch. Ah well, times change, wants change, you get disappointed. You let people down, you hate them, you love them, and it is just easier to walk away. He should not have left her. He could have picked Hartright up at any time.

He stopped about five feet ahead of her. The moments went by, each just looking at each other, with Rosie shifting her weight and Shem smiling at her obvious discomfort. He was not calm. All he felt was rage. Rage at her for leaving him. He could not let her get off lightly, but then this softness started to creep in and this made him even madder at himself for being weak.

He was mad at killing Mestor, mad at not killing Hartright yet. Mad at Mr. H for insisting they have a meet now that he was back. Mad that Rafe was not there to share it with him. Mad that Ray had dared to touch his woman. He was even mad at Earl. His beloved dog now seemed to favour Rosie, and still the dog had not surfaced. That was too much!

He had given instructions for her to be kept at Pevensey and hoped she would have ignored the obvious gossip around his disappearance. He had then returned to find that she had decided she needed her family. What protection would her family have given her? He could imagine that Bob had nearly had kittens when she went off on one. Rosie's family had more or less got rid when they thought she was carrying that dick heads baby. William had been told about the rape, so his alliance with Hartright had been previously put in jeopardy, but it still had not deterred the man from setting up his own smuggling sideline. Some people just wanted to be slapped!

Bob had warned him about charging over to Alfriston and taking her back and making a scene. There would be questions. What had she told them? He had to tread careful. Then he had thought about William, and then in his madness convinced himself, she had gone back for him. He was just mad that she had defied him. Then what had happened, he went in there and saw her face and then went ballistic? It was hardly the ideal reunion. The blackness had engulfed and consumed him. It seemed that all his return had bought him was the hump and people not living up to his expectations. She would be scared, anxious and after seeing him again at his worst, he knew she would runaway if he played it wrong. God! Why was he having to play it well? When she had run off?

'You were told to stay put.' He barked, angrier with himself than her. He stepped forward.

'I did what I thought was best.'

'And look where that has got you?'

'Well you proved unreliable.' She always rubbed her hands down her legs when she was nervous and that's exactly what she was doing now. He tried to focus and tried to push the blackness away. He remembered the day they had met and wanted to smile to the memory. That was years ago, and a far cry from where they both were now.

'Now Master Smith, eyes to me and not to that little Pixie if you please?' Gunthorpe had said behind his back. She had just been dragged away by her huge brother and was laughing at the absurdity of it all.

'Pixie.' Shem repeated.

'Back in the country not two minutes and he has skirt falling all over him.' Bob had remarked.

'She was cute wasn't she?' Shem was looking for their affirmation. He had wanted any little diversions then to steer his mind from the awful truth of what had happened to them.

'Oh behave man. We have some work to do, and you can't go falling in love with every little floozy.' Gunthorpe had knocked his passion down straight away.

'No, but work starts tomorrow. Tonight is for fun!' Shem had teased and he had glanced at Gunthorpe with those sad doe eyes!

'Oh hark at his Lordship. You dirty minded rascal.'

His mind's eye took him to their other meetings and he remembered that horrible encounter when Rosie had been at deaths door. He saw her as they had found her, and then he saw her as clearly as anything, laughing with him at something silly. He had to protect her at all costs. He would have run to the end of the world for her.

'You know you are going to have to think hard about this one, we have walked into a nightmare here, so try and be on best behaviour. You can't just grab the girl and run.' Bob had said last night and knew that he had the younger man's respect to give out the advice. Shem was not a man who took to anyone telling him what to do.

'Alright Mum.' He had remarked sarcastically. He could not get rid of the anger, it engulfed him, and he just wanted to hit out even more. Had he not had enough blood lust just recently to last a lifetime? It was never enough and there was more to do now he was back.

Rosie just stood there lost. He stepped menacingly towards her.

'Shem, I....' She started, but he just glanced straight through her. He saw her start to back away, he grinned, then he grabbed her and flung her back heavily to the wet surface, with a thud. His whole body shadowed her and held her fast. His thumb stroked the long scar across her cheek, and he found himself looking deeply at the horrid thing, which spread from her ear out ward. He could feel the tension, the fright penetrating her whole being and he laughed when he heard her plead, 'Shem, please.' He had complete control over her and he could just squeeze her neck right then and there and throttle her, be done with her forever.

She tried to breathe but found herself panicking and panting. Her head throbbed. She felt all the veins in her neck scream for release. She could not open her eyes. She did not wish to look at the man who had, for a second time, her life in his hands. She had seen it a hundred times in her mind, being reunited with the one she loved. She would run into his arms and he would whirl her around and around. They would laugh and cry and it would end like in the fairy stories. Nevertheless, this had turned out to be a nightmare. He petrified her completely. She was paralyzed with his intensity. Her eyes were fiercely closed to the outside world. This could not be happening again!

As quickly as he had grabbed her, he released his hold. He got up from over her, stepped back a pace, and watched as she cuddled up to herself. She was frightened senseless.

He leant back down casually beside her, his forearms resting on his legs, which he deliberately moved to press up against her. 'Should I have killed you when I had the chance?'

His deep voice penetrated her cocoon and she groaned at herself. Was he backing off? 'Why are you saying that to me?'

He touched her cheek again and watched as she nearly jumped back out of her skin. He laughed. Still her eyes were closed to him.

'What is your problem?' He grinned at that, he liked it when she was brave.

'Just answer my question.' He willed her to open her eyes. 'Why are you here?' He was slowly calming down; she could hear the reasoning in his voice. She would not get cocky again.

'I needed to come home.' He touched her hair and let it float through his fingers. She had lovely hair. She snatched her head away. He shrugged and sighed.

'And where is home, perhaps with lover boy?' His voice was so deep and so near. Her breathing was still shallow, she was still so scared. This was the final test.

'Please, Shem, just .......' She whispered back at him. Slowly she opened her eyes and stared straight into his green glaring eyes. She tried not to blink, but was weak and found herself physically shuddering. He watched her eyes glisten with unshed tears.

'Been shagging the traitor for comfort while I was away?' He grinned in pure pleasure at her unease. He knew very well that William had been nowhere near, he had received a full report on Master William's actions over the last few months. Shem sighed and checked himself. He settled back on his heels, almost ashamed at the way he was trying to behave so indifferently to her, yet as soon as he had seen she might be in danger had tried to protect her. God! He had just killed Valentina for her sake! He shook his head; he knew that was a lie! Was he going mad? He had frightened his little pixie again. The last time he had let the madness run away from him.

Then he checked himself with his insanity and confirmed to himself that he was getting soft and that was not going to happen here. He just wanted to hurt her for defying him or did he really? God! When his pixie had lost her fire, he would have given anything for it to come running back, when it did, there wasn't a dull moment. She had spirit and she put him on edge. He never knew what to expect.

She had opened her eyes. They seemed to stare at each other again for a long time, each weighting up the other.

She looked so sad, so lost, but he remembered that split second when their eyes had first met, he knew there had been a natural joy at seeing him. His mind was in turmoil. Why did he do this to her?

She was shaking out of her boots but she still managed to hold it together, to try and control and demand from him. What had he done? He was mad as hell with her and he still had the desire to take care of her, she had lost too much weight.

He collapsed onto his behind and rested his head in his hands. He had carried too much for too long!

'I just want......' She heard his voice crack. He wiped away-unshed tears and glanced at her resting his elbows on his knees. He had been so mad when he saw the bruise, he had just flipped. He was shaking in temper. His mind was black, burning, it was hell, and he needed to escape it all! 'I need help to get out of this insanity.' He confessed. He closed his eyes again and for a long while just sat there. She saw his mind working and his expressions change as thoughts and schemes entered his mind.

Slowly her fright dissolved into numbness. There was so much she did not know. So much that he had not shared. They had needed each other's love before to get through such horrible things, but now he needed her to pull him through his nightmares. She did not know that she could do it. However, wasn't this what true love was? She too had to start to grow up and not be so selfish about her own woes. He was in turmoil and needed her!

He could see that he she was so frightened of him. He could hardly blame her. He just could not find the words, but he knew he needed too; he could not afford to lose her too. 'This isn't how it's supposed to be.' He whispered to her and looked so earnestly at her, that she started to cry. He watched her breakdown and his heart nearly crashed with pain. 'Rosie.' He pleaded, he went to touch her hand, but she pushed him off. What had he done?

She tried to hit him, but was too weak, she just found herself backing away from him, grasping for breath between her tears. One minute she felt sorry, seeing him in pain, and then she wanted to reject him.

He started to say something, but she could not continue looking at him. He leant forward again and tried to take hold of her hand. Again, she snatched it away. He softly tried again. She punched him hard.

What could he do to make her forgive him? He could not think straight. He was both mad and then so very sorry. What had he done? He covered his face with his hands and he begun to shake. He let his tears fall freely.

'I won't live like this anymore.' She cried.' You scare me shitless. You go off and come back nearly killing my brother. I hear you do all these things. You kill and maim for pleasure and you even threaten me when this thing takes over you. I don't know that this is love anymore. Is it love, or just the threat of what you would do if I left? What is this?' He was shocked by what he heard.

She watched the man she thought she loved so much, struggle with himself to speak. He had risen to his feet and stood in limbo for a long time, and she could see him weighting it all up in his mind. He then glanced away and then nodding at himself seemingly to have made a decision. She waited.

She wanted it back like it had been before he had gone. She wanted that wonderful time back when he had looked after her, brought her back to life and made her see how wonderful life could be. Had she been deluding herself and remembering a dream like fashion what she wanted to see? She wanted whatever it was back. 'I don't know you, this thing that drives you. I need to understand. You are two people and one is a monster!'

She watched his head lower to his chest. She watched him struggle with himself for a long time. He started to pace back and forth wiping the tears away. Finally, he stood still and she watched his shoulders slump. It was time!

'They shamed me.' He whispered and sighed with relief having said those words.

He had said it our loud. However, he could not look her in the eye. She looked at him in bewilderment, but also relief.

'When I was about twelve and Nathaniel ten, we saw some things we should not have seen and Nathanial was hurt and abused, and to shut us up, Harry my cousin, Hartright as you know him, with others help, decided to shut our mouths permanently.' His voice cracked as he relived the moment.

*Oh my God!* She thought. *He is going to tell me.*

'We watched as they killed my father and I could do nothing about it.' He looked away trying to hold back the floods of emotion. Rosie wanted to go to him, but she held fast, he controlled himself and looked to the stars for distraction. However, his mind's eye went back to the moment all those years ago on the beach.

'When you first met me, we were living with Rosamund after returning from Europe. We had been in hiding. My Uncle, Mestor Mordesan. Hartright and his mother had tried to dispose of us.' He started and he looked sadly at her for her reaction. He sighed feeling that a great weight had been lifted. Rosie felt humbled that he had now exposed himself and was unburdening all those things that he had kept close to his chest for so many years. He sat back down on the ground regardless of the wet.

'We were bundled in a boat........' he carried on and she learned what had befallen both him, Rafe and their father. His voice was shaky.

The boys' hands were tied behind their backs and they had been beaten. They were scared, cold and petrified seeing their father also being manhandled.

'Kneel you bastard.' They heard from the shore watching their father trying to not to kneel on the beach.

'I will not kneel to you or anyone.' His father was defiant in his retort.

'If you give me your life without a struggle, I will spare the boys.'

'What is this for Mestor?' They heard their father command.

'Come, come, Troy, you surely are not that naive?' They heard their Uncle laugh.

'The title?' Troy spat.

'Of Course, the title, the lands, the money, the bloody freedom. I can do as I will and no one will ever question me. Without it, I'm doomed and I do have very expensive taste.' Mestor was ever prone to exaggerate. He waved his hands around as if he were performing on a stage. He never denied how camp he was.

'You have no honour.' Troy had spat at him.

'Oh fuck honour, dear boy, so over rated and out dated.' He laughed at his own joke. Mestor was enjoying himself. He whirled around in delight, playing to the theatre ground he saw in his head. He acted his life out like he was on a stage. He giggled.

'How do I know you will not dispose of my boys?' With Troy out of the picture, Mestor still had two potential heirs to the title.

'Because it will excite me, knowing that they are alive in some God forsaken hell hole and suffering for eternity.' At which point he turned to the boy's and waved. 'I get giddy just imaging what delights they will offer, what they will endure, all due to my power. Oh good God, I feel myself getting all flushed at the very thought!' He took a clean handkerchief from his trouser pocket and wiped his brow mockingly. 'I'd rather hoped to have the satisfaction of doing the same to you, but we need at least one body from this tragedy, hey? So, off with your head!' He said dramatically still giggling like a fool, looking across hearing the racket that had been constant from the boat. 'Shut those bastards up.'

Troy turned to look at his sons' who were screaming now for him, he couldn't help them. He had never felt so helpless. With all the love in the world, he looked at both of them in turn and slowly their screams stopped to look into their fathers eyes. They saw the hopelessness, the acceptance of the inevitable. Between the three of them passed a love, tenderness and each glimpsed that wicked sense of humour that Troy possessed. That slow cocky smile back at them, as if to say, *God, what we got here then, this is a right pickle, never mind, what a laugh?* There were so many things to say, to convey, there was never enough time.

'Mummy does so well in black, do you not agree.' He heard his brother's high-pitched voice fade into the background. Troy loved his boys so much. He knew they would survive. His Samuel would avenge him, he had no doubt. Troy's mother certainly was no fool and she had her beloved Gunthorpe, start to investigate how her youngest son, Hector, had died at sea. She did not believe that the sea, the God Neptune or even the Christian God would dare take her Hector! Hector's death would not go un- investigated and she would make a deal with

Satan himself to get to the bottom of what had happened. Therefore, he was under no illusion that she would accept whatever Mestor said had happened to him and his boys.

'You will not get away with this.' He whispered into the night, not once taking his eyes from his boys. Tears streamed down all their faces. He just wanted to get up and comfort them. They were his world. His two little soldiers!

'Oh Troy, do shut up. I have won. Poor old Mestor the quiet one, will never amount to anything. Well look at me know, just oozing with power.' He was drunk with triumph. 'I am so enjoying myself. Well look, good old boring Hector is dead, and be it that you've done a fabulous job and done all the hard work in the name of honour and the estates. It's now my turn to shine. Secomb has left me and really, I have no choice but to be assertive. To win his admiration! I thought you would at least be a little proud.'

'Mestor, you are a fat pompous poof who frankly, I despise and mark my words....' He never once took his eyes from his boys. 'This is not the end.' He nodded at both his boys in turn, they understood the message. He saw Samuel stiffen in attention, glaring at him, fighting, and holding back his tears, while Nathaniel let the tears stream down his face. Then he closed his eyes remembering them playing amongst the woods, running, skirting, laughing, being together, being happy.

'Oh this is all so poetic, and quite frankly a little dull. I have won, and wish to bask in my own glory, so I wish to get to the point, so there.' Mestor kicked his brother in the side and jumped away clapping his hands in glee, whilst still giggling. He bowed down to his brother mockingly, and was annoyed that Troy still had not paid him the courtesy of looking at him once. He only had eyes for his boys.

'Dear Troy, look at me you moron.' He was denied. 'I said look at me.' Still Troy would not raise his eyes to give him the satisfaction. 'Well, so be it. I am not so sorry to see you go. Bye, bye.'

'NOOOOOOOOOOO.' Screamed the boys in the background, they tried to tear free but their bounds held them fast. They watched in horror, as their father was positioned, he kept fighting, and growling at the men who had captured them and they saw, two of the hired villains hold and punch him into submission.

Then all of a sudden, he just stopped and returned to look at his boys again, he held still. Without any ceremony, they watched as the leader of Mestor's hired gang took his sword over his head and with all the strength, he could muster, bring it sweeping down across and in one clean swoop remove the victims head from his shoulders.

'Then they daunted me, daunted me with his head. They actually started to kick his head across the beach, as if it was a football. Can you imagine that?' Shem looked pleadingly at her. He could see clearly, as if it were yesterday, the way his father's body thumped to the ground. The villains had grabbed his head by his hair and begun swinging it from side to side, and then they had started to play with it. The blood had showered everywhere. Shem recalled then how he had looked at all those men trying to remember their faces forever.

'I wanted to kill the bastard then and there. But what can you do. I was a twelve year old screaming?' He cried sadly. 'We were tied up, having been beaten senseless, and I am realising that my little brother as witnessed all this too and is rolled up in a ball at the bottom of a rocky boat, laying in his own sick. We were being taken out to sea, he was scared shitless and singing to himself; Hush a Bye Baby on the Tree Top. We did not know what we had in store. Can you imagine it? Can you imagine that night, then every night thereafter? Reliving that horror! Pissing and shitting in your own pants, waiting for that moment when you heard them bringing you food, water? We had been shackled by the ankles. It rubbed constantly against my skin. God! My ankle was red raw. I had shoved some rags round Rafe's to protect his....God! It was horrific! They were never taken off, even when we were allowed on deck. That was blinding, the sun burning my eyes so! We were constantly cold, sore, alone and there is me having to stand there and say to Nathaniel, this is pretty bad here mate but you wait, I'll soon have us out of this shit hole and we will be on our next adventure and then they will see. We'll show them, hey Nathaniel? We are the Mordesan brothers for God's sake!' He trailed off lost in the memories, and she could see in his eyes, that he was faraway reliving that time, when he had to stand up and be brave, try to get them through it. 'The bastards beheaded him in the middle of the beach. Beheaded my father!' He still could not quite believe it. 'I looked straight into his eyes.' Tears streamed down his face.

'Shem, Samuel, look at me.' Rosie went to him and placed her hands on his face making him look into her eyes. He was so worn, tired, and again exposed to the hell and nightmare he had endured!

He had just confided who he was, and she realised the burden he had been carrying all that time. The reason why he needed to avenge his father. He was the rightful heir to the Mordesan Estates, which Mestor had stolen and destroyed. It all fell into place.

'You were twelve, twelve years old, what could you have done to help, to save him? You were a child, not yet a man. There is no shame in that. No shame.'

'There was for me Rosie, you see it was my entire fault, if I had kept my mouth shut, would my father have confronted Mestor? Would Mestor have had the nerve to kill my father if not been given the push? God! My father treated him well, he had everything he wanted. He was a generous man in everything. Mestor did not want for anything. I should have kept my mouth shut.'

'Your mouth shut about what, about what Samuel?'

He shook his head, and looked away. He wiped his eyes and then softly pushed his fingers through her hair and slowly brought her face to his, he kissed her forehead, then her nose and lastly her lips.

She looked longingly into his eyes. How far they had both come. It was a new start. They would pull through. 'Let's go home; I need to see my son and that bloody deserting dog!' He smiled weakly at her. He had closed up again. That was all she was getting for now. She rose to her feet and nodded. She held out her hands and he took them, and she pulled him up. They faced each other as they had done so many times in the past. She would be his anchor.

'We all have our demons Rosie and I would love to promise to you that there be no more, but I can't.' He had witnessed the death of his father, discovered her battered and bruised body, and lastly watched his brother die. He knew there would be more horrors to come. He would tell her when he was ready of all of his woes. He had started to really let her in and she knew without a shadow of a doubt that he needed her as much as she needed him. She had worked herself up to a frenzy of lack of confidence. She had been frightened of what ifs! She knew that her insecurities were always her downfall. However, this man truly, deeply loved her. This evening's revelation marked a new beginning. They then leant against each other. They would do anything in their power to ease each other's pain.

## Chapter Fifteen

He softly blew into the sleeping boy's face. Seb laid all curled up, warm to the touch. Shem felt himself choke up. He had missed his boy so much. He had been away far too long. Rosie had stayed downstairs in the kitchen of Shaun and Nana's Farmhouse and told him where to find their son. Shem knew from old the way, but Earl led the way in any event.

Earl had finally heard his master, found Shem, and pounced and play fought for ages and ages, until both had been quite exhausted by the welcome.

Shem opened the door, his eyes become accustomed to the dark and he tip toed to the side of the cot bed, which had been set up by the side of a larger double wooden bed. The fire in the crate was just smouldering but he could feel the warmth contained in the room. It was Rosie's old room and was quite small with just a great big bed, which was piled high with wool blankets and a beautiful velvet red quilt, a chair and chest of drawers. He smiled in recognition, having been smuggled into the comfortable room secretly years ago. He remembered the bed had been exceptionally comfortable and some of the most intimate moments of his life had been spent there, shared with his pixie.

He looked down at his little angel Seb. His son looked as if he had grown a little and was not so chubby around the face; his hair was longer and fuller, with ringlets. It was plastered everywhere and all fluffy just as his was in sleep. He felt he was always playing catch up with the boy and it was not the way he ever thought it would be when he had children. He thought then of what his grandmother had said, when he had last visited her, about him finding a proper wife and having children in wedlock. Here was his family and no other would do, whatever his Grandmother had wished and said.

Seb curled his nose and murmured in his sleep. At this point Earl decided to give Shem some assistance and pounced onto the bed. He went straight to Seb's face, and with such delicate care, he lightly licked his cheek and nose. Seb moaned and wiggled his nose.

'Earl no, no.' The boy moaned no longer in quite so deep a sleep.

'Wakey, wakey littleun.' He heard a soft familiar voice whisper to him and still in sleep, Seb smiled. Shem could not resist the temptation and wanted to wake him and not let him sleep on. It was rather selfish of him, but he remembered how his own father would wake them from sleep if he was to return late at night.

'Tell him Dad to leave me alone.' Seb said still in his sleep. Shem pointed to the dog to lie and Earl stretched out by the boys warmth, with Shem stretched out to the other side.

'Seb, wake up.' The boy heard again and felt a soft blow against his face. His eyes started to flatter. Shem watched as his son's expression change from blissful sleep and warm contentment to reality dawning. He snatched his eyes open and glared straight at Shem. His eyes lit up and he grinned from ear to ear and then struggled from beneath the blankets to fling himself into Shem's waiting arms. They laughed, cuddled and then Earl started to bark in excitement at the reunion, running back and forth in glee.

'Rafe said you would come back!' Seb beamed. Shem then looked deep into his boy's eyes and saw the passion there.

'Seb, you are still half asleep. Rafe has left us!' Shem found a lump in his throat.

'Dahhh, told you before, he is here.' Shem felt slightly uncomfortable and decided to ignore that and to steer the conversation away to other things.

'Tell me everything that has been going on.' Seb had looked out to the window and saw it was still the dead of night.

'Is it still night?'

'Yes.' Seb rubbed his eyes.

'Can I go back to sleep first?'

'No, I wanted to wake you straight away so you....'

'But I am tired'

'Tell me.'

'No.'

'Tell me.'

'Noooo.'

'Spoilt child. I'm gonna tell ya mum.' At this Seb chuckled and gave Shem a further big cuddle and manoeuvred back into the blankets, curled up by Shem and closed his eyes. Shem lay back with him and stroked his boy's face. 'I love you Seb.' He whispered. It rolled off the tongue without any thought. He was his boy and looking down at him, he then realised that he was his future. Whether as his purpose had been to revenge the wrong that he and his brother had suffered, he now needed to start thinking more about Seb and what effect his actions and plans would have on him.

'I missed you.' Seb kissed him. 'I don't want you to leave me again for so long.'

'I'll try not to.' He tickled him.

'You'll be gone again soon.'

'I promise I won't.'

'You will, your Uncles' need you.' Seb drifted into sleep and Shem lay curled up with him thinking long and hard at what his son had said.

How could Seb know of them at all, and along with that, of all the worry and concerns that he had been made aware of? How could he know that even now, his Uncles were on their way back to Burwash to make sure that their sister, niece, and Rafe's new twins were fine? Seb managed to unnerve him again and he needed to be mindful and speak to Rosie.

Bob had given Shem information about the various sightings that their informants had passed along the line. It would appear that Hector had pulled the Burwash Gang more into his fold and promised them more shares and cuts in his business ventures. Harry Hawkins and Hector had only met because of Bob and Shaun however had formed a strong friendship over the years. Only now, it seemed that they had cemented more ties and Shem did not like where it was going. He knew that he only had a matter of time before Hector would know of his deceit over Hartright and then there would be a price to pay. However, Shem was not finished yet and he had plans afoot for the attack. However, Shem had something that Hector had lost a long time ago; he had passion to succeed, whereas Hector was just playing to keep people in line for an easy life. Shem wanted to further exploit the smuggling business along the South Coast. He wanted to expand his brewery business. He had money to invest on exploring the possibilities of coal being found on the land at the Hall in Cornwall, and he had money to get the land there working again for him. As Master St Clements, he had established himself as a good investment risk to deliver trade from the East and working with his cousins

Oliver and Luca would open more doors. Even Meir Plancy was interested and liked what he saw.

Hector needed to be shown that his time was up and Shem was the main player now. Whatever it took, he would do. He had the determination and guts and the added advantage of men who were loyal to him. Secomb was another story.

He looked back at his little boy and thoughts of Rosamund played on his mind. She had said that she had seen a blond haired boy who carried the light near him and never paid much attention to her premonitions, but now it played on his mind. What if Seb could really see Rafe and why would Rafe still be here if ghosts did really exist? Seb had fallen back into a comfortable sleep and Shem whispered into the night. 'I know I said I missed you plep, but really don't you think your taking it too far? Why for heaven sakes aren't you chasing skirt in heaven?'

At that point, the door slowly opened and Rosie tiptoed in with candle in hand. 'He fell asleep while you were talking?' She teased.

'I did not realise how boring I had become.' He dare not tell her he was talking to ghosts. He slowly lifted himself up not to disturb Seb and spread out on Rosie's bed instead.

'I would never associate the word boring with you.'

'That's true, I would say the word that springs to mind right now is how magnif...........' She placed her finger over his mouth and tutted in mock annoyance. He caught himself in time and said instead. 'Shall I just grovel?'

The smell of wet seaweed lingered and the air was damp as the dawn was wakening. The sky was already blue and there was a smooth breeze. It was a wonderful morning. The tide was going out and the beach was pocketed with small water pools. The surf softly rolled in, all quietly leisured and relaxed. The beach, like Pevensey, was pebbled up the small slopes and as it flattened became sandy, and where still wet, slushy and muddy. This oozed coldly through Rosie's toes and made them tickle as she walked bare foot through the soft surf, avoiding the deposits of clusters of larger stones that scattered across the beach. Where the sand was clear and smooth, she saw a few shells and worm whirls.

Way out was a small frigate. The sun cast a shadow across the water of it and its appearance was magnificent in the calm settings. She knew without a doubt that Ned and Shem's men would already be alert to it and know it's business.

All types of Seagulls glided effortlessly in the breeze and Rosie noticed small orange and cream poppies dancing amongst the pebbles nearer the beach verges, which were also edged with long grass. The grass' seeds bent with the weight of the stalks, making the grass look as if it were bowing.

She had needed to be on her own in order to gather her thoughts after the previous night's events, but knew that she would have been followed for protection.

'Morning Rosie.' He appeared to come to her from nowhere and him being there knocked her back.

'Oh hello.'

'Sorry I did not mean to scare you.' She would know William's voice anywhere.

'No, no it's alright; I was away with the fairies and should have been looking where....'

She cuddled her shawl nearer to her. Jester the dog bounded up to them and bounced up at William with gusto. He did not even flinch at the power of the dog and for a few moments, he play wrestled with the dog and once settled, he returned his attention to Rosie. It was impossible; they were standing there as if nothing had happened. He hadn't changed much, just a few more wrinkles around the eyes, he looked tired. She had been dreading seeing him and all the emotions she would feel. Now she was tired also and all her inhibitions just disappeared. They both watched the sea calming down after being in a rage for a few days.

When William had heard that Rosie was back, he could not contain himself, he had wanted to run across as quick as possible. However, he had got word from Shaun to keep his distance. He had begged Shaun to ask for Ray and Ned's forgiveness. He still felt he was on borrowed time and had deliberately kept a low profile and had sent messages to Bob continuously for instructions. Bob had sent word he had wanted to meet up that morning and William was anxious for his future. He knew now that having Shem back on the south coast was going to ruffle a few feathers.

Rosie held herself better, with a new strength and confidence, however she did look tired. He tried to look discreetly at her scar but her hair was flapping everywhere as usual.

With all his heart, he hoped Shem had paid Hartright back and made him to suffer for an eternity. He and Shaun had mulled over Shem's absence and agreed it had to do with revenge on Hartright, and settling some other old scores, no doubt. The rumours had been rife and all Shem's gang members had offered was that Shem was away on business. Some had said that the French authorities had detained him for smuggling. Some had said that the authorities in London and got hold of him and he had been hanged. Many, who feared him, had placed bets, hoping that that he had met his maker! In any event, Shem was an enigma, a mystery, and appeared to walk with the Devil.

'You're up early?' He laughed at that. 'I know you too well. I took my chances and thought you'd be here.' He immediately confessed.

She nervously fiddled with her hair as the wind took it and whipped it into her face. She looked over his shoulder hoping that Shem would discover she was gone and come and find her. Now that William was here, she did not know how she felt. She had dreamed of all different scenarios with the two men in her life and within days, both were back in it!

'Hmmm, it's so peaceful and no one is around!' William felt awkward in her presence and was desperate for some sort of conversation. He looked towards the beach and took in the whole view from their vantage point on the beach. He knew he could never have kept away today having heard from his servants last night what had happened in the Tavern. He wished she would just let rip at him and they have it out once and for all.

Rosie turned and also scanned the view and looked back the way she had come along the beach. She watched the waves hit the surf and foam up, then run away and be followed and overlapped by a new wave. Jester was thundering through the waves without a care in the world. She smiled at him and found William watching her. She turned her head in embarrassment. Small red circles formed on her cheeks. He smiled at her unease. He shrugged his shoulders and he too then turned away.

'It's like nothing can touch you here.' He started to say. 'Time stands still.' He sighed. 'If only! It is quite magical. Well I'm babbling. God! I am nervous.' He confessed.

'No, no you're not babbling. You're right, I used to come here to escape, but now it's comforting and just...well yes, it is magical.' She stopped feeling she had said too much and could feel herself shaking all over, but relieved that she had said it. 'I love this part of the beach. I love just being here, come rain, sun, snow, and sleet. It's soothing.' She had always loved this place and she had really missed it over the last few years. She felt she was running away with the conversation again. William picked up a pebble and flung it for Jester.

'I am so sorry Rosie.' He offered in a whisper. They both watched the dog head in completely the wrong direction for the pebble and they jointly grinned at the dog's silliness. 'I pretended I did not care, but I did, and all too soon I realised what I had lost....' His voice broke as he choked back his emotions. He shrugged again and called the dog back, and again flung another bigger pebble. 'I've made a complete mess of everything!' They did not look at each other. 'Do you have to rush off?' He softly asked deliberately watching the dog rather than her.

She felt herself go all warm. How could she allow herself to feel this way after all he had put her through? He had abandoned and used her and made her feel insignificant. She was tired of having such bad thoughts, being so depressed and angry with everyone all the time. Shem would go mad at her chatting to him. She closed her eyes to the blackness and remembered thinking last night that she and Shem were heading for the light.

Unconsciously they both felt for each other's hand and firmly held fast. He was such a huge part of her history and so she had to let go of that for her own sanity. Time moved slowly as they stood there for an age just holding hands and looking out to sea.

Neither could see Shem standing on the grass verges by one of the old fishing wharfs on the beach. When he had woken and felt she was not there, he had immediately panicked. Seb was curled up in his arms, and ever so slowly and lightly, so as not to disturb him, he had got out of bed and gone in search of Rosie. He had ordered Earl to stay and protect his boy but was not surprised when he firmly refused and followed him.

He knew where she would be, blowing the cobwebs away as she would say. He had seen her almost immediately and then witnessed her surprise at William's presence. He had wanted to go and rip the man's heart out and found that he was just managing to contain himself. He tried to be rational. He had been like a man obsessed last night, accusing her of all sorts, and then seeing sense and then they had both been completely drained when he confided in her. Now he found himself feeling exactly the same jealous reaction. She was his and she stood there talking to her old lover! He wanted to kill her.

The green-eyed monster absorbed his ever core and he managed to convince himself that yesterday had all been an act, she was a manipulating bitch. Like all women. She had her claws in him and made him look like a fool. He would have them both right now on the beach. He whipped the back of his coat back and grabbed the handle of his dagger, which was placed, through his back belt. He fingered the handle with raging intensity. She had betrayed him.

'How could you be with a man like that?' William could not hold it in anymore. Their hands fell apart.

'What?'

'What does he do for you that..... ?'

'I don't know what you mean.' She did not want this. Why did he have to spoil it?

'He is an animal.' William declared. All his restraint had gone.

'No.' She would stand by Shem regardless.

'He kills people for a living.' William groaned.

'I don't want to hear this.'

'He orders peoples deaths. Husbands, fathers, brothers, and sons. Even women when he has to.' William had been kind before and now he had turned completely. 'Look around you and see the fear on the people's faces. It's not respect they have for the great Shem, its fear.'

'No you are wrong, He looks after people.'

'In your warped mind. He is a vicious mad man, out to rule the world. He is a lunatic, a greedy horrific monster.'

'That's enough.' She would never tell him or anyone how her thoughts had run along the same path.

'Enough. I have not even begun to get started. And what does that make you?'

'Don't.'

'A parasite, that's what. You feed off him. You love the attention.'

'He looks after me!' She defended and knew that was weak given, she had no idea where he had been recently. She hated the fact that William had manipulated her as he had done so any times in the past. He was just a spoilt man who could not have what he wanted. Why could he have not left it and they parted on good terms. She was so tired of it all.

'Does he? Really? Why did you not go to him when you found out you were pregnant?'

'I....'

'Because you knew that you could not. You did not even know where this man came from. He was just a passing fancy that you hooked up with by chance. You never made plans with him, but he knew that like a sucker you were, you'd be at his beck and call any time. My God he must have been laughing his head off at you.'

'He loves me.'

'Oh well, then that makes it all right then.'

'He will do anything for me.'

'Well he hasn't before now and you did not take that chance, because deep down you knew that you couldn't rely on him. You built the man up in some fantasyland and reality just wasn't an option. My God! All the time you were with me, you were whoring with him. If you hadn't been raped and forced into his path, he would have just thrown you off.'

'You don't know what you are saying. He looked after me.' She would not let William and his jealousy ruin everything. He had gone too far.

'Did he? Really? I don't see him killing that prick that raped you.'

'It is complicated.' She would never tell a soul what she knew. Why did she not just walk away?

'Is that what he said?'

'You don't understand.'

'Neither do you.'

'He loves me.'

'No, he is using you until something better comes along. If he can kill Chater over a witness statement that possibly, just possibly could have put some uncomfortable questions to his precious brother, what does that say about you?'

'That's rubbish, Chater and his family are in France.'

'You know nothing of him and his lot. I think you are delusional if you believe that. My God Rosie, how do you think this makes me feel?' She looked away. 'I truly loved you.' He sighed. 'God help me! I confess, I still love you and yes, and I am a selfish prick that wants it all. But when I found out that you were supposedly dead my heart tore.' He could not look at her. 'I felt lost, alone; I always pretended to myself that you were a stop gap. That I'd go and find a fabulously wealthy woman and live happierly ever after. What did I find? A woman who pulled every string. I was gob smacked, suckered and could not define pure lust from love. I had love with you Rosie, pure love, and I never saw it.' He looked to the sky and she saw his eyes glisten. 'I wanted adventure, be a bit of a player, you know. But Hartright worked on me and I fell for it. I betrayed you, my friends, and I lost Shaun's respect.' He looked hard out to sea. 'They asked me to spy on Hartright for them. Make it up to them or I would suffer. They threatened to kill me Rosie.' She stepped back and closed her eyes to it all. What did he want from her? She wrapped her shawl tight around her, more in comfort than cold and shook her head with it all. 'Yes, I had taken liberties and if it weren't for Bob and Shaun's friendship, I'd be dead now.'

'No, that's not true.'

'Oh Rosie wake up. They have your brothers in tow now, and it's a matter of time before they are made to make an example of me. God! They've ransacked the House, stole the horses, and got my father and brothers all up in arms. I've got Lennard breathing down my neck and bloody Paully just waiting in the wings to snap it.' She could say nothing to his misery when over these last few months had been torture for her, when Shem had abandoned her and she had no say in any of it.

'And all through this, all I think of is what Hartright did to you.' She did not want to go there, never again, it was far too painful, and there had been too much suffering already to keep reliving it time and time again. 'I understand that you are still on drugs to ease the pain, and that your brothers aren't aware of half of what happened to you, are they? Why is Hartright half way across the ocean and not dead yet?' He grabbed her arms and looked hard at her in desperation. He would say anything.

'Because I have not said it was him.' She blurted out.

'What?'

'I have not said it was.' She grasped, hardly able to breathe.

'Everyone knows it was him.' He looked long and hard at her. She had closed her eyes.

'I can't allow myself to think on it and ...; she raised her hands to ward it off.

'My God! Rosie, you are not a martyr. He must die.'

'And then Shem will be everything you accuse him off. I'll not do that and have that on my conscience. Nor will I give Shem the permission to kill anyone for me.'

'So this is about you not facing reality?' She closed her eyes again to the whole thing, why was he pushing and pushing. 'This is madness!'

'I can't walk away now.' She whispered more to herself than him. She belonged with Shem.

'You can walk away with me.' He whispered.

'No, I can't William.' She responded in kind.

'I love you.' He mouthed.

'And I loved you with all my heart, but now I am protected by Shem.'

'You don't love him?'

'I never said that.'

'Then tell me, look into my eyes, tell me that you love him and want to be with him for the rest of your life.' She nodded and he stepped back in denial. 'Tell me.' He pressed and watched her choke back the tears. 'Listen to me Rosie. He will kill you in some shape or form in time. I'm getting out and I want you to come with me. You need to come with me.' She shook her head. It was all too late.

'No William.'

'Rosie. My God women! You owe it to yourself.' He realised that nothing he said or tried to do, would change her mind. She was lost to him now. She was all cuddled up against the onslaught from him and his wants and demands on her. He had lost her a long time ago. She was not coming back. Slowly he resigned himself to the fact that this part of his life was over.

'I have made up my mind to go to the new world.' He stated. 'At one point, we were all going to go.' She remembered all of their conversations, their dreams, and aspirations. Had any of them really got want their hearts desired? 'I will write to you, and let you know where I am, should you ever need......' He did not finish the sentence. They both just stood rigid looking out to sea, neither wanting to look at the other and let it finish and to let it go.

'I hope you find what you are looking for William.' Rosie looked sadly into his eyes. William swallowed hard. He stepped forward and held out his hand. She took it and he kissed her hand and bowed. He then raised himself high and slowly turned and walked away heading towards the other bank which lead to Seven Sisters whilst Rosie turned and headed towards the cliffs.

Shem let out a breath and was thankful that at least the dog had not given him away. His eyes were like black slits. The jealousy was over powering. He found himself crossing his fingers, hoping she did not look back to watch William walk away.

'You touch one hair on her head and I will kill you.'

Shocked at the outburst from behind, Shem turned and looked straight into the eyes of Benedict Hunter, notorious pirate of the Caribbean. What he was doing standing on Cuckmere Haven watching Rosie and William, God only knew? Earl was allowing him to tickle his ear. The dog had truly become soft! Shem stepped back, folded his arms, and shook his head at the nerve of the man. His heart was still black as were his eyes.

'You forget yourself, Benedict.' He almost growled with a mocking gleam on his face.

'No, you cross the line boy when you look as if you will lay a finger on her.' Benedict's eyes went back to search for Rosie. The man had a wonderful full hearty voice that was used to commanding any situation.

'Who is she to you?'

'That's my business, now I am warning you, leave well alone.' He looked back at Shem and stole a further glance at Rosie to make sure she was safe. Shem laughed menacingly at that. He jumped forward but stopped immediately seeing Benedict raise a cocked pistol to his head. Only a desperate man would dare have the nerve to threaten him so. Earl snarled at the stranger sensing the danger in the air. He positioned himself to attack Benedict at any moment. Shem waved at him to stay. He knew this man was no threat to him at all, if he had wanted him dead, he would have killed him already. He intrigued him and this visit to Cuckmere had indeed turned out to be quite revealing and putting him back in the foulest of moods. The man was not stupid and knew that Shem would have back up not far away. He had known this man only by sight, a quick nod of acknowledgement as their paths had crossed in London and the docks, but never had they been this close up. Claude had been right to be so suspicious.

'You dare stand there and tell me what to do. I have had enough shit already. I'll rip ya fucking tongue out, you fucking plep!' Shem snarled and Benedict knew this was not a man to give out threats freely. He had found out as much information about this man as possible.

'George put the gun down man.' They both turned to see old Shaun yelling and racing towards them. Shaun was too old to be running across the verge towards them and Shem knew that there was more trouble ahead now, Bob wasn't far behind. Shem saw that Jesus had the horses up further. Earl remained where he was ready to pounce on Benedict at any moment.

'Oh fuck, that's all I need.' Benedict almost whispered and Shem saw the man's shoulders drop. Shem watched as Benedict lowered the gun and cocked it before shoving it back into his belt. He raised his eyes to the heavens in irritation and half turned away from the approaching men.

'You've got a nerve man, after all this time and to show up stalking our Rosie and then pointing your pistol at him. Do you know what damage you could have done?' Shaun was breathless and in no mood to be trifled with. His long thick grey hair was damp to his shoulders and he tried to catch his breath. He was shaken in temper and everyone knew he was too old for any excitement.

'Don't start.'

'Don't start, I'll tan ya fucking hide.'

'I'm the one with the pistol here.'

'And still light in the head it would appear.'

'Do you have to?'

'Do I have to?

'Why are you repeating everything I say?'

'I am not repeating everything you say; I am just flabbergasted at your nerve.'

'Well you knew I'd come back sooner rather than later and just as well. From what I hear, it hasn't been a bed of roses for her and this one here.' He pointed his thumb at Shem in disgust. Shem just stood and stared while Shaun and Benedict argued. 'I heard he was a right psychopath. Seems Mr. St Clements or is it Shem here is ready to pounce? I am not the one you have to be weary off, he looks like thunder and it's all aimed at my girl.'

'My girl?' Shem edged forward; Bob tried to block his path. Shem would have him, he was no psychopath.

'You always knew how to make an entrance and exit boy.' Shaun moaned, rubbing his chest. Shem knocked Bob's arm away and then Bob piped up.

'Shem this is George Cavendish aka Benedict Hunter. He is Shaun's second eldest son. He is Rosie's Dad!'

'You what?' They all looked at Shaun, then Bob, then again at Benedict or should they say George?

Earl jumped away and pounded down the beach, he began to bark in excitement, and they all turned to see Rosie laughing at the dog as he greeted her as she walked towards them. Jester then made himself heard and started to bark excitedly and found himself being silenced by a growl from Earl.

'What's going on?' She called in all innocence; Shem's mind was a whirlwind of emotions, on the one hand, he wanted to punch her for her deceit and on the other smile welcoming at her.

She came to Shem and tried to cuddle up to him but he turned slightly away and everyone's attention went back to the stranger. She put her arm on Shem's and he looked so distracted and distant. She knew then that he had seen her with William. She needed to explain, but then she got angry. In between, her mind was racing, someone had said something to her, and she had not been listening.

'Rosie love.' She heard a familiar voice call. Shem looked then at her and she looked with a question in her eyes to him and squeezed his arm.

'Rosie love...' Came the voice again, this time she stopped and closed her eyes, she felt the party drift away. It wasn't going away. She dug her fingers into Shem's arm. Slowly she opened her eyes and before her stood a grand man. He was an older version of Ned. His shoulders were broad and strong. His hair had once been blood, but now was dark and hitting his shoulders. His skin was leather brown from exposure to the sun. His eyes all closed from squinting at the sun no doubt, and all wrinkly. He was clean-shaven, which exposed his two brown moles on his cheek. His clothes were immaculate and of exceptional quality and wealth. He was a hard looking man, but now he looked down at her in anticipation, sorrow, and guilt.

This was not fair. She had done the same to her brothers and he now stood before her and she had believed all this time, that he had deserted them and was dead to them.

She shook her head in denial and felt her heartstrings burst. Last night had been bad enough, then seeing William had drained her. When she had woke this morning, she had hope in her heart and now it pounded, fit to burst at seeing her father standing before her. She swayed in panic, stepped back, and let go of Shem. Her eyes darted looking for an escape.

The party of men seemed to have walked a distance off to give them some space. Her eyes tore into Shem. He must have felt it and he slowly turned to face her. His look did not give her any comfort. She went cold with anxiety and all too quickly felt ever so alone again. Her father stepped towards her seeing the look of confusion, hurt, regret, loss, and anger, all in one.

She looked frail and Benedict aka George wanted to swoop her up to him. What had he stumbled upon on the beach? She obviously needed looking out for. George pledged from that moment no one would ever hurt her again. It had broken his heart to leave his children, but what choice had he at that time?

'Shem.' She gasped. It was hardly a whisper, and automatically he stepped forward, instinct making him go when his mind played tricks, telling him she was using him and last night meant nothing, She had deliberately played up to him and behind his back had arranged to meet up with William after all. He would kill both of them.

He'd also kill the show off Benedict or George, whatever his name was, regardless of whether he was Rosie's dad. He did not like him one bit.

George grabbed Rosie's hand and tried to tuck her to him.

'Don't you dare touch me?' She screamed. She snatched her hand away. Earl growled. Shem stepped forward to go for him but felt Rosie's whole body stiffen.

'Shem, Shem. Shem.' She called her voice rising higher and higher. Everyone looked at her in panic. She was backing away, shaking her head, and moaning to herself.

'What's happening?' George looked bewildered. Shaun made to go to her but Shem stepped in front of her for protection. He raised his hand in defiance.

'Don't you dare touch her?' He warned.

'Leave it George, it's too much, can't you see.' Shaun added.

'Make him go away, I don't want him here. He is not my Dad. My Dad's dead. My Dad's dead. Tell him Shem, Shem tell him.' She was going mad now and pointing at George as if he were the devil. She then decided to spit in his direction. Shem turned and grabbed both her hands and held them fast.

'Look at me Rosie.' He commanded bending down and looking directly into her eyes.

Shaun turned to his son and motioned for him to walk away and he looked at his father in bewilderment, conveying that he should not leave them alone.

Both looked over their shoulders as they walked away and saw that Shem had calmed her down, they decided it was best to leave them to it. George spat in contempt at the situation. The reunion would wait. It was all too much for her. Diplomacy had never been a strong point of his and looking at his father, he gave him a filthy look. His manners also had not improved since he had been away.

'Who is he? He dare say he is my Dad. He touched me. How dare he think he can touch me? My Dad is dead. My Dad is dead.' She moaned letting all her anxieties get the better of her. Her mind was whirling, going around and around, with everything caving in on her. She felt like she was going to drown. Her heart was racing and Shem wasn't listening to her. He slapped her hard across the face and she crumbled to the floor. Shem slowly lowered himself and crouched down beside her. His heart ached for her pain, but his head needed to stay focused. She rubbed her cheek as she gave him a filthy look but knew that the slap had brought her back to reality. She sat up and felt his hands on her knees as he bent down to her. She felt the tears well up and fall freely down her face.

She had completely lost it for a moment and Shem had known then that he could not allow that to happen. He loved her too much and how could he ever doubt her? His insanity would be his and her down fall if he did not manage to control it. He felt guilty for feeling that way and now when she cried, he knew he would do anything to make her happy again. She melted into his arms and they sat curled up to each other. Why was everything such a trial?

George stole a look back, watched the pair, and found comfort in what he saw, but knew there was a reckoning coming.


On arriving back at the Manor house, Shaun had gone off to collect Ned and Ray. Shem, Rosie, and George had spent a few awkward moments before Rosie had nodded for Shem to go and see after Seb. Shem had held her hand tightly for a few seconds, conveying that she was strong enough now to cope and knew he was just a call away. He knew that Seb would be up and ready, knowing that Nana would not have any nonsense and he knew that Seb had been so excited at the prospect of going home to see Phoebe and Harry, that he would have done everything asked of him to get him ready.

Rosie stood by the fire in the kitchen, poking at it, to bring it back to life. She did not wish to look at her father. He had seen her at her weakest and now all the barriers were back in place.

'I was waiting for an opportunity to ...' George started but Rosie interrupted him abruptly.

'You shouldn't have bothered.' She turned to face him feeling a little bit braver than down on the beach. She could do this.

'Now that's not nice.' He drawled, she had always been fiery. He sat down at the table as if he had never ever left.

'Not nice! I couldn't give a toss what you think. You have been dead to us these last few years and all of the sudden, you think it's alright to swan in.' Rosie had heard these words flung at her not that long ago and knew at that moment how hurt Ray had really been. She and her brother were more alike than she thought. She stood with her arms folded in defiance.

'I had to get away, you don't understand.' Rosie sighed, knowing that the excuses were on their way.

'Understand. Like fuck.' She almost spat.

'I am still your father and you will not talk to me like that.'

'I will not stand here and listen to this shit.'

'You will stay where you are young lady; I think you have alot to answer for.' George found that she was now a woman and not a young girl who he could order about that easily.

'Fuck off.'

George could not believe her nerve and would do anything to salvage what was left, but watched as she marched from the room and slammed the door shut hard behind her. The next minute she smacked straight into Ray outside in the courtyard. She bounced off his chest and struggled to keep her balance. He made no move to help and just laughed at her in spite.

'You just can't keep that shut can ya? Bowed out on another row have ya? What, has Shem also seen what a conniving bitch you really are?'

'Ray...I..' She started to say and then just stopped, what was the point, his face spoke volumes?

'Typical, what time you leaving? The sooner you put some distance between us the better. You just make me want to be sick.' He turned from her and this made her even angrier.

'Giving it large now, you fat fucking bastard, see how hard you are when you go in there and see what is in there, then come out and ...'

'Rosie, no.' Shaun sterns voice boomed across the yard. He and Ned were approaching. 'Ray!' Shaun said in warning.

'This better be good.' Ray barked.

'Curb the attitude with me boy. I've warned you before.' Ray lowered his eyes in embarrassment. All three siblings stood together and Shaun sighed hard as he looked long and hard at them.

'The last week or so has not been easy on any of us; in fact it's still a little bitter and raw to say the least.' He looked towards his own house and the manor back door leading into the kitchen. He could see the flicker of the fire through the glass windows. Shaun sighed. 'But we have a new problem now.' He could not think of any other word to describe his wayward son. George was a selfish man, there was a reason he was back, and Shaun was under no illusion it was not for his grown up children. He and Nana just had to be there for them because he knew it would only end in pain. Rosie's meeting with her father had not gone well, and it was clear if she had run out on him already, that Ray would do the same, both sharing the trait of not having alot of patience. Ned would always try to find some good in the situation and try to appease one and all, but it would amount to nothing. He and Bob needed to have words and to keep an eye on George aka Benedict and find out what he was about.

Ned and Ray looked to him in anticipation. 'Go into the kitchen, we have another visitor.'


'Your timing could have been better.' Shem mused as he sipped his tea standing looking out of the window at the party gathering in the courtyard. He was thankful that at least the tea was good. Seb and Nana had gone out the front way to have a little time together before they left. He knew Rosie would not wish to stay any longer than necessary now.

'Certainly, from my point this morning it was spot on.' George referred to observing Shem on the beach watching Rosie. 'William is a good bloke, a little too cock sure some times, and that's he's weakness, but knowing that she was yours, and knowing he is on borrowed time with you, do you really think, he would have declared his undying love and asked her to run away with him?' George also drunk his tea, he sat at the kitchen table, resting his elbows and swirled the tea at the bottom of his cup.

'The thought had crossed my mind.' Shem did not wish to look or really speak to the man however, he would share that.

'Obviously, I could see that on the beach and it reminded me of why I am now where I am Shem. I loved my wife to distraction and allowed my demons to tell me things that were not there and true. We all have doubts and want ultimately to be loved to death, but what I let go of was the trust. And that was my downfall.' It would not hurt to show empathy with Shem, George thought.

'Don't lecture me old man.'

'No, you know it all.' George sighed sarcastically.

'I was taught to have respect for my elders, but I refuse to conform on some issues, but as my woman's father I will let you live, but don't be fooled that I care.' He turned to face him. 'If you dare fuck me off again, I will kill you.' George did not doubt the threat at all. He knew that Shem was not a force to be reckoned with. Shem was in a different league and one that George was very comfortable in too, and soon Shem would all too clearly see the wood through the trees.

Shem knew that this man needed to be watched and he was under no illusion that him being there was not a coincidence, what with his name cropping up regularly in reports since Claude had spotted him in London all those months ago.

At that point, the door opened. The tension between them was replaced by apprehension. Shaun entered shielding the party who followed for a few seconds and George rose to his feet. He had been dreading this moment and wished for all the tea in China that he could turn back time and have all his children look at him with all that love that had once been there. He saw three of his four children heading in to the kitchen and his heart pounded in anxiety.

**Chapter Sixteen**

It was drizzling outside. It was persistent, cold rain, which penetrated everything. A small mist had formed and the night had long since closed in.

Lydia sat beside the fire, lost in thought and sipping her brandy. She had hoped that the drink and fire would warm her, yet she was cold all over. The room was just lit by the fire and there was a wonderful glow surrounding the fireplace. However, all was lost on the sorrow, which oozed from the woman's every pore. The heavy-duty curtains had been pulled to keep the world at bay and to try to muffle the sounds of the rain. However, to no avail.

Every now and again, the fire would sing, crackle, and burst and small sparks would jump out and dissolve as soon as they hit the cold stone hearth. Lydia had positioned her chair and small table  as near to the heat as she could, and on the table beside her, she found her eyes kept wondering back to the open letter that she had not since long received.

She had dressed for bed in a lace cotton nightdress and beautiful embroidered cream nightgown. Her hair was all lose, and shone in health; she had been intending to plait it but just could not find the energy. She was pleased that her hair still had its lustre about it but she had discovered a few grey hairs, which depressed her. She sighed as time was catching up with her and still she was on her own. She had enjoyed a bath and covered her thin body with lovely jasmine oil.

She could not believe what she had read in the letter and had been annoyed that neither of her children were around for her to sound off on. Hartright had long since gone and not even her constant bombardment of Constance could make the girl conceal where he was. She had to admit that perhaps Constance was telling the truth and did not know where Hartright was and so it was no surprise when Constance announced she too was going away to visit her friend Lady Skelton, in Herstmonceux, in East Sussex. She would have to write to her and convey the news.

Lydia was all alone and she had no one to share anything with. She gulped the brandy down and quickly poured herself a further drink. She tried not to look at the letter again but could not help it. The letter contained all her fears and she knew that all her dreams for her son were all in tatters now. The letter had advised that the rightful heir, Samuel Mordesan had been found and this had been verified at the family solicitor's office. There was no explanation of where he had been, what he had done and how he had been verified, but the news was enough for her to realise that if she thought her life was a mess now, it was going to become worse when Constance and Hartright found out! What would Mestor do? How would his reinstated nephew take to his Uncle more or less bankrupting the estates? Without a shadow of doubt, she knew Lady Theia would be in her element. She had dared not to enquire about her after their last encounter. She could have died of a heart attack at the news and she would have loved for that to happen. Lydia suppressed a grin at her wickedness.

She wiped her brow, feeling all her old emotions take hold again. For too long she had lived a lie, always waiting for that something to happen. It was just in reach, nearly there, just around the corner. She had lived her life on hold, waiting for that better thing to happen and along the way, miss out on all those choices she should have made to ensure she would be secure in old age. Time was slipping and her social circle had dwindled for her to have options in obtaining a half decent catch. She was fool, a lonely bitter frustrated fool. She had debts, a poor reputation, and no income of her own. She had no property and could only survive on the charity of her daughter. She despised Constance so much. She was young, beautiful, and was full of confidence.

Lydia had been livid about Constance and Williams break up, having hoped that the alliance would have helped her own scheming. That too was all ruined now. She was just so tired of it all, living a life constantly in regret and anger.

She went to pour a further drink when she realised that the bottle was indeed empty. She needed another drink and tutted as she tried to get up to her feet. The world whirled around her and she half giggled at that. She held out her arms and tried to balance herself then staggered forward to the door to call for another bottle.

It was an age before she heard the door open. 'At last, did you not hear me call? My God! Are all the staff here completely ancient and useless, all blind, old, feeble and completely stupid? God! If I was running this place, I'd have you all removed....' She took a step back coming forward to collect the bottle, when she saw an unfamiliar person come through the door as if he owned everything he saw. He was not carrying any drink. The corridor light made a halo all around him.

He looked exquisite in his deep blue velvet coat, which was richly lined with a red silk. He wore black silk pants and a crisp white shirt with a black silk cravat. His hair was loosely held back in a soft ponytail. His tricorne was under his armpit, he gave her the most elegant bow, and as she focused on him, she held her breath. It could not be. She found herself trying to stand to attention and she shook her head trying to clear the vision.

Shem took a threatening step forward. She stepped back. He smiled at her unease.

He watched as Lydia argued with herself as to how to react. Her mind was playing tricks on her. He stood before in all his glory and was the image of Troy. However, how could that be? Troy was dead. Had been for years. She felt uneasy and felt a nervous sweat begin to build at the back of her neck. This upstart did not intimidate her, she would certainly show him. She glared right at him but could not keep it up. She knew she swayed back and forth and then discovered she had closed her eyes to the haze of it all. She opened them not yet completely sober but able to focus better. She grabbed the letter from the small table and held it to her chest. As much as she had argued with herself earlier that the man would be proven an imposter, there was no denying he was a Mordesan. He had the air of his father, his looks, but the fairness of his mother's side. She had not been able to put this man out of her mind and here he was in all his glory. The rightful heir to the Mordesan lands and titles.

She had long since thought of him and his brother. She had assumed he and his brother were dead and good riddance too. How dare he think that he could just show up here at her daughter's without an announcement, be accepted in, and shown to her quarters? It was despicable and showed how he lacked any form of breeding. He was common.

Her face twisted in hate and she looked him up and down, and then spat. 'You can't just waltz in here and expect me to bow down to you. How do we know you are who you say you are?' She started pacing the floor but really did not get far as everything whirled around her. She stopped. 'You think you have won, you are nothing. My Hartright will kill you, and we will inherit after all.' She heard herself threatening and thought that she still had the old fight in her. She had always been spiteful and she saw the look of utter contempt that he had for her.

'He will kill me?' His voice was so familiar, so strong and carried so much authority yet she heard the mocking tones clearly.

'Oh yes, indeed he will.' She was defiant regardless of the drink egging her on.

'How pray tell?' She did not see the scornful knowing expression.

'He has influential friends who will crush you.' She almost spitted the words out, for a moment forgot how anxious she was, found her courage, and leant forward in temper.

'Oh Auntie Lydia, grow up. It's over. I am back now and well; where is your precious Hartright? Could he be chasing his tail across Europe to get to his Uncle who he will find is dead?' He stated rather dismissively. She stepped back in shock trying to avoid her chair. They had not shared any formal introduction and immediately started with unpleasantness and it just escalated and got gradually worse than anything she could ever have dreamt of.

'No.' She clutched her throat. 'You lie. We would have heard.' She gasped. She felt faint. He grinned at her discomfort, and then his stare turned into a stony glare, which was very unnerving. 'He can't be dead. He was in fine spirits. Hartright is his legal heir. He will challenge you. You're an imposter and not the legal heir!' She was deluding herself and babbling insanely. She turned to rush to her four-poster bed for support, still holding firm to the letter.

'Oh well. Shit happens.' He shrugged his shoulders and she saw still that stony glare of indifference. She was horrified at his language, but then slowly it dawned on her what he meant. She did not feel quite so intoxicated now, just tired of it all.

'You have killed him?' She choked, and found the courage to look over her shoulder at him, his evil grin crept through her, and she shivered in both cold and apprehension.

'No, you killed him.' The implication was clear, giving reference to past events. His black eyes tore into her.

'I had nothing to do with that!' There was no point in denying anything anymore but she would try to hold her ground in any event and try not to admit she had anything to do with those actions that happened years go.

'You had everything to do with it Auntie Lydia. You planned it all so that you could be queen bee. You even sacked my Grandmother from her own home. I'm surprised you didn't kill her off too. But then you figured that you could still get an allowance while she lived, she could never be seen to let you down, but once dead, it reverted back to her sisters does it not?' She wanted so much to strike at him at that point, but instead decided to turn towards him and spit at him. He laughed at her effort, looked down at the mess on the floor, and gave her a filthy look.

'You are nothing but a high class whore. Did you ever mourn your husband's death; I am interested as I am not sure whether Hector made it look like an accident, or your doing?'

'Don't be so absurd, how you could even begin to suspect me of something so vile? My God! The man was killed at sea, and for you to even suggest that I had a hand in Hector's death! If I had done such a terrible deed, how could I have continued to live under Theia's roof and protection? Surely, you could see that would be too much to bear. My God! The woman is a saint.' The words almost choked her, she was a hypocrite. She could not meet his eyes. She had completely ignored or not heard what he had said about her husband.

'She's a saint?' He laughed wickedly at that point. 'My Grandmother wants nothing more than for you to also meet your maker.' He stepped forward menacingly. Lydia stepped back in panic.

'You are a liar, a cheat. I'll scream and watch them come and rescue me!' She sat back on the bed having assumed that the noisy servants would have heard the commotion already and be curious as to what was happening.

This man was evil through and through and would never compare to the young boy Samuel. She remembered Samuel as decent and courteous, yet this creature was in league with the grim reaper himself. Yes, he must be an imposter, she had been wrong about him, the more she thought about it, and the more she knew, he was not a Mordesan? This could not be happening.

'Like they came running a moment ago? Get over yourself. No one will come for you, because no one likes you. They despise you. Like your children, who only suffer you for show? You have no friends. Any family you had, have long since closed their doors on you. Servants, who are poorly treated, will take a bribe.' She looked to the door and hallway for help. 'Even your husband hated you. No wonder Hector left you.' He stood before her now.

'My husband never left me. He died in an accident at sea.' She looked up into his eyes aware that they were so close. He towered over her, she wanted to creep into her bed and hide under the covers until he went away.

'No, he left you for another woman.' He leant forward and she arched her back. 'He is alive and well in France and stands between me actually killing your precious children.' He leant down ever so near, she could not move an inch, and she smelt how fresh he was when he whispered into her ear. His hate was boiling over now and he knew he could not contain the blackness.

'You lie.' She choked back now arching further away from him.

'Then how did I escape?' He stepped back and mockingly flung out his arms letting his tricorne fly to the floor.

'I don't believe you.' She almost collapsed in submission, the reality all too much to bear, but then she tried to recover and looked up in defiance, too weak to move. 'Hector loved me with a passion.'

'And you loved everyone else.' That alone smacked her hard. She rallied herself together.

'Yes, even your father if the truth be known.' Her spiteful tongue mocked. 'The final straw was when he too turned his back on my affections. My God he needed me after your mother died, and then he discarded me like I was nothing.'

'You lying bitch.'

'Oh come, come Shem, surely you can see there is more to this story.'

'Don't you dare try and say you and my father were together.' He was intrigued at her now growing confidence.

'Why, is that so repugnant?' Within an instance, he was above her, grabbed her by the neck, and started to squeeze tightly. She punched at him and he flung her away. She laughed at him and he would have finished her then but again smiled to himself at her cheek.

'You are so like your father, you make it easy.' He saw the lie in her face. She was a wicked bitch. She would say and use her body in any way to get what she wanted.

'So you worked on Mestor to kill my father, because he hurt your precious feelings and rejected your attentions?' He played.

'Your righteous father could not stand to be in the same room as me, especially when he discovered that I was with child.' She screamed. 'He was going to send me away. I was a disgrace to him and the family name. The scandal would destroy the family. He had it coming.'

'So let me get this straight, what you could not stomach was the fact that my father saw right through you and your lies, schemes and deceit.'

'No! I am a survivor and I have survived through all this.' She flung back in temper.

'You must be so proud dear Aunt, and what of your precious bastard child?' He flung that at her to see how she would react.

'Your half brother, Samuel.' She declared. He laughed at that.

'Is that the only hand you have left? '

'How can you prove he is not?'

'Because you stupid bitch, your precious bastard was taken in by someone we both know and is a ringer for their father.'

'You are fishing for information and it is clear you know nothing.' She remembered all too clearly the day she had the bastard and had made it more than apparent that he was to be given to the orphanage if he survived the night. He had been weak at birth and not expected to last and once out of her sight, she had scarcely given him a thought.

'No you're the one looking desperate. I know everything, you stupid whore. I know that Mestor refused to marry you because he wanted Secomb back and thought that by showing Secomb how clever and ruthless he could be that this would win him back. Only it all back fired and he had to leave the country in case too many questions started to get asked.'

'You know nothing, you lie.'

'Dear Aunt, I am my father's son and I do my homework, you should know better and play with the hand you were dealt with. You could have had such a wonderful life with Hector. He loved you so at one time. However, you messed that up. You messed with him and even now he doesn't know whether he loves his new wife or

Secomb.'

'What do you mean?'

'Secomb left you to go back to Mestor? Or was it to run away with the other brother he just happened to fall in love with?'

'You can't be serious?'

'Where was Secomb then and where has he been all this time? He certainly hasn't helped you at any time; yet he has helped Constance, why is that? Could it be because he cannot stand you?' He looked at her triumphantly. She looked away. 'Was it worth it? You have had so many chances. You gave away his precious child, who thankfully is so pure and true and not sick and tormented like you or your vile off spring.'

'You lie; you know nothing about my son. Nothing!'

'Again you under estimate me woman. I know that the boy you gave birth to is everything you are not and I would never, ever tell him who he really is. He is good and strong. He is loved, is in love, and is happy with life.'

She turned away from him, trying to imagine what he looked like. She had hardly given him a thought over the years. She had been so lost in herself.

'Is it possible that for once in your miserable life you could actually tell the truth and tell me that you encouraged them all to get rid of me and Nathaniel?' Lydia turned back to face him shaking her head and smiling.

'You want me to tell you about events that I have no real memory of? Dear, dear boy, you are like your father, you believe that everyone can be saved.' She laughed to herself thinking she had the upper hand now. 'Not everyone wants to be saved, but live for the moment. My pregnancy at that time, was a burden, it got in the way of me having a good time. That's what I wanted all the time. Every day and every hour. Do you really think I seriously thought about planning ahead? Did I want to live in that house with all those boring conventional people, who were so in love with each other? My God it was sickening to watch your mother and your father.' He did not like her speaking of his parents in any way. 'Oh so lovey dovey, when all I wanted was to escape and be fucked and liberated.'

He could not believe the filth that spilled from her mouth. 'People pretend to love to be empowered and take risks, but then when it gets a little too hot, they run like weaklings. Pathetic fools. We could have continued to have such fun.' She was lost in the past now, it was so vibrant in her memory, and so near she could almost touch it. She had been especially beautiful and loved by everyone. They all had wanted a piece of her and she had risen to the occasion and indulged excessively.

'No regrets then Lydia?'

'Hardly!'

'Maybe they saw how sick you really were.' Referring to how she was all on her own now.

'No.' She mused and after a fashion lost in her thoughts and physically calming, she added, 'It all went so horribly wrong when Mestor and Secomb lost interest.' She shrugged her shoulders. She wanted to speak and he would let her. She was giving him answers. 'They did not want to play anymore when it got a bit too...,'she smiled in memory at some of the more sordid aspects of her life, which she was not ashamed of. 'You see, we are all from the same cloth. We love danger and we sailed too close to the wind, and when one such as I, gives them what they wanted on a plate ....' She laughed wickedly, and then remembered her parent's servants snarling at her and saying she was the devils child. She had been born naughty. 'Most days, I was completely out of my head. I did what I wanted, when I wanted and with who I wanted.' She sat down drained of all energy now. Her voice was more hushed. She appeared to withdraw into herself. 'I have no recollection of my son, and I gave him no name!'

'Stop playing games.' Sentiment had never been strong with her.

'Does he know about me at all?' She was looking through Shem now, back at the fire, which needed some help. She cuddled herself.

'He has a family. I will not destroy that for him.' She accepted this and calmly whispered.

'Yes, I wanted your father out of the way and you and your brother. I wanted control. Only Mestor decided after all, that I just wasn't worth it and he wanted to return to his sordid affair and chase after his precious bloody Secomb.' Her shoulders dropped and she appeared to accept that it was time to confront the demons. 'He used me, my children and turned them into monsters that enjoyed their incestuous games.' He held his breath at that. 'And yes hurting Nathaniel.' It was out. She had said it. She closed her eyes and sighed in relief. 'Mestor was not a fool; he knew I only wanted him for the title, the security. But what he could not abide was that I was carrying Secomb's child. Mestor loved Secomb to death.' Nathaniel had been far too pretty for his own good, but did he really deserve that torment. Was it any wonder that Samuel was hell bent on revenge at the betrayal? She had deluded herself for years and now allowed herself to be sickened by herself and what she had done in order to get what she had wanted. 'Secomb opened the doors to all out desires, he manipulates and destroys and still he has so much power over all of us. My children see him as a friend.'

Samuel slowly walked around the bed.

She cuddled herself into a ball and let her tears fall freely now, realising that her bitterness at life was all her own making. Hector had been good and kind, why had it never been enough. Had she really been the Devil's child? Why had she enjoyed those things others said were wrong? Was she bad to the core? She had always been selfish and indulgent and really had no time to think on what her actions did to others. Was it all too late? She always thought people had been envious of her beauty and that's why they steered clear, in jealousy. However, she knew now it was because she was a horrible person.

'Just tell me his name.' Her mind kept going back to the baby boy who she had been dismissive of. With both Secomb and Mestor's rejections, the pregnancy had been a burden, an inconvenience which would be covered up and forgotten. As soon as the child had left the room, she had been planning who she could visit to see who was on offer in the marriage market. She had needed a new husband with titles and land, and did not care how far she would have to go to obtain. She had done it before, she could do it again. She would show them all. How stupid and selfish had she been and became? She was so tired of it all now.

Shem came to sit beside her on the bed and appeared to have lost all fight. He gave his Aunt a weak smile and softly reached down to touch one of her tears. He bent forward and with all the care in his voice, he could muster, he whispered.

'Rye, it mean's gentleman in Romani.'

'Rye.' She repeated and closed her eyes. She was so tired; the drink was taking its toll. She sighed and felt sleep try to engulf her whole being. Her boy would be in his teenage years now, tall and handsome with her vigour for life and Secomb's striking looks. She would make amends. Everyone deserved a second chance. Samuel's visit had not been so bad after all. She fell to sleep.

Shem smiled down at the woman sleeping and stroked her hair away from her face. How could someone blessed with such beauty be so sour and cause such hurt and deception? She really was nothing to him. His eyes had not turned back from black. He pulled a pillow from behind him. He puffed it up, casually turned back, and slowly lowered it across the sleeping woman's face.


'You're becoming quite the lady killer Shem. Almost one of those serial killers you read about in the pamphlets. You seem to have a thirst for it.' Mr. H was deliberately trying to wind Shem up. They had agreed to meet in one of Luca's beautiful new builds in Covent Garden. It was immaculate and oozed classical taste throughout. They met in the day room, which was a cowslip colour with massive bay windows to allow the light to flood in. Shem found himself focusing on the outside streets and escaping as quickly as possible.

He smiled as he saw his men patrolling outside, his mini army as Lord Lennard had remarked! They had all the streets guarded and blocked. No one was taking any chances. Mr. H, Luca, and Shem were all powerful and successful in their separate ventures. They were all now looking to go into more legal ventures, but none of them could quite yet cut the strings to their illegal activities. A war was simmering and everyone was on edge.

'I have to say, that the killing of my wife was rather ironic. Poetic justice and all that!'

'I expected Kebo and Pasha to report back.' Shem looked across at Bob, who had taken up a chair in the corner. He promised not to say a word.

'They have always been loyal to me Samuel.' Mr. H made a point of stressing that fact. Mr. H was annoyed that Shem was not more anxious. It wasn't too often that one of his Captains' had a visit from him. However, Shem had turned the South Coast into a blood bath and things were getting out of hand. He needed to tie up loose ends. He noted that Shem was still grinning. Did he know something that he did not?

'Lydia would never succumb to a divorce and wanted me to suffer for eternity for my roaming ways. She was a stupid bitch. I hope she suffered and pissed herself screaming.' Mr. H scorned looking into the burning fire and smiled at the thought. He was a man who genuinely loved woman and had fallen in love with Lydia Hartright Messacomb, the first time he had laid eyes on her. He had been bewitched and seduced into a relationship that was doomed. None of her family had told him of her failings and he had learnt the hard way. She had an evil jealous temper and fits of deep depression that left her almost disabled for months on end. She loved with a passion that was over powering, and had given him two children, that he had suffered for! She had been laid out for months with the pregnancies and had threatened to kill the unborn children she carried, and at one point, she had actually been stopped from throwing herself down the stairs. However, when the babies were born, her motherly instinct had taken over and she had become obsessed with her children. They were her world, they could do no wrong, and the love was possessive and sick. To him, she had turned into a hissing maniac.

He had never been an overly handsome man, just tall, with a commanding presence. Women were drawn to him and he had a way of making women feel that they were the centre of his world. He had an air of authority over him, he was charming and friendly, but to men, he was a ruthless calculating bastard, and he had an arrogance that made men dislike him. His hair was slightly thinning now, but retained its dark brown shine. He had dark eyes and full lips. Every movement of his was calculated and determined. He had always reminded Shem of a great general who masked his will with ease.

His dress had always been of the highest quality and today was no exception. He wore a full thick cloak lined with fur and his riding boots were of the finest leather. When Samuel and Nathaniel's mother had died, Mr. H's wife Lydia had promised to also help and take some of the responsibility for the boys. Samuel and Nathanial remembered their mother as a warm gentle woman very much like their Grandmother, The Dowager Theia Mordesan, but their Auntie Lydia treated them wretchedly. There had been no love there at all and it got worse when Hector, her husband had apparently died.

Hector Mordesan had allegedly died when returning from one of his business trips to France. He and crew had all perished in a dreadful storm that took the boat way off course, and the wreck ended up along the south coast of England, and far away from Falmouth, where it was supposed to dock.

Hector, alias Mr. H had planned a whole new life for himself in France. He did not intend to ever go back to his life, his home, or any titles or monies he could have potentially inherited. He had no remorse for the wicked way he had allowed his mother to assume he was dead, she had never deserved that and Shem could not understand how her trusted Gunthorpe had kept that amongst so many other secrets. He had wondered what Gunthorpe's gain out of all this was? However, when he saw the way he was passionate about protecting his grandmother from any form of hurt and harm, he knew the truth would have tortured her so. Hector had no heart and no remorse for his actions.

Whereas, his father, Troy, and brother had no had on their destiny. It had been believed they were all too lost at sea, rather than, as agreed by Gunthorpe, to let their Grandmother live with false hope. She was not to know that the boys would be found after being sold into slavery and that her righteous buffoon of a son, Mestor, was suspected of having his brother Troy killed, so he could inherit the title.

It had been agreed by all, that if the boys were found, that they needed to be protected until such a time, when they could stand on their own two feet. They needed influential people in their court to cement their claim. If they had been exposed too early, they could very easily still have been killed off, to satisfy the blood lust that Mestor or any other fortune hunter had.

Shem refocused on his Uncle, who had rescued him and who he had admired so much for saving his life. He was feeling guilty about being dishonourable to the man, who had given him back his life, but he saw it as a bit late in the day for Hector to feel guilty about leaving the woman he had married and hated, and the children they had. There was no love lost there at all.

Troy Mordesan, Shem's father, as head of the family, had immediately given Lydia assurances that she would always have a home at their hall and to never feel that she or her children would ever be discarded, when Hector had apparently died. What no one had planned was that she and her other brother- in- law were in cohorts to get rid of Troy and claim the estates for themselves. She wasn't looking forward to him looking for another wife and possibly more children to secure his line on the property. Lydia had wanted more! They had always been the assumption everyone concluded. However, Mr. H and Shem had more to discuss.

'You can't kill him, he is my son and under my protection.' Hector turned away from the warm comforting flames and commanded Shem about Hartright, his son's future.

'I'll fucking kill you if you get in my way.' Shem spat.

'I'll ignore that stupid comment.' Hector replied, he was his nephew and he could take a few liabilities but he was beginning to get out of hand and needed to be put back in his place. Hector rocked his leg up and down as he sat cross-legged. Lesser men would have had their throats ripped out for that lack of respect to him.

'Do you know what your children actually did?' Shem was finding it hard not to blurt out exactly what he had done to his precious cousin, but watching Hector's ignorance made up for any disadvantage he felt with this encounter, as it was panning out.

'You leave them alone. I think the score has been settled with the death of God knows how many people, along with Mestor and Lydia.' He rolled his eyes as if bored with the whole issue. 'Hartright and Constance were children and did not kill anyone.' He stated and usually by his tone, Shem would have recognised not to push any further.

'As good as.'

'Oh now, now, Shem, both of them are innocent.' Hector's whole manner was condescending. Shem knew he was lucky that Hector did not just cut him down and he was pushing his luck, he had every reason too. He had made a move, Hector was still none the wiser to it, and this empowered Shem.

'You taking the piss?'

'What more do you want?' Hector looked back hard at his nephew with just a hint of annoyance. 'I hunted down and killed all those bastards that murdered my brother on the beach that night and left Mestor for you. I searched for you and rescued you. I have provided and protected you. You now have a good living. You've had your revenge with Mestor. The Estate is being put back in your name.

No one knows your alias. You have other identities and can choose to be one or the other. Whichever suits your whim? You have a good cover story. You have your name and title back. The world awaits. What more do you want?' Hector made himself comfortable by leaning forward and tapped his fingers together. He looked deep into Shem's eyes. They had all suffered too much and at some stage, it needed to stop. His voice was fierce with warning. 'You will not touch one hair on their heads.' Shem wanted to laugh in his face. If only he knew!

'Even though you know they are vile misfits, and you expect me to leave that shit face alone after he killed my brother?'

'They are my misfits, not yours.' Hector repeated with malice.

'You're too soft.' Shem spat and threw himself back in his seat. He tried to calm himself and went to have a sip of his drink. Shem had recently acquired some of the best new chocolate drink and had started to import it via Luca. Shem decided that he did not really like it after all. His face did not need to turn sour, it already was. In fact, his whole day was turning out very disagreeable. The sooner he got home to Rosie and Seb the better.

'They haven't exactly had it easy with me leaving them when they were children.' Hector defended.

'Oh my heart weeps. Don't try to justify their behaviour because you left.' Shem was getting more and more angry. 'So it was alright for them to shag each other, then my brother and then to get rid of my father, so Mestor would not be exposed as a raving poof and having it away with his niece and nephew.' He just could not stop himself now. Enough was enough. 'It's alright for Hartright to rape my woman and kill my brother?' Bob had jumped up from his chair and held out his arms towards the pair of them, both had risen in temper.

'Shem no, Shem,' Bob was trying to look into Shem's eyes to make him see sense. But his eyes were black now. 'No, it's all lies about the hanky panky!' He said over his shoulder towards Hector.

'What did you say?' Hector was like a man hunting his prey, ready to pounce. He shook his head in denial. Bob looked at Shem with an expression of what have you done? The atmosphere had gone from frosty to freezing. Hector slowly moved his gaze to Bob for clarification. 'Why did you not tell me all of this before?' He

hissed, this all being too unreal to contemplate. 'All these accusations and lies...?'
He looked both questioningly and challengingly at Shem.

'Hector, I only found out......' Bob tried to explain.

'You fucking liar, we told you.' Shem interrupted. He made to go forward and Bob
shoved him back.

'Shem, please you were young, you'd been through so much, I thought....' Bob tried
to say.

'You thought we were making it up? Bob, making something sick like that up?'
Shem looked at him incredulously. Bob saw the raw hurt and bewilderment wash
over the man. 'So you thought Mestor's only motive was greed?'

'I can't say anything, I just assumed........' Bob was dumbfounded.

'I don't believe this. I don't believe this.' Hector was shaking his head in denial. It
was bad enough that both he and Shem had lost a brother by the hand of another
family member but now the added extra's, it was vile.

Shem was livid with frustration and Bob was trying to fathom out what next to say.
Hector needed to take a few minutes to calm down, looked back into the fire, and
was shaking in anger. Shem had fallen back into his chair. Bob was looking for help
and what to say to each of them.

Hector decided that the meeting was over and quickly made his way to the door.
He stopped, with his hand on the handle and said through gritted teeth. 'By God!
This isn't over yet, but I can't stomach anymore of this now. As I said Samuel,
leave well alone and we will talk again, and Bob I'll see you later.' He then left and
the slamming of the door boomed throughout the whole house and left both men
feeling as if doom was just holding off while they caught their breath.

For a long while, they just looked at the door. The fire crackled. The tension was
still rife. Shem was fuming and started to pace the floor. The meeting had not gone
quite as planned, but it would seem that Hector was none the wiser to what he had
done, nor was Bob.

'I don't need his permission.' Shem spat at no one in particular pointing at the
door.

'They're his kids.' Bob tried to reason.

'And they deserve to die.' Shem screamed, letting his emotions get the better of him, he had no remorse. He should have killed Hartright. 'Hartright molested my brother. When my Father confronted him, he denied it, said it was a pack of lies. They then went to Mestor and said that my father was going to disown him. My Father never let it be known that he despised Hartright and Constance. They were his responsibility but he hated them and that woman. That bitch had Mestor wrapped round her little finger. All of them were up to their necks in vile fucking sex fantasies, getting one up on each other and to fucking impress Secomb. They all got my father killed.' He stopped to breathe and wiped his brow. 'I thought you told him all this?' Shem glared at him incredulously. After all these years, was everyone still at mixed purposes?

'Don't do it Shem, let him sort it.' Bob tried to plead with him, but he could see that Shem had closed him out.

'I've waited too long and taken orders from that man for the last time.' Bob could not believe what he had just heard. How could he have lost his respect for him? He could not let Shem make a move. Hector would kill him. Hector was far more powerful than Shem could ever give credit for.

'He's your Boss.'

'Was my Boss!' Shem was torn, since his father's death he had been governed by so many, Bob, Hector, and Gunthorpe. With the protection of Kebo and Pasha who appeared to keep an eye on everything that happened. Everyone had spies watching other spies.

'Shem?' Bob was pleading.

'No, I have done everything he asked me. I have been patient, I have my name back now, and I am my own man. I do what I fucking want and if I say they die, they fucking die.' Shem had only told Bob and Mr. H what he wanted them to know about his trip. They believed he had just gone to Italy for revenge on Mestor. Both Kebo and Pasha were loyal to their adopted brother Hector and would die for him; but they had never had much time for their niece and nephew and had seen with their own eyes what had happened. They had helped Shem right a wrong and they would not tell Hector what hand they played.

'He will kill you.'

'Let him fucking try. You coming or staying?' Shem looked hard at Bob, searching his expression for any sign of loyalty. At least he had forgiven him. Bob sighed, was it all really forgotten? He doubted it; they all lived to avenge actions of yesterday! Shem was at the door.

'You seem to forget I am retired.' It was a cop out, there was a war coming, and he really did not want any part of it. Bob slumped into Hector's vacant seat by the fire. Shem turned and looked at him. Bob was an old man in a young man's world. He looked like he should just stay by the fire, light up his clay pipe and be waited on and looked after. Shem lowered his head in sadness.

'Look Bob. I'm sorry; I should never have put you in that position.' Shem replied in a softer tone. He sighed, knowing Bob was torn and he was not being wholly fair, but that's just what life was. He should not have asked, and he should let his friend just go. He had tried at the beach before he had left for Italy, but destiny had not allowed Bob to let go. Shem lowered his head to his chest and let out a huge sigh. How many more would he lose? He had to control this blackness that was even now creeping back in. He needed to see Rosie. His pixie's spirits had improved since their fight and every time he visualized her now, she had a golden glow all around her.

He went to Bob and smiled meekly at his friend, he threw out his arms, Bob raised himself up, and both wrapped their arms around each other. 'I do love you,' he whispered with a lump in his throat hiding his face into his friends shoulder. Bob slapped him on the back.

'I love you to pup.' They hugged tightly, then as quick as they had embraced they then parted and Shem walked out of door. Bob slumped back against the chair and wiped the tears from his eyes!

Shem shut the door to the house and motioned for his horse to be brought to him. Paully and Claude had been waiting with the horses and saw something new in their leader. He had a fierce determination and manner about him which ironically matched the stance of Mr. H, who had not since departed in his immaculate carriage, accompanied by many of his henchmen, all riding beautifully bred horses from Spain. The horses were smaller and more robust, and looked wonderful and shiny. Rafe would have been in his element.

As Shem mounted his horse, he just saw black, fire and had an uncontrollable urge to just destroy everything and everyone in his path. If people had not known, better they would believe that Satan no less was in their path. The heavens seemed to agree, and the sun disappeared for a time behind a dark black cloud. A thunderstorm was on its way.

## Chapter Seventeen

They had been travelling long and hard from Cornwall after seeing their mother and just wanted to get back to spend some time with their sister before they made the trip to the coast and back to France.

Hector had not been best pleased with them when they had met up after his meeting with Shem in London. He had accused them of siding with Shem, which they had desperately denied however not wholly been forthright with the truth. They would never tell him the truth and it was only Bob who had known them on the beach when Shem had left England, a few months ago.

They had told Hector that they were going to see their mother before their return and he had not once asked how she had faired when they last saw her. It was too painful for him and both Kebo and Pasha could not believe that he could be so cold and do something so wicked to their mother and let her believe he was dead. Then he had surpassed himself when they had told him about what had happened to their nephews. He had moved heaven and hell to get them and after months and months of searching, they had found them. Hector has been beside himself on keeping them safe and protecting them at all costs until they were strong and ready. As they had all agreed, it had been both Samuel and Nathaniel's decision as to what they wanted to do with their lives and if it were to avenge their father and get their home back, then that's what he would help them do. He had not relied on Samuel being so passionate about his revenge, along with making his own empire and with that discovering, he had power and the chance to make and shape matters. Hector would have loved to see such energy in his two first-born children, Hartright and Constance, but they had been too influenced by their mother. At least he had good strong son's now who were more than assets. He knew he had forged a new dynasty in them.

Kebo and Pasha had received word from Bob that he had become increasingly concerned, having seen their sister's husband, Theo in London at the time of the recent meet. On further investigation, it had been discovered that the Burwash gang, had met up with Hector, along with a further gentleman who was yet to be identified. Luca was looking into it further.

Before Kebo and Pasha had even reached the front of their sister Sade's flint stone house, she had come running out. She had no regard for the drizzling rain, and wore no shawl for protection. The tears rolled down her face and Kebo caught his sister in his arms. It had been too long and they all missed each other so much. Many were petrified of Kebo and his reputation was in many cases justified, and his little sister meant everything to him. It wasn't tears of joy alone at seeing them after so long, Pasha could see something was wrong. Sade had always been sensitive and it had previously worn on him how fickle she could be.

'What, what?' He feared the worst. Whilst still being held by Kebo, Sade grabbed Pasha's hand and squeezed it.

'Theo has taken Amelia and the twins to Hector. She went with him. My baby went. He has taken them with him back to France. They are going to live in France.' Sade cried through her tears.

'How long ago did he leave?' They all made their way into the house. Both the men tore off their oil clothed rain cloaks and made for the heat and light of the huge fire.

'She was happy to go; she was so excited. You can't imagine how it has been for her. Hector promised her a better life.' She had been cooking and offered them hot soup, which both were happy for. They made their way to the table with Pasha and Kebo feeling very uneasy. Any mother would be upset at her child leaving home naturally.

'He sent word to Theo yesterday and they left first thing this morning. I can't believe she has gone. I should have gone to the port myself, said goodbye from there. I did send word to Little Paully.' Little Paully had been torn between his loyalties to his father and staying with Shem, after the two had their disagreement. Rafe had been Little Paully's friend and he had no course to spy for his father or leave the service of Shem. The horses needed him and Rafe had taught him well. His mother understood this well, so he kept away from his father.

'My God! They will be long gone by now.' Sade saw the sheer panic in their faces and did not like the way the conversation was going. Both of her brothers looked to the heavens for help. She did not understand what was happening. She was so upset and knew that her brothers would comfort her for her lose. She had lost her baby and her new Grandson and Granddaughter, Raphael and Gabriella.

'He would not harm the children would he?' Pasha remarked looking intently at his brother.

'I don't know.' Kebo almost did not wish to say. Sade looked from one to the other. What was going on?

'Kebo?' Sade begun to panic. What was it with these two? All these questions? What were they not telling her? She was becoming more and more afraid. What had she missed?

'No, of course he would not.' He turned to Pasha snarling. 'This is leverage.' He realised.

'What do you mean leverage?' Why were they talking above her? Sade was working herself up into a state. Both men had come to the same conclusion and shared it.

'He thinks by taking the twins that Samuel will not touch his children. He thinks that having Mestor and Lydia would have been enough.' Pasha explained. Sade covered her mouth. What did this all mean?

'No. No I can't hear anymore.' She was becoming hysterical.

'We will get her back.' Kebo went towards his sister and rubbed his hands up and down her arms in comfort. He could not bear to see her so distraught. She had always been protected and looked after. His heart ached for her. She kept looking from one to the other.

'What have you done? Where have you been?'

'We have to go, perhaps there has been a delay, and we may get there in time?' Kebo stated to Pasha trying to convince them both. Pasha nodded in agreement.

'Time, what do you mean? I don't understand, you owe me an explanation!'

'Was this a sudden decision or had Hector put this on the table before?' Pasha stared at his sister returning his attention to her.

'I don't know.' Sade was crying and shaking. This was all too much. What did they mean?

'Mygar, Sade?' Pasha barked, he had never been patient. As soon as the words were out in that fashion, he wished he could take them back; he hated to speak to her in this way and wished with all his heart this was not happening.

'Theo was mazed. He said we would have to send her away.' She looked from her dark brother to her light brother with equal love and pleading to do something. Both went and held one of her hands to encourage her. Theo, like other fathers in the same predicament would not be happy that his most beloved un-wed daughter had got herself in bother and then to produce twins, so double the trouble!

'He was mad, mad as hell with Rafe and Shem. He said that it was all a game to Rafe. He said Rafe treated him like a fool. He had no real regard for our baby especially when he saw that Rafe had another woman with children living with him. They do not know who Shem and Rafe really are. I did not know either! You kept that so well hidden. I can't believe you played me and now I know. You let me believe that Samuel and Nathaniel were dead. Am I the only one who did not put two and two together? That hurts so. You made me look and feel like a fool.' She lowered her head in sorrow. 'All this time, such a lie. Did Rafe know who I was, he must have. I remember he used to suddenly just appear, I would see him watching me and did not realise it was him. Then he would disappear. Why did he say nothing? Why would he do that? He must have known that I would never have exposed him. I loved that boy. That was cruel.' Her mind went to better times and she remembered the day she had left home to be with Theo all those years ago.

'My God! You have not let on?' Pasha groaned.

'Do you really have to ask?' There were so many secrets for her to carry. It had been agreed to never tell her that the boys had been found and were the notorious troublesome lads down the south coast. Therefore, Sade's family was none the wiser.

As far as Theo, Harry and Idris knew Mr. H was Sade's half brother and had assumed that there had been a scandal and that Sade had to be placed somewhere, as far away as possible to avoid any further rumours. The fact that two mysterious men visited her every few years was not strange. They would often bring her post and as soon as she had read her letters from her mother, she would hide them away.

She remembered the excitement years ago when Kebo and Pasha had come to fetch her before she had moved to the coast and married Theo. They had arranged to take her to France on a holiday to see their homes. It had been so exciting and they returned on Harry Hawkins little frigate and on that journey she had met and immediately fell head over heels in love with Theo, Harry Hawkins's son. She had never returned to the Hall, and witnessed Lydia's destruction of it.

When her mother had settled in Croxley, she had made an effort to visit her. Theo had been told that her mother had been left a small house in the country and she had never filled him in on every aspect of her previous life. She knew that they all thought of her as a bastard child who needed to be displaced, and in their mind, fate had dealt them the same hand with Amelia.

'No, I should have known better.' He whispered in comfort. 'I am sorry but really, only a few knew, Sade.' Pasha tried to sound kinder and hoped his new words gave some assurance. 'The other woman's name is Daisy. Rafe never loved her, Sade. He loved Amelia.' He tried to reassure her.

'You can't know that for sure. Rafe was a womaniser. Nathaniel, whatever he called himself, even as a child was a charmer. He had Annatasia around his little finger.'

'Mygar woman he was besotted with Amelia. All he ever spoke about was going home and taking her with him.' Pasha lied and Sade closed her eyes and saw her home before her. She missed them all desperately and she wished her mother was there now.

'What about the other woman, this Daisy, and his other bastard children?'

'Do not concern yourself with her. She is of no consequence. Samuel will always provide for her, as would he still for Amelia if allowed. This Daisy, she has no spirit, she is weak. She is not like Amelia.' Kebo stated and Pasha asked.

'When was Amelia approached to go and live with Hector?'

'He was here a few weeks ago.' Sade cuddled herself and shook her head in disbelief at all the events. 'He promised her the world, a new identity, a cover story so she would be accepted, the children to have no blemishes. A new start. He promised her the world.' She sighed and tried not to continue to cry so freely. 'It was so lovely to see him; I know I was sworn to secrecy about him. It is so sad, our poor mother. All these secrets, it's too much to bear. Hector was always so good to me, he loves me, and he would not hurt my baby. He is looking out for her. I can't hate him.' She stopped to wipe away her tears and tried to compose herself. 'He then came back to see if she had made her decision.' She closed her eyes, not believing that Hector would dupe her so. He had always confided in her as a child and she had been the one he had come to discuss his plans to pretend that he had been killed at sea, so that he could start a new life and be happy. She had been the one to confront him with all the negatives of his actions, and her whole argument had always been on the side of the children he would leave behind.

She had said no good would come of it and time had showed her that that was indeed the case. How could they have kept his secret over all these years, seeing how his selfishness had destroyed his children? Who in turn had no hearts, and just followed his example, showing their own selfishness and greed to succeed in their warped minds, and not caring who they hurt along the way. She knew Hector had another family, more children, he rarely mentioned them, what was their fate?

'I cannot believe it!' Pasha turned on his heels looking to the sky realising that Hector had fooled them all.

'What?' Sade asked.

'He had it all planned. He is always one step ahead.' Kebo looked directly at Pasha.

'We need fresh horses now.' He crushed back the kitchen chair, so angry with himself for not believing that Hector could stoop so low. He stormed out and could be heard shouting to the stable hands to get the horses ready. They jumped to attention. Sade pulled on Pasha's sleeve.

'What do you mean?' Pasha stopped and looked down at her. He bent down, kissed her on the forehead, and lovingly circled her face with his hand remembering the first time he had set eyes on the girl. She had been in the depths of the ship, it was as black as coal, and all he saw had been the whites of her eyes, with glistening tears that looked like floating diamonds, pleading with him. Her little hand had stretched out to him and then he had just grabbed and pulled her to him. She had been so small, and then she had withered like a snake in his arms and begun calling and pointing back. It was then he saw Kebo face down with blood all over his head. She had scrambled down and the pair of them had managed to get Kebo free of the carnage. They had all been on a ship, which had been attacked. Kebo had wobbled and fell as they had ascended to the top deck, which had been like bedlam. Everyone was panicking and screaming as the ship was under attack. It was as if they moved in slow motion, dogging the fighting, staggering against the heat of the fires and choking as the wind whipped the smoke towards them. The air was thick with smoke and their ears rung with the boom of cannon, gun blasts, and men screaming in pain and victory. He remembered grabbing whatever he could and wrapping robes around all of them and then they all knew what they had to do. Without any hesitation they had climbed, the side of the ship and within seconds were hitting the cold water desperately holding on to the ropes and each other.

'Get a message to Shem to explain what has happened now. And Sade, listen to me, listen.' She stared into his eyes. 'You must trust no one. It goes without saying, but we keep our business to ourselves. Take your children and go home. Mother is expecting you to visit; she has the Hall back now. Go home Sade. We need to get Amelia and you back under Shem,' he corrected himself, 'God! Samuel's protection, as soon as possible. I need to know you will do this? Gunthorpe will know what to tell Mother.'

'What do I tell Theo? I just can't go home. I can't just go. The business, the ....'

'For God's sake woman. Now do as I say, now, please go home.' She hugged deep into him and they clung onto each other so tightly, she seeing how desperate it had become. 'Benatugana.' He whispered and kissed her forehead. She wished him back, 'God bless.'

Kebo then came back and took his precious sister in his arms and that cuddle told her that he would move heaven and earth to get to the bottom of what really was happening and that his niece would be safe. He kissed her goodbye and then mounted his horse. Sade saw him tut to himself in frustration. He had forgotten after all the commotion that he had a letter for her in his sidesaddle, which he untied. Pasha smiled at that and they both looked at Sade as she leant up to take the letter. She saw her mother's writing and smiled up at them in thanks, hugging the letter tightly to her. She watched and waved as they thundered away. They came and they went, always their visits so quick, like a flash and then they were dust disappearing from view.

She bowed her head in sadness; she felt so much sorrow and emptiness. She was drained but she had no time to tally, she had been given a command and whatever Kebo and Pasha ordered, she would do. Her husband's love had waned and she had suffered enough. She needed her mother's comfort and love.

'When he gets wind, he will kill them.' Pasha voiced the unthinkable when they were resting much later having agreed that Hector would depart from Rye.

'No, he would not do that to us.' Kebo could not believe that Hector would kill his own sister's daughter and her children in revenge for what Shem had done to Hartright, once he found out his fate. He knew his brother and how he worked. Hector had always been selfish.

'Kebo, he will have his revenge and he will kill to make a point.'

'If he harms any of them, I will kill him.' Kebo pledged. 'We should not have let Shem take it this far.'

'It was that or let him kill the fool. This way at least Hector will know there is hope that the imbecile Harry can be rescued.'

'If he still lives. Men do not last long on the slave galleys.' They both sighed and each rested for a time lost in their own thoughts about happier times in their youth. They had taken shelter and watched as the rain whistled down, fighting now against the wind!

Pasha dreamt of them all playing cricket on the lawn at the side of their old house, it had been a glorious summer day. His mother and father were laying on the lawn tickling each other in glee. The man he called father, the man who had plucked them from the sea after his vessel had been the one to wreck the one they had been previously on. Pasha remembered the mighty man looking at the three waifs and strays and laughing loudly.

'Got myself richness there that no man can deny. Three little darlings and no mistake my loves.' He had showered them completely with love from that moment and not a day went by when they did not feel the love of the whole family and that very special man.

He remembered the competitive athlete Troy with his curly hair. Hector, elegant and sleek, always being umpire and then the fat Mestor, who had been so clumsy. He would go to catch a ball and all would just shake their heads knowing that he would no doubt drop it. He was useless and one of the last to ever be picked for any team. Pasha remembered that with any game, Kebo run around like a lunatic, all-excitable and trying to play every position. Gunthorpe would always play and his word was final no matter what Hector said. Sade would just fuss around and get in everyone's way and like Mestor, be there just to make up the numbers but always trying to ensure that everyone was looked after, and then she would cry thinking she wasn't appreciated. They had been wonderful times.

Kebo's dreams took him across the waters, to his home in France. He had been planning for a long time to move back home to England. Now was the best time to get out of France and invest his money in the new business of mining with Shem, as well as enjoy the success of his American investments. He and Pasha had a vast network of merchants and so called pirates that they had done rather well out of. He saw his wife as clear as day, all five feet of her. She was so small to his massive frame, but she commanded him with just a look. He needed to make her safe and he needed her to meet his mother.

Then as quickly as Kebo and Pasha had rested both automatically got up, they laughed at themselves, they were so in tune, and they did not even need to speak at times. They now also shared the anticipation of the future and wished to every God on earth, that Shem did not play into Hectors hand and make a further move. Hector baited people and Shem, although smart, was no match for the experience and cunning of his Uncle.

God they hoped with all their hearts, Amelia, Theo, Raphael, and Gabriella would walk away from all this mess.

'You saw Harry get on the ship and leave?'

'Blessed be God, you are so tedious.' Secomb yawned as his friend asked him again. Secomb had the ability to always look highly bored at everything. He kept his wicked sense of humour well hidden and kept his voice low and hardly ever-showed emotion. He spoke in quick short quips and his pronunciation was exquisite. He was immaculately dressed. He always smelt wonderful and wanted to always look his best. His hair had started to grey, so he had shaved it to an inch of its life and wore a beautiful white wig. He had young blue eyes that glowed. His whole appearance deflected from the real man and his agenda.

'It doesn't feel right.'

They both stood on the top of the beach looking out to the party who were boarding the small frigate, which bobbed up and down on the surf. The day was rather grey and there was a persistent drizzle. Hector was impatient to leave and get home. He was tired and needed time to reflect and plan ahead for what would come. He sighed for it all. Shem had unnerved him.

'She is a beauty.' Secomb purred.

'Hands off, she is my niece!'

'Not by blood!' He further teased.

'She is family.' Secomb heard the smile in his voice.

'If you thought that much of her, she would not be here!' He retorted. Hector did not like that, but Secomb was a man he trusted. Both of their eyes returned to Amelia.

She was a pretty little thing and the image of her mother, Sade. She had no idea how much power her twins held. Hector grinned at that. He was just disappointed that he could not get all of Rafe's other children as well. However, Shem had Pevensey so tied up with security that gone, were the days when anyone could walk into the village without raising an eyelid.

Hector mused that it was a shame he had not been so careful with Shem and Rafe, and held a firmer grip. Now he looked on the loyalty of Bob's family in Burwash to do his bidding!

Theo had been persuaded and seen sense that his daughter would be best served moving away and starting a fresh. As far as Theo was concerned, Shem and Rafe had produced too many bastards for his liking and whereas his father was neutral and his Uncle Bob's loyalty was wholly with Shem it would appear, his was not! Theo had no allegiance to Shem and his gang, even though they had been more than good to him; he was now in league with Hector. Theo would love to see the expression on Shem's face when he realised that he had been hoodwinked.

'You seriously believe that this will kerb the upstart?'

'He is too big for his boots. I tried to bring him down a peg or two but I underestimated him.' Hector declared. Hector was not a man who liked to lose at anything. He left a bitter taste in his mouth. He sighed.

'I hope you are right.'

'I know my nephew. Family is everything to him.' Hector was aware that he was trying hard to convince himself and he realised he did not know his nephew at all.

'I would have gone for his off spring and not Rafe's.'

'This is the next best thing. But there are always opportunities afoot.' Hector rocked on his heels and Secomb laughed.

'You dog!'

'Always have a plan B.' He laughed. 'And C and D.'

'You expect him to yield that easy?'

'No I expect Kebo and Pasha to do that.'

'Why should they stay loyal to you?'

'Because they now the same fate awaits their families and should I really have to, I can destroy them and their businesses.'

'You have them?' Secomb stated impressed.

'Of Course!'

'You sly, sly dog.'

'Plan C, D and E.' Hector was milking every moment.

'You would not seriously hurt any of them?'

'No.' The answer was direct.

'So how?'

'They don't know that. But....I have them, that is enough.' Before he had left, he had sent out invites for a family get together and his extended family even now where on their way to his lands for a welcome to Amelia, but really for their own protection! They would come willingly, having been told that Kebo and Pasha would meet them there; they had no reason to disbelieve.

'Could you win against an all out assault?'

'It will never come to that. Plan C involves having Meir call in the debts.'

'What if your mother finds out everything?' Hector did not answer. He could never allow that to happen, or ever be a threat. Why did Secomb suddenly bring that up? Did he think that he was wholly naive to his agenda in all of this?

'Would you do that to me Secomb?' Hector looked directly into his eyes.

Secomb tapped his walking stick at the pebbles beneath his feet. His walking stick was not needed; it was just a fashion accessory with a hidden sabre. He sadly smiled and shook his head.

'All these lies, deceit. It does sometimes become quite tiresome! Would Shem use that against you?' He deflected. Hector sighed inwardly and become more convinced that Secomb had too many secrets and needed to be watched even more than he was currently.

'What else can we do, I'll not be mocked, as was Mestor?' He chose to ignore the comment about Shem and play along with Secomb and his games.

'Poor Mestor.' Secomb stretched the words out and contrary to what he said; he had no remorse for the man. He was ancient history and long since gone from his life. His little affair with Mestor had been fun, but more serious on Mestor's part than his. He had not realised that by ending it with Mestor that things would spiral out of control and lead to Mestor's obsession to prove how he could achieve anything he had his mind to and had single handily organised the killing of his eldest brother for a family title and the abduction of his nephews. Mestor had then moved to Italy where his lifestyle had been more acceptable and he could indulge all his fancies and be happy, and he had not given stuff for what he had done. It had been Hector's duty to then try to find his nephews. Secomb rather liked how he had played all of these men and how they had bent to his whim. It had been all rather entertaining but he found he lost interest all too quickly.

For Hector, it was all he could do, to right the wrong that he had laid on his mother. He had deliberately planned his own death in order to start a fresh and get away from his wife and children. In that he knew he would have to leave all those he loved behind. Only his sister Sade, who he had confided in, had let it slip to his brothers Pasha and Kebo and before he knew it, they were with him in France.

He could not bear to hurt his mother even more and felt it would be best not to shock her by discovering that he was indeed alive. She, as far as she was aware all her natural children were dead, and she wasn't exactly close to any of her grandchildren. If he thought of her alone, he could not control the guilt, but seeing her face with disappointment at him, he could never bear. He sometimes tried to convince himself that it was because he loved her too much, that he could not hurt her anymore. He had been informed she wasn't well and her memory was failing.

He hated to think of her suffering so.

'Mestor was a fool. A stupid, fat fool! Don't pity him.' Hector had given it all up for a life of his choosing, not anyone else's, he was his own master, and nothing would destroy it.

'Never, as long as you know what are you doing? I'll be by your side always!' Secomb declared wholeheartedly.

'I'd expect nothing less.' They stared at each other sharing many things in that look. Hector knowing full well that Secomb had been playing him for years and Secomb thinking, Hector was so gullible. However, both agreeing that there was still that spark between them and those stolen moments could not be easily given up. But Shem knew and every day his intelligence brought him more and more power.

Bob reflected that much of his time was spent on the beach, watching people come and go from his life. He loved the beach; it was one of his favourite places in the whole world. No two days were the same. The tide would come in and out and would be repeated throughout the course of the day, ever changing the layout, be it that shingle banked in different places, and heavier stones were deposited in different places to expose the sand. Sometimes the sea was a beautiful turquoise colour, sometimes grey and miserable. The contrasts were endless.

He was supposed to be retired, but the call of adventure was too much. Of course, he could settle down and enjoy his winter years; maybe he could ask a certain person to share it with him.

Bob looked out to sea and watched his brother's small frigate sail effortlessly away heading for France with Hector and Amelia on board. The parting had been hard for Theo who had walked back up the beach with head on his chest when the party had got going. Lord Secomb had settled in his carriage and was soon off after having words with Theo, who then turned back and looked back at him. Bob wasn't one to dislike many people, but he did not like or trust Secomb, and the feeling was mutual.

Hector had told him that he was taking his Niece back to France with him, and her Grandfather Harry, his brother, would see that she was settled before his return. It did not rest well with Bob, but who was he in the scheme of things to judge? Hector had requested his presence to say good-bye and watch over a load that had been brought in and help it on its way and then watch as his brother and nephew saw Amelia off. Shem would be livid at the turn of events, but Theo was Amelia's father and it was his decision and he was sure he had best intentions for her.

Hector had a good life across the water. He had a lovely estate, a beautiful woman, and some good-looking lads of his own. He chuckled at that, he was making plans for Amelia and match making and she was not even his. He wished her all the happiness in the world. He always dreamt of happy endings but could not see one for Shem until he had avenged everyone and found Hartright! He chewed on his unlit clay pipe and wallowed for a brief moment in Shem's misery and heartbreak at losing Rafe. *Oh Rafe!* Bob choked back the tears. After all these months, it still got to him.

'Silly sod.' He said to himself, he felt he had failed the boy. He had loved him and God he missed the pup. He would be so proud of all his children and the twins were adorable.

Hector had arranged with Bob and Harry Hawkins to meet him on the beach at Cuckmere after he had made one of his normal runs to France and back. Ned and Ray had immediately alerted Shem.

Once the cargo had been unloaded, Amelia and her twins were first to be rowed to the small vessel which would take her away for a whole new life. It had all become quite emotional and Theo had not been able to let his daughter go and Bob had to subtly intervene which had choked him to watch.

Bob kept worrying that he needed to see Shem and put matters right and tell him directly that he had been at the rendezvous when Amelia went to live with Hector in France. He owed him that much. He could not leave it like that. In fact, who was he kidding? He could not leave him. Shem was family and Shem would know anyway. Shem still needed him, and God he needed Shem. He had served his purpose with Hector. Bob had property out towards Eastbourne, which nestled just the other side of the South Downs and was a stop gap before Pevensey and Shem. He'd pop over during the week, it had been a few days's since their last meeting with Hector in London, and the dust had settled.

Bob found himself waving one last time at the disappearing boat and then he turned slightly having heard the crunch of footsteps on the beach behind him.

'I am not that old that I need the company or help getting back up the beach. You know what I mean?' He moaned with a smile when he saw both Theo and Idris heading back towards him. He thought that after the Goodbyes that both would have been long gone. They had shared a joke or two earlier, one of them had been laughing at him and his bandy legs. Both Theo and Idris laughed nervously at that and each stood either side to him. There was something about their manner he did not like, it unnerved him. Then he remembered Hector's last words to him before he left.

'You should have taken retirement when you could old man; you should not be out in the cold.' That's when it dawned on him. He sighed to himself and taking his pipe, he placed it in his top pocket and padded it. How could it come to this? He looked at the sea before him with all its majesty, smiled, and nodded to himself. He swallowed hard and smiled meekly. Such was life. For the most part, it had been good!

'Hector thinks otherwise Uncle.' Theo lunged forward and grabbed him in an embrace and at the same time while Bob went to push away, Theo plunged a dagger deep into his stomach. How could Hector, ever have got Theo to do this? Theo was shaking from head to foot, but he held his Uncle firm to him and biting his lip, he stabbed him again. The blood oozed over his hands. He screamed inside and tried to hold his Uncle tightly, but Bob was as strong as an ox and managed to push away. Bob was too weak. They looked into each other's eyes and Theo saw sorrow, disappointment, acceptance, and regret. Theo cuddled him to him. Bob desperately held on with all his might. He found he could not feel his fingers. They were numb. He felt the life suck away. He slowly fell to his knees. He looked up at Theo and tried to smile. A tear found its way and trickled down his cheek. The world was turning black before his eyes. He swayed. His body slumped.

Theo turned away, feeling bile build up in his throat. He could not believe it had come to this? He would not let the man go and only after a tug from Idris did he lay his Uncle down on the pebbles, as gently as he could.

He knelt beside him and shivered feeling his whole front soaked to the skin, with his Uncle's blood. He swallowed back the bile. He looked down at Bob and rocked back and forth in grief at what he had done. He laid his hands on him and felt he was still so warm to the touch. He leant forward and gently stroked his face. He swallowed back the lump in his throat but could not stop the tears rolling down his face. Why did they have to succumb to this? Why did he have to do this? He felt like his heart was breaking. He ripped his coat off and covered Bob with it. Was this really worth it? He turned away and vomited.

'You fucked him and us over mate.' Idris whispered into the night, he crouched down and sadly looked at his lost friend, and felt hollow inside, and he too felt a twinge of bitterness that it had come to this. He too fussed over his friend and made him comfortable. 'Goodbye mate.' The tide pulled away and the night crept in with the misty cold. They silently turned to leave with Idris helping Theo up the pebbled beach and headed back towards the cloaked figure of Benedict Hunter who had now appeared. He wore a smirk of satisfaction on his weathered face and spat in contempt.

'Stand and deliver.' He roared at which all his men rolled over and started to laugh at the absurdity of the expression that many poets and newspaper articles were saying was the shout of the local highwayman. Shem tried to contain himself and not giggle.

They stood on the road to Brighton by Birling Gap and had been given the nod that a coach was coming their way. The Lady Constance had recently received word that her mother had been taken ill. She had been visiting Lady Barbara Skelton at Herstmonceux, and was returning home via the main London Road from Brighton. The more direct route, the Wartling Road was impassable apparently due to the poor weather.

Constance had deliberately collapsed in shock at the news of her mother and wanted nothing more than for the woman to die. She wanted the attention on her alone and so everyone had bent over backwards to ensure she was comfortable. They had even sent a messenger back to her home to enquire on Lydia's health, and Shem had ensured that the staff had been paid well to respond, that Constance should make tracks home in haste. Only then, after a few days of complete bed rest, had Constance found the strength to get her things together and endure the trek. She had heard no other news, and waited desperately to hear from her brother, who Secomb had told her was half way across the ocean, heading for his new life. She longed to see Hartright, missed him so, and could not wait to hear from him. Surely, he would ask her to join him there. Why not? There was nothing here now for her. She thanked God for Secomb and his resources.

Shem stood firm in the centre of the road with pistol cocked and aimed at the approaching coach, whilst his men stood to the side of the road holding onto their horses. They could see he was just about holding it together and they all put their hands over their mouths to try to stop laughing. This, after all, was serious business!

Tom O'Sullivan, the driver of the coach, also suppressed a grin and slowly drew up the reins to his horses. He nodded at Shem and put his hands into the air, in surrender, knowing full well who he was.

The gang knew that Tom would offer no resistance, as the previous evening he had been merrily drinking with Paully and Claude and had accepted his new offer of a driving position for the gang, and knew he was on a good earner.

'What's happening?' An insistent voice called within the coach.

Shem swaggered forward and winked at Tom, who casually flung the horses' reins to Paully; he then jumped down from the coach and let Paully take his place. Paully loved driving coaches and was itching to go. Tom peaked his cap, and then caught the monies, which one of the other men had flung, and headed back to town.

'Mr. O'Sullivan, I demand to know what is happening.' Still there came no answer and the gang heard the voice inside scream. 'Maisy, see what is happening this instant.'

'But ma'am.'

'Don't ma'am me, I'll tan your hide, get out.' At which the coach door was opened from the outside and Shem put his head in.

'Morning ladies.'

'Oh my God, ma'am,' Maisy panicked and hitched her legs up to shield herself in fright.

'Maisy would you be so good as to leave the coach, I need to talk with the Lady?'

Shem almost spat the last word out. Maisy turned to her mistress in concern, she was hesitant about what to do, and feeling that at any moment, she would faint. How did he know her name?

'Don't you go anywhere?' The Lady roared defiantly. At which point Shem produced a pistol and aimed it at the very beautiful Constance Mordesan. Maisy decided that she had best do what the man had said, and managed to stand up. Shem took hold of her arm to steady her, as he could see she was shaking and was bound to fall over. He noticed the other arm was bandaged and tutted in annoyance that the poor thing had suffered.

Slowly she climbed down from the vehicle and was immediately placed in the hands of other dangerous looking men. They seemed to surround and engulf her. She was petrified. She squealed and tried to pull back, but then a familiar person winked at her and she found herself facing Claude, who just squeezed his arm around her tightly and led her down the hill, away from the coach. 'Now you're a pretty thing, what you doing working for a dragon like that?' He teased. 'Don't worry; we are not going to hurt you.' She suppressed a knowing grin and pinched him under his chest. Claude was such a rascal and she knew everything was going to be all right. God! How she had missed him so.

Shem climbed aboard the coach and banged the side at which the coach lurched forward.

'What is your business? I have no money or anything of worth on me.' He looked across at Constance and found that he felt nothing for her. He thought he might, but there was nothing, just a mild irritation that he had once quite liked her. She was dressed all in red. He found that fitting. She looked radiant!

'You don't recognise me Constance? He remarked in his normal voice, uncocking the pistol and calmly placing it to his side, away from her. She flinched at his forwardness in using her first name.

She watched his every move and then looked back to his face. She leant back in the cushions and studied the man; He was rough looking, a rogue with a glint in his eye. He carried himself well, she liked what she saw. Her confidence grew; no respectable highwayman would dare brave a robbery without concealing his identity. He was obviously high born from his tone and manners.

'So we have met, I can hardly think where, I am not one to venture into squalor.' She purred. He laughed at her nerve.

'Ever the bitch.'

'Now, now that's not nice, insulting me when I do not know you.' She drawled.

'Oh you know me. Look closer.' She looked him all over and saw nothing that could help, and was conscious that she should be scared, but he had put her to ease.

'Are you kidnapping me for ransom?'

'Oh no, something far more exciting!'

'Oh do tell, it's all really too much, it's killing me?' He laughed again at the irony and her sarcasm.

'I thought you'd like to be smuggled on to a ship and sent across to Africa for the slave markets, they like your colour hair. And let's be honest you'd be good at your job, having had loads of practice. You do like a good seeing too, don't you?' Constance did not like the vulgar turn and he watched as she slightly re-positioned herself on the seat. 'Oh, did I touch a nerve? You don't like that idea for yourself, but was prepared to send others there?' He left it hanging and watched as her face drained of colour.

'No.' She half whispered.

'Yes.' He mimicked with a snarl back and watched as she clenched her fists, she then pounced forward with claws out, hoping to scratch his eyes out. He swiped her arms aside and followed through with a slap across her face. She backed up and then swung forward with a punch that he avoided and then with the back of his hand, he slapped her again, at which her nose burst and blood poured down her face. God! He had wanted to batter her senseless, but had to keep his nerve. Her glance could have killed lesser men.

'What have you done? What have you done?' She screamed, and in a rather unlady like fashion wiped her nose with the back of her hand. 'I hate you. I hate you.'

'It's mutual darling.'

'My brother will kill you for this?'

'Oh I wouldn't count on that happening any time soon!' He laughed. 'I seem to recall he tried to kill us before. What makes you think he will succeed this time?'

'He will rip your heart out.'

'Ohhh, stop being so dramatic.'

'As God as my witness, he will kill you for his, you just wait.'

'Just shut the fuck up, you stupid bitch. Did you really think that you would get away with what you did to me and Nathaniel?'

'So this is revenge, for sending you away. Looks like we have done you a favour. Look at you Samuel,' she laughed at that. 'It is you isn't it Samuel?' Her face was ugly when she was angry. 'You are a man now, a rogue, a powerful man very much in charge.' She spat the words out, pulled out her handkerchief, and started to wipe away at the blood, which had continued to flow from her nose. 'So you hold me for ransom, and Hartright pays you back!'

'No Constance, you misunderstand. There is no pay back.'

'There is always pay back.' She roared at him. 'Oh my God, is this all so you get your title back? Well that's not going to happen, Uncle Mestor has declared Harry, Harry is all the rage, successfully sorting out that smuggling problem. That arrest warrant will disappear once he has brought you to justice. It all fits. You are the notorious Shem Smith alias Samuel Mordesan and oh, I forgot, the Frenchman, St Clements. Do you honestly think that Uncle Mestor will hand it all back to you? My God he hated you.'

'Hartright sorting out the smuggling problem, what alot of shit you talk Constance? You really don't know anything.' How could she be so deluded?

'Oh Samuel, it's only a matter of time before the fat bastard keels over with a heart attack. My God that Nancy cannot live that long with his life style in bloody Italy, so naturally Harry is the next in line.'

'Don't tell me you haven't been across to Italy and tried to kill him yourself yet? God you are slipping Constance. But then he doesn't need to disappear and let your little secret out, does he? By successfully getting rid of Nathaniel and me, you played a good hand. I have to say well done for that one. Pity you did not consider the finer details, but then that has not always been your strong point has it? You were always a selfish thick bitch.'

'Oh poor Samuel, so bitter! Do tell, was you buggered by the ship's crew?'

'I can see you really get off on that, don't you? How much do you charge? You sick cow?' He winked at her. 'But here I am.' His mocking ceased. 'Alive and now only too ready, to tell the world how we caught you fucking your brother and oh our fat Uncle too.' She did not bat an eyelid. Hector would be mortified at the whole truth. 'So now the revenge? So what do you have planned then my darling Cousin?' She was not defeated yet and she would never yield to her cousin the Right Honourable Samuel Mordesan. She, her brother, mother and Uncle had understood that they had disposed of their cousins. That they had supposedly been kidnapped and sold into slavery so that neither Samuel nor Nathaniel could be in the running for the family title and to tell the world what they had stumbled on. They had meant nothing to her. Her brother was her life, she loved him dearly, and with a bit of cunning, she would have Samuel, or whatever his name was now, eating out of her hand. She had always fancied that he had more than liked his beautiful older cousin when they were younger.

'I thought we'd play a little game before I make my final decision.' The coach stopped. She laughed at his suggestion or lack of it and thought he was not so hard, rather slow, weak, and indecisive. She looked out of the coach window and smirked not knowing what went through his mind.

Shem smiled to himself and would enjoy seeing the expression on Hector's face when he learned that Shem had been playing him while he had planned against his own nephew. Hector was so predictable and Shem had known what he would do, and even now had people watching his every move, it was only a matter of time before Kebo and Pasha would get wind and attempt to rescue Rafe's children and Amelia. Shem had friends everywhere and if Kebo and Pasha were unsuccessful in getting them back, then his friends would not be.

Hector had not considered one thing and that was that Shem knew the shame Hector carried. If Hector's mother were ever to find out he was alive and what he had done to her, he could not live with that. Therefore, he would not knowingly or actually cause the deaths of any of her family and those she loved; he could not tarnish his memory to her. Nevertheless, his actions had started everything. He had deluded himself for his own pleasure.

Shem had no such qualms.

'Perhaps a spot of cricket, hey old girl?' He mocked remembering also those hazy summer days back at Mordesan Hall playing cricket and enjoying each other's company. She looked at him in disgust.

The coach door was flung open, Shem handed the pistol through the door to the waiting Paully and still facing his cousin, he backed out of the coach. He signalled for her to get out. She leant forward deliberately showing off the fullness of her breast.

'Or perhaps some flying.' He remarked. He looked across the sea view, spread out his arms, and stretched his whole body. Feeling the fresh air and smiling at all its glory. The wind danced with his hair and cloak. He winked at Paully.

'Flying did you say, I hate flying, - flying as in- kites, is it?' She was not amused and watched as he twirled round and round madly making himself dizzy. She saw that he was really a damn fool. The sooner she got out of here the better.

'Who said anything about flying kites?' He whirled back to her and as quick as a flash grabbed her by both hands and yanked her forward. He pulled her from the coach and swung her into his arms. She felt his power, which was rather arousing. He smelt wonderful but she also felt a little apprehensive, her cousin was stark raving mad!

'What are you playing at man?' He had brought her out of the coach and she looked across and saw they were a hundred or so yards away from an Alehouse. She had heard of it, the Beachy Head, at the end of the world. God, he was going to hold her up in an Alehouse!

Shem carried her forward, and then sharply turned away to the left, she started to struggle and tried to free herself and fling herself away from him, all the while looking at his fierce face. Paully stood lost as to what was happening.

'This isn't funny now, let me go and tell me what it is you want.' She was a little frightened and could not look away from his eyes. Her struggling ceased. Paully was frozen to the spot.

'To see if you can fly.' At which point he tightened his grip on her and as quick as a flash, lifted her up and with all the might, he could muster, he flung her away from him. She tried to grab him back, but his push away had been too powerful, she did not once stop looking at him. Then she knew!

'Bye, bye.' He mocked in memory of his Uncle. He waved and watched her disappear over the cliff edge. The wind took her screams away.

Paully was in shock. He rather gingerly came to stand by Shem's side, slowly and hesitantly they edged forward, a little bit at a time, and rather sheepishly tried to look over the side of the cliff. Neither succeeded, their nerve went and both stepped back. They both let out their breaths' and Paully wiped his brow mockingly. He could not believe what Shem had actually done. They then took another step backwards, just to be safe! Shem begun to laugh and held his stomach where it tickled.

'Ohhh God, that was close!' Paully chuckled slapping Shem on the back 'Jesus, you do have a strong throw, I did say you should join the local cricket team. Shall I pull some strings with me Dad?'

### THE END

Printed in Great Britain
by Amazon.co.uk, Ltd.,
Marston Gate.